DE

DESCENT

Sabrina Broadbent

Chatto & Windus
LONDON

Published by Chatto & Windus 2004

2 4 6 8 10 9 7 5 3 1

First published in Great Britain in 2004 by
Chatto & Windus
Random House, 20 Vauxhall Bridge Road
London SW1V 2SA

Random House Australia (Pty) Limited
20 Alfred Street, Milsons Point, Sydney,
New South Wales 2061, Australia

Random House New Zealand Limited
18 Poland Road, Glenfield,
Auckland 10, New Zealand

Random House (Pty) Limited
Endulini, 5A Jubilee Road, Parktown 2193, South Africa

The Random House Group Limited Reg. No. 954009
www.randomhouse.co.uk

A CIP catalogue record for this book
is available from the British Library

ISBN 0 7011 7685 7

Papers used by Random House are natural, recyclable products made from wood grown in sustainable forests; the manufacturing processes conform to the environmental regulations of the country of origin

Typeset by Deltatype Ltd, Birkenhead, Merseyside
Printed and bound in Great Britain by
Mackays of Chatham PLC

One need not be a Chamber – to be Haunted –
One need not be a House –
The Brain has Corridors – surpassing
Material Place –

Emily Dickinson, 1863

There is love of course. And then there's life, its enemy.

Jean Anouilh, *Ardèle*, 1949

One

21st December 1988

OUR NEW home. I'm sitting on the basement floor surrounded by packing boxes, pot plants and veneer. 259 people have fallen from the sky in Scotland and you are in Budapest.

The coal-effect gas fire is on. I move my face carefully towards its glowing coals until it nearly touches. No heat. I stare at it. Surely there could be no point in a coal-effect gas fire which is just that. Effect. They have left a lot of their furniture, all their swirly carpets, veneer cabinets and a rampant china horse. They have kindly left us their television in its cabinet too. Its aerial likes to hang upside down from the net curtains. This I worked out for myself after a slow-motion tango. Just me and the aerial.

The news cuts from the newscaster to JFK airport. Close-up of the Arrivals monitor. Irrefutable, white on black, it says, 'PA103 . . . Down.' Some cries are audible. I reach for the phone.

Misdialling your hotel, I try again, concentrating on the unfamiliar numbers. Silence while the technology does its invisible stuff. Air waves? Radio waves? Magic? God knows. The ringing tone sounds like a ship lost in the fog. At the stream of Hungarian-hotel-reception-speak I try to imagine the place that you are in. Sounds like the panelling might not be veneer. And the flock wallpaper might be real flock. The receptionist and I suffer a communication breakdown.

'Hello. Do you speak English?' I ask in a voice that I hope says I quite understand if you do not.

'Em . . . Little.'

'Can. I. Speak. To. Mr. Morrison?'

'Miss Termorrison?

'No.' I laugh kindly. 'Mister. Morrison.'

'Spell it please.' Not amused.

'Muh. Oh. Ruh . . .' This takes a little time. When I've finished we listen to the other's breathing until the receptionist realises it's her turn.

'And is surname please?'

'That is his surname.' I allow myself a hint of impatience. 'His first name is Mark. Mark Morrison. He's with the *Snow Queen* film crew.'

'Moment please.'

Police and rescue workers wander across the television screen. Blurred yellow ghosts in the dark. Floodlights illuminate the nose of the cockpit. 'It lies felled in a field like the severed head of a huge fish,' bellows the reporter, stunned for a moment by his own poetry. Cut to a close-up of the cheerful, cursive blue script naming it *Maid of the Seas*. The reporter clutches his microphone urgently, an expression of horror on his face. 'And now the search begins for the all-important black box which may tell us why Pan Am Flight 103 dropped thirty thousand feet out of the night sky. Engine failure? A bomb? The cause of this disaster may not be known for some time.'

Holding the phone between my head and shoulder, I wait. On my knees. I use a biro to slice the brown tape on a box on which I've written, 'Basement'. I try to inject some sense of occasion into . . . the occasion of our new home. I fail to feel excited but take a celebratory gulp of the wine I've poured myself. Leaning over I smell the carpet. The fusty, unfamiliar scents of other lives lived. Their remains are all around. In the dust on the skirting boards; in the black smudges on the light switches. In Budapest the breathing and telephonic clicks continue convincingly.

'Hello?' Your voice. Testosteroned just right. And only just connected to your consciousness. We begin our clumsy telephone dance.

'Hi. It's me.'

'Hi.' Spoken right into my ear. I hold the phone close to my mouth and take a long breath in.

'Were you sleeping?'

'Just dozed off, I think.'

'Sorry.'

'What time is it?'

'It's seven thirty here.'

'Shit.'

There's a pause.

'I'm supposed to be in a meeting.'

I let the silence lengthen and watch the fluorescent shapes move among the wreckage. The reporter talks to camera. His bad-news face is earnest and serious. Relieved that something monumental has happened. Here, at last, a catastrophe worthy of us all. 'And all around . . . a vision of hell . . . the smell of kerosene . . .' He wrestles to convey the horror.

'Have you seen the news?'

'No. What?'

'There's been a plane crash.'

'Where?'

'Scotland. Just now. An hour ago.'

'Hang on, there's someone at the door.'

I catch fragments of conversation and imagine an actress in need. In her dressing gown. On screen a man and a woman weep into each other's necks. His hands clutch the fabric of her coat. A young man looks up at the monitor. We witness the moment at which he is changed for ever. The camera cuts away to an empty Pan Am booking desk. I finish off my glass of wine.

'Sorry about that.'

'What? Who was it?'

'I've got to rush.'

'What's the matter?'

'It's a disaster. Looks like fucking Dilly Nettles is pulling out.'

'What? She's not going to do it? After all that crap about rescheduling?' We are allies against the vanities and vagaries of actresses. 'Why? What's going on?'

'She's refusing to do the sex scene. Says she doesn't want to be naked.'

A pause is allowed for a suitably indignant response to be inserted by me. But I can't seem to find one. I am watching a fleet of ambulances make their way slowly across the field, blue lights flashing. Two rescue workers straighten up and lift a stretcher.

'I didn't know there *was* a sex scene in *Snow Queen*.'

'It's a dream sequence. She's read the fucking script and was fine about it. Now she says she can't do it.' I can hear you struggling with your clothes.

'Well, does she have to be naked? Can't you just . . . ?'

'How can we do the sex scene without seeing her body?'

Various fully clothed sex scenes of our own play through my mind. The rescue workers stagger as they pick their way through rough grass. Cut to a computer animation of the aircraft's flight path dot-dotting its way up England and into Scotland.

'So what's going to happen?'

'God knows. How's the house?'

'Big. It smells funny.'

On screen again, the wreck in the field lies helpless. Beneath me, I feel a muffled rumble and subterranean tremor. I open my eyes and say, 'Oh, and we live above a tube tunnel.'

'What?'

'I can hear the bloody tube. The floor shakes. What are you doing?'

'Having a piss.'

'You know they think there may have been a bomb on board that plane?'

'Christ. Really?'

'Those poor people.'

'Look, I'll have to call you back.'

'OK.'

'Love you.'

'Good luck . . . with Dilly.'

22nd December 1988

Last night I spent our first night in our new home. I slept high up at the top of this tall house. I didn't sleep that well actually. Partly because you weren't there. But also I needed to be able to hear the mad axeman's footsteps on the stairs. And I was trying not to hear our neighbour's repeated playing of his Kylie Minogue record at full volume through the bedroom wall. I try not to wonder what 'I Should Be So Lucky!' is an accompaniment to for a forty-year-old man living alone with his mother. I hope Kylie provides some solace.

Unplugging the phone, I take it with me down to the kitchen in the basement. Pushing aside the nylon nets, I let the sun pour in through the kitchen window. It feels almost homely, despite the alien décor. I consider humming but the only song in my head is Kylie's.

It's early and I make tea and chuck the teabag in the sink. God knows which box the bin is in. I open the cupboard under the sink and see a rat. I close it quick. Adrenalin pops, ides and omens scramble my brain.

The only thing to do, I decide, is to release the rat. I open the back door, close off all other exits, climb up on the counter, lean down, open the cupboard again and retreat to the back of the work surface. The wall tiles by my knees are decorated with field mice. But they're on ears of corn, not crouched in kitchen cupboards. Time passes. The rat isn't coming out. Paralysed with fear probably. Planning a full-scale invasion maybe. One of us has got to do something. I lean down and, with hammering heart, do a high-speed peek into the cupboard.

The rat, I now realise, is dead. Jumping down, I find a Sainsbury's bag, put my hand inside it and, holding my breath, pick up the soft body. With a disgusted exhalation I stuff that bag inside another and, arm outstretched, rush up the stairs to the front door and dump the bag on the steps. Slamming the door, I breathe in. Almost immediately, a frenzied squealing of metal on metal makes me open the door again. Despite the rat bag. Donovan's Aggregates swings at alarming speed towards me. The driver is revelling in the freedom of an empty truck, pulling at the wheel with one hand, lifting a cup to his mouth with the other and accelerating with abandon. Our house shakes. I watch him career up the wrong side of the road, presumably taking care not to spill his tea. As I shut the door, the thundering begins again. We live on a bloody rat run.

Back in the kitchen I recall that apparently, in London, you are never more than ten feet away from a rat. I stomp back up the stairs, open the front door and kick the Sainsbury's rat bag down into the gutter. Mr Ali from next door is getting out of his Nissan. I smile and say hello. He beams back at me. I hope he didn't see the bag thing.

You ring me. You always ring. I love that about you. You are umbilically attached to the telephone.

'Hello?'

'Hi. It's Mark.'

'Hello.'

'How's the house?'

'I've just found a rat.'

'What? A live one?'

'No, dead.'

'Where?'

'In our bed.'

You hesitate, calculating my mood.

'Not really. Under the kitchen sink.'

'What have you done with it?'

'I've thrown it out.'

'Shit, that's disgusting.'

'What are you doing?'

'I'm on the loo. Eating breakfast.' I know your pre-shoot nerves. 'I miss you,' you add, possibly as an afterthought.

'I miss you.' I wish English was . . . what? More. 'How's Dilly Nettles?'

'Looks like she's going to do it,' you say between swallows.

'Oh.' My heart sinks a little. 'Good. You managed to persuade her then?'

'She's really sweet about it actually. It's her agent who's being a wanker. I had to promise not to show her breasts. She feels self-conscious about them.'

'Does she?'

I cup one breast in my hand. Peer down my jumper and stare at both of them. I have to admit they're looking sort of tired.

'Well, she's fine about showing everything else . . .'

'Like what?' You're guzzling something noisily.

'Legs, arse, stomach, fanny . . . just shy about her breasts.'

'Oh.'

I stand up and look down at my legs. Twist round and eye my arse.

'Did you call the builders?'

'Well, I will do.'

'They should start as soon as possible.'

'Although it'll be a bit cold. Without the back wall. In January.'

'It's only for a few days. They'll put a thing up.'

'I wish you were here, Mark. It's weird here . . .'

I switch on the TV. A reporter is shouting into the wind. I turn the sound up. He is breathless. 'Well, James, words cannot describe this scene of utter devastation . . . the acrid smell of fuel still hangs in the air . . . this is a disaster the like of which we have not seen in this country since the Blitz . . . and all around the first light of dawn brings home the scale of this awful human tragedy . . .'

'God, those poor people. Mark, are you still there?'

'I'm still here. Trying to make the telly work. What time is it?'

'No idea. Are you my time or some other time?'

'I think I'm going to have to go.'

'OK then.'

'I love you.'

'And I love you.'

'Don't forget to call the builders.'

2nd January 1989

'The main body of the *Maid of the Seas* tipped forward, broke into several pieces and began to plummet.' Sitting on a plane on the runway at Heathrow, I read the papers which are full of intimate details about how death happens thirty thousand feet up. 'The people on board the beheaded 747 were hit with a shock wave of cold, noise and dark.' The crew smile more than necessary. They have checked my seat belt twice. I stare at my thighs, contemplating the experience of losing them to some unimaginable violence.

The plane hauls itself away from the earth and heads for Budapest. Defying all logic and normal systems of belief, we climb to thirty thousand feet. It's the first time in three years that I've been on a plane without you. A three-year high. In my mind, I replay the moment I walked into the ward office to meet some television researcher for a documentary on dementia.

Suddenly, you. *A coup de foudre* that left us both looking at the other's feet. Battered, brown suede on yours. Fake ocelot skin on mine. I felt I'd found what we're told we're looking for. My other half. Found, I would have said, the perfect man, except you were very much *boy* really. You looked about twelve. Maybe falling in love is the shock of recognition. So there we were, staring at each other's feet, too shy to look each other in the eye. If we had dared to, if we had dared to do what you're supposed to do, look deep into the other's eyes, we might have seen ourselves, tiny and inverted, within the globe of the other's pupil. Falling.

At the airport, I allow myself a frisson of excitement in case you have managed to find time to collect me. Instead I see GENEVIEVE O'DOWD scrawled in black marker pen on a piece of cardboard. I hate to see my name like that. Awkward. Implausible. The driver leads me to an impressive-looking car. I don't have to tell him where to go. Which is just as well because I don't know.

Lying on the bed in your hotel I study the room. It looks as though a suitcase has exploded. Your pants, socks, thermals and a blizzard of paper lie around the floor. Resisting the impulse to tidy up, and offending the one mean streak in you – mini bar prices – I open the mini bar, select a beer and sit down to read your script. It contains a lot of fur and roads and rock music. The dialogue is mundane, broken and inconsequential. Very real. Oh, and there's a beautiful woman who is adored by a lugubrious youth. One glimpse of her sulking behind the patisserie counter and he's bewitched. He decides to risk everything for the possibility of loving her. Abandons his friend, his car and his job back home. In the end, she goes off with *his* friend. I yawn and study the day's shooting schedule. Now this really is extraordinary. Everybody gets collected. Everybody gets lines. Everybody gets lunch. Everybody does quite a lot of nothing. A bit like school.

You told me on the phone to make the most of being here. So this afternoon I have sat in sulphurous baths under Ottoman domed ceilings with lardy women. Been scrubbed and pummelled by retired shot putters and hosed down with icy water. Watched chess players play on floating boards in the hot springs of the municipal lido, steam rising from the surface and snow piled up round the sides. It is understood that this is my reward for patience and loyalty. I've listened to taxi drivers explaining that they have doctorates in chemistry but cannot earn enough in their day jobs so they drive taxis by night. On the way back to our hotel, I noticed that outside Dilly Nettles' luxury hotel there was a scene. A man had snatched a guest's handbag. The hotel manager looked bewildered. The police seemed to consider spraying the lobby with machine-gun fire but thought better of it. Then I passed the set, illuminated in the dark. Hoping to sneak a look at you, I was struck by the sheer scale of the operation, even for a television drama like this. 'Mark Morrison, *Snow Queen*,' was chalked on a clapperboard, signalling the magical shift to film. With film you have inched your way a little closer to your gods and achieved a little godliness yourself. Your crew milled around, faithful and loyal like soldiers, or serfs.

The focus and effort that go into this project are beyond anything I've known on the wards at the psychiatric unit. I could feel its pull. Cables snaked the ground. Women spoke into walkie-talkies. A crane of lights was manoeuvred into position and I glimpsed your face turned up at Dilly's who leaned down from the back of a truck. She was wrapped in fur and you looked directly into her eyes, mouth laughing, face energised. I walked away fast. This is your beginning but pride for you battled with fear. I couldn't feel my feet as I walked back to our hotel.

By the sink in the bathroom, spattered with shaving foam and swollen with damp, is a copy of Hans Christian

Andersen's version of *The Snow Queen*. Taking it into the bedroom, I lie down on the bed and flip through it.

All at once, the great sledge stopped, and the person who had driven it rose up. I roll over towards the mini bar and retrieve a large tub of peanuts. *It was the Snow Queen.* I brush the crumbs from my chest and roll over onto my stomach. *'We have driven well,' said she, 'but why do you tremble? Here, creep into my warm fur.'* Feeling distinctly bilious, I am none the less compelled to start on the Twix. *Then she seated him beside her in the sledge, and as she wrapped the fur round him he felt as if he were sinking into a snowdrift.* Outside, large snowflakes start falling from the blank Hungarian sky. *The kiss was colder than ice; it went quite through to his heart, which was already almost a lump of ice . . . he felt as if he were going to die, but only for a moment; he soon seemed quite well again, and did not notice the cold around him.*

I look at the phone on the table by the bed. It rings.

'Hello?' I say in unison to an echoed hello.

'Genevieve? Is that you?'

'Mum. Is everything OK?'

'Sorry to ring, darling, but I just wanted—'

The sob escapes her. I hold my breath and wait.

'I'm all right. I'm all right.' There's a tremulous sigh. I can feel my heart. The bed cover smells of goat's cheese and something else. Salami perhaps?

'I'm sorry. Oh dear. It's just. That Lockerbie thing. I know it's silly. But the thought of you up in a plane . . .'

There's a muffled rustling of tissues. I can see her fumbling for them, holding the receiver between her head and shoulder.

'Mum? Mum. I expect you're missing Bill . . . New Year and everything . . .'

There's a distant honking as she blows her nose. I think of the Canada geese that Bill used to watch, standing motionless, binoculars raised to his eyes.

'There. That's better. Not Bill. No. Must sound awful I know. Bill and I. We. Well. As you know. We should never have married really. But.' She breathes in deeply and sighs it out. 'We did. And so.'

I stare at a patch on the ceiling and try not to think of my mum and Bill. A mercy marriage.

'Bill was . . . nice, Mum. Of course you miss him.'

I lie very still and listen to her soft gasps. I know what's coming.

'Not Bill, no. Or your father. Or even you. Because now I know you're all right. But.'

Out of the tunnel roars the ghost train. If I lie very still, hold my breath and shut my eyes it will thunder past and be gone.

'Mum? Where are you?'

'I'm all right. I'm at Uncle Frank's. I'll be fine. Just wanted to check. You know. That you were safe.' We retreat, still in one piece.

She wants to get off the phone now. But I don't let her. I attempt small talk. I look at the Budapest guide and read bits out to her. I tell her about the hotel, you, the filming; the swim in the outdoor pool when my feet froze to the concrete; sitting naked in the steam bath with lots of huge women with plastic bags on their heads and being flayed alive by the giant with a loofah. She exclaims in horror and hoots with laughter and I hate Bill for persuading her she needed marrying in the first place. Stupid, stooped, sad old Bill.

Later, you forget to introduce me to Dilly Nettles in the hotel lobby. She is shockingly short. Barely fully grown, I think with satisfaction. Her face is lunar. Pale. And she has the sort of lips and eyes that can hold the gaze of a camera – I see that. I study her face and try to understand exactly what it is. It seems to have something to do with lips like a vulva and eyes like Bambi. Maybe. Maybe it's just as simple and as sad as that, I say to myself dismissively. You giggle and jest deliriously with her. I stand near you, my face inches from your head. A tall man in leather with a floppy, self-conscious haircut approaches and places the palm of his hand on her neck. He leans down and kisses her on the mouth.

'Hey,' he says. 'How're you feeling?' He examines her face with concern and kisses her again. For about five whole seconds.

'I'm so cold,' she says to him, tears welling up in her eyes, and the threat of a sulk on her lips. 'Let's go up.'

He takes her arm. You turn round abruptly. We bang noses. I am undeniably a little too tall.

'Oh, hi,' you say.

'Hello.' I beam at you. Ridiculously pleased to see you. You kiss me briefly.

'Come on. Let's get a drink.' I follow you. A faithful old retainer.

We pace the empty streets looking for a place to be festive in. You are elated and walk fast, searching for a bar. The only place open seems to be McDonald's. Above us, the beam of a plane climbs in a slow arc through the dim stars. Watching it strain through its trajectory, I feel suddenly tired. This is how it is now. You're taking off and I'm ready to land. What I want is to sleep in your arms for the longest time. You hail a taxi coming fast down the street towards us. It stops and we climb in.

'Is there anywhere open for a drink?' you ask him. 'Bar?' you ask again in Hungarian. He shrugs and names a hotel.

'Great,' you nod enthusiastically.

The driver executes a violent U-turn and we thunder
along the wide cobbled street. Holding your hand,
momentum pin my body against the back of th
definitely have a plan. It is a great relief to k
us does.

Two

4th January 1989

WE'VE SPENT a weekend camping in our house together. We lie entwined under the familiar duvet. I open my eyes to a close-up landscape of your skin and run my palm over bone and muscles beneath. I kiss your neck or whatever bit of you this is and wonder at the unlikely good fortune of having found you. When we found each other, we were both running at high speed away from something else. We collided with our heads turned back over our shoulders watching the recent past or perhaps the imminent future recede. And for a few years, the momentum of the collision carried us forward in a delicious, directionless spin. Breathless. Now, at the top of this high house we've bought, I sense the weight of it pulling us down. You squeeze me hard. Don't fall.

I can hear you blinking. A bad sign. You are waiting for [illegible]onovan's Aggregates and the 38 bus. Sad Neighbour is [illegible] silent. I'm wondering whether to make the long [illegible]wn to the kitchen to fetch coffee or whether to [illegible]here with you a while longer.

[illegible] boxes are still piled high but there's good [illegible] and a new washing-up bowl. In the [illegible]otapes lie scattered by the VCR. [illegible]t you let me watch them. But I don't know what to make of them. Some seem shockingly bad, banal even. I wonder how the actors can bear the boredom of take after take of the same scene. But I am starting to see that their reward is the alchemy wrought in the cutting room and the dubbing studio.

It's warm in the house when I get up, thanks to the previous owners. They were Spanish migrants who lived here for thirty years. They raised their family here, then, seeing that the Angel was going down in the world, escaped to Enfield. But they did leave the giant rosemary bush in the back yard, an industrial heating system and a bidet. All of which I appreciate. We couldn't find our old one, so you have bought a new coffee machine. One of your random acts of profligacy. I wait while it splutters and soon the smell of coffee begins to make this strange kitchen feel like home. Maybe this house was the right thing to do after all. I just wish there wasn't so much of it.

The doorbell chimes. Obviously the doorbell will have to go. It chimes again, followed by a thunderous assault on the door with the knocker. I race upstairs to deal with the emergency evidently taking place on our doorstep. As I open the door the familiar stout figure of your father wheels round in pantomime surprise as he comes back up the steps towards me.

'Oh. So you're in then.'

'Marion! Hello! Your son and I were just about to enjoy a wild morning of abandoned sex! Come in.' The sex bit I leave in my head.

Marion. Or Ron as your dad understandably prefers to be called. Named after Marion Michael Morrison. Or John Wayne as he understandably preferred to be called. I prefer to call your dad Marion though.

'I was just passing so I've brought one or two things you left behind at Christmas.' Marion gestures towards the Rover. On the pavement by his car is a poinsettia, a garden tub planted with variegated evergreens and two bulging bin bags. 'Anyway I thought I'd come and see how you two are settling in.' Donovan's Aggregates thunders round the corner towards us. 'Gordon Bennett, what on earth is that?'

'Come on in.' I smile at him and let him inside. 'Come and have some coffee.'

'What's that you say?'

'Tea? Coffee?' I ask, leading him down to the kitchen. 'I'm just making some.'

'Oh. Well, are you sure I'm not interrupting anything? I don't want to cock up your weekend.' Marion is charmingly oblivious to the Freudian high-speed skid that often breaks through the lid inside his head. 'I'd love a cup of instant.'

I open a few cupboards, pretending to look for instant coffee. My relationship with Marion consists of quite a lot of going through the motions.

'I'm afraid it'll have to be tea.'

'Not that funny foreign stuff, is it? Is he in?'

'Now which he would that be?'

'Pardon?'

'If you mean Mark, he's still in bed.'

'Is he?' Marion applies a look of utter disbelief to his face.

'I'll go and get him. Hang on.'

I pass you on the stairs, staggering down in your pants and T-shirt. You pause to pull my dressing gown open and slide your hand between my legs. You'll be gone tomorrow.

'Is there someone here?'

'Your dad.'

You remove your hand and take a very promising erection down to the basement to greet him. Reluctantly, I go upstairs to get dressed.

When I come back downstairs, I find that the bags and pots have been brought in from the car and are sitting on the carpet which, until yesterday, was cluttered with other bin bags and boxes. My heart sinks at the sight of yet more Stuff.

I open one bag and glimpse a scented candle-making kit and a beaded car seat.

'A party? Tonight? Oh,' says Marion. The 'Oh' is sort of sung and protracted, signalling slight disbelief and probably a fleeting hope for an invitation. Marion loves a crowd.

'We just thought we'd christen the house before I go back to Budapest.'

'Well, are you going to get the place sorted before your friends come?'

'No, Dad, that's the point. It doesn't matter how wrecked it gets. The builders are coming tomorrow. Where have you been, Genevieve? I've been calling you. Your coffee's cold.'

'Sorry. The bidet takes a bit of getting used to . . .'

'When do you go back to work then, young lady?'

'Day after tomorrow unfortunately, Marion. The day after the builders start.'

'Are the builders coming?'

'Yes, Dad, I just told you. They're knocking down this back wall. Up to the second floor—'

'Blimey. That'll be a bit chilly, won't it? In January.'

'Then they're knocking through these two rooms,' you stride to the doorway and start swinging your arms architecturally, 'ripping out the stairs, taking out the bathroom and—'

'Oh. Have we decided about that?'

'What do you mean? It's hideous. And then here at the front . . .' you pull back the nets. 'Dad, is that your car out there? Looks like you've got a ticket.'

'You *what*? I don't be*lieve* it.'

'It's a parking meter, Marion. You have to put money in.'

'*Shine* on. I'm only stopped off to visit my son. What do they think they're playing at? Hang on, there's the warden.' Marion takes the stairs two at a time and disappears, slamming the front door behind him.

5th January 1989
I walk to the shops on this grey, mild day. Everything seems in neutral. The pigeons huddle. Even the weather can't be arsed. People are dazed after the long Christmas break. Too much food, too much drink, too much television, too much news. It's just too much. A collective spiritual hangover hovers over us all. Every shop has a sale. *PRICES SLASHED!!! UNBELIEVABLE REDUCTIONS!!!* And this offered as if it is some completely unexpected surprise or act of kindness.

In Boots, a woman stands beside me at the prescriptions counter. She is whispering, 'I've died . . . I've died . . . I've died . . .' in varying tones of incredulity and horror. For a moment I consider whether she could be right: all of us standing here by the Deep Heat, Durex and Anusol, waiting to be served by assistants in white coats and name badges. It soon becomes evident to everyone that the woman is saying what we thought she was saying. We avoid eye contact. I'm on holiday, I think uncharitably. I don't want to have to think about auditory hallucinations until tomorrow. When it's her turn to be served she switches immediately to a confident middle-class accent.

'Can I help you?' says the white coat. No irony evident.

'Oh yes, I'll have some of that and a bottle of that please,' says the woman pointing to the shelf. A pink concoction that looks kind of gastric and a large brown bottle are offered questioningly. 'Yes, thank you very much,' says the woman who's died, getting out her purse. She pauses and looks down in dismay. I can see she's thinking of speaking the unspeakable again but she doesn't. She maintains a perfectly normal façade until the transaction is complete. After which she turns to go and the whispering, now quite loud, continues. 'I've died . . . we've all died . . .'

On my way home I buy coffee, milk, tea and bin bags and when I get home the builders are sitting outside in their white van. I let them in and take them down to the kitchen.

Alan and Bob drink cups of tea, wander around outside, look doubtfully up at the back of the house, use the toilet at length and then leave. You ring me.

'Hi. It's Mark.'

'Hi. How's it going?'

'Just about to go on a recce for the pick-up shots. Are the builders there?'

'They've just left.'

'Have they done much?'

'Not really. They've gone to hire a Kanga or something. They asked if we had a ladder. I gave them a key. And, Mark, I think I might be pregnant.'

There's the smallest of pauses. Could be the time lapse.

'What? Haven't they got their own bloody ladder?'

12th January 1989

Straddling the toilet, head at pelvis level, I'm trying to pee onto a white plastic stick. I straighten up and I click the cap on the stick then sit down and count to 120. Of course keeping it, if this comes up positive, is out of the question. I've just been promoted, your work is taking off, the house, the building project, us. This would not be the time to slam the brakes on everything. Taking the cap off again, I can see the blue line in the second perspex window is definite. I am pregnant. It seems miraculous that we should be capable of such a thing.

You ring. Panic over. The film is saved. I'm not sure I can remember what the last panic was about but anyway I am glad for you. I tell you my news. You are silent for a moment and in that silence I understand that your decision will be mine.

'What are you going to do then?'

'Do you mean what are *we* going to do?' My voice is cold. 'I'll have an abortion, I suppose,' I add quickly before you can speak. I'm matter of fact. No nonsense. No problem. My friend Helena had one under local anaesthetic. She said it was quite frightening but I admire her courage and would like you to admire my courage too.

Anyway a local is much more convenient. No need to take time off work. Just an afternoon. No questions asked. I put the phone down and write 'Abortion' at the bottom of my list of things to do.

13th February 1989

Last night I dreamt that you were standing in my childhood bedroom with a man who I think was my father. He was pointing at a small hole where the stuffing was coming out of the side of my mattress. He said, 'Mark, look, poor Genevieve. Her stuffing's coming out.' You looked over at the bed, screwed up your eyes trying to see and said, 'Is it?' and gave an embarrassed laugh.

Outside the Angel tube station in the drizzle, a tide of people, eyes down, faces set, move down the steps and towards the ticket office. To catch the fare evaders, the Department of Transport has installed automated ticket barriers. The noise they make sounds like something that might happen in a slaughterhouse. Helplessly we march onto the escalator and glide down into the tunnels. Standing on the edge of the platform we are like a congregation offering up a silent prayer. I watch the tiny dirt-coloured mice wander about on the tracks. The train thunders towards us like some kind of revenge. The mice take their time getting out of the way.

'Please. Allow. Passengers. Off. First.' We try to obey orders but most of us, faced with the prospect of witnessing the gape of the tunnel, the mice and the ads again just can't bear to.

Climbing the steps of the psychiatric unit, nylon uniform swishing tightly against my thighs, I try to remember the thrill I had when I was new to the job. Seven years ago.

Then I'd looked up at the Victorian façade and felt such excitement at being given a job. My first real job. A career was a very seductive notion then. One's whole life mapped out: promotion, holidays, sickness, maternity leave, pension. I was excited and full of *One Flew Over the Cuckoo's Nest* intentions. Single-handedly, I would heal sick minds and revolutionise the Victorian asylums. The thrill has gone now and the steps feel steeper each time I climb them.

It's true that the smell of the place has never been right. Like the first time you embrace a lover. You know, however long you might kid yourself otherwise, that if you don't like their smell, the bit just behind the ears or on top of their head, *their* smell, well, then it's done for. You might as well say goodbye there and then. Save yourself a lot of bother and sniff out another. The smell in a mental hospital was never going to be great. 'Susto,' the Bolivian cleaner calls it, waving her hand around her head and grimacing. 'Soul loss,' she adds, shaking her head knowingly and resuming her mopping. She's right, there is something tangible to the taint of human misery in the air in this building; over the years it has leached the enthusiasm from me. Or perhaps it's just that, at the age of thirty, I'm a little too old to still be in uniform.

Lesley's back is turned to me as I put my head round the door of Administration. Unprepared though I was at first for the contorted minds of the inmates, theirs were not as scary as the interior worlds of the hospital staff.

'Hi, Lesley.' I look in fearful admiration at the navy tailored trouser suit and short dark hair. Lesley is Head of Administration at the hospital and has never been known to stare into space or mutter, 'Now what did I come in here for?' There is no reply, so I pick up my mail and leave.

'A moment, Staff Nurse O'Dowd.' I reverse into the office. Her left arm is extended backwards while the rest of her is still interrogating a slightly frightened-looking diary. Her biro stabs the page triumphantly and she looks at me, letting her glasses drop on their string to her chest, eyelids closing briefly in triumph.

'What's that?' I ask, understanding immediately that she requires an explanation for my half-day absence before Christmas. I can't believe how cowardly I am. My heartbeat is actually racing and, yes, I really am blushing. Who needs enemies with a persona like this?

'The hospital requires a leave of absence form to be filled out for the twenty-second of December.' She's tapping the date with one hand and pulling a triplicate form from a tray with the other. That was the day I went to John Lewis to do Christmas shopping. Well I couldn't be sure there'd be anything in Budapest. Plus I thought we might be busy making crazy Hungarian love all day long, rather than buying appliances for our families.

25th March 1989

Angus is a giant bear of a man with red-rimmed eyes, long hair and a massive face. He strides along beside me in the evening cold, coat flapping. I feel awkward. Can't really understand why I'm out with him on this bitter night. Seeing him makes me miss you, makes me feel lucky to have you. You are the only person I have ever met who admits to hating Tolkien and never having got any further than 'In a hole in the ground there lived a hobbit.' You're exactly what I was looking for, I think smugly. Except at times you can be a little hard to find. Like tonight, you're playing your other role – not The World's Most Perfect Lover or The Boyfriend Who is Almost a Girlfriend but The Man Who Isn't There. Tonight you are somewhere abroad and I have agreed to see Angus.

As well as being tall, Angus is sort of artistic and possibly a little dangerous. Helena likes to choose dangerous men, given to driving fast and indulging in extreme sports. Angus is not like the others, however. He's much more Bohemian.

And rather penniless. The endings of Helena's relationships are always explosive. At the moment she is trying to evade Angus but has asked me to meet him.

I am a little wary and unsure of how to conduct myself. Angus is an old friend of yours. Helena is an old friend of mine. Loyalties are muddled.

'Why is it that London has never allowed its population to enjoy its river? I mean Parisians can, Florentines can . . . Come on, Angus, think of some more cities with rivers.' I look at him but he's shut. 'London seems to have some sort of a problem with looking at its river. Why is that, do you think?' Here you are, Angus, a lively conversation opener, snatched out of the blue, neutral and unloaded without too much about me or her or him or you. But Angus is looking sort of thunderous. Once the pause exceeds thought or shyness and begins to become rudery, I save myself some embarrassment and continue. Besides, I'm finding this river topic suddenly interesting. 'Maybe it's because Parliament is built on the river and so MPs think London does overlook the river.' I squeeze myself round a JCB.

'It's because the English can't bear to face anything they can't control – emotions, death, history, the future,' says Angus suddenly. 'That's what the river symbolises.' He turns his back on me and walks on. He is ending the river conversation. 'When did you know Helena was going to leave me?' he shouts back.

I hurry to keep up with his one-league strides and wonder whether I might end up trussed and strangled and tossed in the Thames. Of course, being her friend I probably know more about their relationship than he does. Some of her stories about him pass unnervingly through my mind – covering her from head to toe in plaster of Paris and then going on a bender all night; lacing her dad's birthday cake with dope. Or was that her Colombian boyfriend?

'Well,' I begin, thinking rapidly. Facts are not my strong

point. I find them unreliable. Never there when you need them. 'I knew you weren't getting on very well. Um . . .'

Angus lets rip an alarmingly loud laugh. Like Bluebeard. 'Oh! She told you that, did she?' he roars, jumping heavily down off a block of concrete. Not bending his knees on landing like he's supposed to. 'You know that I thought she was dead!' he says, striding forwards into the dark and the wind. 'She should be bloody dead!' We are getting uncomfortably close to the leaden river.

'Dead? Who?' The cold has done something to the muscles round my mouth. I sound like one of my patients.

'Helena! She was supposed to get that plane. And you know what?' I try to get a look at his pupils. He must be on something. 'She must have got the nod from that CIA FBI damn spook of a father of hers and so didn't get *that* plane home for Christmas.'

'Angus, I spoke to her on Christmas Day. She was with her family in New York. They were all really shaken about the crash.' And Helena couldn't wait to get back for some more of what'sisname on the telly as I remember.

'Oh she got there in the end. But instead of the Lockerbie flight she sneaked off for a night with that smug git of a newsreader and took a different flight the next day.'

He is crying. Standing huge above me and moaning through clenched teeth, his ragged hair whipped up in the knifing wind.

'God. I didn't know.' And this is partly, horrifically true. I didn't know about the Lockerbie escape. Didn't know deceit could be on that scale. I can't even remember what it is exactly that Helena's dad does.

'They must have been expecting something like Lockerbie since they shot down the Iranian airbus last year. Three hundred families shot out of the sky by mistake.' Angus gives a hollow laugh.

'God,' I actually shake my head in disbelief. 'Helena must feel . . .'

'You see that?' he says pointing up. I look stupidly up at the sky with him. What am I looking for? I wonder desperately. A plane?

'That!' he shouts, pointing at the art deco Oxo Tower. It looks like it belongs in New York, not London. Oxo? Bovril? Marmite? I'm not at all sure of my cultural bearings at this moment. 'What does it say to you, Genevieve?'

I stand still and look. There is the rumble of traffic on the embankment, the roar and howl of a plane circling London. I can see the blinking lights of the plane and the concrete box that is the National Theatre. And I can just make out the ironwork letters at the top of the Oxo Tower.

'Oxo?' I reply half expecting him to hit me like an exasperated parent.

'Can't you *see*?' He wheels round with his hands in his pockets, head thrown back at the sky.

'See *what*, for God's sake, Angus?' I shout back at him. 'What am I supposed to be *seeing*?' Why am I suddenly having to deal with visions and hallucinations in my social life as well as at work? Give me a break, for God's sake.

'It's a sky-sign, isn't it? Those damn Yanks. But you can't see it, can you? Mark would see it. Ask him.' He turns away and starts making for Waterloo Bridge. 'Fuck it. Just forget it.'

Oh, I think to myself. The fury of loss. It's all someone else's fault, isn't it, Angus? I trudge behind in his furious footsteps as he lopes off towards the bridge. Why am I following him? Daddy's Girl, I sneer inwardly.

Back in the house, I drop my keys on the stairs and descend tentatively to the basement. The back wall has come down and in its place Alan and Bob have erected a piece of hardboard. It's chained to a scaffolding pole. The red light of the ansaphone winks in the dark. I press PLAY and hear your voice, sleepy, treacly, mumbled. It's 1.30 in the morning in Budapest. I can't ring you now. And anyway I have decided

I hate the telephone. It's lazy. No way to conduct a relationship. And bloody Angus has made me feel stupid. The thought of you asleep hurts. I check the chain round the plywood and climb to the top of the house.

2nd April 1989

I stand in the kitchen with the sun on my back and stare at my list.

Call builders
Call council
Call architect
Ring bank
Ring bed shop
Ring sofa shop
British Gas
Chimney sweep
Paint stripper
Bin bags
Insurance
BT
Car tax
Abortion

'We did the sex scene today,' you tell me on the phone, amid sploshing bath noises. Like imagining an act of infidelity, it's the details that occupy me. I can't work out where you are in the scene. If you're a part of it or just watching. And what the difference is. Kneeling at the end of the bed with a viewfinder? Hanging off the camera crane near the ceiling? Underneath the duvet with a floodlight?

'How was it?'

'Don't know. I'm just looking at the rushes now. We had to do lots of takes. But Dilly was really great about it all. A bit nervous.'

'OK about her breasts then?'

'We didn't show them. She had a little vest thing on.'

My breasts are swollen and heavy. It's how I first suspected I was pregnant. Strange that the breasts swing into action so early on. No doubt milk production is a complicated process. Ask a farmer. Or a cow.

'Apparently, some people knew there was a risk of a bomb on the Lockerbie flight.'

'What? Why didn't they abort the flight?'

'Exactly.'

I want to tell you all about Helena and about Angus's conspiracy theory but he's made me a little paranoid. I take the phone away from my ear and examine the mouthpiece.

'Are you still there?'

'Sorry. I was just . . .' I lift the phone and study the base of it.

'How was Angus? Did you see him?'

'Yes. He's not good. Very upset about Helena.'

'It was so lucky she wasn't on that plane.'

'Yes that. And the other thing.'

'Oh the new guy. He's not really a newsreader, is he?'

'No. He's in charge of Current Affairs.' We both laugh, cruel and safe within our own immutable bond.

'I love you,' you say, still giggling.

'What does Oxo mean to you, Mark?'

'Oxo gives a meal man appeal.'

'Your profundity is very sexy, did you know that?'

'Let's leave my fecundity out of this.'

'I love you.'

'I love *you*.'

'I miss you.'

'I really miss you.'

'Goodbye then.'

'Are you still pregnant?'

'Yes. You should see my breasts. They're huge.'

'Mmm. Sounds lovely. Are you going to see someone?'

'I've got an appointment on Thursday.'

5th April 1989

The lino in the waiting room of the Soho Hospital for Women is flecked with red, yellow and blue. These colours are part of the design, I am fairly sure, rather than evidence of previous patients. *Hello*, *OK*, *Marie Claire*, *Tatler*, *Help* . . . (no, I'm sure there's not one called that) offer plenty of tips about orgasms, diets and handbags but, strangely, not much mention of abortions. I feel reassured that this is a hospital for women where presumably abortions are all part of a day's work. Which was not the case when I'd turned up at a clinic last week and been surprised when the woman paused before filling in the hospital form.

'I have to ask you whether you are certain that you want this abortion.' Fair enough, I thought. She's only doing her job. 'Because you know there are plenty of couples around who have everything, *everything* except a child. They have a beautiful house, school fees, a pony in the paddock.'

It took a moment to fully comprehend that yes, this headmistressy woman in the floral frock was suggesting I might want to be a surrogate mother to a wealthy couple. I had felt helpless and panicked. Could this be done to me? Was there something I didn't know?

Now, undressing in the curtained cubicle and putting on the pale paper gown, I am suddenly fearful. The gown is flimsy and back-to-front and doesn't do up. Designed for emergency access presumably. Whatever the reason, it makes walking across the room somewhat undignified. I try to hold it modestly over my bottom. I am beginning to regret opting for the local anaesthetic.

The surgeon is a small, tired-looking man. He comes into the cubicle and discusses 'the procedure' with me. I lie on the high bed, conscious of my white legs and untrimmed toenails.

I wish I could remember why I had felt compelled to be

brave about this. It was to do with being able to cope, so as not to inconvenience you who would have had to look after me for twenty-four hours. You thought you were going to be away. It was so I didn't have to take a whole day off work. And face the wrath of bloody Lesley.

The surgeon leads me through the double doors of the operating theatre. A masked nurse is taking instruments out of cellophane with gloved hands. She doesn't look up.

'Climb up onto the bed,' says the surgeon.

The bed is high and lit by powerful lights. No wonder it's called a theatre. Underneath one end of the bed is what appears to be a giant pickling jar and a piece of hose. I clamber up and lie down.

'Put your feet in the footrests,' says the nurse. Looking sideways, I see her approaching with a giant, wet, brown swab on a stick. Jesus, what a terrible job, I think, suddenly ashamed at the careless way I had brought them all to this point.

'This may feel a bit cold . . . try to relax . . .'

I try not to but cannot really avoid seeing the needle, which is, of course, horrifically long. Then I feel the needle. But this isn't what I fear most. What I fear most is the suction. And when that starts with the unmistakeable sound of the vacuum pump, the deep, uterine ache begins. I stare at the ceiling, trusting that someone has worked out a pain threshold. I was probably born on a bed like this. Will quite likely end up some way or another on a bed like this. At the sound of liquid dropping into the container beneath my feet I begin to wonder whether I could manage to faint. The surgeon and the nurse say nothing to each other at all. It doesn't take long.

'All right, you can get down off the bed now,' says the nurse.

As I walk to the door I want to turn to look at the bottle under the bed. But the nurse is already covering it in a sheet of yellow plastic.

In the gloom of the side room I am told to lie down for ten minutes while my paperwork is completed. There is a dull pain low down in my womb. I feel like crying but I don't. I take off the paper gown and start to dress. Then I sit on the bed and wait. I can hear the low voice of another woman talking quietly to the surgeon next door. I wonder how many of these he does a day.

'Your husband is here,' says the nurse. I look up. And there you are, standing in the doorway, half in and half out. You. I love the sight of you. You are awkward as you kiss me hello.

'Are you all right?'

'I'm OK.'

You've brought me something in a bag. Inside is a large sticky rum baba with a bite taken out of it. You busy yourself with picking up my things.

You hold open the swing doors and we walk out together, leaving the pickling jar behind us. I wish it goodbye in my head. Offer an apology of sorts.

Back at home you make me a cup of tea and then head off in a rush. You are late for somewhere. I sit on the bed with the white box of painkillers from the hospital and listen to the monotonous hammering and drilling from the basement. A vase of freesias scent the room. I wait for a feeling to make itself known but none comes that I can put a name to. 'Especially For You!' On the other side of the wall Kylie and the neighbour are at it again. 'Especially For You!' I switch the radio on. A government spokesman informs me that bovine spongiform encephalopathy presents no health hazard to people who eat the meat of infected animals. From the basement I can hear the demented rant of a radio DJ. Demolition is in full swing down there. The damp, dead smell of excavation has replaced all the air in the house.

Three

4th June 1989

I ENTER the day room and sit next to Lily Shuttle who is pretending to be asleep. She is collapsed in her plastic-covered armchair, knees apart, stockings fallen, mouth agape in her heavy fenland face. Her eyes are shut tight. Her hands grip the armrests like a falling rock climber.

'Did Danny come and see you then, Lily?' I nudge her playfully.

She lets out a shriek and moans, '*Oooh*, Nurse! Don't *pinch* me! *Help* me! *Some*body help me! Will *some*body *help* me please?'

The fluorescent colours of daytime television flicker silently at us from the giant padlocked monitor suspended in chains from the ceiling. A help-line number does indeed scroll across the screen.

Lily begins rocking and I turn squeakily on my plastic chair so my face is in her line of vision. Or will be when she opens her eyes. Her face is caught in an involuntary grimace and her tongue reaches down from the side of her mouth.

'Did he bring you these sweets then, Lily?' A crumpled paper bag is on her lap. Danny, her son, visits once a fortnight and always brings them. Lily holds them tight in her fist from one visit to the next. But when Danny comes, Lily pretends to be asleep, waking only as he scrapes his chair back to leave and then looking at him reproachfully.

'Will *some*body *help* me *please*?' implores Lily, eyes shut tight, the words scanning perfectly in time to the rocking of her body. Sid, the auxiliary nurse, is seated in a wheelchair on the other side of the room. She has black hair tormented into spikes and one green eye and one blue. She does a skilful wheelie and glides across the lino towards us making siren noises. I should disapprove but at least Sid is evidence of life in this realm of the living dead. I am very fond of Sid and she always has some interesting ideas about psychiatry. Currently she believes that listening to the insane is pointless, that their words are just cries of distress. This makes something of a mockery of my research proposal: *Just Gibbering Wrecks? Voices from the Madhouse*. Sid contends that you are more likely to crack the code of insanity by looking rather than listening. She aims the remote control at Lily who is looking at her slyly through one half-open eye. Lily rubs her hands and pats her knees. Her toothless mouth chews continuously. Sid claims Lily is only pretending to be mad.

'She spat out her largactil. Twice.' Sid points at the pink stain on Lily's crimplene. 'And Danny only stayed for a minute. Didn't even sit down, did he, Lily?'

Alice, who is seventy-two and sitting opposite us, moves across the room and heads for the sink in the corner. She is tiny and thin and walks with a perfectly straight back and a sexy lift to her hips. Her white hair is pulled into a flawless bun and her chin is raised. At the sink, Alice removes the rag from her skirt pocket and begins her washing routine. She stands, turns the cold tap on and slaps the rag around the porcelain. Then she wrings it out, her fists turning upon each other until it becomes a twisted rope that doubles back on itself. It is almost dry when she has finished.

'The strength in that grip,' says Sid. 'Alice ran away again yesterday. Winston found her on the South Circular.'

'Jesus, she's going to get herself killed one of these days.'

'That presumably is the idea. Sister Stone says we have to take that rag off her again. I'm refusing.' Both of us watch Alice as she completes her routine. Each morning and evening Alice stands naked at the sink in the bathroom and uses it to wash between her legs. This is what she has done for sixty years since she was committed to the asylum by her boss shortly after going into service. Alice has never been known to speak. No doubt words cannot express what she feels.

Sid changes the channel on the television. Tiananmen Square, China, is the caption. The sound is down and it is difficult to make sense of what we are seeing. In the vast arena of the square there are students with banners and people with bicycles. It looks like a carnival. The faces are laughing. Cyclists wave as they pedal by, some with girls on their backs. Octavia, over the other side of the room, is suddenly up and out of her chair, wandering with small jerky shuffles and whimpering, 'Oh dear oh dear oh dear oh dear oh dear,' and picking up and putting down anything she comes across. I see Massive Mabel eyeing her belligerently. However crazy Octavia is, she retains the sense to give Mabel a wide berth.

On the screen above Octavia's shuffling routine, a diminutive figure stands in front of a tank. For one horrific moment it looks as though the tank might run the figure down.

10th July 1989

The other day you returned home with a diet book. We've become fat on love. We are eating only porridge oats, water, rice and spinach for three weeks and will thus transform ourselves into thin people. Personally, I think the more of you the better. But you want transformation. You have an idea of perfection. I see it in the rough cut of your film. Eyes. Ice. Mouth. Youth. Freedom. And it is a convenient time to starve ourselves because we have no fridge. Or stove. Or kitchen. But we have a microwave in our bedroom. And then there is the rigorous exercise routine, the other strategy in the battle against our bodies. I cycle to work which is fifteen miles there and back. You walk the five-mile round trip to the cutting rooms. When we get up in the morning we weigh ourselves religiously. We make enemies of our poor bodies. There is a compelling fascination in seeing myself disappear but I wonder a little about where the vanishing me has gone. I thought matter could be neither created nor destroyed, so where am I? And where have you gone? I don't find you more attractive the less you become. You look lean but also a little mean. I now know the meaning of the term 'wasted'. And I start to get the uneasy feeling that I am being watched and weighed up.

The news is on as we bolt our food, kneeling naked on our bed.

'This isn't at all bad,' you exclaim as you always do. 'No!' you slap my hand as I reach for the salt packet.

After knocking back a litre of water we go to the cinema to see *Women on the Verge of a Nervous Breakdown*. I'm becoming used to the feeling of emptiness in my belly – a watery, light feeling. In the dark, I run my hands over my flat stomach and along the slimming contours of my thighs. I feel like someone else. Just as the film is about to start you leap up and disappear into the dark, weaving down the sloping floor towards the green glow of the Toilets sign. Lateness, the near miss, close shaves. You seem to need them. Your favoured mode of travel is flying by the seat of your pants. I know you'll miss the beginning. You often do. Whereas I appear to find it impossible to be late. The punctuality gene is quite a cross to bear. It means a lot of waiting.

I relax into the beautiful Spanish lament of the title sequence, loving the darkness around me, the light of the story drawing me in and the company of strangers. There is something different about the first shot of the heartbroken woman asleep on her bed. She looks real and solid and very sad. But more than that, there is something unusual about the camera, the way it tracks her body and holds its look on her exhausted face. It is as if this camera does not leer at or long for women in the way we are used to.

I see you peering down the wrong row and then you are back and reaching for my hand in the dark. Your slender fingers close round mine.

'Have I missed anything?' you whisper hotly into my ear. I lean into your ear to try to begin an answer but your face is already absorbed by the light of the screen. You hold on tight to my hand.

10th September 1989

We wake in the chill damp of our sleeping bag to find an Alsatian's muzzle inches from our heads. A voice from further up the beach shouts in Greek and the dog dances round us, flicking dog spit into our hair. We lie completely still, not sure whether to be afraid or not. I enjoy the moment, squeezed tight against your thumping chest like twins among the nylon smells of childhood. A whistle rends the air and the dog bounds off. We poke our heads out and can just make out the man's shape waiting by the edge of the sea. The man and the dog are almost invisible as they move off towards the scrub at the edge of the beach. Out of the corner of my eye I catch the dying dive of a shooting star.

Our holidays are the best times. It's like it was before we lived together. When it was either your place or mine. Living together is probably the last thing lovers should do. Living together is what we did with our parents.

Here in Greece, it is almost impossible to believe that the house, the builders, work, the tube, the Angel exist at all. We live on honey and yoghurt and fish and cheap wine. We have nothing to do but read and the faint boredom makes us lustful. Also, I have to confess, we are both looking pretty damn bloody lovely. Our bodies are lean and brown and mainly naked. We feel compelled to make love in places of historic interest. Churches, volcanoes, ruins. We love a metaphor. I have tried to teach you to swim without fear but your mum got to you first. When she heard we were going on holiday she delivered an oft-told cautionary tale. 'Well don't go in the sea Mark because no there's no need to be laughing I'm absolutely serious as Dad will tell you won't you Ron what do you mean what you know very well what that time we were in Malta and I'd only gone in to rinse the sand off my feet and I sat down in really shallow water and suddenly this giant wave came out of absolutely nowhere and covered me completely and I mean *completely* and before I knew it I was dragged along the seabed and turned over and upside down and I didn't know which way was up well when I did finally get my head up for a breath I put my arm up in the air waving like this at Ron and I called out once Ron! but of course he wasn't paying a blind bit of notice and then *fortunately* a very nice foreign man heard and heaven knows how but he was just beside me right there and he put his arm out like this and grabbed hold of my hand and oh the relief when he got me out of the water and up on my feet of course Dad was none the wiser but what I'm saying to you is *don't* go in the sea it's very very dangerous so be *care*ful.'

I love swimming in the sea. Under the water the world above is almost silenced. Like being in space. I try to teach you to enjoy it too. But you won't get your face wet. And you cheat by bouncing one foot on the seabed, your head jerking with the effort of keeping your chin high. Once, you managed to swim with me out of your depth. There was a moment of delight in the freedom and the having done it. Then seized with the panic of nothing below your feet, you turned away, angry and deaf to my entreaties to stay. You doggy paddled madly to shore and stretched yourself out on the hot stones under the burning sun.

15th September 1989

We're strapped into our seats staring out of a porthole at the shimmering tarmac of Athens airport. My tan is already vanishing from my legs. I study the bolts of the wing panels. I stare at the back of the seat in front of me. I take a look at the emergency card in the seat pocket. I check out the sick bag and the flight path map in the magazine. In the aisle, an air hostess is going through the emergency routine for us to the usual voice-over.

'In the event of the aircraft landing on water . . .' surely a contradiction in terms '. . . your lifejacket is under your seat . . .' A collective surreptitious foot search by passengers ascertains that this is patently not the case. She does the pretend puffing bit, the pretend pulling bit and then she does the twirl with the tapes tied in a double bow round the front. Her mask of slap and death's head grin fail to conceal her boredom with this safety mumbo-jumbo. And I don't blame her. It's a bit embarrassing for all of us really. Why are we going through this rigmarole? Presumably even standing up is unlikely in the event of a fall from the sky, let alone removing your stilettos.

The routine done with, the cabin crew perform a perfunctory checking of seat belts, slam a few lockers in case anyone's dozed off during the floor show, ignore the woman across the aisle whose seat appears to be collapsing and stalk off to be seated for take-off.

The plane moves gently towards the runway, pauses as if thinking about it, begins to howl like a missile and hurls itself down the concrete, causing the cabin fittings to shake and rattle alarmingly. I look at your eyes for traces of fear. Nothing there. You squeeze my hand and kiss me. No sign in you or others that the end might well be nigh.

And then, contrary to all laws of physics and metaphysics that I'm aware of, the plane hauls itself very slowly off the earth. It tilts sideways till we are almost at right angles so we can feel the fearsome impossible weight of us and the fatal pull of the planet, then wobbles and tips and regains its balance, just before it's too late, and is soon nosing spacewards, apparently weightless in a gentle, smooth ascent.

If gravity can bend space, how the hell can it let this plane up? I ask you silently. You pull me close and kiss my neck. You like to sit at the window and watch the slanting, disappearing terrain beneath, to see the solid earth drop from beneath us and become a map. Even the reckless tilting, undercarriage clunking and random flapping of wing flaps, which to me are all evidence of panic and confusion in the cockpit, leave you completely unmoved. We judder through and beyond the clouds, enter a void of calm and finally I can relax.

We have consumed our little portions of food and now sit with a tower of plastic, cellophane and bottles stacked in front of us, unable to move. Which is presumably the point. I am reading R. D. Laing, famous and allegedly mad psychiatrist, who has just died. He tells me that we are all murderers and prostitutes. Well just one journey on the tube in rush hour would tell him that. The air hostess appears and jerks a coffee pot at us. I hold my cup in the air and she fills it to the brim with searingly hot coffee. The murderous prostitute does you, then turns to the row behind us.

'We are bemused and crazed creatures, strangers to our true selves, to one another,' continues Laing. But now, up here, cruising smoothly at thirty-three thousand feet, side by side in space and holidayed, it doesn't feel as though we're strangers. It feels like we're twinned, connected somehow. I don't know if that is love. You tell me that it is. And I want to believe it is true in the same way I want to believe this plane will stay up. I look at you, your head bent over a Penguin Classic. Crystals of salt trace the tiny hairs of your ear. I read some lines from your book because that is an irritating habit of mine and because I want to know what's inside your head. The fragmented lines look like modern poetry. Maybe the Penguin Classic cover is a decoy. I look again, stealing the words hurriedly.

'Godlike the man / who sits at her side'

Glancing at the top of the page, I see it's Catullus and two thousand years old. I read more.

'nothing is left of me, / each time I see her'

The thing is I have no idea if this is how you see me. I have a feeling, though, that it's what you are looking for through the lens of your camera. All at once, the plane dips, then drops, then shudders earthwards for a moment. All eyes fix on the air hostess and the coffee pot, both of which defy gravity by remaining upright.

'What the hell was that?'

'Just turbulence.' Without taking your eyes from your book, you hook your arm around me in a shut-up-and-keep-still kind of a way.

'Don't you ever feel afraid?' I ask your chest. Maybe dying like this wouldn't be so bad.

'Love you,' you intone, like a Hail Mary, eyes still glued to Catullus.

I return to Laing. 'From the moment of birth, when the stone-age baby confronts the twentieth-century mother, the baby is subjected to these forces of violence, called love.' I think of Mabel and Lily and Octavia and Alice and decide Laing is right. I think of you and me and our parents and hope he is not.

'Builders should have finished the kitchen by now,' you tell me, finishing off the miniature bottle of Retsina and abandoning Catullus for a minute. I really would rather not have a discussion about the builders.

'But they were still waiting for the plumber when we left. They'll have taken two weeks off. Mark,' I struggle upright with my Ronnie Laing, 'do *you* think that "love is an act of violence which ultimately destroys its potentialities"?'

'What?' You grab my book, look at the cover and toss it dismissively back in my lap, 'That's bollocks. Look, Alan promised he'd have it finished by the time we got back. You did give them the thousand pounds before we left, didn't you? And we must remind them they'll have to put an RSJ in. You better contact the Building Inspectors, too.' I write myself reminders on the flyleaf of Laing. I'm not looking forward to landing.

'What about just sex then?' I ask. 'Does sex destroy its potentialities ultimately, do you think?'

'Probably. If you run out of ideas.' Needless to say, having goaded you into responding, I feel this mild remark lodge in my heart like a poisoned arrow. It's probably a warning, I think gloomily. 'We must go to that place, you know, in Wales where they sell old floor tiles. We can get Dad down to help clean and restore them . . . Shit, did the radiator guy get back to you? You know that mosaic we saw on the church ceiling? It would be good to have one of them on the bathroom floor . . .'

Hazily, I daydream about our holiday, the noise of cicadas and distant tourists, the faint fear in the back of my mind of serpents and scorpions, and the slipperiness of our bodies and our minds in the heat.

'And that's not a big job, is it?' you continue. 'Connecting up the gas pipe? We should tell them tomorrow to dig a channel along the floor so we can have an indoor water feature.'

'Mmm. Like a Roman bath, you mean?' I nibble your earlobe in an effort to stem the tide of Home Improvements.

'What's that?' You turn to look at me. I brush my lashes across your cheek again, something my mum used to do.

'A butterfly kiss.' You pause. I can see me in the pupils of your eyes. I'm not sure if it's insect love, talk of plumbing, Laing or Catullus that inspires you as you slide your hand down the front of my shorts.

'Come on,' you say, pushing me to my feet. 'I've never screwed in a plane.'

You have no shame at all. Unlike me. I am more or less

constantly racked with worry about what others might be thinking. You're shy but you're not ashamed. I'm ashamed but not shy. Is this a good thing or not, I think, as you knock imperiously on the toilet door, say 'Sorry' to someone waiting in the queue and slide in.

The grey interior and weak lighting above the mirror gives us both a corpse-like sheen. Half on and half off the tiny metal sink we set upon each other like, well, like murderers or prostitutes. Thirty-three thousand feet up we are defying gravity, both the Newtonian and the parental kind. Just as you come ('No, of course I didn't, Mark. How could I in that position? And in less than fifteen seconds?') the bonger bongs and Captain Hesketh informs us we have begun our descent and would we please return to our seats, fasten our seat belts, ensure our seats are in the upright position, fly with them again soon and have a safe and pleasant onward journey. And that it is raining in England and unseasonably cold.

Alan and Bob are just leaving as we turn the corner into our road. Alan scratches his giant paunch unhappily and nods at us.

'Good holiday?' He stands looking off to the middle distance, one hand down the front of his tracksuit bottoms. He attempts a smile but looks like he might cry. Bob stares at my breasts and jingles the keys in his pocket.

'Great, thanks,' you smile and shift your bag to the other shoulder. 'Before you go, can we just talk through one or two things?'

'We've took out your bathroom,' says Alan defensively.

'Shall we just go in for a minute?' you suggest. Bob lights up a Lambert & Butler and leans against the van.

'Yeah. Course. When we get back. Yeah? Just got to collect some cement. Be back around . . .' Alan looks at his imaginary watch, '. . . half hour?' Bob stops staring at my breasts and unlocks the van door. A shower of polystyrene cups falls into the gutter as he opens it. Inspired, he wrenches out the ashtray from the dashboard and empties that into the gutter too.

Inside, the house feels cold and damp. There's that nameless smell of what must be old London, long dead, dug up. A layer of dust covers every surface. Rubble litters the bare boards. Dropping our bag in the hall, you make your way eagerly downstairs. An open milk carton, used teabags, the *Sun* and empty packets of Lambert & Butler lie scattered on the kitchen floor. The sink appears to have been mistaken for a urinal. You take down the plywood wall and stand in the gaping hole surveying the back yard.

'They've dug the foundations,' you observe. I stand next to you and look at the crater in our back yard. 'And they've taken out the bathroom,' you add looking up to the second floor where the ripped and torn remains of the avocado suite are exposed to the elements. 'You see the glazing will go all the way up to the height of the ceiling there.' Looking up, I notice Sad Neighbour glowering at us through his top window. 'Fucking yuppies,' says a thought bubble above his head.

'I can't believe we still don't have a wall though.' I have to say this. I know you won't like it. But the wall is important to me. I turn round but you've gone.

'I can't believe it!' you shout from upstairs somewhere. I clamber over the rubble and make my way upstairs towards your voice. You are standing in the sitting room staring at the fireplace. 'They've put the damn fireplace in backwards!' You are actually pulling your hair like a cartoon character.

And it is true. The cast-iron fireplace is cemented in with its rusted flue and back plate facing outwards into the room, the ornate front buried into the sooty interior of the chimney. The marble lintel looks as if it's sloping downwards at an angle. Or that could just be the house.

31st October 1989

As winter approaches, the walk from the tube to our house offers a choice of being jumped by a mugger or crushed by Donovan's Aggregates. Once the clocks go back it becomes hazardous as early as five o'clock, by which time we are plunged into darkness.

Tonight it is Halloween and the Angel is teeming with Youth, some only a few feet tall, most of them masked and all of them demanding money with varying degrees of menace. I stride along the centre of the road with the other street-wise commuters, leaving the Youth to prey on the hapless old folk who are too slow-moving to dodge White Van Man, High-speed Bus and Juggernaut.

Having sprinted the final few yards to our house, I open the front door, inhale the damp mortar air and crunch my way over the rubble downstairs to the kitchen. I look around and see that Alan and Bob have not been. It's been two weeks since we saw them. A volt of rage zips through me, coming to a dead end in my head where it tightens into a skull ache. I take the phone and dial Alan's number. The phone, like everything else in the house, is coated with a film of gritty dust. After a very long time, Alan answers.

'Alan, it's Genevieve.'

'Who?'

'From the Angel.'

There's a wince from the other end before he says, 'Oh, yeah.'

I can't work out why this money-in-return-for-work relationship, which seems to operate quite well in other spheres of life, is so problematic with builders. Be firm. Don't apologise to him. Talk straight.

'Sorry, but I was just ringing to find out if there was any chance you knew when you might be able to get the water turned back on . . .'

'We're waiting on the plumber. He was supposed to come Thursday.'

The door knocker raps urgently.

'Hang on, Alan, Mark's just arrived.' I race up the stairs and open the door. Three hooded ghouls stand on the step with white face masks in scream mode.

'Trick or treat.'

'Sorry, I'm on the phone,' I tell them, slamming the door to a volley of abuse followed by a couple of soft thuds. I race downstairs again and pick up the phone. Amazingly, Alan is still on the line.

'Look you said yesterday he was definitely coming today,' I pant, switching on Alan's industrial lamp to get a bit of light in the kitchen. Bouquets of wires splay out from the walls like skeletal hands.

'Yeah, that's what he told me.'

'But we haven't had any hot water for two weeks.' I pace the room as far as the phone cable will let me.

'Thing is, right, he's got held up on another job.' There is more banging from the front door. I hide along one wall next to the window so they can't see me.

'Well get another plumber.' I throw three old copies of the *Sun* and a couple of *Hustlers* in the tea-stained swing bin. Something wet hits the glass.

'Then it'd be an even longer wait.'

'Look just give me a date. When does the plumber say he can come? I'm not joking, Alan, I'm going mad living in this mess. And why have you got to wait for the plumber anyway? There's tons of stuff you could be doing. Putting the floor down for one thing.'

'Can't do that till we put the heating pipes in. Otherwise we'd just have to dig your floor up again.'

'Well the bathroom then. Why don't you just finish that?'

'Same reason.'

'No I mean the walls. Build the walls of the bathroom.'

'That's the joiner. Now he did come – last Wednesday I think it was – but he couldn't get in. You wasn't there.'

'I was at work. We both were. How do you think we pay you, Alan?'

'Hold on a mo, I think me battery's going . . .'

'Hello?'

At the insolent monotone of disconnection I slam the phone down. The door knocker beats heavily once again.

'Oh piss off.'

Your voice calls from the hall and you and Angus come down to the half-light in the kitchen. You kiss me, ask why there's egg on the door, whether the builders have been and if there's any drink in the house.

'Children threw the eggs, Alan's just put the phone down on me, no we haven't. Hello, Angus.' I look warily at him, trying to gauge his mood. He gives me a hug and looks at the chaos around him.

'Let's eat out then.' You pick up your keys and look at your watch. 'We can catch a film later if we hurry.'

Part of me needs to sit in front of the telly in pyjamas but sitting down isn't possible until we get rid of the dust. And I know that for you the whole point of living in the Angel is so that we can avail ourselves of the bars, restaurants and cinemas which are opening near by. I don't want to disappoint you and, usually, after the first glass, the exhaustion of the day dissipates. I pick up my bag and we leave.

The spooky children are hanging around on the corner. They take one look at Angus and disappear. It's great walking along with Angus. You don't have to walk in the middle of the road for one thing and the beggars never ask Angus for money. I trot between you in an effort to keep up. A firework explodes in the hallway of a block of flats followed by a black cat that streaks across our path.

'Don't you just love these ancient English traditions, Angus?' I say. 'Do they have them in Scotland?'

'Of course,' says Angus. 'It's the same as here. Me and my sister would go guising just like those kids. But we weren't allowed to eat pork on Halloween. That was forbidden by the Witchcraft Act which I don't think they got round to repealing until the 1950s in fact. And we didn't trick if there were no treats. Trickery is quite a recent American import.'

There's a lull in the conversation which I quickly divert away from any Helena potholes.

'Work was crazy today,' I laugh. 'I'm knackered. I think it's the tube journey that does it. That and the early start. I'm going to start taking the car, Mark, and just hope that it gets me there.'

Another firework blows up inside a dustbin somewhere near by.

'Last time you tried that it broke down on Vauxhall Bridge in the rush hour.' He opens my coat and peers at my clothes. 'That's a funny thing you've got on, Genevieve. Where'd you get it?'

'That's my uniform, Mark.'

Angus gives you a shove towards the gutter and we dive in through the door of O'Donnell's and into the warm tobacco and alcohol fug and clatter of the bar.

9th November 1989

'Are you watching?' says my mum down the phone. 'Look at the news!'

'What?'

'The wall! It's coming down.'

'Hang on, I'm going to put you down this end but you should still be there when I get upstairs.'

I take the stairs two at a time, turn on the television and pick up the phone. The scenes from Berlin are shown on every channel.

'When the wall went up,' says my mum, 'we listened. On the radio. We.' There's a shout from outside, in the square opposite our house, where the winos are on the sofa. One is gesticulating with a can and shouting into the air in front of him and the other one has keeled over sideways. In Berlin, the crowd swarms around, and over, the wall. The reporter's voice comes in broken bursts, searching for the right register – awe, concern, disbelief.

'Oh. Look. Climbing the. Helping their. Oh. Lord,' cries my mum.

I join in with a few squawks of amazement while part of me wonders in dismay at the crumbling of the seductive, romantic notion of Communism. What will become of Red Square in the moonlight and the slow, balletic goose-step of the Red Guard in the snow at the entrance to Lenin's tomb? One of the winos opposite has got to his feet now and is beginning a slow-motion vertical swim to the kerb like a joke drunk. A bony dog, nose hoovering the ground, weaves its way around them, lost in an olfactory world of its own. Drawn to the beleaguered sapling planted by the council, it craps on the path beside it.

'Jesus, that bloody dog!' I shout at the window.

'Oh! Look. Do you see? That man?' cries my mum.

On screen, East Germans climb on each other's shoulders to reach the top of the wall, hands pushing up at their legs and backs. On top of the wall, West Germans reach down to haul them up. Everyone wears an expression of ecstatic joy, except for the soldiers who stand and stare, embarrassed and uncertain. A man with a hammer begins thumping at the stone. Others rush to join him, pocketing lumps of graffiti-scrawled mortar and shouting with glee into the camera.

'It's like. Like the end of the war. When. Oh. Sorry.' I can hear gasps and wet sniffs. I hold the phone tight to my head.

'I've got to go, Mum.' I look down at my regulation hospital shoes. 'I'm on duty in an hour.'

I hate the way I shy away from her pain but it's always felt like something we may not survive. Only now Bill has died do I realise, with a sour sense of guilt, how much I relied on him to deal with all this.

'There's this thing between us,' I told you once, the words falling one by one from my mouth as I tried to explain about my mum and me. 'The twin that didn't survive. Then my dad—'

'Genevieve,' you sighed, 'that was years ago.'

'Yes, but I kind of . . .' I falter. 'I think that . . .'

In fact, I don't know what I think until I form the words. 'I wonder how she must have seen me, as a baby.' No, that's not really it.

You pulled your arm out from beneath my head. I looked up and noticed the film of dust on the ceiling lamp above our heads.

'I think she's probably over it by now. Bill's really . . .'

'It feels like there's a dam or something, waiting to burst. It scares me.'

I watched a tiny pulse in your neck start up while the words lay scattered between us on the bed sheet. I felt ashamed, as though I'd confessed to a belief in the occult. You don't believe in digging up the past. Middle-class, liberal shite.

'Is that crack up there getting bigger?' you asked, looking up at the ceiling too.

23rd December 1989

It's my early shift and as I go down the escalator into the tunnel, the night workers are coming up. We pass each other as we glide, yawning, in opposite directions. As I sit on the train heading south on the Northern Line, too bleary-eyed to read, I think back to this time last year. I tried to ask Helena about the Lockerbie flight once. And her dad. Was it true that he'd known? She'd lifted her head and looked me full in the face and said, 'Angus is mad, Genevieve. I never had a ticket for that flight.' There was a small silence, just long enough for me to understand that I had trespassed and then dizzy Helena returned, managed to spill someone else's coffee, pulled her scarf off her neck to help him clear it up and had his phone number within about fifty-five seconds.

Mary is seventy-six and was committed fifteen years ago after her husband died. This morning Mary lies on the floor by her bed in a pool of urine and shit. As she does every morning. Sister Stone is built of tungsten and wears her uniform like a bomb casing. She is talking to Mary sternly. As she does every morning.

'We'll have to put you in a cot, we will, if you keep doing that, Mary. And you won't like a cot. With bars on, will you? Like a baby? You're not a baby, are you?' She has one arm hooked under Mary's armpit and I have one hooked under the other.

'Oh, John. Whatever's happened here?' sobs Mary, close to tears and surveying the mess on the floor with bewilderment.

'Come on, up you get now.' Sometimes Sister Stone sounds almost kind. 'Goodness gracious, we can't have you getting into such a mess so near to Christmas, can we now? You see, Nurse, if we don't restrain her at night, she will do herself a real injury and then the powers that be will be down on us like a ton of bricks.'

We lower Mary into a wheelchair and pull the sodden sheets off her bed. From the other bed on the other side of the room, Alice watches us, sheets pulled up to her nose. It is 6.15 in the morning. Mary starts to weep noisily. She is one of the few patients on this ward who cries. It's unnerving. I crouch down beside her and take her hand. Her nails are embedded with shit.

'I think I should be getting back now,' she tells me, face wobbling. She looks in despair at her soaked nightie. 'I should be getting back now. I've got to get his tea on.'

'John is dead, Mary, as you very well know. Now, Nurse, I suggest you take Mary down to the bathrooms and clean her up. She might as well get dressed and wait in the day room.' Sister Stone is flapping a clean sheet over the plastic mattress cover. I consider bludgeoning her to death with the bedpan. 'Well go on! We haven't got all day! There's twenty old ladies to wake, dress, feed and medicate.'

'Why don't we let them lie in? I mean, they don't really have to get up for anything.'

Sister Stone selects a look from her repertoire of withering stares for blithering idiots, delivers it and returns to subduing the sheet on the mattress.

'What happened, Mary?' I ask as I wheel her down the corridor. I like listening to these women talk about their lives. It amazes me how it is the dull routine that is retained. Maybe that's what love is. Not passion, or the wedding or giving birth but getting the tea on at 5.30 every day and sleeping in the same bed as someone else for decades.

'John always sleeps on that side. Always. And then one morning I turned over . . .' She stops herself with the past tense.

When the others come on duty, they join me in the bathrooms where we lift and shuffle the women in and out of the cubicles. Winnie, head bowed to her chest, delivers a constant high-pitched litany of household chores, fingers and thumbs moving as if preparing a pastry mix. 'Now where'd I put that . . . ? Just pop this in the . . . you'll want to skim that first . . .' Apart from her fingers, her body is rigid with a sort of rigor mortis. If you try to dress her, or in anyway interrupt her domestic soliloquy, she cries out in distress. When I first met her I thought she must be in pain. Sister Stone does not believe that the mad can feel pain. After a while, I think I am starting to wonder too. I try as gently as is possible to prise Winnie's arm away from her side so I can lift her nightclothes over her head. The cries get a little louder. I talk to her, telling her about my journey in this morning, what I've bought your family for Christmas and how we're driving down there tonight to spend Christmas with them.

'Oh Come Let Us Adore Him,' is belting out of the wall speakers by the time breakfast is over. This is probably Winston's idea of a joke and I look round to find him with an arm round Lily and an arm round Mabel, singing loudly as he escorts them down to the day room. It's only nine o'clock but the women have been up for at least two hours and are seated in their chairs in the day room to endure the next three hours until it's time for more food. On Sister Stone's ward everyone has to hurry to get nowhere and to do nothing. The Christmas decorations have been up on the Long Stay Geriatric ward since 31 October. The radiators are on full throttle despite the warmth of the weather outside and on the stereo the peculiar sadness of the Christmas compilation pervades the atmosphere. A few bony fingers tap the arms of their chairs to the rhythm of Bing, Noddy and Sir Bob. Mabel looks as though she might celebrate by murdering Octavia who is finding herself compelled to remove all the Christmas tree decorations. I make a note to check Mabel's sedation before Santa arrives this afternoon.

In the crush on the tube, face flattened against the wool and fur of my fellow travellers and despite the atmosphere of viruses, exhaustion, pungent body sprays and seasonal panic, I feel a rush of excitement about Christmas. I still love it. And you are a voracious present buyer. With a gratifying surge of generosity, I pay the homeless person slumped outside the tube station a whole pound coin instead of the usual twenty pence.

'What have we got my mum?' you ask, helping me through the door with my bags.

'A lamp, some perfume, a book, a photo album and a tree.'

'I'll try and get her some bathroom scales then. And my dad?'

'A compass, a map, a book about hot air balloons, a jumper and a garden shed.'

'What's his main present then?'

I look at you. 'Hand On Your Heart!' Kylie is bouncily bursting through the wallpaper again. She is a bloody singing exclamation mark. 'Hand On Your Heart!!' she yells again. Hopefully, when the doors are slammed shut on this mean little decade, Kylie will get locked in with it and stay there. A Kylie-free nineties. I look forward to it.

We pack the tiny car with the presents. They won't all fit. We swear and ferment a little mutual hatred and disdain, laying down some seriously lethal stuff for use at a later date. I'm thinking, If only you didn't have this thing about giving so much stuff to your family every Christmas and you're thinking, If only I could afford a proper car. Then I think, Why do we have to go to your family every Christmas anyway? In the end there is nothing for it but to leave our presents to each other behind and drive the two hundred miles of motorway with the boot of the car wide open. Once we get south-west of London, the temperature inside the car begins to drop noticeably.

To my shame, I always defer to your wish to drive. I notice I am not alone in this piece of feminine feeble-mindedness. I look carefully at all cars overtaking us and see a determined-looking man at the wheel and the vacant stare of the woman in the seat beside him. Like a lobotomised passenger. The problem with this is that the driver can always not talk because he has his mind on the road. And important things like Getting There and Not Getting Done for Speeding. Trying to have a conversation with you while you're staring straight ahead reminds me a little of talking to Lily Shuttle.

'I hope my mum's all right,' I say for starters. My extended family, what there is of it, is awkwardly scattered across the country. And I can't compete with the superglue that holds your family together. Your family is nuclear.

'Why shouldn't she be? Your uncle will be there with the kids.'

'Because it's Christmas and we're going to *your* parents again.'

'She was invited, too.'

'Well maybe she wants to spend Christmas in *her* family home not the home of some people she's met twice.' I twiddle dismally with the radio knob. 'Do They Know It's Christmas?' asks Band Aid. I quite like that one.

'For God's sake, turn it off.'

'I quite like that one.'

I find the news. It sounds like things are hotting up in Bucharest. We listen in silence, trapped in the slow lane, soporific cat's eyes leading the way back to your past.

Four

26th December 1989

'THE ANTI-CHRIST is dead!' I tell Marion, repeating the jubilant words of the Bucharest radio announcer and because I've been fighting an overwhelming urge to say or do something outrageous for several hours. Marion is hovering in the doorway. I've hidden the remote control so he won't turn over to watch the golf.

'You what?' says Marion. 'Now where the blazes did I put the blinking flicker?' He lifts up the seat of the chair and tosses a few cushions around.

'They've shot Mr and Mrs Ceauşescu,' you tell him. We're lying in a stupor on the settee as though dropped from a great height. Stunned into submission after sixty hours of television, microwave dinners and sparkling wine in room temperatures generally only found in the Caribbean at this time of year. But sex has saved us. We're in love again.

'Mr and Mrs *who*?' His searching has become slightly frantic. 'Mark, have you got the blasted flicker?'

'Out the way, Dad, I can't see.'

We are transfixed by the television replays of grainy video footage showing an elderly couple shuffling off to a yard to be shot by firing squad. Funny how small and ordinary tyrants look after their fall. We are treated to a satisfying close-up of Mister, toppled in a truncated X shape, a spatter of blood on the bullet-ridden wall behind his head. Next to him lies the Missus, looking like she's just had a fall outside Marks & Spencer, apart from the stream of blood leaking from her head. We both hope Mrs Thatcher is watching. It is a surreal and fitting end to a year of unthinkable upheavals. Book burning in Bradford, tanks in Tiananmen Square, Berlin, Romania, our back wall, Dilly Nettles. It feels uncomfortably as though real life is catching up with the big screen.

Jubilant, tearful crowds embrace the soldiers waving the Romanian flag with the centre torn out of it. One soldier on a passing tank throws white flowers down to the people. I've seen this on screen before in other revolutions and wonder whether all tanks are equipped with carnations for just such an eventuality. 'It means I have not lived for nothing,' a weeping man tells a news reporter before he is swept up in the crowd.

'Lord above, whatever is going on there?' asks Marion, at the replay of Mrs Ceauşescu shouting at the men in yellow boiler suits who are tying her hands behind her back.

'The Romanians are having a revolution, Dad.'

'Having a what? A revolution, did you say? Whatever for? Now come on, you two lovebirds. Where's me flicker? It's the golf on ITV.' Marion winks at me. I wink back.

'Shall we go back to London today?' I whisper in your ear.

'I thought we were staying up for New Year,' you whisper back.

'Heavens to Betsy,' says your mum, watching Marion upend both armchairs and empty the wastepaper basket. 'Whatever is he doing now?'

'But I don't want to have a sit-down-buffet at The Fiveways Motel at six thirty with your parents' friends and then watch the New Year on the telly,' I hiss back. 'We did that last year. And the year before that. We could go to London. You know, Sex and Drugs and Rock and Roll.

What young people do.' I beam at you in what I can only hope is an alluring way, full of promise and extra-special favours in the connubial department. You look tormented, then sullen, then vacant. I've lost, I know it, so I lob a pathetic loser's missile, hold up my copy of *A Vindication of the Rights of Woman* which I have been hanging on to like a life raft and which some previous reader from the library has helpfully highlighted. I point at a heavily pinked bit and whisper some of Mary Wollstonecraft's words of wisdom. 'A slavish bondage to parents cramps every faculty of the mind.' I give you a meaningful look and settle down to feel depressed about my lack of slavish bondage to my own parents. The thing is, I tell myself, given the lack of anyone else to continue this interesting dialogue with, when you pair off with someone, one set of parents has to go. And my parents are obvious candidates because they are so complicated: a little lacking in the marriage department. The fact that my dad took one look at the disaster surrounding my birth and scarpered means it's not really a level playing field when it comes to the game of Happy Families.

1st January 1990

'Who on earth is that?' asks Marion.

'Angelica Houston, Dad.' You lie with your head in my lap and one foot dancing in the air at shoulder level. We are watching a tape of *Crimes and Misdemeanors* that you've been sent. We haven't moved from this sofa since Christmas Eve. I am stuffed with snacks.

'What, her who's married to Jack Nicholson? Good grief, is it really?'

Your mum puts her head round the door, sees that our mouths are empty and darts in with a plate of sausage rolls. Marion picks up the TV guide and starts fidgeting with the remote.

'Dad, leave the flicker, I've got to watch this for work.'

'Ooh, now she is tall, isn't she?'

'I find it rather encouraging that Angelica Houston is still married to Jack Nicholson,' I say.

My mind strays to Dilly Nettles and my stomach falls a little at the prospect of watching *Snow Queen* on the telly tomorrow night. With her long hair, wild eyes and flimsy frame, I can see that Dilly is a faery child. A Keats' 'Belle Dame'. Certainly 'sans Merci', I think, recalling your tales of her ruthless dumping of her boyfriend, two actors and the gaffer by the end of the shoot.

'Love is a paradox,' a character in the film is telling us, like a patient parent to a confused infant. 'When we fall in love, on the one hand we are seeking to re-find the people to whom we were attached as children.' I steal a look at your parents and think of my mum and the photo of my dad. 'On the other hand,' continues the character, 'we are asking the person we love to correct all the wrongs that these early parents or siblings inflicted on us.' Well, maybe that's a possibility, but all this talk of parents. I don't think Woody Allen has taken into account Sid's theory of heterosexual love which she calls the Jenny Agutter Complex. Sid says that when boys watch *Walkabout*, the image of Jenny Agutter's pubescent body is burned indelibly into their cortex so that they are destined to wander the outback of life for ever, searching for a naked schoolgirl treading water in a billabong.

Just then, on the screen, the beautiful young woman (who has a bit of a Jenny Agutter hairline) falls in love with the man twice her age (no hairline there). My heart sinks. Obviously Woody Allen has heard of the Jenny Agutter Complex after all.

'This isn't by thingummyjig, is it?' says Marion.

'Woody Allen.'

'Really? A bit short on laughs, this one, isn't it?'

2nd January 1990

We are all glued to the screen watching *Snow Queen*. You keep disappearing. I wish you wouldn't. Especially when the sex scene comes up and there's just me and your mum and your dad and Dilly Nettles groaning in Hungarian. Some of it is beautiful, especially the snow and the ice. I hadn't realised before how snow alters the sound of everything. And where the acting is clumsy, the soundtrack does wonders. Afterwards, my mum rings. Your auntie rings. Everybody rings. Your mum cuts out all the TV schedules she can find with your film mentioned in it and sticks them into a scrapbook.

'So,' says Marion, topping up our glasses. 'What's she like, this thingummy, Lily, is it?'

'Dilly? Really nice.' You stuff another salmon vol-au-vent into your mouth.

'Hasn't she got a lovely smile?' says your mum wistfully.

'So. Is she being whisked off to Hollywood, then?' says your dad, turning up the volume on *Sports Roundup*.

'She's doing a Ph.D. in Philosophy.' Your voice is sticky with cream cheese.

'Is she? So. A bit of an all-rounder then?'

'1989 has been quite a year, hasn't it?' I'd like to change the subject before Dilly as Renaissance Woman takes root as a Conversation Topic for Marion.

'It certainly has,' agrees Marion. 'Apparently the Cold War is officially "over". I mean, credit where credit's due. Say what you like about Margaret Thatcher, she certainly got rid of the Reds.'

'No, Dad, the people had a revolution, remember? Thatcher doesn't do revolutions. And anyway, she wasn't there. She didn't even go to the Berlin Wall because she was too scared.'

'Scared? Mrs Thatcher? She's driven a bloomin' tank, you know.'

You and your dad are off and I would join in but there aren't any gaps. You machine-gun him with derision, denial and dogma. But Marion enjoys it. This is called Having A Conversation in your house. Still, it's true, things have changed a lot. Why, only three years ago you were making boring old documentaries about mental hospitals and corporate videos for the Welsh Tourist Board. And I was . . .

I make a mental note to rise meteorically and become Senior Consultant in Psychiatry with all possible haste.

Later in the pub, faces flushed with the heat of the open fire and warm beer, I try to talk to you.

'But weren't you . . . aren't you . . . do you . . . would you . . . you know?' This is as articulate as I get until after another pint I blurt out: 'But don't you want to sleep with someone as beautiful as that?' The fire hisses. It burns white hot at the collapsed centre.

'Genevieve! For God's sake. I would never sleep with an actress. They're nightmares. Monster egos. It's just a fucking job.' You return disconsolately to reading about the promising new British talent which is you in the Arts page of the paper.

5th January 1990

Back at our house we discover that very small burglars have relieved us of our kettle and radio. They got in through the coalhole by our front step. Presumably in full view of the occupants of the square opposite us who were possibly too pissed to realise that disappearing through the ground is not the customary means of entering a property. Alan and Bob have decided to prolong the holiday. On page three of the *Sun*, a woman's breasts stare up at us like giant eyes from the floor where the cooker should be. She has a Santa hat on. You phone Alan.

'Listen. If you don't fucking get your fat arse round here

now, I'm sending someone over to break your legs.' In fact what you actually say is, 'Oh. Is he? Sorry to hear that. Yep. OK. No problem. Nope. Yep. OK. Yeah. When he's feeling better. Bye.'

Upstairs, I open the door of the room we nervously call the nursery. I register the smell of soot, floorboards and exhaust and see at once that something has happened here. All our photographs have been emptied out of one of the packing boxes and spread over the floor. Close-ups of our faces grinning into the camera stare up at me from the floor. We look tanned and relaxed and happy. And innocently open to the scrutiny of the lens. No hint of the self-consciousness and imperceptible turning away that has begun to creep into our photos now. Some naked ones of me have been left on top. What's really creepy is not that someone has gone through our intimate stuff but that they want us to know that they've seen it. I don't know who has done this. The child burglars, perhaps. Maybe Bob. I put them away wondering what we thought we were doing when we took the pictures anyway. They're not the sort we're going to put in the family album. If we ever have one.

I wake in the night thinking I have heard someone coming up the stairs. I lie frozen, listening, propped up on one elbow. I stare over your sleeping form into the gloom. Inchoate, the now and the past, reality and fantasy, drift and settle in my mind. I realise that what has woken me is not a noise but a dream. In the dream I was on one side of the river and you were on the other. The water had risen and was rushing in a dangerous torrent just below the arches of the bridge. I knew I had to cross it to reach you but could risk being swept away if I did. As I began to inch my way on all fours you stood up and held out a hand. And I saw it wasn't you, but Angus.

11th February 1990

You phone me from Spain where your film is showing at a festival.

'Why don't you come out this weekend?' You've forgotten my exams.

'I've got an exam on Monday. I have to revise. Who's there with you?' My scalp contracts as I say this, which is a brand new addition to my collection of physical manifestations of dread.

'Um, Dud . . . Dak . . . and Daz.'

'No Dilly then?' I lean over and lick my knees. I taste of salt and rubble and metal.

'God knows what she's playing at. Cancelled at the last minute. What are you doing?'

'Kissing my knees. Watching Nelson Mandela give his speech.'

You tell me about your idea for your next film. You're going to make it all up as you go along. But starting with the end. And writing each day's shooting the night before. But backwards. The Stone Roses have agreed to be in it. You're going to shoot it in Portugal. It's going to be about a schoolgirl from Cardiff who runs away to see the Stone Roses play in Lisbon.

'Ooh. We went to Lisbon,' I remind you unnecessarily.

'Yeah. I thought she could stay in that little place we found overlooking the beach.'

'Do you remember that lovely Fado bar where we . . . ?'

'I'm going to suggest she gets a job there. As a waitress. Or a singer.'

'And there was that amazing view from the top of the cathedral – do you remember?'

'That was a great view. And the view of the city was pretty good too.' We snort together at the memories of our sacrilegious acts and say goodbye reluctantly. I hope there isn't a God. Although Nelson Mandela looks worryingly like the Second Coming. The crowd on television are singing

'Nkosi Sikele Africa'. It is a song that it is impossible not to be moved by. Rather different to 'God Save the Queen'. I wish I could catch one of these world-changing events. Be a part of something. Instead of travelling the tube, living in the grimy old Angel and sedating the mad. I resolve to stay in and revise Schizophrenia instead of going to a film with Helena.

17th March 1990

Winston and I take the drugs trolley through to the day room. The women are already queuing by the door except for Lily who has her head tipped back, mouth open, groaning. I check the list and let Winston do the measuring and administering.

'Doctor,' says Mary, 'I wonder if I could fetch up John's pills while I'm here?'

'Of course you can,' says Winston. 'I'll pop them in a bag for you and you can pick them up on your way out.'

'Thank you ever so much, Doctor,' says Mary, beaming at him. 'He's ever so good you know,' she murmurs to me on her way past.

Winnie, Octavia, Alice and the others file past and we dose them up. I wonder what the pharmaceutical bill is for this country. And what proportion of the nation is currently medicated. It's not that I disapprove of the drugs. I know that some of them are miraculous in their power to realign the brain so that it no longer sees the demons. It's just a sense that with the approach of the millennium, people are becoming ever so slightly hysterical. On the Northern Line anyway.

Mabel has reached the head of the queue. She is nearly as tall as Winston. She fixes her beady eyes on the cabinet.

'Not those,' I tell him as he reaches for the pericyazine. 'We've changed her over to a depixol depot, remember?'

Winston asks Mabel to wait, so he can give her the

injection when the others have finished. Mabel shakes her head vehemently.

'Exactly, Mabel. Not good for your ticker, is it, all those pills? You won't be able to do the egg and spoon race unless you're in good shape, will you?'

Mabel looks at me and then at him. I smile vacantly. Lily lobs a payload of abuse at everyone in general.

'You stand a good chance of beating Lily this year, Mabel. Just have to practise that running a little more,' continues Winston. 'And you know what Sister Stone keeps in the office for people who have injections, don't you?'

Mabel nods. Winston nods. I nod.

'Smarties,' says Mabel.

'Exactly,' says Winston.

'Will some bloody body help me please? I'm dying over here!' shouts Lily. 'I am fucking pegging out! And none of you cares. Call yourselves nurses? It's a bleedin' disgrace!'

Mabel trundles off to wait by the door for Winston, rubbing her large dry palms together in anticipation.

'Mrs Shuttle,' calls Winston, 'your turn.'

Lily pushes herself to her feet, sways precariously, aims her body at the trolley and propels herself our way.

'It's not right and you know it,' she moans. Winston hands her the measure of largactil. 'And I'm not having that filth.' Winston takes it back. 'Don't you dare.' She makes a shaky grab for it. 'Take the clothes off of me bleedin' back, you would.' She downs it in one, belches and returns to her seat.

At the window I see your face. My heart actually does leap.

'Ooh, Lover Boy is here,' says Winston, closing up the trolley and locking it. 'Where's he taking you tonight, then?'

'We're going to some posh film thing,' I say, waving at you in delight. 'I've got to wear a frock and lipstick.'

You give me a quizzical look and shrug. You don't know how to get in and somehow, you've managed to get yourself inside the quad. Acute Admissions are behind you and Geriatrics are in front. You are surrounded by lunatics.

I unlock the french doors and you step inside and kiss me hello.

'Ah, that's nice,' says Mary. 'She's brought her little boy to see us. Isn't he lovely?'

24th April 1990

It is over. Alan and Bob have gone. Not exactly finished but gone. One day I came back to find all their tools had disappeared. And Alan's phone number didn't work any more. And that was it. We never saw them again. It was kind of a relief. The smell of drying plaster has replaced the smell of wet concrete. There are not many walls left in our house now and it is a bit like living in an aircraft hangar. But undeniably beautiful. ('What a fantastic . . . space!') The building project has drained us of all our money, ('So come on, then, how much did it cost?!'), all our energy ('You didn't strip all the doors yourself, did you?'), very nearly all of us ('You both look so . . . slim!'). Our conversation recently has consisted solely of washing-machine spin speeds ('You'll need the extra spin once you're washing for a family'), the relative merits of beech, oak or maple worktops ('Blond woods give a marvellous light, soft feel to a room') and flue widths ('Otherwise it won't pull properly and you could get carbon monoxide poisoning.' 'Oh. Do you think Alan knew that, Mark?'). Our free time has been spent choosing furnishings in department stores, cast-iron baths in architectural salvage yards and on our hands and knees restoring vast areas of antique floor tiles with toxic substances. The skin from our fingertips has worn away. I can't feel much now. So here we sit in the unfamiliar space of our new home, the wreckage of last night's dinner party stacked in the butler sink. But still, it is not enough. You want more. You are sketching your plans for a roof terrace. I'm not sure I can survive a roof terrace project. Losing my back wall was bad enough. If the roof goes, who knows what might happen. If it does go ahead, I hope and pray there'll be a period of unemployment for you and double shifts for me.

'What?'

'Sorry. Did I say that out loud?'

You lift your pencil thoughtfully from the piece of paper and point it at me. You are getting An Idea.

'Then in the summer we could have a Bedouin tent on the roof. To keep the sun off.'

4th July 1990

The rush and hiss of testosterone is almost audible in England these days. For four weeks everyone with a Y chromosome has been swept up in the cultish rhapsody that is the World Cup. Every four years I make a concession to this homoerotic festival and, like many women, possessed as we are of just the why? chromosome, I try to learn the lingo, understand the rules and attempt to get transported by the spectacle of the matches. Mind drifting somewhat, as it is wont to do during all the many hours of television-watching that the World Cup necessitates, I find myself wondering whether, like the story of *The Emperor's New Clothes*, anyone else has noticed that the trophy that we keep getting shown being kissed and held aloft by leaping men, looks exactly like the head of a giant priapic gold penis. Do not say this out loud, Genevieve.

But what's nice about the four weeks is that the roads are empty whenever there's a match on and everywhere is strangely quiet. Like living in the country. What's not so nice, what with repeated shots of past winners kissing the giant penis, endlessly repeated shots of men whacking balls into the back of the net and the hours given to grey-haired football has-beens sitting around in their Farrah slacks criticising the players, is the unashamedly transparent fact that it is, after all, a man's world.

We're watching the semi-final between England and Germany with your parents and several of our friends. Most of the women are faking it, I suspect. Your mum is doing a lot of bustling in and out with cups of tea. But she's been married long enough to know not to knock the game. She shows an admirable semi-detached interest in what's going on without displaying any immodest sexual fever or foul language. 'Oooh. What a shame' and 'Oh, they do look tired now, don't they?' is, she knows, all that is necessary. Helena, on the other hand, is trying much too hard. Her attempts to join in with 'Where's the defence? *Where's the bloody defence?!*' and '*Jesus Christ* that was definitely off-side,' are just irritating. And because she's half American, not to mention the fact that she is also a woman, no one takes any notice of her comments anyway. The match gives the men everything they need, even, once Gascoigne's been shown the yellow card, lessons in crying.

'The men are getting hysterical,' I tell your mum in the kitchen. She staggers slightly as she moves towards the dishwasher with a towering trayload of dirty cups.

10th July 1990

An ominous crack has appeared in one of our walls which make us suspect Alan and Bob didn't put an RSJ in when they took the back wall off. We are in a state of profound and permanent sleepiness which could be due to the building work, the ageing process or carbon monoxide poisoning. And the council has sent a letter that suggests our extension is against the law and will have to come down. And you have discovered that the television company that liked your idea for the schoolgirl road movie in Portugal seems to not like it quite so much any more but may like it again if the script has a little less swearing by the female lead and a more mainstream soundtrack to attract a wider, younger audience. Someone suggested Kylie Minogue. So now you have to decide whether to make a crappy cop series based in Hull or a crappy cop series based in Birmingham. You're on the phone to your agent cajoling him to give you a better deal on the Birmingham one. We have looked at the scripts. They're dire. We have watched the tapes. They're dull. We talk through the options. There aren't many because we're broke. You say yes to the Birmingham one.

Angus comes round and the three of us sit outside in our coats, drinking, listening to the roar of the traffic and occasionally catching the unmistakeable whiff of cat shit. After a few glasses it is almost possible to imagine that we are in some hacienda courtyard. That, anyway, is the idea behind the pots of geraniums that the local cat population use as litter trays and the snail population use as their larder. Angus says the snail invasion is the result of the drop in the sparrow population. I don't think he's right. Sparrows eat spiders not snails, I'm sure, but it is true that I only see pigeons and magpies now. And snails and spiders. Perhaps birds are just getting bigger. Maybe we'll have vultures in Trafalgar Square before long.

Angus and I smoke his roll ups. I know I will regret this tomorrow morning, especially combined with the red wine, but I don't care right now. I'm flirting with Angus because he's being sad and funny and because he helped me across the terror torrent in my dream. He tells us how to rectify Alan's botched jobs. He asks you about your work. Bravely, you talk up the Birmingham job.

'And have you seen Helena recently?' Angus asks eventually, looking at the ground, rolling a giant spliff. He looks rather handsome in a ruined kind of way and I think that Helena, who has been giving me daily instalments detailing her cocained sexual adventures with the newsreader, must be mad to have let him go. In my head, Angus and I lie panting in one another's arms, drenched in river water. He kisses me for about half an hour. Then we come home and he fixes my boiler.

'Um. No. I've spoken to her. Once or twice.' ('God, Genevieve, I mean, honestly, we were at it all night. And I mean *all* night. I couldn't walk the next morning.')

There's a silence. You disappear inside to fetch more wine. Bloody hell, I think. Angus is *your* friend. You could at least commiserate with him. The first lungful of the joint feels like a frontal lobotomy. Wherever Angus gets his grass from, it occurs to me that it may be responsible for his episodes of bizarre behaviour. Reeling slightly and attempting to remember what we were talking about, I hand it back.

'The thing is, she said sex with me was the best sex she'd ever had . . . and . . . she was my best friend . . .' He's on autopilot now. I've heard all this before. 'I can't imagine you would ever do a thing like this to someone, would you, Genevieve?'

I do my best to look like a good person but I'm not fully in control of my facial expressions at this point. Have we done Helena? Something about rivers? God no, don't mention rivers. Or Oxo towers.

'Well . . . you know, I don't think Helena is very happy, Augus . . . I think she's kind of experimenting with . . .' Please come and rescue me, Mark, before I say cocaine or newsreaders.

By two in the morning, Angus has only reached the middle of his monologue about what real love is. There seems to be no way of stopping him.

'You two seem to have the perfect relationship,' he tells us. People always say this. I wish they wouldn't. I badly need to go to sleep. We've done prolonged and noisy yawning, we've done lovers' caresses suggesting that bedtime is imminent, we've done 'God have we really drunk all those bottles?' We've commented on how early we have to get up the next morning. I'm beginning to fear that when we said come round for a drink he thought we said come and live with us for ever.

And then Angus starts to cry. Not out-loud wailing or childlike whimpering but strangled, glottal sobs stuttered from his mouth like a death rattle . . . aghagh . . . ghlooo . . . zzzteee. It goes on for a long time and I think it would be nice if you comforted him and you are nearest. So I wait for you to put an arm round him, offer a kind word.

You sit completely still and stare into the shadows of the yard. The weeping increases in volume. I try to meet your eyes but you are unreachable. *Touch* him, I say silently. This is unbearable. *Say* something to him. But you do not move. You are frozen.

I am suddenly sober when I see it.

Five

2nd August 1990

I'M SAD for you because you hate your job. We lie tightly entwined on the weekend nights and you leave on Monday mornings very early. So early the traffic has barely begun and every now and then I can hear a bird braving it in the plane tree outside our house. It is rather touching that you hate leaving home. When the alarm goes off at 5.00 I feel a kind of despair at the prospect of beginning the separation again. I go downstairs to make you coffee and to help you pack. You stay in bed until the cab driver bangs on the door by which time I am desperate with anxiety on your behalf that you will miss your train. You leave in a panicked flurry so that we do not have time to say or feel any of the things inside us. The door slams and I hear the cab disappear.

When you ring at night you sound like a child at boarding school, knowing it's not going to get any better.

'It's only for six weeks,' I tell you, not very helpfully, accompanied by Kylie bawling 'Tears On My Pillow!'

'And then I'll be out of a job and we won't be able to pay the mortgage at all.' I know this is what you'll say. It's a reminder that your work is a dog-eat-dog world but rich and mine is safe but poor because I'm a public servant. 'Tears On My Pillow!' clamours Kylie, sounding anything but sad.

It's true that we haven't been able to withdraw any cash for a week and I've had to rely on the loose change that falls out of your pockets at bedtime to buy the milk. And strangely, the building work cost fifty per cent more than Alan quoted. And took three times as long. And wasn't finished. But apparently that is completely normal and happens to everyone we know who has had the builders in. I sit down in the kitchen and stare at the pile of unopened letters from the bank. Gingerly, I open one of them dated March. It is a very nasty short letter informing Mr Morrison and Miss O'Dowd (Ms damn it!) that our account is overdrawn by . . . JESUS! . . . five hundred pounds and fifty-seven pence and that we have been fined thirty-six pounds as a result. I open another envelope from the Building Society which informs us that our bank has been unable to pay our standing order due to insufficient funds and that our home is at risk. Shit. This is much more serious. Repossession is rife. I read about it all the time. No one knows what happens to the sad families pictured outside their front doors with their stuff on the pavement. In a panic I do some sums. We both earn the same and we seem to work all the time but we don't have enough money and we can't afford this house. I've just been promoted, probably too soon if the truth be told, but there is nothing for it but to try and get promoted again.

On my way to work I go into the betting shop and put our last fiver on a horse. The man on the radio said it was his tip for the day and at 30–1 it could solve all our problems. For the week. And he works at the BBC so he must know what he's talking about. Coming out of the bookies five pounds poorer, I take a close look at the prostitutes loitering by the phone box. I wonder how much they make a day. When I look up I see an old billboard for *Pretty Woman*. Julia Roberts has been sent by Hollywood to tell me that prostitution is a career option. Is this a sign?

11th August 1990

'Borislav is going crazy on the men's ward.' Winston selects the jam turnover and then changes his mind and wonders about the Bakewell tart. 'We've been forbidden to have the news on at any time. At lunchtime when he saw the coverage of the Croatian elections he started getting agitated. Then, there was a shot of the red chequered national flag and he started screaming and attacked the television with the fire extinguisher. We're all in the shit for not securing the fire extinguisher to the wall.'

'I don't understand the Balkans,' I say. My New Year's resolution was to come clean about my ignorance. I promised myself that if there was anything I didn't understand I would ask for clarification. I can't be the only one who doesn't know anything.

'Apparently they used a body double for the shots of Julia Roberts' legs.' Sid is leafing through a magazine that hasn't heard about the war in Yugoslavia but has heard about *Pretty Woman*.

'I mean, I thought the Croatian elections looked rather wonderful, what with all those doves and olive sprays. Why shouldn't they elect their own president?' I say, still intent on solving the Balkan question but staring in fascination at Julia Roberts' mouth.

'It's Nationalism, Genevieve. Nationalism is bloody dangerous.'

'To Borislav, a Serb, that chequered flag is as bad as seeing a Nazi wave a swastika at him. The Croats used to be fascists in the war.' Bloody hell. That is typical. Sid knows about the Balkans as well.

'And they killed hundreds of thousands of Serbs,' says Winston. 'They're not going to forget that in a hurry.'

'Borislav's never forgiven himself for being in England during the war. We had a special session about it so we could understand the guy a bit. But having said that, he is a psychopath even if he was on the right side during the war.'

'So who is on the side of right now?' I ask. 'Whose side am I supposed to be on? The Croats or the Serbs?'

'That's the whole point about civil war. You can never get to the bottom of it. It's the murderous rage of families and bloodlines. Lethal stuff.' Sid lights up. 'Especially when you slam a lid the size and weight of communism on top of it all.'

'Well and truly repressed,' says Winston. 'And the return of the repressed, when the lid finally blows, is not a pretty sight. Look around you.'

'Hey,' says Sid, 'will someone please explain to me the Richard Gere appeal? Is there anyone who can put their hand on their heart, stand up in public and say, "Yes, I find this man attractive"? There isn't, is there? It's a con. Women don't really like men like that. Is it a Hollywood gay plot or something, Winston?'

'Richard Gere? I wouldn't say no.'

'There you are. I knew I was right.'

28th November 1990

There is a riot in the day room. The air is filled with whistles, yelps, gasps, catcalls and flying paper cups. Several staff are on their backs on the floor kicking their legs and punching the air. '*YYYEESSSS!!! SHE'S GOING! I CAN'T BELIEVE SHE'S REALLY FUCKING WELL GOING!!!*' Winston is waltzing Octavia around the room. Sid has two cigarettes on the go and is making yipping noises and Lily has produced a brand new refrain: '*Shut* the fuck *up*, Nurse.' It's bedlam in here.

'How dare you! She's the best thing that ever happened to this country.' Sister Stone glares at us. She stands by her altar, The Drugs Cabinet, holding a 5ml plastic beaker in one hand and a bottle of Lithium in the other. Mabel towers motionless beside her, hands loose by her side, eyes fixed on the beaker. Above Mabel's head, Margaret Thatcher, looking suddenly old and clutching her handbag, emerges from the door of Number 10, pauses to speak to the waiting reporters, begins to cry and totters towards the waiting Jaguar.

'Nurse O'Dowd, I believe that is the telephone ringing,' Sister Stone says, bristling. I take a last look at the jubilant scenes on the television and run down the corridor to the office. I think it might be you. Struggling to unlock the door, I hope it will be you. Breathless, I grab the receiver and it is.

'Amazing news. Are you watching it?' you say, shouting above some office chaos of your own.

'Unbelievable. They keep showing that shot of Angus chasing the police horse in the Poll Tax riots. Did you see it?'

'I know.' We're both laughing.

'He's a national archive! Maybe there'll be tanks. And soldiers with carnations.'

'And guess what? They've said yes to the Portugal drama. Next autumn. I'm going out there in the New Year to cast it and find locations. We could go together.'

The future is suddenly filled with promise. Laughter gurgles up in me. Passing motorists are honking their horns. We arrange to meet after work to celebrate the end of an era. There's a roar of voices from Acute Admissions. I stick my head out of the door and look down the corridor.

'I've got to go, sweetheart. It's pandemonium here. I think there might be a breakout. Of staff that is.'

Back in the day room I see that over in Acute Admissions the staff are banging on the windows at us across the lawn, punching the air and shouting, 'YEAH!' Behind them the patients drift and hover and jerk in their habitual routines. Sister Stone leaves the ward in disgust and Winston turns the sound up on the television.

'Oh, John! It's Greta Garbo on the television,' says Mary. 'Doesn't she have beautiful hands?'

Six

17th January 1991

'UNDER COVER of darkness and a new moon, Operation Desert Storm began at about three a.m. this morning. First, nine warships, including US battleships *Missouri* and *Wisconsin*, began firing Tomahawk cruise missiles at targets in and around Baghdad.'

The news on the radio is not good. I am five days pregnant with our first child. You don't know this yet but I know this. We had a sort of conversation about children. Not exactly what you would call a planning-a-family type of conversation but an equivocatory kind of conversation around the topic of conception.

'What do you think about us getting pregnant then?'

'Aren't you on the pill?'

'Well yes, but I thought maybe I'd come off it. And we'd, you know, have . . . um . . .'

'An abortion?'

'Now why would I want another of those?'

'Are you telling me you're pregnant?'

'No I'm not. But I thought we could have a baby. It might make me stop smoking. And drinking. And assuming that we're going to have them one day then . . . you know . . .' I can't quite bring myself to say I'm not getting any younger. Because you actually do seem to be getting younger. What is the secret of your eternal youth? Never having to live in the house when the builders are there, possibly.

'Well, obviously, some day, it'd be nice.' You stuff the rest of the French tart into your mouth and nuzzle my ear. Wetly. 'Maybe we could start . . . trying . . .'

Great. Permission granted, I think to myself.

So I chucked my pills in the bin and two weeks later I know we conceived. I felt it actually. You'd laugh if I told you that but it's true. I felt the beginning of something. A meeting of, well if not minds, matter.

And now America and Britain have decided to have a war, as if we haven't had enough of those for one century. We watch the news bulletins sitting up in bed in the dark winter morning. We are shown aerial video footage of Baghdad crisscrossed with a gunner's viewfinder. We are colluding with the bombers whether we like it or not. We're in the bloody cockpits, for God's sake. Twentieth-century computer crusades. Infrared imaging, collateral damage, night-vision technology. I try to believe the tacit lie that in this hi-tech war the targets are only buildings and munitions dumps. But at the dull flash of the bomb on impact I feel sick and very afraid.

19th February 1991

I'm naked in the bathroom when you ring.

'I thought you'd be at work. I was going to leave a message.' I can hear the sound of a tram and snatches of Portuguese in the background.

'Well I'm here. I'm not on duty till two. I can't wake up these days. I feel like I've been asleep at the bottom of the sea. What message were you going to leave me?'

'Come out this weekend. It's beautiful here. I miss you.'

I twist round and view my body from the side. I think I can detect a swelling in my belly. My breasts are heavy. I look like someone else. My body seems to be taking over. It's nice.

'But we're broke.' I stand on the chair to get a better view.

'We can sort something out. What are you doing?'

'Taking pictures of myself in the nude. With mirrors.' I depress the shutter so you can hear the clack-snap. It sounds like certainty or truth. The shot is of my mother's long, slender back. I take another picture, this time of my mother's large, rounded arse ('childbearing hips, darling') and what I assume are my father's legs. I'm documenting my descent. I wonder which parts of you have been selected down there inside me.

'Hmm. Kinky. How are you feeling? Sick?'

'Not sick, slothful. I have to lie down and snooze a lot.'

'Really?'

'Mmm. Slothful. And terribly lustful too.'

'Slothful and lustful?'

'That's right. I'm being transformed into nothing but a sloth of lust.'

'Perhaps I should come back for the weekend then.'

'I think you'd better. I can feel a bit of a nap coming on right now.'

'I love you.'

'Hurry up then.'

'I'm on my way.'

26th March 1991

The gene-mapping poster on the wall looks a little like the Desert Storm Operations map in the newspaper on your lap. On one are the small white blotches that are tanks lit up by the infrared imaging from a bomber's cockpit and on the other are coloured blue lozenges representing CF genetic mutation. The doctor looks even younger than you and leans towards us in his chair. He is kind, but unable to conceal his excitement, as if he's just discovered a rare pair of breeding pandas after a long trip through the jungle.

'It's extremely fortunate that you agreed to take part in the screening trials at the hospital. As a result, you are going to be one of the first families to benefit from the discovery of the CF gene in 1989. And we'll be able to track you throughout the whole of your reproductive life . . .'

Why is he calling us a family I wonder, half pleased, half appalled? I stare out at Coram's Fields beyond his head. He's handing us a leaflet called *Cystic Fibrosis: the Facts*. But we know them all already. It is a recessive gene, carried on Chromosome 7, and mainly affects Caucasians. We have more in common than we thought. We are both carriers. Mutants. There is a one-in-four risk that our baby will be born with cystic fibrosis. Maybe that's what we recognised when we fell in love. 'Hey, darling, there's something about your DNA.'

'. . . clogged bronchial passages . . . plugged liver bile ducts . . . abnormal function of sweat glands . . . rarely survive beyond thirty . . .' The doctor is leaning forward in his chair. He is speaking quietly but is intent on conveying the full force of the facts. 'It's important that you find out immediately whether this baby is affected.'

If we didn't live in the Angel, near to this teaching hospital doing the trials, we would never have been offered the test. How different then would our future be? And what is to be our future, now that our past seems to be catching up with us?

'People only began understanding and naming the disease in the fifties but we think it was recognised as early as the seventeenth century when it was known that a child that tasted salty would die shortly after birth.'

I envisage our ancestors, dotted about dark, cold, Northern Europe, licking their newborn babies. Salt tears. Bloody hell. What we don't know about where we've come from.

15th April 1991

So The Foetal Medicine Unit at the big teaching hospital takes us in. The National Health Service suddenly swings into action in an unrecognisably competent and impressive way. Vast sums of money are about to be spent on us. Entirely free of charge. Because we are no whining malingerers coughing and sneezing in the doctor's waiting room. We are an emergency. And a medical curiosity. I feel quite proud.

Mr Hallam, the consultant, is tall, balding, rounded and possessed of the voice and self-confidence bought by a private education and Oxbridge. And that is also the reason he feels compelled to wear a bow tie and yellow braces. His speciality is Chorionic Villus Sampling, which, I am soon to discover, is exactly as unpleasant as it sounds.

He's talking to my mum as he snaps on his rubber gloves and stares between my legs. Oh. You're not here again. You're in Lisbon trying to persuade a Fado singer to be in your film. Well it may involve semi nudity but mainly, the character is just a fantastic singer. As well as having hauntingly deep, dark eyes. You are going to try and be back in time to pick me up.

'Really?' says my mum, looking over the hill of my raised knees at Mr Hallam. 'The recessive gene survived because it gave protection from cholera?' She draws a long breath in.

'Oh, yes. There has to be a reason for it not being eliminated from the population by natural selection.' He adjusts the lamp and bends lower. 'And while we can't be certain, from what we know of your family history—'

'Ouch.'

'Yes, you may feel a little discomfort, Mrs Morrison. I'm just inserting a . . .'

'*Ms* actually. O'Dowd.'

'There we are.'

This is what Sid calls the Metal Fuck. I can hear him

screwing it open. As though he is struggling with a particularly stubborn bottle of claret.

'And cholera, you see,' he glances up at my mum who is blinking hard, 'or some similar diarrhoeal infection, is the reason for its persistence in the population. You see, with acute diarrhoea . . . Nurse, pass me a Number 4, would you please . . . the victim dies through loss of fluids and salt. But—'

'Ow!'

'Sorry about that . . . during the devastating cholera epidemics that have peppered history . . . just relax now if you can . . . CF carriers, the heterozygotes, have enough of a defect in their chloride channels to prevent the cholera from taking hold . . . but not enough to have the ultimately fatal symptoms . . . of cystic fibrosis.'

'Good gracious,' says my mum with a desperate cheerfulness. 'Do you suppose that's why I never get an upset tummy? Are you all right, darling?' Her mouth wobbles and I suppose she's wondering, What if I'd known this when I was pregnant?

'Nnnn.' I'd quite like this to stop now. Mr Hallam's forearm appears to have disappeared inside my vagina. Along with quite a few instruments. Vaginas and mothers do not mix. Well, obviously in a fairly profound way they do but it's not something to dwell on. You should be here, Mark, when there's a man doing this to me. Not my mum.

'Nurse.' There's a pause. My mum squeezes my hand. I can see she's thinking she's about to witness a miscarriage.

'Sir?'

'Nurse, Mrs Morrison's cervix is tipped right back at an unusually acute angle. I'm afraid we're going to have to go in through her navel.'

The nurse adjusts her face and her trolley for a more serious procedure. A large tear drops from my mum's cheek and lands on my fingers which are crushed within hers. I start to sob, face screwing up like a child. I wish you were bloody here. It's probably your fault my cervix is all misaligned anyway. Mr Hallam comes up the head end and starts talking to me kindly.

'Now, we're going to put a cannula through your navel just . . . here . . . and that will allow me to insert a fine needle with which to extract the sample. You can watch it on the ultrasound. You may just feel a little scratch as I put the cannula through your stomach and then a bit of a period pain as it passes through your uterus wall.'

The sensation of the cannula going through my navel is, unsurprisingly, like having a thin sword pushed into my gut. On the ultrasound monitor I can see the tip of the sword pushing at the uterus wall. Our baby is pulsing gently in its bag of fluid. I can see its mouth when it half turns and moves towards me. Now I understand the appeal of E.T. He looks just like a foetus. I am about to say this out loud when the point of the sword breaks through and I see the baby jerk away in fright. I start to cry again. This time I cry for our baby that has already made a mother of me. My own mother is having a bad time of it too. I've lost all feeling in my hand. I feel, confusingly, like a child.

When I'm dressed and sitting on the edge of the bed behind the floral screens, Mr Hallam comes and sits down beside me. Mum is down the corridor trying to phone you. He's removed his bow tie. He looks directly at me.

'Have you and Mr Morrison discussed what you want to do should the test prove positive?'

Tell me what we should do, I plead silently, looking back at him. We have no idea.

'You know, CF-affected children are often very bright, extremely engaging young people.' He takes his glasses off, looks at the lenses and puts them back on again. I think of the ultrasound image of our baby that I have just seen. 'They are almost always quite special. Perhaps because they spend so much time off school and in the company of adults. But if you had a CF-affected child, you would not be able to live a normal life.' I look at his eyes and he looks back at me. 'They require physiotherapy several times a day. You would spend many, many weeks of your life, with your child, in hospital.' I want to ask him how the abortion would be. At sixteen weeks I know it would involve giving birth. I very much need to know how, exactly, the baby will manage the dying. 'Family holidays would be very difficult, if not impossible. And you would have to live with the knowledge that your son or daughter would be unlikely to survive to adulthood.'

'Do you have children?' I ask him.

'Three.' Mr Hallam smiles, unfolds and refolds his arms. 'The oldest has cystic fibrosis. Now I'm going to leave you with the nurse who will discuss the details of a therapeutic termination and I shall ring you with the results as soon as we get them. It'll be three to five days. Is it all right to ring at work?'

18th April 1991

'My Bonnie lies over the ocean . . . Oh dear oh dear oh dear . . . My Bonnie lies over the sea . . .'

Octavia is singing in a reedy voice and managing to cry at the same time.

'That makes you sad, does it, Octavia?' I ask, after quite a long pause, my pencil poised.

'My Bonnie lies . . .' Octavia's voice is a whisper now. 'Oh . . . bring back my . . . Bonnie to me . . .'

She's up and off at this point. She doesn't get very far because the door is shut and we're in a small room. At the door she stands and whimpers with her back to me.

I'm trying to piece together a case history about her. Most of Octavia's original notes were lost many years ago and so her history is a bit of a blank. But I have seen the original leather-bound ledger containing her admission details. It was rescued from the council skip where it was smouldering during hospital building works. All that is left concerning Octavia's admission is a faded sepia photograph of a girl squinting up into the sun, her mouth open as if taken by surprise. Under it is written her name and a few singed details about her stepfather who arranged the admission. Sister Stone says she thinks she remembers someone saying Octavia had had a baby out of wedlock. My requests for more details sent Sister Stone into a seething whir of fury. I remember her snapping on her surgical gloves in preparation for somebody's manual enema and saying, 'Nurse O'Dowd, I cannot for the life of me see why prying into Octavia's past can be of any use to anybody now. What I *can* see is that right now Octavia needs to have her dress changed and be taken down to the day room *before* the tea trolley arrives.'

The problem is that Octavia doesn't actually speak. She only sings and whimpers. The door opens abruptly and Sister Stone looks in. All day she has had a visible vapour of fury around her because I've said I can't lift any patients for a few days. Back trouble, I tell her. This is like a miner telling the pit owner he's got to stay in the fresh air. She has shouted at everyone more than usual and makes a point of lifting some of the old women on her own and letting them drop painfully onto their chairs. I wonder whether ECT might do the trick for her. She leaves a glare in the room with us and slams the door shut.

I sit as still as I can, afraid that the baby, traumatised by the CVS, will decide to leave go and fall from me. In the hospital gardens, pear blossom is heaped on the branches like whipped egg whites. Everywhere, nature is running riot – all doing that memory and desire thing, just like the poets said. What the hell does Octavia make of it? I wonder. She has become still and silent, her face to the barred window. I get up and take her by the hand, filled suddenly with a deep sadness for this irritating, broken woman. She lets me lead her back to the day room. I hold her frail hand in mine, walking close against her, our arms and hips touching. I don't care what is the matter with this baby. I just want it to survive to nine months and be born.

At night it is a relief to put out the light and lie enclosed in the warmth of you. We are sad and gentle with each other but we have spent most of the evening on the phone talking to other people about it. And the phone has rung a lot. From your Production Assistant ('No. It's got to be done at night. Well just tell them we need the whole beach cleared. Yes, day after tomorrow. And don't forget the dog. And the donkey.'); from your Producer ('Well I guess we'll just have to work for nothing again.'), and from an actress called Felicity Blow ('No, no, no. I think your character is essentially a very complex woman. Sensual and intellectual. Strong yet vulnerable. Beautiful yet flawed . . . Really? Allergic to donkeys? That could be a problem I suppose. What about mules? Do they have the same effect?').

In bed, in the dark, I try to talk about our decision.

'So, if this baby has cystic fibrosis . . .'

'Look. Let's wait until we know. There's a seventy-five per cent chance that the baby is fine.' You squeeze me. Not quite hard enough. You kiss me. For not quite long enough. Tomorrow you have to leave again. Maybe tomorrow we'll get the results.

'I'll call you when I find out, shall I?'

My voice sounds disembodied. I wait for a response. There is none because extraordinarily enough you have fallen asleep. Men seem blessed with a kind of narcolepsy that kicks in at, or soon after, moments of high tension in bed. Now if someone could bottle that and sell it to women they'd make themselves a fortune.

19th April 1991

The only reason I'm upright as we hurtle through the dark is because fifty other bodies are packed tight around me. There is nothing to hold on to so I put my trust in them. I stare at the page of the newspaper held two inches from my face and try to make the numbers mean something. '150,000 Iraqis; 18 UK; 141 US (20 to friendly fire).' It's the score at the end of the Gulf War that's been played nightly on our television screens for forty days and forty nights. 'Move right down inside the carriage please.' Although you can hardly call it a war when only one side is doing all the dying. I feel ashamed to be British. I try to imagine the shock waves of desolation radiating out from each of those deaths – the mothers, the fathers, the daughters, the sons, the sisters, the brothers, the husbands, the wives, the lovers, the friends . . . 'Right. Down. Inside.' Supposing there was a way of measuring global grief? 'Mind. The. Gap.' Supposing there might be a point at which the atmospheric levels of it become dangerously high and threaten to alter the spin of the world's axis? Or change the weather. Like ozone? 'Mind. The. Gap.' 150,000 Iraqis. Jesus. That was some punishment. Perhaps the Americans will give up bombs for Lent.

There's a seat next to Winnie at breakfast. She half looks at me as I sit down. And I look at her as I always do in an attempt to see the woman inside who once flew solo across the English Channel. No one fitting that description looks out at me from her eyes and I begin the messy business of trying to spoon porridge into her mouth whenever it opens. 'Well they should only take a moment to dry . . .' she says and I get half a spoon of sludge in there. The air in the room is heavy with the smell of porridge, scrambled egg and tea. Radio 2 is piped through the PA system which doesn't help. 'I give them a good rinse through first with soda . . .' continues Winnie. In goes the spoon. In the kitchen across the mud-coloured corridor, they appear to be having a pan-throwing contest. Cooks' rage. Why are they so angry all of the time? I'm sure they put soul sap into this food. 'Oh, that'll never do, will it?' Winnie shakes her head at me, too quick for me that time. The hospital policy is to fill the vacuum left by the loss of souls with food that is as close to mortar as the kitchens can make it. No doubt something to do with keeping body and soul together. Sister Stone patrols the room like a furious mother, occasionally snatching the spoon from a bleary-eyed nurse and shovelling the stuff into a toothless, resisting mouth. When Winnie says, 'Just give me a minute, I've the blessed pans to do first . . .' I'm ready for her and in it goes. There seems very little point to all this feeding, given that within the hour, Sister Stone will be admonishing the women in the washrooms for having been constipated for the last fifteen days. Purging, after all, has been a favoured method of psychiatric treatment since Bethlehem Hospital records began in 1403. Winston says there is no point in blowing the whistle on Sister Stone. Everyone knows about her and she'll be retiring at the end of the year. 'WHAT HAVE I TOLD YOU ABOUT COMING THROUGH WHEN MY FLOOR'S WET?'

It always makes me jump when Winnie gets to this point but it's usually a sign that she's had enough and isn't going to open her mouth any more. Still, at least Sister Stone doesn't actually chain patients to the beds. Although I imagine she may have done in her time. But maybe she'll never go. Like Kylie Minogue.

In the staff canteen there is a surplus of puddings but no main courses left. Bread and butter pudding or jam roly-poly. Both named to accurately describe what you'll look and feel like after eating them. There's probably one called Susto Surprise. Sid approaches with her tray and looks disparagingly at my pile of revision books.

'Food and television are bad for those women,' she says, sitting down with a bowl of spotted dick. 'What they need is live music, theatre and sex.'

'A bit like us then.'

'Of course.' She pulls a packet of ten Embassy from her uniform pocket and lights up.

'Heard anything yet?' she asks, twiddling the stud in her nose.

'Still waiting. I think, maybe, today.'

'You should get Mark to ring them. He might as well do something useful for a change.'

'He can't. He's in Portugal. You know. Preparing. For his next film.' I sound like an adoring schoolgirl. Sid inhales deeply. She has black nail varnish and very laddered tights. I envy her mass of hair and large sexy body. She is extraordinarily, fascinatingly unselfconscious.

'Well he's a wanker then. He doesn't deserve you.' Even coming from Sid, this shocks me. I open my mouth to defend you and she chucks me a fag. I leave it lying on the table between us.

'No thanks. I've stopped. Anything toxic makes me feel ill now. Maybe that's why pregnant women look blooming. They're just not poisoning themselves like they used to. And getting lots of sleep and sex.'

Winston appears at the door. He spots us and does his camp weaving walk over towards our table. A dropping sensation in my guts tells me what he's going to say before I hear it.

'Gen. Phone call.'

In the ward office the white receiver lies waiting on the desk, its cord coiling across a stack of patients' files. Sister Stone is opening and shutting the filing-cabinet drawers with a series of slams and tuts. I turn my back to her and crouch over the phone.

'Hello?'

'Is that Genevieve O'Dowd?' Mr Hallam's voice. It's what I expected but it has an alarming effect on my heart rate. 'Sorry to call you at work—'

There's a final metallic crash behind me and Sister Stone pokes my back with a pencil.

'I hope that is not a personal call, Nurse.' She taps the notice on the wall warning employees away from the phone. 'Emergencies only, remember,' and she bustles out of the door.

'. . . so I wanted you to have the news as soon as possible.' He clears his throat.

Outside the window, the blossom seems to vibrate. I have no idea how to prepare myself for what he may be going to say. The notice on the wall in front of me says, Check for Vital Signs. Ring Crash Team. I am aware of Winston and Sid hovering near the doorway.

Mr Hallam is speaking again. 'I'm sure you will be relieved to hear that your baby is not affected with cystic fibrosis.'

I stand upright, put the phone down, and turn and look at them.

'Yes!' shouts Sid, rushing forward and kissing me on the mouth.

'Fucking excellent!' says Winston, hugging me tight. He picks up the phone again and hands it to me. 'Right, you ring Wonder Boy, we'll get the drinks in. See you down the Barefaced Stag in half an hour.'

Dialling your number, the taste of Sid's lipstick on my lips, I stroke the small curve of the baby low down on my belly. A harassed female voice tells me you're away from your desk at the moment.

'Could you tell him Genevieve called and that it's good news?'

'How are you spelling that?'

'Actually, don't worry. I'll ring back.'

I look at myself in the small mirror on the wall and think that I have never felt such happiness, ever.

Seven

7th July 1991

I DISCOVER I'm rather good at being pregnant.

'You look like a bloody brood mare, mate. Gorgeous,' says Sid, slapping my arse as she walks and I sway down the corridor.

'It's true actually, Sid. I behave as if I'm on a stud farm. With Mark that is.'

'Got a fag, Nurse?' says Isaac Woodhead who is seventy-two and famously, but not very unusually, has a twelve-inch penis. Longevity and long penises are God's perks for the mad, it would seem. His admission notes, signed by the local JP when Isaac was fourteen, state that he 'ran naked from Wimbledon to Tooting pursued by the devil'.

'Got a fag, Nurse?' is his only refrain. Sid stops and pulls her Embassy out of her pocket. Today her hair is iridescent pink and matches her lips. Isaac appears not to notice the vision that is Sid. He only has eyes for her fags. He sticks one in his mouth and waits, rocking from foot to foot, while she gets her lighter out. Once lit, he darts off to waylay another member of staff.

'Good sex then?' asks Sid, selecting a glutinous rice pudding from the shelf.

'Incredible. Really. Um have you got anything . . . green?' I ask the woman with the nylon hairnet.

'Green? What do you think this is, a funny farm?' She shrieks with laughter. I know what she's going to say next because it's written above her head on a notice and because she says it at every opportunity. You Don't Have To Be Mad To Work Here. But It Helps! 'You don't have to be mad to work here. But it helps!' she says, nearly falling into the lasagne with mirth.

I look at the aluminium trays lit up by the giant heating lamps. I see only things that are off-white and a tray of brown meat of indeterminate origin. But as hospitals don't do healthy food, I have a Ploughman's. Plenty of susto filler there.

'So,' I say, following Sid to a table, 'I wonder what the evolutionary reason is for pregnant women to want to have unbridled sex all the time, Sid. I can't work it out.' I open my mouth and try to tackle the French stick without dislocating my jaw. Coleslaw oozes from the sides. The bread remains intact.

'So the father doesn't do a runner and leave the mother in the lurch, stupid. Think about it. The sex he was getting before you were pregnant was fine but nothing to the sex he gets while you *are* pregnant. You've probably got magic mucus or something. Seriously. It's probably got some kind of stimulant in it.'

'Shh. For God's sake, Sid.' On the table along from us Lesley is licking her thumb and slowly turning the pages of the *Daily Mail*. Naturally, pregnancy is frowned upon at work. It is disruptive, expensive, inconvenient, unpredictable and completely contrary to the Protestant work ethic of this country.

'Which means that,' continues Sid, taking no notice at all, 'he doesn't start lusting after other women. Even if they have got flat stomachs and thin ankles. Because they're just *wee men*, whereas you,' she says, looking at me, 'have turned into something he's never made love to before.'

'What's that then, Sid?' A dollop of coleslaw drops onto the table.

'A *Womb* Man.'

'You've lost me there, Sid.' I wipe more of the stuff off my nose.

'It's obvious, innit? Men, as we all know, really and truly, desire men, don't they? I mean, that's what the footie's about, yeah? And the fancying women who look like girls. Or boys. Not letting us earn as much as them and stuff like that.' Her very pink tongue licks her spoon. 'Plus the fact that, most of them, just don't like women. Plain and simple. They don't like them.' She snaps her lighter at the end of her cigarette. Sid is very beautiful and very watchable. She should be in films. Except she's too fat. And too frightening. Most film directors seem to prefer little women, I've noticed. Almost boys really. Now why is that, I wonder?

'Maybe. But not Mark. He's practically a girl himself.' Fragments of bread crust fly from my mouth. Sid looks at me.

'So, when you become a *Womb* Man you are desirable not just because of the secret potion in the cervix but because you are no longer one of the Wee Men.'

'Sorry, Sid, but how do you spell that? I'm not sure I can tell the difference.'

Sid's off though in the rapture of the rant. 'Wee Men they've done. Done to absolutely bloody death. But fucking a pregnant woman must be a blast. Especially if you've got her pregnant. A bit like fucking yourself.'

Sid did Cultural Studies at Trent Poly and tends to make everything up as she goes along. But quite often I feel that she is not far from some sort of strange and secret truth. Suddenly I have a really good idea.

'Sid. Come round for dinner Saturday night. There's someone you should meet. Angus is coming over.'

Back in the ward office, I try to concentrate on my work but I have to keep checking the letter from the local health authority. However many times I try to work out my maternity leave it still comes out at six weeks on full pay and twelve weeks on half pay. This means that unless I work up until the fortieth week of pregnancy, I will probably have to return to work when the baby is twelve weeks old. I have no idea whether this is the right time for the baby or not. Will it be out of nappies by then? Walking perhaps? Obviously it won't need any breast milk by then because if it did, well it might starve to death. Presumably someone in Whitehall is an expert on babies and knows that at twelve weeks they can be independent of their mothers. So that's all right then. Because if our income drops even a teeny bit lower than its current level the whole house will come tumbling down round our ears. And down will come baby, cradle and all. Or that appears to be the subtext of the letters from the bank. At least, last time I dared open them which was quite a while ago. And then there's the ante-natal classes where I'll be taught how to give birth. Because frankly I'm a little unsure about that. I read some stuff about breathing that I could not keep in my head and I want to make sure I get it right. So I rang up about ante-natal classes. There aren't any. Well, it's not that there aren't any. But they're all booked up in my area. Although there may be a vacancy in Bromley, in November.

7th September 1991

'Now take it up to the first floor and hold for one, two, three, four, five. Aannd, take it up to the second floor . . . one, two, three, four, five . . . and the third . . . two . . . three . . . that's right, don't forget to breathe, and take the lift back down again, in your own time . . . And twice more . . .'

I've managed to get myself onto an NCT class in Wimbledon and I am completely in the dark about the going-up-in-a-lift thing. I'm lying on my back on an oatmeal carpet in someone's front room, trying to work out exactly which bit of me is supposed to be moving. Looking around the room of prostrate women offers few clues. From the expression on their faces they seem to be doing mental arithmetic.

'And remember, you want to do one hundred of those every day. For the rest of your life. Do them on the bus, in the car, in the queue at Sainsbury's. Anywhere at all. I can assure you your husband will thank you for it.'

A titter ripples round the room, joined by a loud fart.

'And that's another reason to be very disciplined about your pelvic floor exercises, ladies.' The room erupts into guffaws and snorts. 'That whole area is under tremendous strain during pregnancy and during the birth itself, of course. It is very very important to keep it toned.' A dozen heads strain up from the floor to look at our leader, Louise. She is serene and supple and graceful with a Julie Christie mouth. She's definitely over forty and her pelvic floor is clearly the secret of her happy marriage.

During our herbal tea break, I feel like the new girl at school. Everyone knows everyone else and they even seem to have a uniform I've been told nothing about – striped sailor T-shirts, polka-dot baggy trousers and Alice bands. A kind of post-modern Sloane-look. They've all bonded in a frighteningly intense way. The conversation slips about like a rip tide.

'I would definitely prefer to tear rather than be cut.'

'Oh God, yes. Lucy said they cut her from front to back and then she was stitched up by some locum and now it looks like Spaghetti Junction down there. All the nerve endings destroyed. Completely numb.'

'Well, Susan said if you're booked into St Luke's say no to an enema. And shaving. And artificial breaking of waters. They're short-staffed and they run the place like a poultry-processing plant.'

'Yep. Honestly. In the freezer. I'm not joking. And her

mum, thinking it was bolognese, defrosted it in the microwave. Nearly fed it to her husband!'

'Foetal monitoring is absolutely out unless I have to have an epidural. And I really don't want to have an epidural. I just think it would be weird.'

'Well I do. I tell you, my mum said that giving birth was like shitting bricks and having the 73 bus driven down your wusser. Give me the drugs – that's my birth plan – gas and air, pethidine, epidural. I want everything they've got.'

In the slight pause that this remark produces I attempt to insert myself into the conversation and try to talk to a woman rummaging in the HobNobs tin. She has a stomach the size of the Rock of Gibraltar.

'Can you just tell me . . . what is it we're supposed to be doing with the lift thing?'

'Your pelvic floor. Mmm. These are yummy. Are you local?'

'Yes, no, not really. I live in the Angel.'

'Oh you should talk to Sandy. I think she lives round there.' The bricks, bus and drugs woman is pointed out to me. But I'm still none the wiser. 'Pelvic what?'

'Floor. Pelvic floor. You know. Think Bangkok. Ping-pong balls? The Singapore Grip? They're keeping you, you know, *toned*.' She turns back to the others. 'I've told Simon he's not to let them inject syntometrine into the cord until it has absolutely stopped pulsating.'

Back at home I am consumed by the need to create order. Before 5.00 p.m. I get the rust off the metal fireplaces with the new drill bit, phone the chimney sweep, construct some wooden decking over the dank bit outside our back door, polish the grout residue off the bathroom walls, put our book collection into alphabetical order, vacuum the picture rails, erect a curtain rail in the nursery, wash our sheets, throw most of our clothes into bin bags to be taken to Oxfam and polish the stone floor with the Electrolux floor polisher you bought for my birthday. My mum used to have one just like it.

9th October 1991

'Let's Get To It!' squeals Kylie through the wall as I scrutinise my book on childbirth, trying not to confuse the information there with my case study on *The Hallucinating Patient*. I look at the drawings of couples trying out different positions for childbirth. She's wearing a leotard and a pudding-basin haircut and he's wearing a moustache and an understanding expression on his face. Most of the positions seem to involve a chair. The drawings are a little like those in *The Joy of Sex* but without the joy. Or the sex. But the amount of information I have to remember in order to give birth naturally is alarmingly complex. 'Let's Get To It!!' Kylie shouts, with just a hint of desperation. I try to memorise the many and confusing stages of labour and the multiple possible scenarios ('waters may break with slow leak, or pop so that water streams out'), the suggested activities ('try a little light gardening, cook something that takes a long time or go for a walk in the country'), things that you can do to help ('cunnilingus and nipple stroking can help ripen the cervix. Help with the household tasks. Give emotional support.'). Bloody hell, they should put all those in the marriage vows.

When the phone rings I let the machine answer it in case it is my mum or your mum or your dad or our friends checking to see if I've gone into labour. All are on high alert in case you don't get back from Lisbon in time and they have to step into the breach. So to speak. I hear the outgoing message, the recording of your voice, words tumbling over each other in a rush. Having your voice on the OGM is a cunning ploy designed to dupe would-be rapists and murderers into thinking that I am, in fact, not alone because, despite all indications to the contrary, like reality, you are, in fact, living here with me.

'Hello?' There's a pause during which I recognise Marion's breathing. 'Hello? Shine on. It's the blinking machine again. Hello? Mark? Are you there? He's not bloody there again.'

The phone rings again.

'Oh. Hi. Gen? It's Helena. Bit out of my head actually. Whoops. Shit. Are you still there? Sorry, just dropped the phone. Just wondering how you are. I'm in – where is this, Damian? – some club in Soho. Leave a message at my place if you need me. I'm at the ready (snorts of laughter), lots of love.'

It rings again. I wait to hear who the caller is and hear your voice. I reach across and pick up the receiver. Hold you close to my head.

'Hi. Are you OK?'

'So far. When are you coming back?'

'Tomorrow. Should be home about six in the evening.' I adjust the time automatically adding three hours in order to convert your good intentions into reality.

'How long for?'

'I've got the whole weekend and Monday off. Don't worry. I'll be there. It's been a bit of a nightmare here. The financiers told us they were pulling out again yesterday and I've been in meetings all day trying to convince them to change their minds. I think it's going to be OK though. But what they've agreed to is way below what we budgeted for. I think we're going to have to do without one of the characters.'

'How? Who?'

'Well, we thought we'd develop the donkey storyline.'

'You mean have a donkey as a main character?'

'Yeah. Sort of. Felicity's character falls in love with the donkey instead of with Marco.'

'What does Marco think of it?'

'He's pulled out. He's got a job presenting *The Eurovision Song Contest.*'

'Oh. So it'll be sort of *A Midsummer Night's Dream* meets . . . er . . .'

'Yeah! Exactly. What do you think?'

'Mark. I'm worried about ice chips. You need to get some to feed me during labour. But they've got to stay as ice for several hours. How are we going to do that? And the list here says we have to bring something to dress the baby in. And a pillow. And I can't find a bloody hot water bottle anywhere. I need one. All the books say so.'

'Don't worry. It's going to be all right.'

Later, I press Rewind, hear each message again, press Delete after each of them except yours, after which I press Save. I collect fragments of you. I keep them safe. Photos. Notes. Worn out T-shirts. Your voice. Just in case.

Eight

11th October 1991

IT'S TWO in the morning. I'm breathing through my contractions and watching a video of *Betty Blue*. Because you think it is a great film about romantic obsession. And because I thought you might like to watch it with me, what with it being a skin-flick, I mean art film. It opens with a shot of two people making love on a bed. 'I had known Betty for a week. We made love every night,' says the voice-over. On the wall above their writhing bodies the *Mona Lisa* gives me that smile. Maybe she knows something I don't. The film is about . . . er . . . Beatrice Dalle, the actress playing Betty Blue, who has an enormous, swollen mouth that looks like it could swallow a man whole and an insatiable body that the camera has kerb-crawled persistently for nearly two hours. Oh, and giant, nocturnal eyes. I'm not fully concentrating for most of the film, apart from the sex bits, but it looks like Betty behaves quite badly towards the love-sick narrator – trashes his manuscript, burns down his beach-hut, et cetera, but he cannot get her out of his head. Or bed. He still loves her. Even though she is dangerous and mad. Just before the end credits I feel a warm flood spreading across my groin. My God! The book was right! It's all going according to plan.

'Ooh. Mark!' I whimper, experimenting with being

helpless and in need. 'Maaarrrk!' I do a few pants to get myself fully into the role before heaving my body up off the floor and clambering up the stairs to wake you.

'What? What's happened? What time is it?' You leap out of bed in an instant as though you've been caught asleep on the job. Which you have. I flip through the pages of my book trying to find the bit that tells us what to do.

'Waters have broken,' I tell you.

'Are you sure? Where?'

I embrace the duvet on all fours, not quite believing this is happening to me.

'Here. Let me see the book. How dilated are you? How often are the contractions? What page is it on? Shit. Wrong book.' You toss *Mad Doctors, Mad Houses and Mad Men* onto the bed. I gesture towards *Freedom and Choice in Childbirth.* I'm on all fours and the contractions feel rather serious now. Like having a truck roll slowly across my stomach. I think you're going to have to carry me in this position down to the front door.

'Stay there. Don't worry. I'm ringing the hospital.'

The hospital more or less tells us to wait until I am screaming the house down. And bring our own pillow. And bath scourer. I pace the kitchen and check the book. 'You may find it difficult to relax completely.' I put on my coat. 'You may feel restless and irritable.' Take off my coat. 'You may be frightened because everything is overwhelming.' I panic. You panic. You phone a cab. We go to the hospital.

What they don't understand in films or labour wards is that you cannot give birth on your back. A woman on her back with just a hint of lip gloss, a damp fringe and her legs in the air may seem the way things should be to some but there's no way you're going to give birth in that position unless they drag it out of you with you screaming blue murder. No, to give birth you have to get down on all fours and bellow like a cow. Squat down and howl like an ape. Birth takes you right back. Shunts you off down some ancient tunnel of blood, sweat, shit and tears which roller coasters, war, sky diving and the World Cup may attempt to imitate but never actually can. It is a tortuous tempest, an exorcism, a triumph of body over mind and I'm not surprised our dads were too scared to be there. But you. You hold on tight, feed me ice, stroke my back and read aloud to me from the newspaper. You do not leave. And just as I feel that there's been some terrible mistake, that I really will split in two and break apart, that I can't do this any more, the struggle ceases, it's done, the head is through and you are holding out to me the astonishing fact of him in both your hands.

At the gossamer touch of him, the starfish reach of his hand, I am pitched headlong. Falling. At the descent of the milk as he starts to suckle and fixes his gaze on me, I think *this*. This is love.

12th October 1991

Intoxicated, grinning, we flee from metal beds and restraints, tubes, masks and rubber gloves like cadavers' skins. Escape down stairs, through doors, corridors and emerge triumphant onto the steps. Sudden rush-hour hit; screech and roar of Huntley Street. Hovering at the entrance we must look distrait, deranged. Me in pyjamas and you in a track suit stained with my blood. Opposite, a plane tree towers, tired leaves trembling in the fume-filled air. At the sour tang of heavy metals on my tongue I make a dark cave for him inside my coat and inhale his amnio scent. Furtively I bend to lick his hair. I taste the primordial damp and wait while you run, frantic, chasing taxis down the street.

Together we kneel over his tiny naked form on the white expanse of our bed. You make a nest of your arms and a roof of your head and stare down at his wise old man's face. Searching. Gravely his eyes return your stare. I don't know what you see in that long, still gaze. But I see you mirrored in him. We undress and lie with him between us, curled inwards, skin on skin. Back in touch. Hold on to this.

A cacophonous pounding on the door knocker heralds the arrival of your parents. You look at me. Don't go. Pretend we're not here. Stay here with us. But there are stronger, older forces at work here, I am learning that. You are up, hopping on one leg with your knickers in a twist, pulling last week's dirty laundry on inside out, and you're off. I look around for something to put on. But our baby has become clamped to my nipple like a limpet. In our milky embrace, his eyes hold mine in a solemn regard. Disturbing him feels like a betrayal. Skin. I know he needs to feel skin. I find a giant T-shirt still smelling of you and pull it over my head. Just as the tiny O of his mouth opens in despair, I pick him up and tuck him inside, close in the dark against the warmth of my skin.

'*Where* is he? *Where* is he?' your mum sings as she comes up the stairs.

Pulling the duvet up to my stomach, I arrange myself for the visitation.

'Come on then. Where is he?' Marion's voice echoes in the empty nursery below. There's no way I'm going to put him in the room below us. Despite your best-laid plans. Easy prey for Vikings and burglars.

The doorway of our bedroom is filled with your parents.

'Whatever have you done with him?' asks Marion, incredulous.

Modestly I raise my T-shirt to reveal the back of his dark, curly head. Marion steps smartly out of the room. Your mum moves towards me arms outstretched.

'Oh,' she says, her eyes filling. 'Oh. Little boy. Come on then. It's Granma. Come to have a little look at you.' I can see Marion's shadow across the doorway.

Disengaging him, I bring him out from under my T-shirt

and hand him over. I watch amazed, as your mum, with infinite gentleness, takes him to her, unwraps him, looks into his face, touches his hands, his feet, his ears, kisses his head, strokes his hair and then wraps him up again with awesome proficiency and does a slow waltz with him in her arms to the window.

'Little man. Aren't you handsome? Just like your daddy. Yes, you are. Oh, yes, you are.'

I retreat to the bathroom and stand under the shower. It feels a shame to turn on the water. Don't want to wash away the smears and smells of birth. But it's chilly standing naked in a dry shower and so I turn on the taps and let the water stream down my strange, emptied body.

When I emerge from the bathroom, the bedroom is empty. From the basement the thin cry of our baby produces a fine jet spray of milk from my breasts. Panicked, guilty, suddenly desolate, I struggle into my too-tight nursing bra and clothes. More tender and bruised than I'd realised, I hobble, one step at a time, down to the basement.

'Dance for your daddy my little babby, Dance for your daddy my little man.'

Your mum is jigging and swaying, Marion is clapping his hands loudly in front of his face and our baby is bawling inconsolably. You are up the other end of the room, clattering cups and kettles and plates and bagels, preparing an elaborate brunch.

'There we are now. There she is. That's it. Mummy's back,' coos your mum, bringing him to me. I take him awkwardly, unsure how to hold a baby standing up at the same time as trying to unzip my bra cup without him sliding onto the floor. His baggy white babygro has been replaced with a pastel blue one and on his head is a matching flannelette cap with an anchor on the front. Giant John Lewis bags cover the table. The phone rings. It's my mum.

'No. No. No. I'll come and fetch you,' I hear you say.

'Course I will. Stay where you are. I'll be fifteen minutes.' And you're off. I'd love a cup of tea but my hands are full.

'Now we've brought a few things for Baby,' says your mum, pulling a musical mobile from one of the bags. Twinkle, twinkle little star . . .

'Oh that's lovely, thank you.'

'And this is very useful for carrying all your bits and bobs.'

'Oh, that's lovely . . .'

'And you'll be needing these little caps in Lisbon. A baby's skin is very sensitive.'

'Oh, that's . . .'

'And here's a teddy for him, and if you press it just here, it growls, look.'

'Oh . . .'

'And this is a little suit for when he goes somewhere special.'

' . . .'

13th October 1991

'Well some cultures just give their children a number, you know, Marion.'

Somehow, no one wanted to leave and so my mum slept on a mattress in the nursery, your mum insisted she would be fine on the sofa and Marion declared there would be no problem sleeping in an armchair. They study our baby. His eyes and ears and mouth and nose and hair, the shape of his head, all are identified and claimed by different branches of our pasts. I try to keep him close to me and hang on to the hope of some DNA-defying newness in him.

'Shine on, Mark. Do you mean to tell me that my grandson isn't going to have a name?'

'Course he's going to have one, Dad, it's just we haven't decided yet.'

'Well, what names have you thought of so far?'

'Well, that's the point. Every name we think of has a problem. You know, undesirable connotations.'

I can see Marion preparing himself to misquote Shakespeare at this point.

'What's in a rose? A name of any other flower would smell as sweet.' Marion gives me a wink. 'Isn't that what the great beard said, eh?'

'Now that's a lovely name, that is. Rose. Very feminine,' says your mum.

'I had a great aunt called Rose,' says my mum. 'She married someone quite high up in the Foreign Office. I think he was a "Sir".'

'You can't call him Rose,' says Marion, standing with our baby held outwards like an award. 'Ronald, though, there's an idea. Ronald Morrison. Sounds all right.'

'O'Dowd Morrison,' I say.

'Pardon? Ronald O'Dowd, did you say? Come off it. You're not going in for all that women's libbers' stuff now you're a mum, are you? You can't call him Ronald O'Dowd. My bloomin' line'll die out.'

'Dad, we're not calling him Ronald, OK? And we don't know what his surname will be.'

'You know you could give him my maiden name,' says my mum. 'That way we'd bypass your father's line, Genevieve, which he has, after all, rather forfeited.'

'Oh there's a novel idea,' says your mum mildly, rearranging the pleats on her skirt. 'What's your maiden name then?'

'Panter.' There's a bit of a pause at this point so Mum adds, 'It's an old French name for bread seller.'

'That is unusual,' says your mum.

'Gordon Bennett,' says your dad.

'We could call him that,' you say, putting crostini on the table.

14th October 1991

'What about Archie?' I'm going through the names book.

'He'd be called Arsie at school.' You're holding a finger up in front of the baby, then another and counting aloud. 'One, two.'

'Winston.'

'He's not black.'

'Nor was Churchill.'

'Sue.' No reaction. 'Maybe we should name him after your dad.' You are pointing to the window and saying, '*La fenêtre.*'

'Christopher.'

'Too middle class.'

'But we are middle class.'

'*I'm* not.'

'You're the poshest person I know. Other than Helena.'

'Bollocks. *Trois. Quatre.*'

'Iago. Marcus. Paul. Richard.'

'One syllable. Let's have a name with just one syllable.'

'Sam.'

'The whole world is called Sam.'

'What about Isaac?'

'Definitely not.'

'How about Karl?'

'Karl. Yeah. Karl's good. Mark, Genevieve and Karl. That sounds all right.'

'Karl O'Dowd.'

'Sounds like he's called Carlo then. Karl Morrison.'

'If he's called Morrison, every time I ring the school or the doctor and I say, "I'm ringing about Karl Morrison," and they say, "And your name is?" and I say, "Genevieve O'Dowd. I'm his mother," it's an unnecessary complication. It's more practical if he has my name. Come on, Mark, you know I'm going to be doing more of that stuff than you. You're never here.'

'That's not true. And anyway I might be unemployed in three months' time. I could be phoning the doctor a lot.'

'OK. Karl (Morrison) O'Dowd.'

'It's a deal.'

Nine

30th October 1991

MY MUM tries to be brave as I kiss her goodbye and walk through to the Departure Lounge. I have Karl strapped to my front in a sling. The bulging bag that has become my constant accessory is in the pram that will be his bed for the next five weeks. Nappies, wipes, changing mat, sterile water, baby toys, baby clothes, passport, novel.

Immediately I need to pee. How is this to be done? I wonder. For starters I have to leave the pram outside because it won't fit through the door and round the corner. Then I try going into the cubicle with him still strapped to my front but when I turn round to close the door I discover we are jammed against the toilet bowl and the door won't shut. Perhaps I should take the baby out of the sling and lie him down on the floor while I pee with the door open. Alternatively I could give him to someone while I pee in private. Wandering out of the toilets having decided I don't want to pee after all, at least not for another few hours, I spot the Disabled Toilet door. Inside it's fabulously spacious. I can fit the pram, the baby, my luggage and myself all in one room and shut the door and turn round. Luxury. The image in the mirror is a bit of a shock. Where did gorgeous, gestating Genevieve go to? My hair seems to have died and my face is drawn and white. The lower half of me appears to be being used as a fat store for milk production. I wouldn't be surprised to find my teeth have gone black and are on the verge of falling out. I wonder what Sid's explanation for all this would be. Hardly likely to keep the father of my child intent on popping dead rabbits into my pot. Although Sid did intimate that after the birth things get a bit lairy so what happens is that nature plays her trump card – narcissism. She ensures that the first child looks the spitting image of the dad, thereby compelling him to hang around long enough for the mother to regain her sanity and her figure. I miss Sid already. I hope she will come and visit in Portugal.

I sit down to wait for the plane. For a while I am eyed uneasily by the other passengers who are clearly not sure whether I am a tragic figure (lone mother, possibly abandoned) or a raging feminist (artificial insemination by a gay friend). Finally, a nun gets up from her seat and heads towards me, drawn like a missionary to a developing country.

The flight is surprisingly problem free in that Karl stays latched to my breast for almost the entire time, oblivious to the roar and scream of take-off and descent. Problem free that is apart from when he does one truly explosive shit which necessitates a complete change of clothes for him and uses up a week's supply of baby wipes. And has to be dealt with on my lap. It is possible to do many things in an aeroplane toilet as we know, but changing a baby's nappy is not one of them. Sister Moira, however, who has stayed by my side throughout, takes it all in her stride – apart from the take-off and landing when her faith seems to falter and she has to concentrate on her rosary. By the time we land I feel pretty pleased with myself for surviving the first major hurdle of motherhood: international travel.

When I wander out of Lisbon airport you're there but harried and distracted. You're with a runner whom you introduce me to but whose name I don't catch. You seem embarrassed at the clutter and chaos of us. In irritation you struggle to unclip the carrycot from the pram and then struggle to fold the pram. Both operations are new to you and pram designers seem intent on making them as unobvious to the newly initiated as possible. You have hired a car for me but tell me sheepishly that I'll have to drive it to the hotel as you are late for a meeting in the other direction. You scribble the name of the village on a piece of paper and tell me to look out for signs before the exit to Lisbon.

To my consternation, I am shaking as I start the engine. The car is like a furnace. I open all the windows. With the map on my lap and Karl screaming behind my head and the wind in my ears, I drive haltingly towards the exit of the slip road and edge out into the river of motorway traffic bound for Lisboa.

31st October 1991

One sock hangs off a lampshade. The other is balled tight on the floor near its trainer, laces tied in an impenetrable knot, its partner lost. In the corridor the trail continues. A T-shirt dropped at the bathroom door. Inside, the twin towers of your jeans semi-collapsed where your legs last left them astride the porcelain.

Don't ask me why, I know it will end in tears but something compels me to clear up the room while the baby is sleeping. Anyway, right now chucking your dirty clothes in the laundry basket is about as creative as I can get on sleep that is snatched in ninety-minute segments. On good days, like today, I tell myself it's the prerogative of the creative genius to be selfish and chaotic. My God, Leonardo da Vinci was probably shockingly messy. On bad days, like 2 a.m. this morning, I tell myself you're a self-obsessed child who's never grown up.

But it's 9.00 a.m. and Karl has just fallen asleep after only fifteen minutes of walking, jiggling and 'You take the high road and I'll take the low road . . .' and now I'm going to be a really good wife and mother. What else is there for me to do out here? I'm going to hand wash Karl's clothes and my milk-stiffened bra and T-shirts like my mum used to do. I'm going to swat as many flies as I can so our baby doesn't die of dysentery. And now I'm going to pick up all your scripts and shooting schedules and place them in an orderly pile. Finally I will put all the videos back in their covers and stack them neatly by the television. Like your mum used to do.

I wheel Karl onto the balcony so he can get fresh air. But not too much. 'Babies chill very easily,' according to the book. I create some shade with a pair of your jeans strung up from the concrete joist. 'Baby's skin is very sensitive. Do not expose them to strong sunlight.' There is just time therefore for some cerebral stimulation so that I may continue to be a partner who is an intellectual equal. I open Tolstoy's *The Kreutzer Sonata* in which the protagonist spends a whole train journey from Leningrad to Moscow telling the man opposite him why he has murdered his much-loathed wife. According to the introduction, which is as far as I have got in the last three weeks, the story of the marriage is strongly autobiographical. Apart from the actual murder, presumably, as Leo dictated it to his wife. Blimey. I put the book to one side and close my eyes. God, this is bliss. I'm doing nothing. I imagine the dread brown corridors of the hospital, Sister Stone herding her ladies up and down it, 'Hurry, ladies, hurry. We haven't got all day.' I plan my escape.

You come back early and we drive down the coast. Just the three of us. We find a restaurant where our arrival is treated like the Second Coming. They fall on Karl and exclaim at his beauty and perfection, tell us he is the spitting image of you, say something kind about my hair, offer us a glass of the local wine, return to look at you and look at him, clap their hands to their chests and shout to the cook who comes out with a blood-stained knife and agrees that yes, he is very beautiful. We sit on a terrace and eat dinner overlooking the crashing Atlantic and watch the sun sink in a crimson gashed sky. It is ridiculously romantic – the kind of thing you love. At one point a school of leaping dolphins even flash by in gleaming arcs. Karl is taken inside to be entertained by the staff. We look at each other and talk, smiling at our good fortune. You are full of plans for our future. We should go and live in the country, we should take a year off and travel, I should get a job closer to home.

'The important thing is to be happy,' you say.

'I am happy. At this moment. Completely.' I kiss you.

'It makes all the difference having you both here. I love you. Both of you.' I wonder if Karl is about to start the screaming but he hasn't. It's an hour later when you get up to find out where he's got to. He's fast asleep on someone's grandmother's lap.

*

I explored the village a bit today. Everyone says 'Ah *bambini*!' when they see me and Karl. Keep asking how old he is. When I tell them three weeks they look at me as if I'm mad.

*

Manuel has just walked into the room to deliver your tapes. I am topless on the floor doing my post-natal exercises because the books say it is very important to get back into shape as soon as possible. He's seen my breasts before anyway because they are permanently out of my bra as Karl is permanently hungry and upset. It's like having a succubus latched to me twenty-four hours a day. The more he suckles the more I produce and then if he sleeps more than two hours my breasts become so engorged I have to submerge them one by one in a sink of hot water to let the milk leak out. Exquisite agony.

*

I have rarely had the use of both hands at once since Karl was born. This makes eating quite hard. I eat toasted sandwiches in the bar. That's either ham or cheese. Once I had cheese with tomato, which was nice. I miss Mum.

*

I really like Consuela who cleans our room every day. She changes my milk-drenched sheets each morning and talks to Karl. I don't understand a word she is saying but we both look forward to her visits.

*

You're right, it is idyllic here. So peaceful. What with the sea over there. And the fields. And the sleepy little village and things. And we're lucky to have this balcony. Lovely for me and Karl to have so much fresh air. And sun in November!

*

Mariana on the desk downstairs tells everyone that the reason my baby is crying all the time is because he's alone with me too much. I feel quite hurt when I hear this. What am I doing wrong? This morning she beckons me over to the desk, sticks her arms out and nods her head vehemently.

'*Aqui, aqui.*'

She takes Karl in her arms and makes shooing motions at me with one hand. Empty handed, baby-less, I leave Karl with her, pull open the door of the hotel and stand stupidly on the pavement. Now what?

It's strange to walk without a baby strapped to my chest. I sit in the empty square, watch two dogs fucking and then wander back to the hotel. Karl is fast asleep in the arms of Mariana's grandmother. I feel an overwhelming gratitude to these women who know what to do and a creeping certainty that I'm hopeless at this mother business.

*

Today, Karl's screaming took on a different tone. I undressed him to discover that the skin of his bottom and genitals is flame-red, almost blistered. How could I not have noticed before? When did this start? How did it start? Was it the cheapo nappies I bought from the village shop? Can babies die of nappy rash? Will he ever trust anyone with his penis again? Feeling guilty, desperate and helpless, I lie him naked on a towel, fan his bottom with a newspaper and look up nappy rash in the phrase book.

*

You sleep through the nights like a stone. Most mornings you leave at six. There is a twenty-minute window before you leave in the morning when Karl is awake and not screaming. He lies on his back between us like a jerky chicken, spluttering and kicking, delighted to find us both there. He pauses every now and then to grab your hair, pull your head towards him and stare up at you in uncertain amazement.

In the evenings you finish at eight or nine or ten. Sometimes later. You are very good about stopping by to see us even if you have to rush out to a meeting where the latest production disaster must be averted.

*

Consuela knows what to do about Karl's rash. She has gone to fetch cream. Felicity Blow said they could hear him screaming all the way down at the beach. They were shooting the scene where the teenage girl has her toes sucked by the priest. I tell Felicity that that wasn't Karl screaming, that was me. She laughs hysterically at this very amusing joke and then stops suddenly and gives me a meaningful look.

'Are you all right, Genevieve?'

*

Last night Karl slept for forty-five minutes. The rest of the time I walked round the room and out onto the balcony with him. He screamed. I screamed. I thought about jumping off but decided against it as it might mean you'd have to miss a day's shooting. I rang Sid sometime in the night. She told me I should take him to the doctor. She said some bad things about first babies and first films, egos and eggs and some other stuff I couldn't really hear because of the crying. I wish she was here. I am taking the bus into Lisbon so I can visit the doctor. I'm afraid Karl is terribly ill. What if there was a mistake and he has cystic fibrosis after all? The stupid bloody phrase book does not have cystic fibrosis in it. I lick Karl's face but can't tell whether it's too salty or not.

The doctor is very kind which makes me want to cry. He feels Karl's tummy, looks at his nappy rash, weighs him and writes a prescription for wind and sore skin. He asks me if there is anything else. How are you? he says. I'm fine. It's beautiful here, I tell him, grinning like a lunatic.

*

Last night I had three and half hours' uninterrupted sleep. It's the best thing that's happened to me for weeks. I feel deeply in love with both of you. Now I'm determined to become a better wife and mother. I listen to the tape you told me to get, *Teach Yourself Portuguese*. I learn to count up to seven before Karl wakes up again.

*

It's two in the morning but you are still out shooting the sex scene in the stable. I expect you may have to do several takes. Karl smiled his first smile today. There was a hesitation in his stare up at me during the chin-tickling session (which, according to the book, can help with smile development). Then a dent, then a dimple appeared to the left of his mouth. His eyes actually twinkled. And he smiled! What a moment! I couldn't believe it. I have been trying to get him to smile for days because the book says it happens at five weeks so he is a bit behind. Or I am possibly not funny enough. Or not very good company. Or something. When it happened I felt bloody fantastic. OK, Consuela was standing behind me, waving over my shoulder, but she had the good grace to pretend to be swatting a fly when I turned round in triumph.

*

I sit on the narrow balcony with our naked baby face down on my knees and I'm trying to do the back-pat-thigh-shake routine that Portuguese mothers seem to know about but which they didn't show us at the NCT classes. It's something I remember the Ethiopian midwife in the hospital showing a mother, too, and I wonder if maternal incompetence is just a North-European trait, common among the English and the Irish, like cystic fibrosis. The patting and jiggling is not really working though and the crisp, bright afternoon air is rent with Karl's screams. I snatch lines of advice from the Penelope Leach book which lies open beside me. In the absence of anyone else to talk to about how to look after a new baby, she seems to offer compassion and humanity, if not always a solution. 'There is very little you can do for a baby suffering from "colic" . . .' That's what worries me. Those quote marks. Suppose he is, in fact, dying, not suffering from colic at all? I turn him over and lift him onto my swollen, monster breasts. They spray milk at the sound of his screams. A needle jet gets him in the eye. '. . . Your helplessness, together with the fact that the dreadful bouts of screaming . . .' he stops, belches with sudden and violent force and the screaming stops momentarily only to start up again with renewed desperation, '. . . occur at the time of day when you are most tired and in need of peaceful times together . . .' His quivering mouth finds my nipple and sucks for a second. He lets the nipple go and begins to shake and sob, revving up for another bout of banshee wailing. '. . . and remember; however awful the colic may be . . .' he kicks and twists like a tortured soul, '. . . it will not harm your baby.' He is beside himself, literally. '. . . neither will it last for any longer than . . . ' We both are. '. . . twelve weeks at the very most.'

⋆

I have carried Karl's carrycot down to the bar this evening because, miraculously, he fell asleep at nine. Zak, one of the crew, talks to me a lot and looks like he might cry when he looks at Karl. I guess at some kind of marital explosion going on with Zak which I would rather not hear about. I try to avoid him but often he's the only one there. If he says to me one more time, 'Ah it's a magical age. Enjoy it while you can – they grow up so fast,' I shall asphyxiate him with a muslin square. I can tell he's only seen his children at weekends since they were born and doesn't really know what he is talking about. He tells me you are a genius and how glad he is to be working for you and how amazing some of the underwater shots are that you got last night of Felicity Blow pretending to nearly drown in the donkey's water trough and then Felicity tells me what a brilliant dad you are and how sweet it is that you've brought your family out with you. She's right. You are a hero. Not sure what of.

⋆

I have taken to frequenting the restaurant at the other end of the village. It has four tables and is always empty except for me, the large bosomy woman who owns it and her daughter. They practically dragged me in off the street one evening when Karl and I were doing our circuit of the village, Karl screaming as usual and me wandering aimlessly like a car crash victim. They took Karl off me, made me sit at a table, poured me a drink and slammed a plate of steaming stew down in front of me. But the best bit was what they did with Karl. With him face down on her knee, the mother sat in the doorway, jiggled her thighs and he was fast asleep in three minutes. So here I am sitting at a table eating a plate of stew with huge hunks of bread and slabs of butter. I have both hands at my disposal and even have the Tolstoy propped up against the bread basket. I am looking around me and taking an interest in my surroundings. If there was someone else here who spoke English I would no doubt converse with them. I write a hyper letter to Sid telling her how great it is here and urging her to come out and see us as soon as she can.

*

Can't carry anything today. There are a lot of stairs. Not just in the hotel. In the whole damn village. And the carrycot and the pram and the bag and the baby are all a bit heavy suddenly. I think my back's gone. Probably followed my sanity which I think finally walked out the door sometime yesterday. Today I am staying in the room. I am staying in bed. If I just lie on my side, Karl can suckle and we can both drift in and out of sleep. If we just stay here I have a feeling he won't start the crying at three. I watch the clock. When he stirs, my nipple is just by his mouth. No bras, no nappies. We're on a pile of towels which are getting soggy with milk and pee and sweat. I think though this is probably how it was supposed to be. You know, when we were grunting about in old caves and things.

*

I think we are both possessed. Beside ourselves. My milk looks like it has turned to water. He cries while he's sucking it. As if it's poisoning him. The crying is demonic. The noise of it tears through the silence of the sleepy village. His screams seem causeless and are without consolation. I watch, helpless, as he wails in terror at some appalling shades and spectres of grief. I begin to be haunted by the notion that it is something he has seen in my eyes, something he has seen in our history. God knows. If you were here. If you could hear it, I could tell you what I mean. Or you could tell me I am not mad.

*

It is nine thirty when you walk in the door. Karl has just fallen asleep in our bed. I'm lying beside him, not daring to move in case he wakes up again. My nipples feel like they've been sandpapered. You kneel gently on the bed and kiss us both. We don't speak. You lie alongside my back and hold me tight.

There's a timid knock on the door. The knocking repeats itself, still quiet but persistent and urgent. We wait for the noise of the slip of paper under the door that usually follows an unanswered knock. Nothing but another knock. You sigh and get off the bed and open it. Through the open bedroom door I watch Felicity Blow fall into the room sobbing very well indeed.

13. INT. MARK'S HOTEL ROOM. NIGHT

MARK ushers FELICITY into his room. She is crying noisily.

MARK

(Patting her shoulder)
What's wrong? What's happened? Here, sit down.

MARK waits for the wailing to subside. He finds emotion difficult without a camera.

FELICITY

It's . . . it's Dave. I got back tonight and he was gone!

From the bedroom comes the sound of a baby crying. MARK crosses the room and closes the door.

FELICITY

(Holding her tiny head in her tiny hands)

Oh God. Have I woken him up? Here, I'll go. It's just, I needed to talk to someone.

MARK

(Patting her shoulder and staring at the floor)
No, sit down. Don't cry. Look, he's probably just popped out somewhere. He'll be back.

FELICITY

(Handing MARK a crumpled piece of paper)
He left me this. He's not coming back. If he's taken a flight already I'm just going to have to fly to England too. I can't carry on if he's not here!

From the bedroom, the noise of a baby's screams are intensifying. Outside a donkey brays mournfully.

MARK

(Looking helplessly at the bedroom)
Let's go down and have a drink in the bar. What happened? Did you argue about something?

FELICITY

(Racked with renewed sobbing)
I don't know! I don't understand. I thought everything was fine. I don't think he can handle me and Pepe.

MARK

Pepe? But he's a donkey.

FELICITY

I know! That's what's so crazy! What is wrong with me, Mark? Why is it that every time I find someone I really like, it always goes wrong? You and Genevieve are so lucky.

MARK

(Helping FELICITY to her feet)

Come on. We'll phone the airport from the bar. He won't have left yet. I'll drive you there if necessary.

FELICITY

(Checking her face in the mirror)

Look at me. I look terrible. Oh God, look at me.

BEAT

I'm so sorry about this, Mark. And you being so kind just makes me want to cry again.

FELICITY breaks down again. They leave.

FADE UP BOB DYLAN's 'Just Like a Woman'.)

*

It's one in the morning and I've strapped Karl to my chest like an unexploded bomb. I'm bored and lonely and I'm going to try and watch the shoot. You don't like me doing this. You think it looks naff having the wife and baby watching. I suppose it does a bit. But there's nowhere else to go. I walk through the dark streets towards the lights of the set down in the field towards the sea. The lights turn the dark into day. It always amazes me that you can make this happen. I pass runners and lookouts with walkie-talkies, all doing not very much. I stand on the edge of the field, near a group of curious villagers, looking down on the set below. Every now and then I recognise the shape of you, moving in and out of the darkness. Like Christ on the shores of wherever transforming loaves and fishes, even this film, made for the small screen, low budget and soon to be forgotten, promises the miracle of transformation. I shudder, standing there in the dark. It is no longer warm and I'm afraid Karl will give me away. Nothing happens for an awfully long time.

After a while, Karl jerks himself awake from some precipitous dream and opens his mouth to yell in shock and surprise. I scramble to my feet and hurry out of ear-shot. I start running down the dark track that leads back to the village, holding the back of his head so it doesn't bounce about too much. Looking down I see him looking up at me in amazement, head wobbling, arms outstretched. He is smiling an enormous smile. I've cracked it. Why didn't someone tell me? All I have to do is keep running. I set off at a brisk jog down the path to the beach.

*

'Look—'

'Don't shout, Mark. He's asleep.'

'Look. I'm sorry I haven't been around more but it's very stressful for me, too, you know. It's not that I want to work long hours. I have no choice. It's the job. Look, why don't you take the car tomorrow and drive down the coast? You could take windsurfing lessons. Do a bit of sightseeing. It's lovely down there.'

'Do you realise that you haven't changed a nappy yet?'

'What are you talking about? What's that got to do with anything? I haven't had a chance. I've been working since two days after he was born. Someone's got to earn some money round here.' You look desperate.

'Why don't you try having a bath with him? He's sweet in the bath. He loves it.'

'What's having a bath with him got to do with anything?'

'I hope this film is going to be worth it, Mark. You've hardly looked at him since we arrived. You've held him about twice.'

'I've seen him every day. That's the whole point of you being here. So I can be with you! Look, it's difficult for me too, you know. This is the biggest thing I've done so far and if I fuck this up I won't get another chance!' It's strange the way once the shouting and the swearing starts, how tempting it is to return to it. Like smoking. 'And we won't be able to pay the mortgage on your fucking salary.' What's that film, *Bad Timing*? This is all such bad timing.

'My fucking salary was the same as your fucking salary before this film.' The swearing. When did it start? I really don't like the swearing. But on the other hand, there is something strangely satisfying about the violence it carries. 'Why do directors get paid so much money anyway? Perhaps you should think about giving your family some emotional support. Sod the money.' I stop because the next line is I'm going back to my mother.

Karl joins in with some screaming. You throw up one hand in disbelief. You switch to kind and conciliatory.

'Why don't you *do* something, Genevieve? You're out here, in this beautiful place, lovely weather . . . but you never leave the village. Why don't you go into Lisbon and find out about Portuguese lessons? Do some exploring. Structure your time a bit.'

I burst into tears and say, 'I want my mum,' but what I mean is I want you.

The three of us stop and look at each other in exhausted despair. We are wordless, sorry and tearful. It wasn't supposed to be like this. We attempt a clumsy cuddle. You stroke Karl's body, tracking the lines of his face, swallowing and blinking audibly. Your face looks suddenly old. Shadowed and sad. Haunted.

Ten

AT MY mum's it is autumn and raining. A safe and familiar interior world. Shreds of my own babyhood come into focus every now and then. Red coals in the grate. The blanket with a corner the dog chewed. Bye baby bunting . . . The cream cot with drop-sides that will take a finger off like a guillotine. Lavender's blue dilly dilly . . . The sound of my mother's feet.

In sleep, I drop deep down out of sight, out of this world. It is like a death. Oblivion. When Karl cries in some distant place, I hear Mum come and take him but I don't surface. His birth could have been a dream. You ring, but I don't hear the phone.

In the steamy fug of the bathroom I lie in the bath alone. Myself. Bliss. No baby in my arms. My breasts float like torpedoes, fine trails of milk clouding the water at their tips. Karl lies naked on my mum's towelled lap where she sits by the window. The whole length of him reclines fearless and easy, head tilted back over the edge of her thigh, face upwards, one tiny hand spanned in a gesture of greeting. My mum's head is inclined, each hand round a tiny foot or fist. 'Yes,' she is saying. 'Yes. You *are*.' And between them, a full frontal stare. Intense, infalling, in love.

I don't mind the damp air here or the drizzle or the dying colours and you feel very far away. I look out at the day and think how much you would long for bright sun or a dramatic snowfall. You dread the incontrovertible sadness of the English weather. But here at Mum's I sit for hours, deep in cushions with my nipple in Karl's mouth, talking nonsense and droning on to him about ploughs and fishes and boughs and wishes. I realise that mothers look at their babies obsessively. This must be disconcerting for the fathers, I suppose, because the mother literally cannot take her eyes off the baby. And maybe it's disconcerting for the babies, given that the eyes are the windows of the soul and all that. But I guess my soul must be all right now, with no hint of *susto* or whatever, because Karl's eyes lock on mine while he sucks, hands paddling the breast like a puppy and every now and then, he makes a superhuman effort to pull his head away, and with milk falling from the corner of his mouth, he looks right into me and smiles.

In the chill, darkened passage between my mother's bedroom and the stairs is a chest of drawers that used to belong to some great aunt. On its polished surface stands our wedding photo. There's a group of us lined up outside the registry office on that cold, windy day. It had felt awkward, so soon after Bill's funeral. We were going to cancel but my mum insisted we go ahead. It's a shock how young we look. Both of us laugh out at the camera like children. Helena's incandescent beauty dominates the photo. She knows how to do the split-second pose for the camera, head tilted down, eyes raised, lips soft and almost parting. Angus stares at her. There are your parents and my mum all leaning towards us, smiling. In the photo next to it is Mum's wedding photo when she married Bill. I study his stooping frame. He was already old when she married him. In one hand burns the perpetual cigarette, a long curve of ash at its end.

I kneel down and pull open the heavy bottom drawer where she keeps the other photographs. It smells of ageing paper and the peaty smell of old wood. Beneath all the albums recording my childhood are the two framed photos that I always retrieve from their storage place. Still damp from the bath, holding the thin towelling robe round my body, I pull out the photos. I pick up the larger of the two. There's my mum, wearing a tailored suit, the waist nipped above the curve of her hips as she bends to get into the car. Her face is turned to the camera and she is laughing with her mouth open and her eyes shut tight against the shower of confetti. Her hand is clasped by the large hand of my dad, half his body off the frame but his face caught in the same noise of laughter and farewells. I can see that his thick dark hair is mine, falling heavily towards his eyes, his other hand coming up to sweep it back from his face in what I can tell is a habitual gesture. Then there's the much smaller photograph of me and my twin brother each cradled in the crook of one arm, my mum's head bent down towards us, a complicated-looking nursing blouse done up with a double row of buttons. It is just possible to discern the serious line of my mum's mouth. In the background is the wooden clothes horse that now stands in her bathroom, draped in the photo with the countless white squares of small babies' laundry. I study my brother's face for signs of Karl. But the image is blurred and indistinct. I've never managed to picture him properly.

Eleven

10th December 1991

I'VE DECIDED I can't live the rest of my life with my mother and sometimes I entertain the perverse fantasy that she is keeping me hostage in revenge for the marital crimes of my father. I slightly fear that my being there just proves there is no escape from our pasts. So I've come home to the Angel to prepare for your return.

Friends have been and left flowers and every kind of small stuffed toy animal. Now I know, though, that the only ones Karl will do anything with are the ones that make a noise and have some method of attaching them to his pram. The rest might just as well be paintings or books for all the playing he'll do with them. They will be added to the mute audience already piling up in his room. I'm halfway up the stairs with an armful of ducks, cows and sheep when the door knocker goes in Sid's inimitable door-knocker riff. And in the doorway, there she stands, huge and beautiful and smiling. Behind her, looking sheepish and tentative, is Angus. Next to him is a Christmas tree. We all try to hug each other but can't really without crushing Karl so we stumble and exclaim and laugh down the stairs to the kitchen.

'Your mummy is a clever clogs,' says Sid to Karl, doing the rocking jiggling thing with him in her arms. 'Oh, yes, she is.'

'Well, they weren't anything that difficult, just—'

'Passed her exams with flying colours.' I'm beaming with pride while I follow her meandering dance round the room. 'And making you at the same time.' She holds Karl up above her head and brings his face down to hers. She's got very white square teeth. I hover next to her. Just in case. 'So what are you going to do now? Now you're a Staff Nurse with an M.Sc.?'

'Well, thought I'd maybe apply for a research grant, you know. Whoops. Mind his head on that cupboard, Sid. Maybe look for lecturer jobs or something, just while Karl is little.'

'Escape the madhouse and do bugger all in a college. Good plan. What did Mark say about your results?'

'Got a bucket, Gen? Or something to stand this tree in?' Angus is standing like a woodcutter grasping the Christmas tree. I feel a childish rush of excitement about Christmas.

'Oh by the way, Angus has got a new job.'

'Hey, Angus! What, a proper job, do you mean? You've not finally succumbed to the Protestant work ethic, have you? Congratulations!'

'I have actually. Prosthetics.' He takes Karl off Sid, holding him gently against his chest, looks at me and smiles. He looks open and happy. Then he turns his back on us and wanders off towards the french doors humming. It's an old Irish ballad and it makes the hairs on my arm stand on end.

'But what happened to the puppet making?' I ask, tears welling at the sight of Karl in Angus's arms and the sound of that song.

'No call for puppets these days,' says Sid. 'But artificial limbs, well, now you're talking. Wooden legs are always in demand.'

'There's a big market for them in Cambodia, Vietnam, you know, all those places.' Angus hands Karl back to Sid and starts looking in cupboards for a bucket.

'Anywhere the Brits and Americans have sold landmines

to, basically,' says Sid. 'The landmine companies probably have shares in the artificial limb industry. Wouldn't be surprised. What the hell is this, Genevieve? A sex toy?'

'It's a breast pump, Sid. So I can return to work after Christmas and express my milk. Then I put it in the ice tray and freeze it so he has my milk to drink from his bottle instead of formula.'

'Wouldn't it be simpler to get a wet nurse?'

'Where do you want your tree, Gen?' Angus has a bucket in one hand and the tree in the other. He looks like Lenin with hair. Apart from the bucket.

'God look, man at work,' I say in admiration, watching Angus place the tree by the garden window. Next he actually kneels down and begins to decorate it. He's brought some decorations with him and everything. Bloody hell.

'I know. He's bloody gorgeous, Gen. I owe you one. And sex is . . .' She mouths the words 'fucking fantastic'. I'd quite like to get my baby back now but Sid is waltzing off up the other end with him.

'So. Sorted the childcare yet?'

'I can't quite believe it, but apparently—'

'There isn't any. I know. I did some research for you while you were away. You could leave him with the manic depressive and her Rottweiler on the top floor of that tower block that you see over there or you can pay six hundred pounds a month to leave him at Little Scamps, the private nursery in Islington run by disappointed Sloanes where he'll be ignored all day long. Or you could bring him with you and leave him at the hospital crèche. That's cheaper but full until 1996. But I think you could sort it.'

'Gen, are you sure you want to leave him with someone else at twelve weeks?' says Angus. 'It's a bit soon, isn't it?'

'Oh, but I have to. We need the money.' Although obviously the money argument has just vanished with Sid's information about the cost of childcare. 'I want to get back. I need to get back into it.' These words become the truth as soon as they exist outside my head which is one of the problems of speaking, I often think.

The phone rings. It's Helena. She's round the corner and wants to come and see the baby.

'How are you? How was Portugal? Was it amazing? Can I pop round now? I'm just up the road?'

'It'd be great to see you, Helena . . . but there're some people here right now . . .'

'He's an absolute animal,' says Sid very loudly as she passes me, '*day* and night.'

Angus has his face in the Christmas tree. Helena says something like, 'Oh, are Angus and Sid there?' She sounds hurt but determinedly cheerful. Says she'd love to see them but she doesn't want to tire me and Karl with too many visitors.

I wish my friends would stop fragmenting. Planning a dinner party these days, if I ever got round to it, would be a diplomatic minefield. Couldn't have the ones who work in television with the ones who don't because the ones who work in television can only talk about television. Couldn't have journalists all together obviously because then who would they talk about? Couldn't have people without babies present with people who now have them because the people who now have them can only talk in hours (sleeping), kilograms (growth) and mls (milk). And they always appear with their baby. Couldn't have actors unless there are people there who have seen their latest work. Couldn't have work friends because they will only talk about patients and hospital management and you get bored. Couldn't really have Helena if the truth be told because she's secretly slept with most of the men. Angus and Sid are the only people I know now who can talk about anything other than how they earn a living and mortgages. Mainly because neither have proper jobs and consequently no mortgage. I think we need a new drug to divert us all.

Twelve

31st January 1992

THE BOTTLES are lined up on the table by our bed. The red digital glow of the radio alarm measures out the small hours each night. At 2.17 I hear him begin to cry and I turn over luxuriating in the knowledge that tonight we're sharing the feeds and it's your turn so I prepare to fall peacefully back into slumber. At 2.21 the crying gets louder, more insistent. I wait, eyes open in the dark, for you to rouse yourself.

'Mark.'

I did him at 1.12 because I just thought it might be easier but if we're going to share the load of these shredded nights I am going to have to make you do this one. Since going back to work, I'm terrified I'll find I just can't do it.

'Mark.'

At 2.26 his crying is shifting gear, revving up to the kind of baby's wail that heralds the end of the world. At 2.33 I give you a gentle shove.

'Mark.'

You roll on your back, eyes closed, breathing the steady sea shore rhythm of the very asleep. You are *fast* asleep. As in *shut*, *secure*, dead to the world. Not just *un*conscious, *sub*conscious. You spend more time with your subconscious than is probably good for me. And God knows what's happening to mine because I haven't been asleep long enough in the last three months to have spent much time there at all. At 2.46 I go in to our distraught baby, lift his flailing, furious form from the cot and suckle him. He guzzles breathlessly, and I avoid his wet-eyed reproach seeking out my eyes in the gloom, staring instead at the fatuous cheer of the Thomas the Tank Engine nightlight. I mustn't fall asleep without changing him otherwise . . . But I'm out of it before he is, like a drunk on a park bench.

It's a mystery, I think to myself at 3.31 as I climb back into bed, to you and to sleep. How do you get to go so deep where nothing can reach you? It's a bit alarming actually. If the building were on fire or wife and child being slaughtered by drug-crazed maniacs, would you wake up? Unlikely, given that waking you up in the morning for work necessitates three alarm calls from the operator and an alarm clock placed on the far side of the room which, despite the heart-stopping, klaxon call it makes, has never been known to wake you. As in 'Genevieve, darling, wake up, my alarm's gone off, ooh must have been twenty minutes ago now and I leapt up, popped downstairs and made you this coffee.' You know I'll wake up so you don't need to. Or maybe your ears just need syringing. I open my eyes, raise myself on one elbow and stare hard into your ears. I can't see much despite the shaft of light from the landing. Maybe men suffer from an excess of ear wax and are actually walking the planet partially deaf. That would explain quite a lot. I snuggle up to you and breathe in the sweet sweat kernel of your head, the scent mark that still delights me and which Karl shares. I love the warmth of you through your skin. You reverse your bottom into my flank and hold my arms tight around your chest. I sleep.

4.17 and I desperately don't want it to be because if it is it can only mean he is awake again. Surfacing feels like being raised from the dead. I sleepwalk to his room and lift him from the cot, his bottom sagging with the weight of his sodden nappy. I pull apart the poppers and the nappy thuds to the floor. Leaving his bottom naked, too shuckered to care, I carry him back to our bed. There is no more crying that night and I take small sips of sleep, wary in case one of us rolls on top of him and dreading the day to come.

'Mark.'

In order to wash Karl and myself and eat breakfast and prepare his stuff for the day in the hospital crèche I need to get up at 6.00. Which isn't really a problem because Karl starts his day at 5.30. I play with him with my eyes closed until 5.55.

'Mark.'

In the bathroom mirror I'm shocked to see a shipwreck survivor. I hope that the shower will do for me what the carwash does for the car. I dress and stuff breast pads down my bra. Don't want the oceanic quantities of milk that leak from me between feeds to frighten the patients. They might think I'm coming apart. In the bedroom I discover both of you, looking like two creatures dropped from the sky, spread-eagled in sleep. It's 6.17. Karl and I have to leave at 6.45.

'Mark.'

I go downstairs to the kitchen. Breast pump, bottles, water, nappies, cream, wipes, spare clothes for Karl, changing mat, money, book, milk cubes. All the space in my head has been filled with things to remember. I feel like my hard disk is full. Total system crash can only be a matter of time. At 6.44 you come downstairs with Karl, both of you scratching your heads and yawning, in what is, I am sure, an adorable kind of way but which right now I am blind to because the script I've been given casts you two as Cute Modern Dad with Baby and me as The Wife From Hell.

'Looks like he slept through the night,' you say, kissing me and dropping the untouched bottles into the sink.

'Mark. He's not dressed.'

The crèche is in a Nissen hut behind the kitchens. I'm hoping it's going to be the answer to all my problems. Inside, the lights are on and the Christmas decorations still up. Clumps of cotton wool have been glued to the windows which are sprayed with fake snow. Shoving open the door with the front of the pram we are hit by a wall of heat in which is trapped a powerful aroma of baby shit, disinfectant and baby lotion. Not unlike the ward. It is run by Pam, gargantuan and with brown circles under her eyes. She's talking to a mother who's unpicking the hands of a toddler from her coat and backing out of the door. He's frozen in a pose of utter terror and bawling at the top of his voice as if he has just witnessed some unspeakable atrocity.

'Leave the Calpol with me then and I'll give it him as and when I think fit. All right? Come on, Harry. Come and have a cuddle with Pam.'

'Muuummmeeeee! Muuummmumeeeee! Mummeeeeee! Mu-u-u-u-m! Na-ah! Na-ah! Na-ah!' At which point words give way to a piercing scream as the mother turns and flees.

Talking to Pam right now is obviously out of the question so I park the pram next to the others and lift Karl out. There's a low table with tiny chairs where some worn-out-looking jigsaws have been laid out. In a plastic box on the floor is a collection of not very clean baby toys. I sit on one of the miniature chairs next to a woman distractedly doing a chunky wooden Postman Pat puzzle with her daughter. She gets up to go, the child starts to whimper and she sits down again looking at her watch.

'Mummy's got to go now, Chelsea.'

'No.'

'Mummy's got to go to work now. Come on. You'll have a nice day with Pam, won't you?'

'Mummy stay.'

I wonder what it is that makes mothers refer to themselves in the third person when they talk to their children. Does this indicate the beginnings of some kind of personality disorder or at the very least an identity crisis? Maybe I should propose a research project on the subject. Or write a children's book explaining to children that mothers are in fact sentient beings just like them – could call it *The Mummy Who Lost Her Id.*

Mummy looks round for a surrogate mother to leave her child with. All three of them have children attached to various parts of their bodies. One catches her eye and shouts over.

'Just leave her. She'll make a big fuss at first but she'll be fine as soon as you've gone. Honest. Go on. Just go.' Another illogical piece of emotional skulduggery guaranteed to make mothers paranoid. Because it seems to be true. Are the children involved in the conspiracy as well? Keighley comes over and sits with the child, eyes glazing over as the little girl starts posting shapes through the holes in a yellow elephant's head. Mummy makes her getaway.

I'm going to have to leave too. Can't have Lesley and Sister Stone thinking I'm not up to all this. My God, if I can't cope with a baby how the hell can I be expected to cope with the seriously demanding world of Psychiatry? I carry Karl over to Pam. She seems dimly to remember me from my heavily pregnant visit.

'What's his name again? Hang on a sec. Keighley! Just give him three spoonfuls of the stuff otherwise he'll be murder all morning. Sorry, Jenny, is it?'

'Hi. This is Karl. Shall I just leave him . . . somewhere?'

'You can put him back in the pram, might as well.'

'He usually has a sleep at about ten.'

'They all have a sleep at ten whether they like it or not.' Pam laughs, heaving herself up off the midget chair and going over to a chaotic table of papers in the corner. 'Here, just pop your details down where we can contact you and what have you.'

'And where shall I leave his bottles and nappies and stuff?'

'Just stick them down under the table.'

When I leave, Karl gives me the Northern Line look. Outside in the grey I succumb to a flood of crying, striding purposively off in the wrong direction.

Winston spots me standing near the allotments blowing my nose on a baby wipe. It is raining and he comes lolloping across the wet grass, head down, grimacing against the weather.

'Gen! It's you. I thought it was Alice doing another runner for a moment. Ooh. You look a little peaky. Not thinking of doing some gardening now, are you?' He takes my bag and gives me a bear hug. 'You are all woman, Genevieve.'

I laugh mid-sob and allow him to steer me back to the ward.

17th February 1992

Crouched under the desk in the ward office, dress unbuttoned, one breast elongated into the suction disc, I pull slowly and not very productively on the plunger. A few fine jets dribble their way down the tube. Ten millilitres. Jesus. I have to manage at least thirty before Sister Stone comes back from her break.

'Oh my God!' It's Winston, clapping both hands to his cheeks and standing transfixed in the doorway. 'Genevieve, where did you get that thing?'

'Shut the bloody door, will you?'

'Hey, that's a pretty nifty little gadget actually.' He's laughing now and doing Larry Grayson faces at me. 'I can think of quite a few friends of mine who'd kill to get hold of one of those. Where'd you get it? Mothercare? We'd better warn them there's going to be a rush on.'

There is no getting away from it. The whole process is highly undignified, not to mention faintly pornographic. Extricating myself from under the desk, I try to stand up, achieve half-crouch position before whacking my head hard. Winston rushes across, knocks over the milk which I had balanced on the chair and rubs my head frantically while I make agonised hurt head noises into his white coat. At which point the door opens and Sister Stone walks in. There is a silence during which I understand that the course of my career may be being irrevocably altered. Winston puts his hands in the air.

'It's not what you think, Sister Stone. Please don't jump to conclusions. Genevieve is a little upset by her poor milk yield and has just sustained a head injury.'

'May I remind you both that this is a psychiatric hospital and not a nursery and that there is a room down that corridor full of ladies waiting to be toileted, fed and medicated. At present there is only one member of staff in that room and *she* is unqualified. And, Nurse O'Dowd,' she adds, looking at the wall but gesturing at my breast which I've forgotten to zip up again, 'kindly make yourself decent before leaving this office.'

I have already worked out the fatal dose of Haloperidol. 400mg slipped into her coffee. Given that the coffee in this place tastes like it's made of old car tyres, the Haloperidol will be unnoticeable. Then sit back and wait for respiratory or heart failure. We could wheel her straight down to the morgue.

In my lunch break, on my high-speed hike over to the crèche for the lunchtime bonding session I decide to give in. I can't do this full-time thing. I'll hand the hero's coat of arms back over to you, Mark.

'Why bother with the bloody breast pump anyway?' asks Sid who can walk and talk and eat chocolate sponge with custard at the same time.

'I'm afraid that if I don't express it, I'll stop producing it and then Karl won't want it any more. Cow & Gate will have won.'

'Don't take this the wrong way, Gen, but you look terrible. Wasted. And your hair's gone straight. You don't think you're suffering from Lactational Insanity, do you?' I feel hopeful for a moment. My condition has a name.

'I looked it up for you. It's what Victorians called pauper women who went mad through prolonging their breast feeding to save money and prevent conception. Malnutrition and anaemia sent them crazy.'

'I don't know, Sid. I'll ask the health visitor.'

'What's Mark say about it all?'

'He's working really hard as well. He's very supportive actually.'

'Just never does anything.'

'He does, Sid. He does the nights now. If he's not working the next day. And we go out in the evenings. To the cinema.'

'What have you seen recently? Anything good?'

'I think we saw *Delicatessen* but don't ask me what happened. I fell asleep. I read the reviews though. It sounded a little like a day in this hospital actually.'

'And have you found a nanny yet?'

'They're too expensive. We can't afford one.'

Isaac Woodhead is walking his distinctive walk down the path towards us, weaving sharply out of the way of invisible demons, hands patting his coat pockets, shaking his head vehemently.

'Got a fag, nurse? Got a fag?'

'Isaac, you bought twenty Capstan Full Strength this morning from the hospital shop. I saw you,' says Sid, handing me her pudding bowl and fishing out her Embassy. She hands him one. 'What did you do with your Capstans, Isaac? If you've smoked them all already, I suggest you go straight to Surgical.'

'Got a light, Nurse? Got a light?'

I begin striding on ahead, unbuttoning my uniform, anxious to get to Karl before he's put down for his nap. He doesn't smile at me when he sees me. It doesn't matter what you say about how convenient this crèche is. Karl's too young to be here. He should be at home.

27th February 1992

I open my eyes with a start to find my face squashed up against his shoulder. I look up at the man next to me but his eyes are fixed on his newspaper. Clearly he does not want an apology. Or even an acknowledgement of my existence. Perhaps he's used to strange women falling asleep at his side. Shame about the dribble on his coat though.

Seating myself upright I try to work out which station we are at. Moorgate? Kennington? Balham? There's a crowd of people on the platform and the doors have clunked shut. As the train pulls away I catch a glimpse of the sign, London Bridge. I can only have been asleep for a few minutes then. I think of Karl and the new nanny and hope that this one will work out better than the one last week. It's a relief to be able to leave him at home rather than drag him all the way to work with me. But nine hours is an awful long time for anyone to be alone with a baby, let alone a teenager with a baby she barely knows. It just never occurred to me that childcare was going to be such a problem. Somehow, birth is made to seem like the ultimate goal. But birth is nothing compared to finding someone you like and trust and can afford to look after your child.

I consider talking to someone at the hospital about getting myself an insulin-induced coma. Highly discredited form of psychiatric treatment now of course but I can't help thinking it might be just what I need. When I asked the doctor at the baby clinic how long she thought it would be before he slept through the night she said when he is two and a half. Just like that. No hesitation. I'm not sure I'll last another twenty-six months without sleep. Although last night I slept long enough to have a nightmare. I was falling backwards, a parachute in a slender stream above me like a giant squid, cords twisted in undoable knots. I knew it wouldn't open in time. I tried to shout up to you perched at the ledge of the plane's doorway but my mouth filled with air and I could see you hesitating, fearing to jump. None of the baby books tell me how long I should expect to exist in this state although *The Book of Margery Kempe* does suggest that even fourteenth-century women found motherhood something of a challenge. It's chilling to read a medieval woman describe the experience as 'going out of her mind'. She took herself off on a prolonged pilgrimage to Rome and The Holy Land. This weekend we are going on a pilgrimage to the West End. You are taking me shopping for clothes.

2nd March 1992

I walk the pavement now, my arms no longer ending in hands but in handles that become pram. It feels a little mad pushing an empty pram, as if I can't leave the house any more without one, but you are striding ahead with Karl strapped to your chest. The pram is just in case he falls asleep and we get the chance to sit down and eat somewhere. I know you are trying your best to restore me to who I was in some distant past life. I don't feel I can tell you that what I would really like on this rare weekend when you are here with us is to be left in bed to sleep while you take Karl to Sainsbury's on your own. Just to share the experiences a bit. I sort of understand you may feel a little adrift yourself. I can dimly see that you too might wonder where the old Genevieve has gone. The person who adored you. The person at home. The person on the end of the phone. The person with her head inside the washing machine. Or was that your mum? The person you slept with. When it could be fitted in to your shooting schedule. When I used to sleep. When I had a career. Could be funny. Kept up with current affairs. You know, all that kind of thing. Your solution is to buy me some expensive clothes in the hope that it might transform me into someone more closely resembling the person I used to be. Or that you meant me to be. Or that you momentarily mistook me for. I trail after you feeling like a hopeless case. You take me to shops I've never heard of. You seem to know about them. Small places tucked away down alleys in Soho. You pull unlikely looking garments from the rails and push me into the changing rooms while you sit and wait with Karl.

The changing room is cramped and hot. I pull on the outfits, most of which I can't even get up past my arse or down past my breasts. Both these parts of me appear to have developed a life of their own recently.

'Let's have a look,' you call from the shop's leather armchair for long suffering husbands. Next to it is a table stacked with magazines. I poke my head round the curtain, wrapping the length of it around my body. You are surrounded by twelve-year-old salesgirls who are in a swoon at the sight of New Man With Baby.

'Mark,' I hiss, poking my head out of the top of the curtain.

'Let's have a look then.' You, Karl and the twelve year olds look over at me.

You must be bloody joking. I'm not parading my poor battered body out in front of that lot. I re-poke my head back inside the changing room. My milk has leaked onto the organdie blouse. Your face appears round the curtain. Karl is being danced around the shop to the sounds of Jarvis Cocker getting himself all sexed up over Es and Legendary Girl-friends.

'Nothing fits,' I whine, stumbling about in the heap of clothes at my feet, and trying to get my old clothes back on again. But you are determined. You are convinced that the clothes will restore me to myself. When I told Helena you were taking me shopping she seemed to be envious. 'Not many men would do that, Genevieve.' It's true. And I should be grateful.

But after two hours I am ready to stop. Exhausted by the multiple dressings and undressings, entries and exits from shops with the pram and Karl and all our stuff. I want to stop. But we press on. There's a place you know . . . Just up here . . .

Eventually I give in. I try on a jacket and trousers that seem far too conservative and far too expensive to me. But they more or less fit. We can't afford them but you seem satisfied with the look. You hand over the money and we leave.

4th April 1992

At our parents' we can sleep. We lend them our baby in return. At your parents' house we escape to the bedroom where we can find some darkness in a house that seems fearful of shadows. We let in some cold air in a house that is hermetically sealed against the very beautiful but dangerously wild landscape. In my mum's house, the landscape is relentlessly flat. Sky is everywhere, but shadows are everywhere too and we are sent to bed at seven in the evening. 'You must be tired, darling,' she tells me as soon as the last mouthful is swallowed. We don't argue because in bed we can find some heat. In the impossible contrasts of our parentage we self-medicate with sleep therapy. There's not much else we can do.

In the bedrooms where we slept as children, we lie tangled together after making love, fitting ourselves thoughtlessly into the well-known places of each other's bodies. My head there, your shoulder here, hands on this, foot feeling that. Breathe in. Drift. The lovemaking at our parents' is characterised by an adolescent frisson. I do my best to be utterly silent as if bound and gagged and you thrash around the bed, determined, I sometimes think, to communicate the scene to the parents in Morse code. Maybe this is a Boy Thing. I whisper porny protestations like 'No', 'Stop', 'Don't' and 'Sshh' as I imagine Marion watching the telly beneath the unmistakeable rhythm of the ceiling light.

We revel in lie-ins that last until eleven in the morning or sometimes even twelve. In the warm dark of those beds, we are returned to ourselves, briefly. So we visit them a lot. Or they visit us. We are not often alone, the three of us. I'm not sure if this is what I want or not but I am easily bribed by the promise of sleep. Right now I would do anything for sleep. Especially when it is sleep with you. Because we don't quite know what else to do with ourselves. Being at home alone, just the three of us, is sort of strange. I suspect it is something you want to avoid. Or maybe you feel a loss too. The loss of your boyhood that is fatherhood. These trips back and forth across England reassure you that you can still be, just, the adored son. And in the gift of Karl some reward, some pact is being struck. A deal. An exchange. For what I can't quite make out.

He is taken from his cot by our bed at first whimper. I fall back into sleep to the muffled sounds of Marion and your mum playing Mums and Dads. They're uncharacteristically nice to each other. Downstairs I know he is being stuffed with love. Dressed and undressed in new clothes, cleaned and powdered, fed and played with, changed and burped, talked and sung to. When I finally go down to see him, for a moment I don't recognise our baby. His hair is coiffed up into a fluffy hairdo, he sits propped up in a sea of cushions and stuffed toys, keeling over in very slow motion, eyes popping in surprise at Marion who dips and bends with the camera, snap-flare, snap-flare, in the intensely lit room. This is the deal. In return for sleep he's being Morrisoned. They are overwhelmingly generous in their desire to be very good grandparents.

10th April 1992

On the tube to work this morning I am disgusted by my fellow travellers. I glare at the ones reading the right-wing press. I glare at the ones who look like they didn't bother to vote. I glare at the ones who probably dithered and voted Lib Dem. I feel utterly disillusioned after last night's general election results when we were dropped into the hands of crazed Tories yet again. What will happen to the hospitals? What will happen to the schools? Transport? The economy? What will happen to Lily and Mabel? Cared for in the community? It is all a disaster of unparalleled proportions and I have a killer hangover. Sister Stone will be gloating and I will be tempted to do dire things to her if she is left unattended in the vicinity of the morgue.

Sister Stone is bustling with a certain extra vigour as I enter the ward. Winston, I notice, is off sick but Sid is sitting by Lily, holding forth like a parliamentary orator on the perils that await us all now we've handed the reins/wheel/joystick over to the Tories for a fourth term. Lily is unusually articulate.

'Ooh, don't she go on?' she is saying. 'Ooh, do shut up, for Pete's sake.'

'Have people round last night?' asks Sid. I nod at her, silently apologising for not asking her and Angus.

'Course she did,' says Lily. 'They go in and out of her house all times of the day and night. That's no secret.'

I beam at Lily. 'And good morning to you too, Lily. Did you watch the election on the telly last night?'

'She 'ad a baby last year, you know,' continues Lily conspiratorially, ignoring me. She beckons Sid closer. 'And so did that Mary over there. She's a one an' all. But she lost it.' Lily relaxes back into her chair, chewing her gums and pulling at her fingers, strangely calmed after this small sputter of bile against other women.

I walk down the corridor to the ward office, feeling the dreariness of this place drain me. Since Karl was born it feels as though my life is conducted in slow motion. Like trying to walk upstream with wellington boots on. When I'm with Karl I walk very slowly as he crawls around the kitchen floor, climbs the stairs and dances with the banisters. At work I walk very slowly in time to the old women's tottering gait as they shuffle down the corridor to be fed or medicated or put to bed. I spend what seems like huge tracts of time dressing and undressing other people, bent over their straining bodies as they defecate and pee. I am intimately connected to what goes in their mouths and ever watchful for words that might come out. I feel I will implode from inertia unless I do something. I feel guilty because I want to leave. But, like the patients, I have no idea what I would do if I got out.

'I'm thinking of leaving the hospital,' I tell you that evening. You have taken to feeding me enormous quantities of food and I'm growing in front of our eyes. When you're away I can live for days on two tins of soup and half a packet of cheese. But when you're here, I feel duty-bound to fill the fridge and you feel duty-bound to fill my face.

'But you've just been given that research grant. Or was that last year? What's it for again?'

'I can't bear being there any more. Every time I go in I feel like someone's pulled the plug out of me. It's just not what I want to do any longer.'

'What, so you want to be a full-time mother? How would we pay the mortgage? Yours is the only steady income we have. And you get a pension.'

'There was a job running the cinema down the road. I could do that. At least your films would get screened.'

'Don't be ridiculous. You get a good pension with the NHS.'

'There's no point to what I'm doing any longer. No one gets better in that place. And now the Tories have got in again there will be more cut-backs. It will become impossible.'

The phone rings. I make no move to answer it because it

is always for you. You hand me Karl as you reach for the receiver. It's your casting agent. There's a problem with someone's visa.

'So,' I continue when the call's finished, 'I thought I might apply for a job in the university.' I hand Karl back to you while I eat my food. The phone goes again. You hand me Karl. It's a cameraman touting for work.

'Hi. Yes. Yes. Hopefully we'll be shooting in Mozambique for three months starting in September. Yeah.' Karl slaps one hand down in my plate of food, producing an impressive array of special effects.

'Well, we're having a meeting with the insurers this week. Yep. Have you heard of Delores da Souza?' I hold Karl's hand firmly as it prepares to come down for another swipe. There's a pause and then a rising squeal of protest.

'What? Yeah, she's Portuguese and really really nice. Incredibly bright. She's a poet actually.'

I turn Karl round to face me and make pretend sick faces at him. He giggles and claps his hands on either side of my face, holds it still between his hands and stares at me. It is quite something to be adored by a miniature you. A blinding head butt ruins the moment. The call finishes and I hand Karl back to you to continue my meal.

'I mean, I suppose university teaching would be quite an interesting break for me because—' The phone goes again, you hand me Karl. It's a journalist.

'Her character? The rebel leader's lover. Well, in the script she's supposed to be thirty . . .'

'Da da da da da da da da . . . thththththththth.'

Karl is pointing at you but you are oblivious. I turn his face towards me again. I don't want him to learn about telephone addiction. He dives down and plays peepo over my breasts. You stare blankly at us, listening to the voice down the phone.

'She is quite young yeah . . . nineteen, I think, maybe

eighteen, but she looks quite old, about twenty-three . . . how old's the rebel leader? Late fifties, I think . . . maybe sixty . . . he was an amazing person though . . . a tactical genius . . .'

Karl turns round suddenly, drops both hands by his side and concentrates hard on your face.

'My family? Oh! You mean Genevieve and Karl? Well, hopefully they'll come out with me for some of it . . .'

I can't complain, I think. Karl and I are shipped out all over the place to be with you. Which is lovely. Mainly. Except that it does rather disrupt my career. So much so that I haven't a clue which direction it's supposed to be going in. You finally finish the call. I hand you Karl. It's your turn to put him to bed but I don't want to tell you that because that would be nagging.

'So the Africa film's going to happen, is it?' I ask, trying to sound neutral.

'Looks like it but we won't know for sure for a couple of weeks. You will come out, won't you?'

'I've used up all my leave, Mark. I think I might get the sack if I take any more time off.'

The phone goes again. You hand me Karl. I give up and take him upstairs to bed.

13th June 1992

'Where's Spot?'

It's 5.15 in the morning and I'm drifting in and out of a coma on the sofa while Karl is transfixed by the video. Contented whistling noises are coming from the bottle that he holds tilted into his mouth. I'm surprised he likes it so much. Because to me, formula milk smells distinctly of petrochemicals. Perhaps it's like smoking. I know I should be playing with him, interacting and all that, but these early mornings are killers. Now I understand why the hospital gets the women up so early and prescribes daytime television. It must reduce the drugs bill quite considerably. Don't get me wrong. I *am* in love with Karl. I love my days with him. I love to bend over his naked body so my hair tickles his tummy. I do all that stuff and I look forward to those days desperately. But at the same time I feel coshed with boredom and sort of dislocated. And starting at five o'clock as they do, the days are very very long.

When you leave at nine thirty, Karl and I go to the park. The park is a kind of limbo place where mothers wander about trying not to get dog shit in the wheels of the pram, flinching from the used needles and burnt silver paper and the bench of drunks who blurt out 'Cunt!', 'Fuck!' and sometimes 'Fucking Cunt!' in a Tourette's syndrome kind of way. Having negotiated these hazards the mothers arrive at the Under Fives play area so that their children can 'play'. Life slows almost to a standstill at this point as the children climb so so slowly one-step, two-step up the brightly coloured ladders then crawl down tunnels where primitive wall drawings inform them that Sharika is a cocksucker and Lee's mother has Aids. After the tunnel it's the swing. I lift him up and stuff his legs that for some reason now only stick out at right angles, into the bucket seat and start pushing. Now it seems to me that there is a limit to how long one can push a swing for without getting a kind of strobe effect *déjà vu*. Which as we all know can bring on an epileptic fit. At the very least. We do a bit of the swing and then we go on the horse on a spring which oscillates between total immobility and a wild bucking-bronco action that eventually flings him out of the saddle.

I think we imagined that having children was going to involve a good deal of frolicking through meadows in sunlight and of course we don't do sunlight much in this country. And there is a shortage of meadows so we have to make do with the municipal park. A few other mothers sit around on benches. We eye each other warily, wearily. Some are mute and ignore their children and everyone else. Over-medicated, for all I know. Others draw deeply on their cigarettes, sitting cross-legged on the broken bench, jiggling one foot up and down and staring at the grey blanket that is sky.

'How old is he?' we ask anyone who makes eye contact. There's a pair of nannies who sit apart from the mothers complaining about their filthy-rich employers – 'And I said, "You can't ask me to do that." She goes, "I'll ask you to do what I bloody well want." Well I'm not having that, being sworn at, she can stuff her fucking job' – while their charges narrowly avoid serious injury launching themselves down vertical slides and persistently toddling off to stand in front of the swings where they get knocked down like skittles with monotonous regularity. There are never any men. Apart from the drunks. And except on weekends when there are never any women. Apart from me.

Back at the house, Jesus Maria Cruz is sitting at the kitchen table because she refuses to go to the park. So she is sitting drinking coffee and talking to her family in Lisbon. I don't care. She is my saviour and has made my life all right again. Mariana, the receptionist in Portugal, sent her. Jesus Maria is her twenty-year-old niece and she has rescued us from our childcare problem. I work three days a week and leave Karl at home with Jesus, as I like to call her. She's a bit feckless, but being Portuguese this doesn't seem as irritating. In fact, I find it charming and quite admirable. Also she can cook and she can make Karl go to sleep. She is a little bit like a slightly lazy wife. Which is what I want to enable me to cope at a basic level. Obviously if she were a highly committed and devoted wife I would by now be Senior Lecturer at the Royal College of Nursing but for the moment I have opted for this.

6th July 1992

Karl is bouncing up and down through the air, laughing hysterically, turning in a slow circle. Each time his feet touch the ground, his toes brace against it for a moment and push him up into the air again. I'm laughing too at the sight of his chubby body, suspended in the baby bouncer, turning this way and that. His laughter is an incredible thing. A fountain of absurd happiness. I don't know where it comes from but between us we seem to have discovered a huge joke. We've kept ourselves amused this way for at least twenty minutes. He catches my eye during a pause in the hilarity, takes off into the air again and there's another peal of mirth. I wish you could see him.

Sid arrives bearing sparkling wine and baby food. I open the door with Karl still strapped into the rubber, canvas and chains of the bouncer.

'Jesus Christ, Gen, so they finally invented a straitjacket for babies, did they?' She takes him from me and goes down to the kitchen. The room is cluttered with devices for keeping mobile babies contained and amused. A full-size swing in a frame that plays 'Rockabye Baby', a wooden playpen and a chair on wheels which allows his feet to touch the ground so he can scoot about the floor. He usually travels in this at high speeds like a demented crab and takes a delight in collisions of maximum impact. The fridge, the walls, the table, cupboards, my legs.

'You know that crawling is essential to his intellectual development, don't you, Genevieve?' she asks, looking disapprovingly at all the paraphernalia. 'And what happened to sand and water?'

'It's either his intellect or mine by the end of the week. I attend to his on Mondays. What's this in aid of then?' I open the bottle expertly. The trick is to hold the cork and twist the bottle. Obviously.

'This,' says Sid, giving Karl a careless bounce that sends him much higher than usual, 'is to celebrate the launch of my new career. My new band!' She produces a flyer with a picture of Sid in uniform and two women in flowery dresses and Doc Martens looking shiny faced and wild.

'Got three pub gigs booked.'

'Fantastic, Sid. I never realised you were actually planning to perform. Interesting name too . . .'

'Yeah, Lily gave me the idea for that. She pointed out the tulips to me in the grounds of the hospital. The frilly, pink ones with lots of layers. "'Ere nurse," she says, "that's disgusting that is. Fancy planting cunt tulips. The cunts." Something like that. And I looked and she was absolutely right. Then I thought what a great name for an all-woman band. A fine example of Truth Bursting Through When You Least Expect It. Talking of Freudian slips of nature, have you seen that mushroom called Phallus Impudicus? It's outrageous, got a little drop of semen coming out the top, flies buzzing round it, a bit of a smell – incredibly realistic. Can't be an accident. Almost makes me believe in God.'

I'm laughing and Karl is laughing and twirling like a dervish. I love it when Sid talks dirty. 'Don't suppose you'll get on Radio One with a name like that though. Give us a song then.'

Sid does an extraordinary rendition of 'Molly Malone' with multiple entendres and sung with a voice like a gale. Karl gapes at her, apparently stunned by the profundity of the song. Then she sings 'Pop Goes the Weasel' in a way that gets Karl so excited he nearly catapults himself out of the harness.

When the performance is over I say, 'I didn't realise Molly dies at the end, Sid.'

'Yeah. Cholera probably. All those lullabies are fantastically dark. That's why they make such good songs. Like opera. It's why it's no good giving Karl all this *Spot* and *Postman Clap* buggery, Genevieve.' She slides an LP out of its sleeve and puts it on the turntable. Evidently we're having a party.

'You've got all you need in the songs and fairy tales,' she shouts above the noise. 'Plus the wooden spoon, saucepan and kitchen sink, of course.' She releases Karl from his straitjacket and puts him in the kitchen sink, and runs the tap. 'Babies are born with an innate understanding of the tragedy and difficulty of life. Deny it and you'll be in trouble. Believe me, I've thought about it: "Rockabye Baby" – non-accidental injury – "Dance for Your Daddy" – incest – "Twinkle Twinkle Little Star" – nihilism – "Pop Goes the Weasel"—'

'Sid, shut up. Don't you sing any other stuff or is it all lullabies?' I hover by the kitchen sink, on the lookout for germs and sharp objects.

'Course we do. But you'll have to come and listen to find out what. Get a babysitter for Friday night. Oh and I'm bringing a man for you. Blind date.'

'What? I don't want a date. I've got Mark.'

'Bring Mark then.'

'He's away till Sunday.'

'Exactly.'

Thirteen

11th July 1992

I RUN, skip and jump down the road to the Angel tube station. Everything is perfect. I am going to work, leaving Karl safe in the arms of Jesus Maria. Home life runs smoothly without me. Jesus will sing in Portuguese and cook wholesome baby meals. I don't have to think about home all day long but it will be there for me when I return, welcoming me back into its warm embrace with the mouth-watering aroma of *Sopa de Peixe*. I'll have stories to tell Karl and will swing him round by his arms and wrestle with him on the sofa and make him giggle and shriek. I will be able to devote myself to my career and will get promoted with breathtaking alacrity. I'll write papers, unlock Mabel's misery, cure her, in fact, and I'll give provocative and moving lectures that will make everyone go really quiet and then applaud wildly. Oh and I have a bit of a thing going on with another man. As well as a loving husband. What more could a girl want?

I take care not to push my fellow travellers as we are force-fed into the train carriage and this morning I enjoy the minutes we spend stuck in the tunnel between London Bridge and Bank because it gives me more time to fantasise about my blind date with Leon. I imagine all the usual stuff: Leon wandering around the house naked with piles of clean laundry in his arms; Leon down in the kitchen with Karl in one arm, preparing breakfast for me with the other; Leon turning the baby alarm off, taking me in his arms and kissing me passionately for the entirety of *Newsnight*; Leon flirting with my mum . . . I don't know where that one came from but it was there.

'The Kunt Tulips were a revelation, Sid. You had the whole place up on its feet. That never happens these days. It's so uncool.' Sid is washing Octavia's hair. Octavia's head is tipped back on the lip of the sink, her eyes wide, feet dangling off the ground. One hand wavers up by her cheek.

'Don't worry, Gen, your secret's safe with me although I can't vouch for Angus, of course. He is Mark's friend.'

'Sid, you don't half talk a lot of bollocks sometimes. All I did was dance with him.'

Sid lathers up Octavia's head and begins a slow, circular kneading motion all over her scalp.

'Just close your eyes, Tavvy.' Octavia's eyes squeeze shut. Her hand comes juddering down and chatters with the other one in her lap. 'Well there was the dance, yes. Vertical intercourse, from what I could see.'

'We didn't even kiss, for God's sake, Sid.'

The dance. Like the hesitation on the top of the roller coaster. The moment just before the delirious drop down. Like the time I was twelve just before I kissed Sam for the first time. That long limbo moment. The belly-melting desire of it but with no idea what it would be like. And then the kiss. Slow, hot, dark discovery of the inside of someone else. Octavia sighs tremulously and Sid wraps a towel round her head before sending her back to her chair. Then she calls Mary over.

'Oh, lovely dear,' says Mary, sitting herself down and smoothing her skirt.

'And then there was the animated conversation when you sat at the table together. You were dazzling him, Genevieve. Like a film star, ha ha.'

Mary's eyes flutter as the warm water trickles back from her forehead. Her mouth relaxes. In this position, released from gravity, Mary looks young, sensual. The way John would have loved her often. A tide of sadness rises up in me. It is just terrible what is lost. Sid sees my eyes fill.

'You were disappearing, Genevieve. Becoming a satellite.' Small sighs come from Mary's mouth.

'I've just been tired. Things'll be easier now I've found Jesus.' I giggle at her. Sid doesn't laugh.

'I'm serious. If Mark won't talk to you, won't *see* you, then you have to make something happen.'

'What do you mean? Of course he talks to me. He phones me all the time. That was a lovely evening last night but Mark is the only man I want.'

Which you incontrovertibly are. You are. I don't have any desire to sleep with anyone else. I can't imagine anyone else I'd rather sleep with than you. Well, imagine, yes, but actually *do*, no. I feel suddenly indignant. 'Look, Sid, as you and Angus very well know, there's no such thing as a one-night stand.'

'She *never*,' says Lily, who's been hovering, hoping for a miraculous hair wash from Sid. Lily looks me up and down and says to Sid, 'Oo was it then? That black fella, I'll be bound.'

'One person is always hoping for a whole lot more than just one night,' I continue, ignoring Lily. 'Which is why we don't do them. And Mark can't help his job, Sid. We have a good relationship. Just because he's away a lot doesn't mean . . .' My words trail off.

'Away a lot, is 'e?' Lily really does resemble Albert Steptoe when she leers like that. 'I'd watch it if I was you.' She chews away at her gums and fishes a boiled sweet out of her pocket.

'His job is his life,' persists Sid. 'And it's about the inside of *his* head. Not yours.'

'Well, Sid, you're wrong. Mark's not like that.' I prepare to stalk off in your defence. 'I'm off to interview Octavia for my research on *Women and Madness*. Because I have a career to consider. Unlike some.'

Sid laughs long and loud at that one.

In the office, Octavia is standing before me in her shapeless floral print dress looking unhappy. Her hair is damp and the smell of shampoo fills the cramped room. Every now and again she sits down on the other side of the table from me. Sitting still is something she doesn't like. So she is very up and down. I flick back through the various treatments and diagnoses recorded for Octavia. It's all depressingly familiar.

Octavia says, 'Oh dear oh dear oh dear.'

I know she wants to get back to the ward in time for Occupational Therapy so she can knit bootees and shuffle to and fro. She starts to fidget with the hole-punch and the pot of pencils on the desk, moving them like chess pieces. Then she brushes imaginary dust from her chest. 'No no no no no no no.' She starts a tremulous humming, snatches of 'My Bonnie Lies Over the Ocean'.

There was an extra verse that your mum sang to Karl the other night that I had never heard of before. I join in with her wavering humming and add the new words over the slurred dah dah dah of her own.

'Last night as I lay on my pillow, last night as I lay on my bed, last night as I lay on my pillow, I dreamt that my Bonnie was dead.'

This is a bit brutal of me but Octavia's madness is maddening. At the word 'pillow' she becomes still. Sits with her head hanging. Her hands flutter like exhausted moths in her lap.

12th October 1992

I wake before Karl, already anxious about the day. Turning towards his cot in the corner of the room I can see his sleeping face through the bars. A jungle of discarded milk bottles and toys surround him. We disagree about the toys. I think there are too many and you think that I'm still influenced by the austerity of my upbringing. You recoil from that with something near fury despite the angry letters from the bank. And so we veer between ostentatious displays of excess and plenty and sudden, irrational belt-tightening when the overdrafts become just too big to ignore. I think I was probably left outside in all weathers with just a wooden spoon to chew on and that you were wrapped up tight and snug watching your mother's hands clap clap clapping one two three. I survey the audience of stuffed toys, faces fixed in expressions of permanent cheer or surprise, lined up round his cot. Once there was the idea that you had one teddy to love and to hold until death us do part. Now the toy industry's over production means the market is flooded with very cheap teddies and so all babies must have ten, twenty, thirty or more and none of them is special. You think I'm weird to think like this about toys but in the end, it's a practical matter. I don't know where to put them all – the teddies, the rabbits, the ducks, the mice, the dogs, the cats, the lambs, the elephants, the lions, the monkeys, the toucans, the fish – I mean fish, for God's sake – since when were they cuddly? None of this bothers Karl, however. He couldn't care less about them. He knows what he's really interested in and that's me and Postman Pat.

I listen to the buses on their early shift, the HGVs and the occasional car speeding down the empty road. Each time they pass, the windows rattle and the house shakes a little. Karl sleeps on. Achingly, gut-wrenchingly beautiful and beloved. I stretch out a hand and touch his head.

'I can see you,' I whisper.

When he was first born he looked like neither of us. Other worldly. Then within a few hours he began to resemble you. Through the year I have watched his face, held his limbs, felt the skin and the flesh and the bone of him as shades and shadows of myself and you passed, paused and sometimes stayed. Sid was right about first children. To the world Karl looks like you but in the nameless areas – the curve between eyebrow and lid, the shape of his mouth when he yawns, the angle of the neck against the shoulder and the line of his back – he is indisputably me.

It's his birthday and I've upset Lesley and Sister Stone by swapping my shifts to spend it with Karl. I'm torn between wanting him to wake and savouring the time to myself. Once I sit up, place my feet on the floor and reach down to lift him, that will be it for seventeen hours.

There was a story in the paper the other day about a single mother who died of exhaustion. I read the six-line column hoping for clues and details about how exactly that had happened. I wasn't surprised that it could, just wanted to know that woman's circumstances. The report was unhelpful. But exhaustion was the word that was used. Perhaps if more of us started dropping dead on the job the world might start to notice. I imagine the high streets littered with mother corpses. Having pushed the twin buggy up the hill for the three hundredth time that year, a mother at the playgroup bends to unstrap her jam-smeared toddlers and her legs give way. With a heavy thump she keels over in the musty swamp of coats, mittens, scarves and bobble hats. In the confectionery-induced tantrum at the supermarket checkout, turning to remonstrate with her purple-faced offspring and before she can give in and agree to the sugar-hit the child is cold-turkeying about, another mother slumps towards the cashier, face down in her pile of bulging Happy Shopper bags that would have broken one hundred yards after she had hooked them over the handles of the buggy. Or on the bus, under the gaze of the driver who stares with the contempt of the professionally pissed off, another mother is struggling to unstrap her child, fold the buggy, pick up the shopping, hold the child, get on the bus, get out the purse, brace herself and keep her and the child upright as the bus accelerates down the road – when her heart simply beats its last beat and that's it, can't summon the energy to beat the next one. The ticket flutters from her fingers, her eyes roll back and she slides down the 'Do Not Distract the Driver's Attention While the Bus is in Motion' sign, spilling pees from her purse and baked beans from her bag.

Karl's eyes are open now and he's talking to his feet. He stops and stares at the flying teddies mobile suspended above his head, their arms outstretched, faces towards the earth. They shake and sway imperceptibly. With small grunts and pants he gets himself onto his hands and knees and pulls himself upright. There's just the sound of his breathing as he surveys the desert of duvet on our bed. He spies my face smiling at him. I blink hello. We lock eyes and look. He begins to run on the spot, nappy shaking, clinging to the bars, saying Mama and laughing his hiccuppy, glissando laugh. At the thought of another day with me he extends his hand, opening and clenching it in a come-here-come-here-you-gorgeous-Mummy kind of a way. I throw back the duvet and in one step reach his cot. This first greeting of the day, when he's full of fevered anticipation at the thought of it, at the thought of me, when I bend to reach his up-stretched arms and hold the damp, sweet scent of him against my body – it is always like the first time I held him – an explosion of love, a sudden shock of delight at the fact of each other's existence.

On the way down to the kitchen I pick the newspaper up off the mat and wince at the headlines and photographs from Belgrade. On the front page there actually is a mother lying dead on the street, a puddle of blood spreading from her coat and a burst bag of shopping beside her. In the kitchen I turn the paper face down and study the television schedule instead. Sid says that's the problem with becoming a mother – it blinkers you, makes you hostage to your emotions. She's right, I suppose. The news reduces me to tears these days and I had to leave *The Hand That Rocks the Cradle* halfway through the screening. Which is only a film and hardly the worst the world has to offer right now. I tell myself I will harden up my feelings and shake up my intellect starting from tonight when Karl has gone to bed. I'll watch that video you were sent that I've been avoiding: *Henry: Portrait of a Serial Killer.*

I'm a little unsure how to mark Karl's birthday having never done it before. There are cards on the mat for him which he opens, puzzled by the expectation in my voice, pressing each one against his face before tossing it to one side. I'm going to take him to the zoo and then home for his birthday tea with Winston and Sid. I can't wait. It's ages since I had a party.

24th December 1992

'Sorry it's just the one, Mark,' says my mum, retrieving the tissue paper from your lap and smoothing it down. 'But Happy Birthday and Christmas.'

You lift the one sock for examination, say, 'Oh, thanks very much,' and lean over to give her a polite kiss.

'It's just that. Well. I had no idea. A sock takes an absolute age to knit.'

Angus is wheezing and shaking on the other side of you, threatening to shower us all with an explosion of sparkling wine. Sid kicks him and goes to inspect the sock.

'But this is a work of art,' she says, holding it up to the light. She turns round to Uncle Frank and shows it to him. 'Isn't it, Frank? Here, you're a man with a discerning eye. Take a look at the stitching on this.'

But Uncle Frank isn't listening. He is sitting next to the potted banana tree with your mum, nodding and looking, murmuring little noises of gentle interest. Two of his grandchildren and Karl are herded near them, grazing on chocolate coins and slurping unlikely coloured drinks. They all share the same shaped head. It's somehow reassuring seeing so many familiar phenotypes in the same room.

'I've started on sock number two, Mark. You can have that for your next birthday.'

'And look,' continues Sid. 'It's monogrammed. See? MM.'

'Mm, that's sweet,' I say and give you a kiss.

'The other sock could have GO on it, couldn't it? Then people will know they're a pair.' Sid looks over at my mum again.

'What a good idea, Sid. The letters do make it all rather fiddly though.'

'Thanks, Mum,' you call over to your mum, pulling out seven pairs of M & S socks from a sheet of gold wrapping paper. You clutch them to you and pick your way through the litter of paper and gifts to give her a kiss. She looks up from her conversation with Uncle Frank and kisses you back.

'You'll get your main present tomorrow. It's a lawn mower.'

'Mum! What are you telling me for? It's meant to be a surprise.'

'Well I thought I should mention it so you'll know to leave room in your car when you drive down tomorrow but now look carefully in that little bag because there's a foot spray in there too and a foot bath and one of those battery neck massagers for when you're flying and a little bleeper that you can attach to your toothbrush to tell you when you've brushed for the full two minutes.'

You look in the wrapping paper, then check down at your feet and look blank.

'Morrison, over here!' calls Angus who has got up and is standing in front of the mirror with a humming neck cushion on his head. His eyes start out of his face and he grimaces hideously like Frankenstein's monster shortly after creation.

'Hold still, Angus,' says Marion, edging into the room with a video camera raised to his eye. 'Oh, hang on, I can't see a blinking thing. What's happened to it, Mark?'

'Try shutting just the one eye, Dad.'

'Ah. That's it. I've got it now. Right, now, where's he

gone? Angus? Where the blinking heck are you? Put that vibrator thingy on your head again.'

'I've lost it. Where'd it go? Sid, get off, you'll burst it or short-circuit it or something.' But Sid is offering my mum a cigar and my mum is doubled up with laughter, arms flailing and threatening to wet her pants. Sid sits opposite her, eyes rolled to the ceiling, a faint humming coming from beneath her backside.

Uncle Frank refills your mum's glass and Karl climbs on her lap to give her a gold coin, smearing her in chocolate in the process. She squeezes him tight and sucks each chocolatey finger in turn. He stares at her, besotted.

'Orson Welles, eat your heart out,' says Marion, winking at me and moonwalking round the room.

I lean back on the sofa with you and put my arm round you. You take it off your shoulder and put your arm round me.

'What do you think my mum and Sid are cackling about?' I whisper, pointing at them with my foot. 'They're getting on very well, aren't they?'

'I expect they're gossiping about you. Are you all right?' you ask, kissing me.

'This is nice. I love you. We should risk an actual Christmas like this one year, instead of driving to your parents' at the crack of dawn tomorrow.'

'But Great Auntie Ida always comes for Christmas dinner. She does the pudding. You know that, Genevieve.' You threaten to withdraw your arm. I hang on tight to it.

'She can come too.'

'We'd never get her wheelchair down the stairs.' We both look over at Karl.

'Maybe we should just have lots of children, more than we could fit in a car. Then everyone would have to come to us for Christmas.'

'Maybe we should.' You kiss my neck.

'Now then, now then,' says Marion. The video camera is

inches from our heads. 'Steer clear of the X-rated scenes, ladies and gentlemen, if you please. This is a family show, let's not forget. A family show.'

6th March 1993
As the plane banks and heads west towards Spain, we attempt a kiss over Karl's head. A hot coffee pot interrupts us.

'Coffee, Sir? Tea? Coffee, Madam? Tea?'

We settle for small plastic cups of flavoured boiled water instead of the kiss. Your television adaptation of *Ghosts* has just been screened and we're blowing the proceeds on a week's holiday. 'Determinedly bleak and perverse,' said one reviewer who had possibly not realised it was written by Ibsen a hundred years ago. Tragedies are not popular on the small or the big screen any more. In fact, they're not really allowed. Upbeat endings are strongly advised by film and television executives. I look at you, your head bent towards Karl as you struggle to help him open his packet of crayons. While the prospect of a whole week together makes me feel happy, it's funny, but I realised the other night as I got into bed alone to the sound of Whitney wailing 'I Will Always Love You!!' through the wall, that I'm sort of used to it. Since Karl was born, I don't mind your absences so much. Your absence is part of you. Part of us.

'*Uno, dos, tres* . . . say it, Karl.' Karl ignores your attempts to teach him Spanish. He drops his juice beaker into your lap and laughs at you.

I return to reading *Spaghetti Junction*, the script for your next film. You are determined to do a feature film, come what may. No more TV dramas. This project seems to be a kind of cross between a spaghetti western and a road movie. It's about Britain's pathological attachment to cars, road works, traffic jams, service stations and tailbacks. Most of it takes place going round and round the tangle of flyovers near Birmingham and up and down the M1 and M6. Apart from motorway service stations and Welcome Break Inns, the main location is the inside of a Ford Sierra. The car is driven by Graham, a Xerox engineer. Graham is on a quest to find his brother who was last seen hitching a lift at Junction 11. The soundtrack is Portishead, and Massive Attack intercut with Radio One. Graham picks up various hitchhikers along the way whose stories confirm our growing awareness of the irredeemable pointlessness of life. The script ends with a double suicide involving the pedestrian walkway over the M1 at a Welcome Break Service Station. I think the script is great but I can't imagine who you will get to be in it. Let alone finance it. No love scenes, no stunning scenery, no redemptive ending. I can see the reviews now: 'Bleak . . . an apocalyptic vision of the British psyche . . .', ' "Shall we just stop for a coffee?" will never sound quite the same again.'

In Spain we hire a car and drive along the northern coast. It rains a lot and so we press on, the nursery rhyme tape accompanies us all the way. I worry slightly that if playing Mozart to babies in the womb has been found to increase their IQ then could it be possible that playing the saccharine renditions of 'Here We Go Round the Mulberry Bush' and 'The Wheels on the Bus' might have the opposite effect, not least on the parents' brains, if not the infant's? But it's too late. Karl is already addicted and cannot travel without these tapes. I long to listen to the news on the radio. I long to have a conversation with you. I long to stop and be still in one place for a while but you are determined to find somewhere beautiful. On we go, further and further west, until eventually, of course, you do find a stunning setting. As you knew you would and I feel unworthy for having been willing to settle for something less.

Lying on my side in the minty moistness of meadow grass, a picnic of olives, sausage and bread half eaten beside me, I watch you through the broad blades of bright grass where insects clamber and wait. You are bent double as you hold Karl's hand and walk with him towards the grove of almond blossom that borders a stream. The only noise apart from the duet of your voices is the rush of water over stones. I should reach for the camera to record this moment but I don't lift my head.

I roll on my back and close my eyes. Like time going backwards I can feel the light-starved skin of my face drinking in the spring sun. A bird sings somewhere near by. And I think that happiness is not a destination or a place that can be inhabited like a home. It's a moment. A small moment. A spell.

Fourteen

27th April 1993

THIS TIME I face Mr Hallam on my own. In my hand I hold a small stone I found in your pocket. Your pockets are full of stones and loose change. The stones are your talismans. You pick them up from beaches and fields. As long as you have stones in your pockets, I think we will be all right.

Mr Hallam has a serious-faced woman doctor with him. I'm told she will do the procedure while he oversees it. We exchange small talk about Karl but Mr Hallam is distant. His eyes don't meet mine and he seems to have shrunk a little. His tie is a yellow tartan and the braces are still red. A nurse with a warm smile smears the cold slime of gel on my stomach, rubs the ultrasound thing around and we all watch the screen. Helena told me they give you a print-out of your baby these days. I'm not sure whether to ask for one or not.

'There's a leg, two arms . . . heart . . .'

To the watery slosh and ter-thump soundtrack, I try to make sense of the snowstorm screen. I think I can see a tiny beating, like a bird.

'. . . and there's the other leg.'

The grainy, black-and-white submarine search continues and then, looming up from the nothingness, for an instant, I see it; a fleeting glimpse of a face that looks familiar.

The doctor seems to be good at what she does. It doesn't

hurt this time. But she doesn't look at me. She is utterly intent on getting that telltale DNA sample from the soup of us in there. I close my eyes, pray not to feel the low uterine ache of contraction and wait for it to be over.

When I open my eyes again, Mr Hallam has gone.

21st May 1993

The sign is huge. It says Up for everything except for the Mortuary, which is Down. Mum hesitates at the metal gape of the doors and I hold my hand flat against the impatient shove of them. Too late, I remember her fear of lifts. She looks like she might cry but is being brave and before I can leave the lift so we might take the stairs, she has murmured a small 'oh' and hopped inside. With a clunk we're sealed in.

'Sorry . . . I just remembered . . . you and lifts.'

Mum stands very straight and still, eyes wet, lips trembling. I'm shocked by her fear. We should probably have a talk, I think dismally. But the lift stops, the bell pings and the number 7 glows red above the door.

'This is us, come on.'

We leave the lift and follow the signs for Gynaecology. A sign above an empty desk says, Wait Here To Be Seen.

'I'll be fine. You go. Honest.' I'd rather wait alone and not risk a tidal wave tale of family catastrophe. There's a time and a place after all. And just before a therapeutic termination is not one of them.

The nurse comes to get me ready and my mum gives me a teary hug.

'I'll wait. Outside,' she says. 'Mark will be here. Soon. I'm sure. Won't he?'

I give her a little wave and follow the nurse through the swing doors.

Up on the trolley, I make a point of looking into the anaesthetist's eyes as he puts the needle into the back of my hand. He is fatherly and kind although he has never met me before. He asks me if I can count to five. Liquid ice enters my veins and I hear my voice say 'two' before the black curtain drops.

10th September 1993

Helena has her ear pressed to the wall in our kitchen and is listening intently.

'There's definitely the sound of a knife being sharpened, Gen. I think you should call the Fire Brigade.'

'What do you mean the Fire Brigade? Firstly, Helena, I think that you may be imagining it and secondly if you're not, we should call the police.'

'Shhh! Shh!' Helena makes frantic shut-up gestures and moves along a bit, trying to get herself closer to the wall. The bulge in her stomach makes this fairly impossible. I watch her and wonder about her and David. When people say 'he's something big in the City' I used to have no idea what they meant. But then I met David and that's what he is. He's very tall, works late, talks posh, votes Tory and is given to sudden barks of laughter. He is always just about to arrive or just about to leave. No one really knows exactly what he does but he earns a fortune and has consequently moved to Notting Hill. And now Helena lives there too. She actually looks rather happy. That could be David or that could just be being pregnant. Or living in Notting Hill instead of Peckham. But being pregnant does take your mind off some of the more existential questions like Why Am I Alive? Which Charity Most Deserves My Money? and What Is This Thing Called Love? Which is presumably why it's so popular with teenage girls in this country. Helena tiptoes over to me, eyes wide open in horror.

'Call the Fire Brigade, stupid, because if the police knock on the door he just won't open it. But if we ring and say there's a fire at number seventy-six he'll be so surprised he'll let them in and then they'll discover his mother . . .'

Karl is marching backwards and forwards carrying the contents of the cassette cupboard, item by item, from the far end of the room up to the end where we are and placing them in a pile at my feet.

'There,' he says each time, pausing to look at me.

'Oh, thank you. So, Helena,' I try to distract her from returning to listen to the wall by bringing up the topic of her approaching marriage to David, 'have you decided on a dress yet?' She ignores me. And anyway, whatever dress she chooses will have to be more on the lines of one of those Renaissance portraits of heavily pregnant women. We saw one on holiday in Italy once. The *Madonna del Parto* by Piero della Francesca. Helena looks like a beautiful wood sprite. Tall and fragile with a pale childlike face and a rounded abdomen like a bursting fruit. Fecund is a word that springs to mind. A bit like the *Madonna del Parto*, in fact – sort of sexy, pouty and defiant. And alone apart from a couple of angels. I can quite understand why David has agreed to marry her. It's just embarrassing that he's so right wing. And a bit of a cad and a bounder to boot, from what I've heard. According to Sid there's some woman in New York and another in Tokyo. Helena's told Angus.

'Hang on, I can hear something.' She's slithering along the wall again. A giant yawn engulfs me and I am suddenly overwhelmed by the desire to go to bed. 'Oh.' She looks crestfallen.

'What?' I look at my watch. If I take Karl upstairs now for his nap, I can have one too. I watch Helena as she comes and sits down at the table again.

'I just heard his mum shouting if he didn't get his backside over here this minute she'd tan the hide off him.'

'Helena, the man is in his forties.' I wander over to collect Karl so I can make an announcement about putting him down for a nap.

'Seen Angus lately?' she asks, not looking at me and collecting up her things. It is amazing how abruptly lives can jump the tracks. One minute you've been sleeping next to the same person for half a decade, the next, you never see them again.

'No. Oh, yes. Well, not really.' Helena's pregnancy seems to have detonated some sort of problem between Angus and Sid. I don't want Helena to pry, so I say, 'I *love* that coat.'

'Oh this old thing?' Helena's not hard to divert. 'I found it in the Oxfam shop in Holland Park,' she lies, smoothing the soft animal skin down her flank. 'Cost a tenner or something.'

There's a crash and a scream from the other side of the wall followed by hysterical laughter. Helena hesitates at the stairs and looks towards the wall. I push her firmly ahead of me with Karl on my hip.

'Forget it, Helena, it's called family life. Hadn't you heard? They fuck you up your mum and dad, They may not mean to but they do . . .'

I look at Karl and say sorry.

15th December 1993

Out on the street, there's a crazed look in people's eyes already. As Karl and I walk home from the Mums and Toddlers group, trailing tinsel and wearing silver foil crowns, I realise time is running out. I haven't done the Christmas cards. I haven't bought any presents. I haven't got a tree. I haven't got any crackers. I have disobeyed instructions and I am in danger of Failing. We go to a charity shop and buy the last pack of cards left. They depict Mary on a donkey being led by Joseph along a stony path. I know just how the donkey feels. Then we buy a Christmas tree from Chapel Market and drag it home together. Halfway home, Karl stops walking and says he wants a carry. I sit down on the pavement beside him and listen while he moans about his legs. We sit there for quite a long time, Karl, me and the

Christmas tree. An old woman with a battered brown handbag shuffles by, pauses and hands me twenty pence.

This year we are having three Christmases. One at the Angel with Sid and Angus, one at my mum's and one at your parents'. It will involve quite a lot of driving and gargantuan quantities of presents, the prospect of which induces a sense of breathlessness in me. Both the giving and the receiving. My fantasy Christmas is just the three of us deep in a snowy forest by a lake where you go out on Christmas Eve and chop down a tree with an axe. There's a scene with a sleigh in it and a few deer wandering about in the thicket and quite a bit of tumbling about in the snow. Especially once Karl's been tucked up in his rabbit skin.

When we get home I find I have left one of the shopping bags behind somewhere. Unfortunately it's the one with my wallet and phone book in it. That's when I know in an annunciatory kind of a way that I'm pregnant again. Alarm and elation wash through me. I look at my watch. If I ring the hospital now, I may be able to book myself in for the CF test before the whole world shuts down for a week.

Fifteen

7th February 1994

THE INSIDE of Helena's and David's house looks like Hollywood's idea of how the English live. I'm not sure which company supplies their sunlight, but their hallway is bathed in it and the air is thick with the scent of cut flowers.

David looks dishevelled but relaxed, as if he isn't just about to jet off somewhere for once. I hand him more flowers. He kisses me the confusing way. One, two and three.

'Genevieve! What happened to your hair?' he laughs affectionately and then claps you on the back. 'Mark! Glad to see you survived the war. That's not Karl, is it? When did all that growing happen?'

We shuffle around each other for a while, you with Karl in your arms and Karl holding on to both your ears while he studies David's display of public school cheer.

'Look, Karl,' you say, pointing and kneeling down at the entrance to the sitting room, 'a rocking horse'. At one end of the vast still room an old-fashioned horse with a long, silky mane stands waiting for a rider. In the centre of the room, plump sofas face gently flaming fireplaces. Everywhere is draped and layered with the sheen and depth of wealth. At the far end of the room french doors overlook an immaculate garden of mature trees which stretches as far as the eye can see.

'Wow. Amazing place, David,' you say, helping Karl onto the horse. 'How much did you say you paid for it?'

'Two hundred and ninety thousand,' he announces, rattling a bottle in the ice bucket.

'You're kidding!'

'Nope. Honestly. I heard that the little old lady who used to live here couldn't bear the thought of being here alone once her husband died. When I heard he was on his last legs, I made her a cash offer.'

You look at me, eyes shining. You want this. But I don't want this, Mark.

'Is Helena upstairs, David?' I say, holding our present in my arms. 'Can I go up?'

'Of course.' He waves me off with a champagne bottle in his hand. 'She's dying to see you.'

I go up the wide silent staircase and push open a door. There, in a throne of linen and silk, is Helena, reading *Hello!* magazine. By the bed is a lacy cradle on rockers. She beams up at me, shifts to make space on the bed and winces in pain.

'Ouch. God. Caesareans may mean the birth is painless but you bloody know about it afterwards. Oh, thanks.' She tosses the present onto a pile of gifts at her side.

'Let's have a look at her,' I say, bending over the cradle to peer at the tiny chrysalis bundle. I pull the cover back gently and look at Molly's face.

We go '*Aah*,' when we see a newborn baby but really we mean 'Aah!' Their faces are a shock. So stern and wise. As if to say, Take me seriously, or else.

'*Aah*,' I say. 'She's lovely.' But not nearly as lovely as mine. 'Tiny.' A little too small really.

'David says she's got my looks. And that as long as she's got his brains she'll be all right.' She does a small laugh and offers me a chocolate. The sort that are individually wrapped in spun gold.

'Helena, what possessed you to live with a git like David? He is incapable of forming a mutual bond with a woman.

Listen to the way he talks about them.' But of course I don't say this out loud.

'How are you?' I say instead. 'Is the milking going OK?'

'The milking's fine. But I'm not sure what I should be doing exactly. It feels a bit odd just sitting here with my tits out all day and night.'

'Oh well, you've had plenty of practice then . . .' A squawk of a giggle dies on my lips as I realise that somehow, comments like that are now banned with Helena. I look around the room. 'This place *is* amazing, Helena. Like a palace. A bit different from Peckham, isn't it?'

'I love it here. The light. And the space. Take a look through there.' She nods at a door the other side of the room.

I pad soundlessly across the floor and open the door onto a chamber of mirrors and chrome and blond wood.

'Two sinks, for God's sake!' I shout, opening yet another door. 'Blimey! Who sleeps in here?'

Another bedroom is spread out before me. I come back through to Helena.

'David sleeps there.'

'Does he?' I shudder. 'Oh.'

'So he isn't disturbed in the night. Quite sensible really. He does have to get up at five after all.'

'I suppose so,' I say, wanting to console Helena and unable to say exactly why David should share Helena's broken nights.

'Seen Angus?' she asks as I know she will.

'Not really,' I lie. 'What are you going to do about work, by the way?'

'I've been asked to go to Afghanistan to do a piece on female circumcision in April. I'm determined to take Molly with me. And the nanny, of course. David's against it, needless to say, but he'll be in New York then so, you know . . .'

'I don't think Afghanistan is very welcoming to women

right now, is it?' I struggle to remember who's in power since the Russians withdrew. 'It's an Islamic state, isn't it?'

'It'll be fine.' Helena shrugs nonchalantly. She loves playing the intrepid journo. I envy her even if she is part time and, as I suspect, protected by her father's invisible influence. 'What about you? Work OK?'

'A bit tedious. No one seems to get better.' I bend to smell a mahogany bowl filled with rose petals. 'But Mark may be going to South Africa to make a documentary about Mandela. And Karl and I may go with him.' I stand and beam at her in excitement at the prospect. 'Better than administering ECT and enemas.'

'I thought Mark's thing was fiction not fact.' A thin stuttering cry begins from the cradle. She sighs. 'Pass me that baby, could you, Genevieve?'

I pick up the weightless bundle and hand her over. The baby strains her head this way and that like a blind baby bird.

'*Aah*,' I say.

'Aah!' yells Helena, sitting up and lifting one leaking great breast out of her shirt. 'These sodding stitches.'

6th May 1994

'There just aren't enough hours in the day, are there?'

None of us says anything in response to this remark of Helena's. There's a crowd of us from the Playgroup and for some reason, Helena has decided to come along too. We stare at the roux of toddlers waddling about near the miniature model of Amsterdam. Lucy continues shredding her polystyrene cup. Susan opens her mouth to say something. We wait, but nothing comes out.

Then Helena says, 'Well there are actually,' and everyone shifts onto another buttock and continues staring.

It's 11.45 a.m. in Legoland and it looks like rain.

'What I mean is, however long the day is, by the time it is finally over, I still haven't cleared up the breakfast. There were two days last week when I never got out of my dressing gown.' We look at Helena who has Molly strapped to the front of her coat and a baby seat over one arm like a hideous handbag. There doesn't seem much point in Molly or Helena being here but she insisted on coming. She thought it would be a laugh.

'This may be just me,' I begin, 'but I'm not sure I really understand this place.' We look around us at the beleaguered queues of mothers with children, some looking in disbelief into their purses while their children start revving up on Quavers, Tangos and Slush Puppies. We gaze in a bovine stupor at the men in anoraks squatting down in order to examine the finer details of the miniature railway. 'I mean, is this it?' I continue. 'From what I had been told about it, my visit here, like a visit to Neuro Disney, would be guaranteed to rank among the most profound of my experiences of parenthood. There are some aspects of motherhood that I'm just not getting. This queuing thing. I mean why should I want to come all this way, pay all this money and stand in queues? I can do that in Sainsbury's. And all this hanging around *looking*. I'm sure it's not supposed to be like this. In fact, when my second child is born, I'm going to refuse,' I say, stroking my rounded belly defiantly.

'What, not take it to Disney or Legoland or Toys R Us?' says Susan. 'You won't be allowed, someone will report you.'

'On Wednesday,' says Helena avoiding our eyes, 'I lost my way to Brent Cross Shopping Centre.' We watch a small boy machine-gun the geese on the lake. Helena turns her head away from Molly and lights up a fag. She takes two deep drags, blowing the smoke up at the blank white sky. 'I was on the North Circular right? I passed Ikea, Computer World, World of Leather . . .'

'Passed Village of the Damned . . .' mutters someone.

'Saw the sign for Brent Cross. Followed it and then, I am not joking, it absolutely vanished. No more signs. And I was hurtling headlong towards Luton. It took me several hours to get back. Brent Cross just wasn't there. Molly was in hysterics by the time I got home.'

We all think for a minute about life without Brent Cross. Mecca of Mothers. It's got special changing rooms and everything. There are no able-bodied people there. Just mothers with small children. We shoot sideways looks Helena's way. How awful to no longer see the signs.

Sixteen

30th August 1994

YOU AND Marion stand veiled in smoke from the barbecue. You are decrying the almost unbelievable complete and utter stupidity of some football manager. Your mum is telling Karl that her neighbour once knew a little boy who had a dreadful accident with a chicken bone and that by the time the little boy's mummy had noticed that he was choking it was too late he had gone completely blue and wasn't breathing at all any more and although they had called the ambulance the driver was Welsh so he wasn't a lot of use really and he took ever such a long time getting there and when the ambulance did arrive it knocked at number thirty-six instead of sixty-three.

I glance at Karl whose eyes are fixated on Granma, his mouth open in amazement. This could be due to the story or the sheer volume of words.

'. . . and all because the little boy's mummy hadn't told him that when you eat chicken you've got to be very very careful because of all the tiny little bones which are very sharp and can be very very dangerous.'

You pass me a plate heaped with an enormous helping of food and topped with a perfectly formed baby chicken. It's a poussin. Sainsbury's sells everything now but cow – you can get ostrich, crocodile, kangaroo, blackbirds baked in a pie probably . . . I lower myself into a chair and get up again. I'm at the stage where sitting is no longer possible. The baby's head has definitely descended – I wouldn't be surprised if it were visible. I hover near Karl, uncertain whether your mum's story is going to end in an actual death or not. Then I feel a warm flood in my pants and I say to no one in particular that I'm about to have a baby.

'Pardon?' Marion looks up, barbecue fork poised over the leaping flames. 'You're what?'

You look up from the glowing coals, uncertain whether to believe me or not. 'Are you sure? Why don't we just have lunch first?'

'Tell you what,' says Marion, 'you finish your lunch, Mark, and I'll run Genevieve down to the hospital.' Marion is putting down the fork and picking up his jacket. 'It's no bother, honestly.'

I would much rather that you drove me to the hospital, Mark, given the rather intimate thing that is going on inside me. I turn to Karl who is on your mum's lap being fed tiny pieces of poussin meat. I want to kiss him and say something by way of an apology for the fact that everything is about to change for ever but all that comes out is a subdued groan. Your mum's been telling me that in the old days women made no noise at all while giving birth. All this screaming and shouting is a bit modern apparently. Suddenly it's very important that I put some distance between your parents and me before I start doing the mad cow thing. A contraction seizes me like a vice and I make a grab for your arm.

'I think we should go,' you say.

Somehow I seem to have got into the front seat of Marion's Mondeo and you are in the back. This is a very bad combination, Mark, wetting my pants in the passenger seat of Marion's car. I don't like even thinking about my pants when I'm with Marion and because he is your dad he's making me think of my dad.

Birth, like death no doubt, is when you need to be with

someone who can look you in the eye, whatever horrors are going on elsewhere. But you can do the birth look, Mark. Or at least you could last time.

'Are you going to put your seat belt on, Genevieve?' asks Marion as we move off in the wrong direction. I let out a shout which makes him go twice round the roundabout in alarm and you lean forwards and pat my shoulder hesitantly. I wish I was in the back with you. But you are telling Marion that he's going the wrong way and he is telling you to stop back-seat driving he knows very well where he's going thank you very much. I open my eyes briefly to find we're in a traffic jam near the Euston Road. Thank God. Not far now.

'Dad, stop the car. The hospital is south of here, not west. We'll get a taxi. Honest it'll be quicker. Stop the car!' You're grabbing the back of Marion's seat and for one awful moment I think you may be about to hit him.

'What are you talking about? There's a clear run coming up ahead. Just tell me where to turn off. Hang on there's an *A–Z* under your seat, Genevieve.' Marion starts rummaging around under my feet. I'm facing the back of the car and clinging on to the headrest and sinking my teeth into it every time a contraction comes. I can taste your mum's hairspray. I try to be quiet but this is much more painful than last time. Marion sees an empty bus lane and puts his foot down, sailing at high speed past the road that would lead us to the hospital. Marion turns on the radio and for a while you are both quiet, concentrating on the football commentary. The entrance to Regent's Park streaks past.

'Stop the car,' I pant. Suddenly it is all happening very fast. Marion seems determined to head west, like a homing pigeon.

'Slow down, Dad, for God's sake! Whatever you do, don't get on the Westway. We do not want to go to fucking Oxford!'

'Mark, I'm going to lose my temper with you in a minute. Now that sign. That sign there.' Many signs accelerate towards us. 'What does it say?' A convoy of Ikea lorries drive alongside, obscuring your vision and prompting another outburst. Through my armpit which I'm panting into, I notice the road ahead is completely at a standstill.

'That's all we need. Looks like there's a match on.' Marion swings sharply to the left and takes a slip road off the overpass where he makes a beeline for a blocked-off road with several police bollards and Road Closed signs. A man in a fluorescent tunic waves us down. 'Bugger that, this is an emergency.' Marion accelerates past him and roars up a maze of residential side streets. The roads are strangely empty. Marion is triumphant. But still completely lost.

Before long we realise that no, it isn't a match, it isn't even that it's a Bank Holiday. It's the Notting Hill Carnival. Marion has got us right into the Notting Hill Carnival which is an incredible feat of navigation given the circumstances and the fact that we live some distance from Notting Hill. We are stationary in the midst of a crowd of jubilant people, we can't move and Marion is uttering hideously racist remarks.

'It's OK, Dad, it's OK. Look stop tooting your bloody horn like that, Dad, and just edge forward gently.' The tooting continues and no break in the crowd appears. 'Dad, open your window for God's sake. Just open your window and let me speak to someone.' You are struggling with the electric window opener which your dad has locked and with the door handle which is child-locked. Marion starts pressing buttons wildly on his dashboard. Up until this point in our history, apart from that 'bugger' just now, the only oaths I have ever heard Marion utter are 'Shine on' and 'Gordon Bennett' but when the Brent float comes calypso-ing by and half of Hounslow shake their booty up against Marion's window he says something so deeply shocking that for a moment my labour ceases altogether. I do not understand how you can be this man's son. What is the connection, for God's sake? Perhaps you're not really his but a love child that your mum has kept quiet about all these years. Then you start screaming and I fear that our baby will be born in some ghastly Oedipal denouement and you're telling me to climb over into the back and you start climbing over into the front which involves forcing Marion's head onto the steering wheel and any minute now there's going to be that shocking frenzied smacking of fists against skin and bone which erupts when men fight and you're calling him a fucking moron.

Someone shoves me in the stomach and that really is it. I've had enough of your crazy family so I open my door with difficulty and fall out into the crowd where I'm held up and stood on my feet again. Suddenly there's a guy with a megaphone and he's shouting 'Let the lady through! This lovely lady is having a baby!' and extraordinarily enough after a few more shouts the crowds part and Marion starts bellowing at me to get back in the bloody car before they turn nasty. 'I'd rather walk,' I gasp, and as it's the Notting Hill Carnival it is suddenly possible to find a police officer when you need one, which I most definitely do and before I know it I'm kneeling on the back seat of a squad car and the driver keeps looking at me in the rear-view mirror and saying things like, 'Don't worry, love. My wife was doing this three weeks ago. I know all the ins and outs.'

Giving birth the second time is supposed to be easier but here I am in the Labour Ward, completely at sea and shattered and lost without you. I bite down on the oxygen mouthpiece, moan and inhale, hanging on until my teeth ache like a high-wire trapeze artist dangling from someone's harness without a safety net. It has no discernible effect. But then, why would it? It's gas and air. I need heroin, morphine, a serious religion.

The thing is, with a second baby, it's bloody bigger, would you believe? And the second baby thing. It definitely isn't easier. What they mean is, you know what to expect. So when you are writhing around, your mind failing to come to terms with the sensations in your body, begging to be shot, somewhere in some stone-age part of your brain you understand that you probably aren't going to die, it's just that an entire baby is actually going to have to be pushed out into the world down your vagina. It's a lesson in grammar, a verb thing. You are going to *have* a baby. I hear the midwife inform me that she's going off duty now and there's a vending machine down in Casualty and am I sure I wouldn't like to phone someone at which point I realise that I am unbelievably, catastrophically tired. It feels as if since giving birth to Karl I've had all the stuffing knocked out of me. I'm not at all sure I can do this all over again. Because of staff shortages the midwives are all agency midwives who come and go and leave me when I shout too much or don't do what they tell me which is mainly, 'Get up on the bed and lie on your back.' This is like asking a boxer to stop putting his hands up in front of his face when the punches come.

Then the door flies open. You. At last. Your face.

You are looking panicked and urgent. You drop the bath cleaner, scourer and pillow and get down on the floor with me. Wordless, I hang on to you. Hang on to the sweet familiar feel and scent of you.

'I think I'm getting flu.' I sneeze. 'God's punishment for finding it so easy the first time round.'

Seventeen

29th September 1994

NOW I feel like I'm really getting the hang of this mother thing. You're not away and I'm still off work for another few months thanks to what you got for *Spaghetti Junction* and the promise of a TV drama about a serial killer in Croydon. And life is just ordinary and slow and manageable. Nothing much rattles me. Not even Ivan's colic, which though not as bad as Karl's, still means there's a hell of a lot of screaming. It starts at five past six in the evening and stops just after the nine o'clock news. I'm developing a theory about colic. The books and the health visitors and the doctors may insist it's digestive or simply a mystery but I know it's nothing to do with stomach cramps or what I've eaten in the last twenty-four hours. It's to do with philosophy. Colic is the last thing it should be called. Colic is something horses get when they've eaten too much clover. What Ivan's going through sounds like what it is. Grief. Inconsolable, raging grief for the human condition. Don't ask me how it is that babies can feel it but they definitely do.

Strangely I don't mind the screaming so much because this time round you're hearing it too. You're not off busy placating some sobbing, sulking actress or worrying about lights or budgets or dropping a scene. You're in the house with me and Karl, witnessing Ivan's glimpse of the abyss.

You know it's not possible to make it better. This is nihilism not wind. Valiantly, you carry him up and down the room saying, 'Don't cry, don't cry.' And you sing nursery rhymes to him at full volume (this, it should be noted, always makes him worse). You take him out in his buggy with him screaming fit to bust and return an hour later, with him still screaming. You drive round North London with him in the back of the car, sounding like some Rapid Response Unit. Quite often, all four of us end up screaming. Nowadays the neighbour is completely silent. Nothing comes through the wall at all from his side now. Poor Kylie. I haven't heard her for a long time. Kylie kyboshed. I never thought I'd see the day.

Despite the screaming, I think that we are happy. Well I am. I can never be entirely sure about you. You spend a good deal of time telling me we are happy but I tend not to listen to these announcements – I've always assumed it's your mum's voice somehow coming through on our frequency by mistake. Filial interference. But, generally, if this is called Family Life, then I like it. The screaming stops at five past nine each evening and by the morning all four of us are piled up in the big bed, snoozing. At these times, Ivan has forgotten his encounter with the dark side of the moon and is merry and delightful. I feel safe and adored and I am getting quite fat. You keep feeding me. It's a bit like the early days when we first met. We spend most of the time in bed, or in our pyjamas. And the outside world feels very far away.

Dimly, through the haze, on the radio or the TV news, I am occasionally made aware of catastrophic, unthinkable events in Rwanda. I hold Ivan's head in my hands, closing my eyes and my mind to the accounts of machete flesh and bone and I offer up some apology, some plea. To whom, I don't know. This is nearly the twenty-first century, after all and we know there is no God.

10th November 1994
I'm standing in the shower, my face against your neck, while the water batters down on our heads. You're pretending to be depressed and I'm pretending not to be nervous. Depressed because *Spaghetti Junction* is being screened for the first time at a cinema in central London tonight. Nervous because I'm afraid the surprise I've planned for you will backfire and you'll hate me for it. My explanation will be that because the film's so small there's been no publicity and because I know how important the first weekend's takings are I've phoned everyone I can think of and told them to be there for the evening screening tonight. I sort of let them think it's a premiere followed by a premiere-type party. Jesus, I hope they don't think I'm buying all the tickets. I've warned the pub next door – they know we're coming. They think it's a premiere too so they're quite excited even though they've never heard of Mark Morrison or the film or the cast but I implied that was their shortcoming not the film's and that they should expect a hundred people. The water is starting to run cold.

'Come on, Mark.' You hold me tight so I can't move. 'We ought to get dressed.' Reluctantly I unwrap myself from you and kiss you. 'You look beautiful. Come on. It's my first night out since Ivan was born.'

It is strange to get dressed without the children round our feet. Strange to be talking just to each other and not to Ivan and Karl. It's been ages since we were alone. Sid says that marriages usually fail just at the point when being alone together is possible again. She says the parents become strangers to each other and fear the return of intimacy. Sid is very precise about the date this happens. It's either when the youngest child is five or when the kitchen appliances start to break down – dishwasher, washing machine, cooker. Keep an eye on your appliances is Sid's advice. I think she's just comforting herself for the fact that Angus doesn't want children. Or so he says. He's definitely gone a bit funny since

Helena had Molly. If I had a theory about the end of marriages, which I don't, it would be more to do with the point at which sex is confined to bedtime rather than all the other far more sexy times of the day. Like breakfast.

'Is there something wrong with the dishwasher?' you ask. I pull up my knickers and look at you. You're lying on the bed in a star shape. 'Come here,' you say. The putting on of knickers always has this effect on you.

'Dishwasher?' My insides flip in alarm. 'What do you mean? Why are you talking about the dishwasher all of a sudden?'

'My glass is all smeary.'

'Oh!' My knickers are coming off in relief and gratitude. 'That just means it needs Rinse Aid.' I join you on the bed.

There's a scream from downstairs and we freeze.

'That was laughter,' I whisper into your ear.

'I think that was pain,' you whisper back.

'If it was serious there'd be a silence.' We listen. Karl is squealing downstairs. But it's squeals of delight not torment. And Ivan is chuckling. Something hilarious is obviously going on down there.

'It's OK. The au pair's reading to them.'

'When does Ivan's screaming start?' you say, raising your head for a moment. Your hair is still wet and warm from the shower.

'Five past six.'

'Mmm. Ten minutes to blast off then.'

We're late when we get in the car and it has started to pour with rain.

'Shit. No one will come out on a night like this.' You look wretched.

'But a rainy Friday is a perfect night to go to the cinema, Mark. Come on.' I make a dash for the driving seat, leap in and belt up before you can say, 'I'll drive.'

'I'll drive.'

'No it's OK. Get in.'

'Which way are you going?' you say as I pull away from the kerb. I ignore this reflex of yours. You can't help it. It's the Marion in you.

'I'm not going to sit through the film, you know. You can watch and I'll meet up with you afterwards.'

'OK but I've asked Angus and Sid to meet us there.' This is a risky confession because I haven't asked your permission. I'm only just beginning to understand that becoming a Great Film Director requires many things. One of them is Diffidence. Another is Cool. Going to see your own film with your wife and friends breaks all the rules. Only some ninny at film school would do that. Unless it's being screened at an international festival, of course. Some of the other attributes required for being a Great Film Director I don't want to even think about.

'You've asked Sid and Angus?' There's a silence. I sneak a look at your profile. You look a tiny bit pleased. I zip through the traffic. I know the short cuts. I should drive more often. I'm a far better driver than you. I nearly say this out loud but stop myself just in time.

'Mark, what you have to realise is that all your friends and relatives are very excited about the screening of your film. I'm sure a lot of them will be there.'

'I doubt that very much.' You attempt a hollow laugh.

'I wouldn't be surprised if your mum and dad were there too.' Damn. What the hell was I thinking of, inviting Marion and your mum? They'll die of shock when they see the final scene.

'They'd better not be.'

'I'm sure they said they might be in London this weekend. Anyway, if it's a full house tonight, it'll increase the chances of it being on for more than a week. Even a wider distribution. Who knows? It might become a cult movie.' I don't even know what a cult movie is. Doesn't it just mean hardly anyone sees it? I decide to be silent until we get there.

I hesitate and then accelerate between a juggernaut and the 73 bus. It's a bit of a close shave. Breast milk leaks onto the front of my shirt.

'Park here,' you say, after we've crawled at one mile an hour for twenty minutes. 'We can walk from here.'

'It's OK. I know a place a bit closer. Somewhere we can leave it all night if we have to.' What's come over me? I keep disobeying you. It's bound to be a good party though. Whether you're there or not. I've asked relatives, old bosses, old friends, old flatmates, Leon . . . Come to think of it it's going to be a total disaster.

'Genevieve! You've missed another parking space, for God's sake!' You twist round in your seat, furious at my idiocy. But I don't care, for once I know I'm right. I do know about this parking space.

'Mark. Who's driving?' I turn down a tiny side street, deliver a prayer up to any deity that's out there and, yes, there is my parking space. It's a rare strip of single yellow line that Westminster Council hasn't noticed yet.

'Tee Hee.' I look at you. 'See? This bit is always empty. No one knows about it except me.' We get out of the car and make our way towards the cinema. We're late. They should all be in there by now.

'Did you see that woman?' you ask, looking back over your shoulder at someone going in the side entrance in a wheelchair. 'She looked exactly like Great Auntie Ida.'

'Mark. Are you really going to make me sit through your film on my own?'

'Hey, it's Mark Morrison!' We turn to see Angus at the door to the cinema. He's waving tickets at us. You grin at him. I can see suddenly that it's all going to be all right.

We find our seats in the crowded auditorium just as the opening credits roll. Your name comes up on the screen. Cheers and whistles go up from the audience. I survey the many familiar silhouetted heads around us and squeeze your hand. It's going to be a bloody good party.

Eighteen

1st February 1995

IT'S MY first day back at work and the au pair decided she wanted to go home yesterday. I daren't take a day off because now I'm part time, I feel guilty enough as it is. We panicked and even rang Jesus to beg her to come back to us, offering untold riches and a part in your next film, but alas, she had fallen in love and could not be tempted. Karl has pus seeping from one ear and cannot possibly go to nursery today and I've spent most of the night wandering the house in order to breast feed Ivan and spoon Calpol into Karl. But you've solved the crisis temporarily and you are staying at home to look after the children. No, that was a joke, but you have sent Marion to stay with me. You've had to go to Venice or Eastbourne or Dubrovnik I can't remember which, to persuade some actress to be in some film. She's probably one of the many scary giant close-ups we've got scattered over our bedroom floor. They fall out when you open your post in bed.

When I stagger down to breakfast Marion is already at the table reading the paper.

'*Good* morning,' he says as I deposit two moaning children into a high chair and a booster seat at the table. I squint at him wondering if I detect a note of sarcasm in his voice. No, he's just being cheerful.

'Morning, Marion.' I won't ask how he slept. It can't have been very well because we don't have a spare bed since all the walls were knocked through on the first floor. And anyway people never tell the truth about how badly they have slept in someone else's house. Karl lets out a piercing shriek which, if his eardrum isn't burst already, will certainly have burst it now. My own ears are ringing.

'Ooh dearie me! What's the matter?' Marion claps his hands in front of Karl and then looks me up and down. 'Aren't you going to work today then?'

'Yes, course I am.'

'Where's your uniform?'

'No uniform for now.' I sincerely hope this isn't going to be one of those mind-boggling conversational loops Marion can get into where I end up feeling like I've been emotionally frisked.

'I got a research grant remember?' I pour cereal into both boys' bowls. 'Tea, Marion?'

'What's that?'

'Would you like some tea?'

'Well if you're making some. So have you stopped being a nurse as such then?'

'For a while, yes.' I hand Ivan a bottle of milk and give Karl a cup of juice. 'I'm doing some research. Hopefully.'

'You're doing what?' asks Marion, incredulous. I take Ivan's bottles out of the steriliser. 'I'm doing some research on women and madness.'

'Women and madness? Whatever for?'

'I'm doing it,' I continue, unloading the dishwasher, 'because I've been nursing for ten years and I want a change. It's a promotion, sort of. Without the money.' I line up enough jars of food to last several days. 'You sure you'll be all right with these two?' I write down Ivan's timetable for the day, draw a map to the park, write down the doctor's number, my mum's number and my work number. 'I should think Karl will just want to sleep most of the morning. I've left all the nappy stuff upstairs and their coats and things are by the door.' Karl is chewing the side of Marion's hand with a desperate expression in his eyes. Marion shifts his palm so it warms Karl's sore ear. 'It's really very kind of you to do this, Marion—'

'It's no bother at all. We'll enjoy ourselves, won't we, boys?'

Ivan's drumming has started up with the plastic spoons and bowls. Karl looks at Ivan in astonishment and then joins in.

'Oh, and if the builders come, I'm to let them in, am I?' shouts Marion above the din.

'What? Did Mark say they were coming today?'

'Well he said they might. He told me to give them a ring. They're building his roof terrace, aren't they?'

'That was the plan.' I curse you silently. 'But I'm sure they won't turn up.' I kiss the boys, precipitating a whole new kind of crying from Karl. 'Although I thought we'd put it on hold until Mark was sure about his next job!' I shout. 'Because we haven't got any money!'

Karl levers himself half out of the booster seat by clinging on to my hair. Ivan realises something is up. He looks shocked, then devastated, then angry. He bursts into tears.

'So. They might start taking the roof off your bedroom then?' Marion can't seriously be wanting a building conversation, can he?

'Marion . . .'

I drop down to retrieve Karl's beaker which has hit the fridge and landed upside down in the cat's bowl. Marion gets up from his chair. I look at him helplessly. It's mayhem in here even with the roof on.

'Could you . . . ?'

I prise Karl's fingers off my hair and try to kiss Ivan without detonating another explosion.

'Off you go, Mummy. Come on, boys. We'll see her later, won't we?' Marion shoos me out of the kitchen. 'One man went to mow . . .' he sings. I pick up my bag and keys and back out of the room.

'Went to mow an meadow!' shouts Karl, spraying cereal from his mouth.

'Look, thanks,' I say, suddenly seeing that I can leave my children with this man who loves them because they are part of him too.

By the time I get to the tube I've stopped crying and look just like all the other commuters. Wrecked and vacant. It's a long time since I've clung on to the rail above my head with one hand and stood in the crush of other bodies mutely enduring their transportation to work. I feel in limbo, released from one kind of constraint only to be delivered into another.

As soon as I'm in the hospital though, and I realise I'm freed of my hateful uniform and the tedium and restrictions it imposes, my home life dissolves. I luxuriate in the long wedge of time that non-nursing work provides. My head is uncluttered and clear. There is an ordered sequence of events to the day. Meetings, archive study, patient interviews. Work. I'd forgotten. There are whole professions within each institution devoted solely to Cooking. And Cleaning. And Paying the Bills. It's a bloody parallel universe. No wonder men guard it so jealously. And spend so much time doing it.

As I'm making my way from one part of the hospital to the other, out of the gloom of the long beige corridor comes the familiar swaying gait of Mabel. She is grinning, moving faster than usual and throwing her hands up and clapping them above her head.

'Nurse, Nurse!' she calls in her little girl's voice. She lumbers towards me and stretches her arms wide. I hesitate and wonder what medication she's on these days. Before I can decide whether to take evasive action she's got me in a bear hug. Her body is unyielding, like plastic and she smells of urine and talc.

'Where you been, Nurse?' she asks in her tiny voice, patting my back. 'Where you been?'

I'm laughing into her chest and when we look at each other there are tears in our eyes. She's shaking her huge white head and saying, 'I been waiting for you. I been waiting ever such a long time.'

'Well, Mabel, I left to have a baby remember?' I take a step back and try to release my upper body from her bear hug. Her grip tightens. I've hardly ever heard her speak before. It's her voice more than her grip that unsettles me. With my face crushed sideways against her body I look down the deserted linoleum corridor towards the doors of the ward. Familiar cries and clatters reach me. I can feel Mabel's shallow rapid breath on top of my head.

'Did they let you keep it?'

I extricate my head, losing an earring in the process. Looking up at Mabel's face I see an expression of clown-like sorrow and compassion. A tear falls from the curve of her cheek onto my lip. She takes my hand and wraps it in both of hers shaking her head from side to side. I notice Winston standing at the corner watching us.

'Let's go and have a nice cup of tea, shall we?'

'That would be lovely, Mabel,' I say, and I let her lead me down to the ward.

7th May 1995

There is a lot of sex and violence in *Kissed the Girls and Made Them Cry*, your serial killer drama set in Croydon. You're getting rather a reputation for making dark and depressing films. Letters of outrage appear in the press. Sid and I watch you on television trying to defend your work. The house smells of cement again. Cables and rubble litter the hall and stairs. Tarpaulin sheets flap where the roof used to be.

'*Aah*. Bless. He looks like butter wouldn't melt in his mouth,' she says. Despite myself she makes me laugh. She's sort of right. Your outward appearance is quite a contrast to what is evidently stored up in your psyche.

'Shut up, Sid. I'm trying to listen.'

'But the scene where the mother is bludgeoned to death in front of her young child,' says the presenter of *Right to Reply*, 'is that really essential to the story? Some accuse you of sensationalism.'

'Well, you have to ask the writer that question,' you reply, leaning forward earnestly.

'Ooh. Neat pass,' says Sid.

'Yes, but, as the director, you are responsible for interpreting the script,' persists the presenter, 'and ultimately for what the viewers see on the screen.'

'Sure. And if I offended anyone then I apologise, obviously, but if they didn't want to see any violence, perhaps they shouldn't have watched a drama about a serial killer.'

'Well we have regulations, don't we, about taste and decency and some might argue . . .'

'It's the shadow, you see,' continues Sid, 'he won't acknowledge it in real life so it gets dealt with through his work.'

'For God's sake, this is Mark you're talking about not Isaac Woodhead.'

I can hear Ivan crying. I stand up and hover. Your bit on the television is being wound up. Looks like you've charmed the presenter who is laughing heartily with you.

'Well, there we must leave it, but thank you very much for coming on the show, Mark Morrison. And now,' he turns to camera with a twinkle in his eye, 'we've had a positive deluge of letters asking why oh why haven't we seen anything of Kylie Minogue recently? So for all those of you who've been missing her . . .'

I race up the stairs to fetch Ivan before he wakes Karl.

When I come down again, Ivan at my breast, the velvet nap of his forehead against my lip, I sit down next to Sid. I'm intrigued by the Jungian shadow conversation. And a bit annoyed. She's always getting at you. Sometimes it's funny, but at other times it's just rude. She doesn't seem to take you seriously. And she seems to forget that if it weren't for us, she'd never have met Angus. The woman has no sense of gratitude, for God's sake.

'And I suppose you don't have a shadow, Sid,' I say, sitting down again next to her and ostentatiously rearranging my breasts.

'Course I do. Look. It's all round me.' She puts her hand on her tummy and pats her way down her to her thighs. 'Solid shadow. Several stone of it.' That's shut me up. I didn't know it was allowed to be mentioned. 'But don't expect me to tell you what it means because that, as you know, is my business.' I look at the magnificent size of Sid. I'm a bit disappointed she's called it her shadow. I always thought of it as more of a political statement – a refusal to be confined to the impossible and demeaning dimensions deemed appropriate for women. Literally a refusal to be diminished. I envied her courage. We stare at the television for a while.

'So what's my shadow then, Sid?' I feel a bit nervous asking this. A bit like a game of Truth or Dare. But Ivan at my breast gives me a modicum of psychic protection I like to think. I'm a mother, aren't I? Nothing complicated about that.

Sid takes out a Marlboro Light and puts it between her lips. She jiggles her foot up and down and doesn't light the cigarette. Instead she takes it out of her mouth and points it at the television where Kylie is miming and gyrating to some unconvincing tale of sexual fervour.

'You've got to hand it to her,' says Sid, 'she never stops smiling. I think she probably believes in the whole illusion herself, don't you?' She snaps her lighter at the end of the cigarette. 'Your shadow, Gen? The elements of yourself you can't bear to acknowledge? I couldn't possibly comment.'

She aims the remote at Kylie and the woman vanishes. She guffaws silently and sits back smoking contentedly.

The front door slams. We hear your heavy tread on the stairs.

16th December 1995

Thunderous drilling from the top of the house battles with the *Teletubbies* tape. Sid has wandered in through the front door that is kept permanently open by the builders. They don't think about doors in the same way as we do. Even when it's freezing like today. Or the streets are filled with thieves, like in the Angel.

'Sid, just don't say anything, OK? Someone's got to do it.' I am sorting the washing and Sid, grazing at the fruit bowl, is observing me with interest.

'Repetitive and pointless tasks,' says Sid. 'That woman in *Rumpelstiltskin* did them. Psyche did them. Women in Colney Hatch lunatic asylum did them—'

'Don't tell me. They were shut in a room and told to weave baskets out of macaroni.'

Don't say Sid's going to go all uber-feminist on me. It's nearly the twenty-first century, for God's sake. The ozone layer is disappearing, genocide is back, Aids is rife, half the planet goes to bed hungry and all she can think of to moan about is who does the bloody washing.

'No, they got them to sort coloured beans into two piles. It took about three hours every afternoon. At the end of each day the two piles were mixed up together again so they could be sorted the next day. It's just a form of' – I slam the washing-machine door hard – '. . . madness,' says Sid. 'It's why if you watch mad people you can suddenly see the equation,' she goes on. I select the cycle and try unsuccessfully to put the powder in the drawer without spilling it on the floor. 'Know what I mean?'

I sit down. Then I stand up and switch on the kettle. I'm

like Octavia these days. I can't keep still. There's too much to do. I decide not to answer Sid because frankly she doesn't have a bloody clue what is involved in keeping a house going with a family inside it. And trying to work. Sort of. Not to mention supervising the bloody builders.

'Boredom,' continues the Oracle. 'That's what they're acting out. Madness is boring because you're stuck in a loop. And if you watch madness, you'll see that. Think of Alice and Octavia and Isaac. They're just going through the motions. Or go to the zoo and watch the polar bear.'

I yawn loudly and try sitting down again. A bucket of bricks on the end of a rope rises up past the kitchen window. Something heavy drops with a clang through the scaffolding and lands on the pavement followed by a torrent of gynaecological abuse.

'Repetition and pointlessness.' She's getting her Old Holborn tin out. I love that smell. 'Think of any long-term patient you know and what springs to mind is the way they enact their madness.' Karl climbs onto my lap. He's hoping Sid will shut up too.

'Karl don't do that.' I take his fingers out of my ears. I don't think she means to but Sid has the ability to make me think my life is a joke. And in some respects I agree with her. Karl tries to stuff his fingers in my mouth. I don't know how it happened. But somehow I got the job of bringing order to your chaos. It is almost a full-time job. And now I'm hyperventilating about Christmas again. We're just having two this year in an effort to be fair to my mum. Last year I was up until three in the morning wrapping all the presents. It nearly killed me. And when Karl woke up at four with an anticipation that no presents, let alone the miracle of the virgin birth, could possibly live up to, you let him open his stocking. By seven o'clock in the morning Christmas had already happened. Ivan had missed it. Call me old-fashioned but I thought Karl should wait until six thirty. Karl gets down from my lap and goes over to poke the tree which is already dropping its needles.

'Coming to see us play tomorrow night, then?' asks Sid, opening a bulging makeup bag and selecting a lipstick. Karl watches her, fascinated.

'I can't, Sid. I can't get a babysitter. And I've got to varnish the banisters.'

'I don't want you to go out, Mummy.' Karl glares at me from the Christmas tree.

'Get Mark to babysit.' She is applying an outrageous colour to her lips without the aid of a mirror. It's wet like paint. I'm filled with admiration. Karl looks as though he might faint from desire. 'And for God's sake, eat something. You are obscenely thin.'

'I can't. I mean he can't. I'm not sure if he'll be in. And anyway, it's just not worth the hassle with Ivan.' I admire my shapely legs when I think Sid isn't looking. 'He screams the house down when I leave.'

'Leon will be there.' She zips up her bag of tricks and rolls her lips over one another.

'I don't want Leon. I want Mark.'

Nineteen

15th September 1996

THE CHILD *in the Grave* by Hans Christian Andersen.

'Oh.' I look through the photocopied pages and I'm not sure what to say. Sid is lighting up a Silk Cut Ultra Mild. Karl is at school and Ivan is asleep. I have two hours to myself. Secretly I had planned on sitting at the kitchen table, alone, drinking coffee and staring into space. But no sooner had I sat down and started staring than Sid arrived.

'It's not for Karl, you idiot. It's for your research.'

'Ah. Explain it to me,' I say, playing with her cigarette packet and contemplating having one.

'It tells you all you need to know about the psychopathology of parental grief. Angus found it in some old book of his. It's an incredible description of what maybe Octavia and certainly some of the others must have gone through. Here.' She takes it from me and starts to read aloud.

'*The father's heart was bowed down, but the mother sank completely under the deep grief . . . The tears of her husband fell on her forehead, but she took no notice of him; her thoughts were with the dead child . . .*'

'This is a fairy story?' I ask, stalling for time and thinking of the photo at my mum's. Of the way her face used to go when I asked her to tell me again about the other baby in the picture.

'Well, it's in his collection of stories. They were family stories, to be read aloud. He wrote about important things, I guess. And the death of a child was no doubt a common event. Listen. After the funeral, the mother pretends finally to be asleep, right? So the husband thinks, Oh, thank God for that, and falls asleep as well.'

'Obviously.' I attempt a laugh, take a cigarette and light it. Remorse spreads through me chased by a headache.

'Obviously. But of course she isn't really asleep. Just lying completely still doing the pretend breathing.'

'As you do.' The third and fourth drags aren't so bad for some reason.

'As you do. So she gets up really quietly and leaves the house and goes to the grave of the child, *where her thoughts constantly lingered.* She's kneeling over the grave and crying onto it. Then she hears a voice. *"Thou wouldst gladly go down and be with thy child," . . . a voice that sounded so deep and clear, that it went to her heart.*'

'Auditory hallucinations.'

'*She looked up, and by her side stood a man wrapped in a black cloak, with a hood closely drawn over his face . . .* Who do you think it is?'

'Death, of course. She wants to die.' I look down at my arms. All the fine brown hairs are raised, trapping the heat, preparing me for flight. Ancient reflex.

' *"Darest thou to follow me?" asked the form. "I am Death."*'

Sid's eyes are enormous. What she's able to do with a mascara brush is truly extraordinary. She's stubbing out her cigarette and finding the next page.

'Listen. *She bowed her head in token of assent.* That's brilliant, that is. She's speechless but not with fear, with loss. So then she goes down into the darkness. *She sank down, and the spectre covered her with a black cloak; night closed around her, the night of death. She sank deeper than the spade of the sexton could penetrate, till the churchyard became a roof above her . . .*'

'Depression.'

'Of course. And then at the bottom, there's this huge space, soft lighting, a kind of constant twilight and she sees her child smiling at her. She hugs him and heavenly music plays and everything.'

'Oh bloody hell. Now it's gone all religious. I was just getting into it. Don't tell me he's an angel now.' I stub out my cigarette angrily, draw my fingers under my nose and smell the sad-old-man smell.

'Shut up, Gen. They're bloody Victorians. Anyway, listen, there's this dark curtain that the child points out. Where all the beautiful music is coming from. The child tells her that beyond it is eternity which is a beautiful place and he wants to be there. Wants to fly away to be with God . . .'

'Sid. I'm supposed to be writing a piece of psychological research not some religious mumbo-jumbo.'

'Religion's just a metaphor. The whole story is. Why do you think Margery Kempe had visions and went on pilgrimages? It's a cultural thing. Anyway, the child tells the mother it can't be with God, because she won't stop weeping for him. *Suddenly her name was called from above; what could it mean? Her name uttered in a plaintive voice.* It's her husband and the daughters weeping and calling her name. Because she's not there. And then she realises that her grief had kept his soul from his immortal flight and she's forgotten the living. She goes back up and they're amazed at how much better she is. They ask where she got her strength from and she says, *"It came from God, through my child in the grave."*'

There's a silence. Just the sound of Sid's cigarette burning as she draws deeply on it. I know what's coming. It's not that I don't like talking about it exactly, it's just that I never really have. 'Your mum, Gen.' She looks at me. 'You're a twin, she told me once.'

'Was. I was a twin, yes.' Mark's aversion to digging up the past has made me superstitious of it. I'm afraid of contamination. 'And so,' I sigh and feel suddenly emptied, 'I guess she was in that place when I was a baby.'

'But she had you, didn't she? To draw her up again.' I try, but fail, to meet Sid's gaze.

'I imagine that's what lots of people told her.' I know but can't feel the horror that my mum must have felt. And that makes me feel callous. Unworthy. On a knife-edge of luck.

'The thing is,' she continues, 'old Hans knew about nervous breakdown precipitated by loss when he saw it, and probably lots of people did see it in those days. But why couldn't psychiatric hospitals, even one hundred years later? The awful thing for Octavia and Mabel and Alice and the others is that they're still stuck down there, in the dark. Instead of being helped out of the pit, they were shut in. Years ago. No one and nothing ever got them out.'

'Maybe you should write this thing, Sid,' I say. I can hear Ivan waking up. I half get up to go to him, not sure whether I feel relieved or disappointed.

'No, singing's my thing. Hey, did you know that the English have more mad old songs than any other European country? Angus read it somewhere.'

'I can believe it. It's our national malady. We're all completely mad. Upstairs and downstairs and in my lady's chamber and the cat ran away with the spoon diddle diddle.' I stand at the bottom of the stairs and listen. Sounds like Ivan's gone back to sleep. I put the kettle on instead. I hope Sid's going to leave before my whole morning disappears.

'Gen. I've just thought of how to overcome the problem of getting Octavia and the others to speak. How about if I come back to the wards and sing some of those old songs and nursery rhymes and then you interview them? We'll tell management it's a singsong. They're always wanting to fill the Occupational Therapy slots. But really it'll be a sort of singing hypnosis to unlock the inner Old Mother Hubbard.'

She gets up and collects her things and suddenly I don't want her to go. I think about it and consider that quite possibly it's a brilliant idea which will be completely forbidden by Sister Stone and Lesley. I'm not sure if it'll work but the madness of the method appeals to me.

21st September 1996

I'm so excited that it's Karl's first day in the Reception class at school that I'm awake long before him or Ivan. Perversely, they both decide to sleep in on this day, something they have never done in their lives before. In the end I have to resort to sitting in their bedroom and singing 'Row, Row, Row the Boat' quite loudly.

As soon as they open their eyes, I have them dressed, fed and stuffed in the double buggy before either of them works out what's going on. Karl should walk really but that will just take much longer. I have it all planned out. Today is my day off but I shan't be joining the other mothers down the café, or sitting in the kitchen reading the paper or even doing the weekly shop. No, I will use the time to work on my research and rekindle my interest in my career thereby securing an escape route from the hospital wards and keeping our careers in a healthy parallel ascent. I think school starts at nine o'clock. By the time I get Ivan back he'll be asleep for his morning nap which will leave me the whole morning to get on with my ground-breaking research into why Mabel, Octavia, Alice and Lily are mad. Actually I'll leave Lily out of it as I agree with Sid: Lily is either pretending or just plain bad.

When I arrive at the school the teacher points out to me that Karl's start time isn't for another forty-five minutes.

'We stagger their start times, so as not to create too much anxiety,' she tells me. A small crowd of mothers of five year olds have gathered in the corridor, many staggering and anxious after the five-year wait for 'full-time' education to begin.

Once I'm inside the classroom and about to leave, I'm told that for the first week, the children only stay for an hour, accompanied by their mother. I erase the shock from my face and replace it with an expression of understanding and don't say that when I was five, I did a full day, five days a week and probably walked to school on my own. But then the next sentence would be, 'and it didn't do me any harm,' which is of course a matter of opinion.

'Perhaps you'd like to take Karl over to the activity table,' she suggests.

I nod, lift Ivan out of the buggy and sit down to a Postman Pat jigsaw.

21st October 1996

It's finally Karl's first full morning. He's fallen in love with a boy called Dean who shares his interest in dressing up and so leaving him is not the trauma it was for the first week. What I hadn't fully realised, however (I was slow to understand that my son starting school would mean many, many, many pieces of paper, all of which had to be read), was that he won't be staying to lunch until Easter. So until then I have to return at twelve to pick him up.

I walk back home at high speed with Ivan in the buggy. By the time I'm home he is fast asleep. He seems to like it fast and furious. I congratulate myself on my skills as a modern mother as I pull the buggy backwards up the steps. Once the front door is shut, I leave Ivan asleep in the hall, go down to the kitchen and force myself to ignore the piles. Of letters from the bank, junk mail, dirty washing, clean washing, plates, cups, pans, dust balls, toys, scripts and photos of hopeful actors and actresses. I walk straight past them and sit down at the computer and begin to type.

Mabel was committed to hospital in February 1927 by her mother, under the Mental Deficiency Act of 1913, for dressing up in her mother's clothes and dancing in front of a mirror. Mabel was thirteen. She was diagnosed as suffering from dementia praecox, the original name for schizophrenia. So what? I can hear my supervisor saying. I can feel the brisk draught of Sister Stone as she passes my back. These are her 'ladies' I'm writing about and no one knows better than her that they will never offer anything intelligible. As far as Sister Stone is concerned they have nothing to say. I swat away the fear that she may be right.

My aim is simple enough. That's what worries me. It's a matter of turning the facts into questions. Why have there always been more women than men diagnosed as mentally ill? And if they are all mad, what's driving them mad? In Mabel's case I'm fairly sure the answer to that question is that being incarcerated by her mother drove her mad. I'm pretty sure she wasn't mad in 1927. Nevertheless, as I tap away on my computer I know that this is a very unfashionable topic. Especially in the nineties. Now we've got Prozac. And Irony. And Wonderbras. Because we've done feminism. It liberated us and it isn't nice to keep harping on about it. Besides, look what it's doing to the boys. They're all muddled up now, poor things. But in the interests of balance I'm going to have to talk to mad men as well. And the other reason I want to do it is because most people don't want me to. And in the end, I know there is no point in continuing to walk those women up and down the corridors, wipe their bottoms, spoon food into their mouths, swab their papery skin and try to talk to them about what's on the telly. Those corridors go nowhere. I riffle back through my notes on Mabel. Through the years she's been described as suffering from dementia praecox, mental deficiency and catatonic schizophrenia. The treatments Mabel's had constitute a history of psychiatry in themselves: laxatives, water therapy, bromium, chloral, insulin, electro convulsive therapy, frontal lobe lobotomy, chlorpromazine, librium, largactil, Perry Como and daytime television.

The phone rings. I get up to answer it and sit down again. I will ignore it. I look at the clock. I have forty-five more minutes. I scribble a note to myself. 'Record a conversation between Lily and her son. Do another search on Octavia's family.' My feeling is that if I can track down who admitted Octavia or write down Lily's fury . . . the door knocker goes. I get up to answer it and sit down again. Then get up again because it may be the washing-machine man.

It's the DHL man and he's in a hurry which is fine by me. I sign and take in the extremely urgent packages of scripts delivered twice weekly from your American agent. Back at the computer I continue writing about Mabel's first days in the asylum when it appears she was talkative and cried a lot. The night nurse writes in a cool, cursive hand in blue-black ink that looks like old blood. Her account of Mabel's first night is chillingly matter of fact. 'Patient increasingly agitated towards evening and cried noisily for her mother for several hours. At 1.30 a.m. patient thoroughly hosed and purged. 3.30 a.m. Patient abusive and violent. Restrained in strait-jacket and left to calm herself. 6 a.m. Patient quiet but refused breakfast. Tied to her chair. Food taken at 9.'

The phone rings. Without thinking I pick it up triggering a sales pitch from Gerry who is ringing to enquire whether I knew that my electricity can now be supplied by the gas board which can enable an average saving of up to £3.58 per month which when you total that for the year is over £40 before VAT and subject to alteration without prior warning. I tell Gerry, as kindly as possible, because it isn't his fault that call centres are the only industry left north of Watford, that I do not want to buy stuff over the phone and I would rather my gas was supplied by the gas board and my electricity was supplied by the electricity company.

The phone rings. It's the builder. He needs to be paid in cash, today. Hundreds and hundreds of pounds. Otherwise he can't pay the plasterer. I look at the towering pile of notes by my side. I look at my watch. I shut down the computer and run upstairs to wheel Ivan back down the road to the school.

3rd December 1996

Today Karl is going to Dean's for lunch which means that I can spend two hours at the hospital where I need to check Mabel's notes so that I can finish off the first section of my research in time for my supervisor meeting in a few days' time. I sprint to the tube after dropping Karl off, rely on the kindness of strangers to keep Ivan's buggy upright as we descend the endlessly long escalator and rattle down the Northern Line with him all the way to Tooting Bec.

I'm indebted to Sid and her singsong on the ward. It was a wild afternoon and caused so much noise that Security arrived armed with hypodermics. But the noise was just raucous singing and an impromptu karaoke which included Alice singing 'The Raggle Taggle Gypsies' and Lily doing 'Three Blind Mice' with several verses added that I'd never heard of before but did sort of explain what the farmer's wife was so angry about. I feel the same sort of excitement about my research as I got after that evening with Leon. I glide down towards the tunnels, chuck my change in the guitar case of the busker at the bottom miming to a Jimi Hendrix tape, past the ads for crappy musicals which suddenly look full of warmth and touching optimism (well maybe we should go to more musicals – I try unsuccessfully to memorise the box office number of *Mamma Mia!*) and wait on the platform reading *Crime, Madness, and Politics in Modern France: The Medical Concept of National Decline* below the gaze of a twenty-foot poster for *Tomb Raider*. It looks like men have given up on human versions of the female form and gone for a cross between Action Man and Barbie. Lara Croft has thighs of steel, an arsenal of weaponry hanging off her waist, blow-up tits and no bottom. It has evidently been decided that the arse must go. Sid's theory is that this is because the female arse reminds men that the object of their desire is a grown woman when actually what they really want is either a child or a man. But then Sid would say that, being the proud possessor of one of the biggest arses on the Victoria Line. And that is saying something.

I look quickly into the ward hoping to catch Winston. The women are having their hair set by the hospital hairdresser. Who invented the blue rinse and why? I wonder. They all look a little alarming with their tight perms on their heads like blue bubble wrap. I have to get the keys to the archive drawer from Lesley so I take a deep breath and walk into the inner sanctum. I'm shocked to discover that there in the middle of the office a small room has been erected with Lesley's name on the door. Sandra really does roll her eyes and mouths something at me at which point the door to the room opens and out walks Lesley.

'Morning, Lesley . . . Ooh. Nice office—'

'It'll have to be quick. I have a Human Resources meeting in ten minutes.' She flicks a look at Ivan, marches past me, taps a computer into life and begins a rapid finger dance across its keyboard. No doubt Lesley has been given her own little office for helping to sell the hospital down the river to the multinational waste-disposal company. No doubt she's got shares in the prestige development of luxury apartments they have plans for once they've tipped all the patients out into the community.

'Could I have the keys to the archive collection? I left you a note to say I'd be in today to . . .' Lesley doesn't answer. I can hear what she's thinking. First she has the temerity to give birth, then she wants to come back – part time mind. Oh and then she asks for leave at all times of the year, causing no end of inconvenience and then she decides nursing's beneath her, she'd rather teach Mental Health Issues at the University of the Angel Islington thank you very much. Then she waltzes back in here bold as you like and starts spying on us all for her research. I ask you. Who on earth does she think she is? She straightens up, smiles, selects a form from a stack of trays by her face and holds it out to me. She's got fantastic frosted peach nails. And I haven't seen that kind of pearly eye shadow since the late seventies. I stare at her in a kind of awe. She gives the tiniest of pouts.

'This will need to be filled in and signed by the registrar before I can release the keys.' I look at the clock and feel the beginnings of panic. If this is a wasted morning I won't be able to get any more done until next Tuesday by which time it will be nearly Christmas and then a whole week will be wiped out.

'OK. Is she in, do you know?'

'She's on holiday until next week.' Lesley exits into her control room and closes the door with a click. I look helplessly at Sandra who is bending down in front of Ivan.

'Come back in ten minutes,' she says. 'The key's in the drawer.'

10th December 1996

Mabel's voice, when it comes, is a surprise . . . I write. *Out of this giant, pale, heavy woman who carries hospital legends of violence around with her comes a high small voice like a little girl . . .*

You ring me. Now we have a cordless phone I wander the house while we speak, moving piles of scripts, collecting VAT receipts and putting clothes away. I'm not sure if I'm doing this for you or for me. It does surprise me that you don't seem to notice. I listen to your worries about the funding for the next film. You are on edge. You have a revolutionary new idea. Not only will this film use real murderers, real prostitutes and real corpses, it will be shot on steadicam with no lights and no makeup. And you won't have to go away too much because you're going to shoot most of it round the Angel.

'Mmm, sounds amazing,' I say, returning to the computer and tapping the keys. *She does not talk to me but addresses her mother most of the time . . .*

'Did you ring the gas people about the electricity?'

'Oh. Forgot. So who's going to be in the film then?' *Occasionally there is another voice which sounds more like the voice you would expect from Mabel . . .*

'I think we've got Carlotta da Sanchez and Sly Humbert.' *It is harsh, cold and suffused with the threat of physical violence . . .*

'Never heard of them.' *This is the voice of her mother . . .*

'Well you should have done, they're asking a fortune.' *Mabel's speech is . . .*

'Did you ring the computer people about the modem?'

'Er, yes. But there were no human beings available. When will you be back?'

From upstairs come the sound of the first thin wails of Ivan waking up. I half stand. Guiltily, desperately, I type a couple more words. . . . *fragmented, circuitous . . .*

'I'll be back tomorrow evening.'

'I've got to go, sweetheart. Ivan's crying. Love you.' . . . *as if she does not expect to be heard.*

I press Save, shove my chair back, grab a towering pile of clean pants and vests and climb the stairs.

Twenty

1st May 1997

THE SITTING-ROOM floor is a sea of wine glasses, bowls of popcorn, outstretched legs and clambering children. Our windows are open to the evening air which carries a chill on it now, but the lengthening days still feel like a gift. Outside the windows, the young leaves on the trees look freshly rinsed. A horse chestnut, its giant candles dancing up and down in the breeze, seems to share the excitement of the evening. The streets are deserted, the traffic has gone. The council has cleared the square of fridges and supermarket trolleys. Anticipation and hope is in the air. It's the General Election and this time it looks as if the Tories are finally going to go.

Karl and Molly squat by the window, pushing popcorn into the barren earth of the window box. Occasionally Karl sends Molly back to collect more supplies which she dutifully does, stopping to peer into Helena's face as she passes. Helena is deep in conversation with Winston's boyfriend, Des. The words 'I think he just needs a little space' and 'I'm thinking of doing a course in landscape gardening' drift up from her lowered head. Des says things like 'you may be right' and 'oh absolutely'. He nods, shakes his head, puts his hand on her arm and refills her glass.

'*He's* gay,' says Winston authoritatively, pointing at a Tory

MP on the television who is kissing his wife. 'And him,' he says again as we cut back to a studio interview.

'Well maybe they've got it sorted,' says Sid, popping another bottle. 'Think how much simpler life would be if we all lived double lives.'

'Sid, you don't really believe that so why say it?' says Angus, poking her bottom with his foot.

'It's true, Sid,' I join in. 'You and Angus are the most married of all of us. Admit it.'

'Watch this space,' she says. 'Chuck us those fags, Angus,' and she settles her bottom on Angus's foot. 'No, you're quite right, Gen. He treats me like a lady and I sit at his feet.' She writhes around a bit, closes her eyes and lights up a Marlboro. 'Luckily, he does have enormous feet.'

The door opens and you appear with a steaming bowl of noodles, the phone held between your shoulder and your ear.

'Course they will, Dad. It's going to be a bloody landslide,' you say, laughing in disbelief at Marion's insistence to the contrary.

'Sorry . . .' begins Helena, looking worriedly over at Sid.

I hope Helena's not going to say anything stupid like, 'Would you mind not smoking when Molly's in the room please, Sid?'

'But would you mind not smoking, Sid, when Molly's in the room?'

'You don't mind, do you, Molly?' shouts Sid. 'That's right, darling, stay by the window. Carbon monoxide is much more refreshing.'

Helena looks at Angus. Angus leans forward and takes Sid's cigarette out of her mouth.

'Ladies don't smoke,' he says, putting it out in the ashtray. 'Wait until they're in bed.'

'But are they ever going to go to bed?' says Sid in a stage whisper, eyes wide in concern. 'You know, I remember when friends would arrive for a soirée with a bottle and a date. Now they turn up with a child, for God's sake. Call me old-fashioned, but—'

'Take no notice of the old witch, Helena,' says Winston. 'No one else does. It's her brush with fame. Thinks she's Maria Callas.'

The door knocker goes and you leave to answer it. Ivan staggers after you, trips and manages to break his fall by kneeling in the puy lentils. I get up to stop him before he gets to the top of the stairs. Angus puts his leg up against the door frame and blocks his way.

'Stay here, Ivan, my man. You don't want to miss this. Look!' He points at Peter Snow on the television who is using his whole body to demonstrate the swing to the Left. Ivan hesitates just long enough for you to reappear with Jakov, a Croatian actor.

'Jakov!' cries Sid. 'You get the prize for being the handsomest boy in the room. Go and sit over there. Helena will tell you all about her clitoris, I mean, clematis.'

Jakov, as well as being handsome, is also that rare thing, an unattached, heterosexual male. He is additionally desirable, of course, because he has known horror and suffering and so probably does crying as well.

Helena makes some small adjustments to her hair, eyebrows, bra and ankles while Jakov is settling himself beside her. It only takes five seconds but when he turns to look at her, a relaxed, beautiful and enigmatic woman smiles up at him.

'Time for bed,' I say to the children. One bangs its head on the window and bursts into tears, another falls backwards against the table and starts to wail and the third gets its whole hand stuck in the video slot and emits a piercing shriek.

'Be good children now!' shouts Sid above the tears. 'And when you wake up in the morning, all the Conservatives will have gone.'

By the time I get back downstairs again, the party has got bigger. To my surprise, Leon is sitting next to Angus. Feeling the heat rise in my face, I look at Sid but she is chatting to Mr and Mrs Ali from next door along with Charlene, one of the other Kunt Tulips. Leon raises his hand and waves hello to me. I step over the legs and go to greet him. A kiss on the cheek. In confusion, I sit by Charlene who is a six-foot, blonde air hostess when she isn't being a Tulip. Charlene is explaining to the Alis why she prefers to play guitar dressed only in her bra and pants. The Alis listen with great concentration, holding a platter of aubergine fritters between them. Simon, the television producer that Helena had an affair with, has also turned up, presumably in the hope of consoling her. But Helena is telling Jakov that she has loads of space in Notting Hill and that she could definitely put him up until he has to start the filming in Rwanda. Consequently, Simon is talking to you about your next project, a romantic comedy about a Slovakian UN Peace Keeper in Kigali. I sit with Angus and Leon, regretting the fact that I dozed off in the children's bed and didn't bother to check my hair or my face before coming down. I look over at you. You look elated and you're chatting animatedly to Simon. I love the look of you. The way you crouch, glass in hand, dark hair falling over your eyes. I look at Leon. He looks scrawny and his skin is much paler than I remember. And I think I just caught him gazing at my chest. It's with a mixture of disappointment and relief that I realise the flying sensation my last encounter with Leon left me with is not happening again.

On the television, the second cabinet minister of the evening stands on a town hall stage and receives a humiliating defeat. We all fall silent, except for Helena, before erupting into wild, jubilant and astonished disbelief.

'Unbelievable!'

'Oh my God!'

'. . . and there's a little bathroom right next door to the guest bedroom . . .'

'Completely unbelievable!'

'Gen, your shirt's undone.'

'Oops. Thank you, Angus. Ivan still can't get to sleep without a quick . . .'

'Shush! Shush! They're showing it again!'

'Turn it up!'

'Watch his face! Watch his face!'

'Serves them right!'

'That'll teach them!'

'Not again. Oh God, a close-up this time.'

'Now this is what I call television.'

'You're not kidding,' says Simon. 'Voting, public humiliation . . . I'm getting a great idea for a whole new kind of TV show . . .'

6th September 1997

Helena and I are sitting on the edge of the sofa weeping companionably. The slow progress of the cortège, the shots of stricken spectators and the sad, sombre stillness of London is utterly compelling. I check the back yard where Karl is still standing dressed up as his favourite film character, Dorothy from *The Wizard of Oz*. Molly has been ordered to stand on an upturned bucket with her arms outstretched. I think she's a signpost.

You ring.

'Hello?'

'Hi. It's me.'

'Oh, hi. Helena's round with Molly.'

'Is she . . . you know . . . OK?'

I look at Helena whose nose has turned red. That's probably the wine.

'Oh God. Look at her poor boys. And that freaky bloody family.' Helena points the remote like a weapon at the television and turns up the volume. The wheels of the gun carriage are the only sound in the surreal silence apart from the occasional wail that rises from the crowd. Even the paternal tones of the BBC are silenced. Perhaps Sir Thingummy is lost for words. 'What have they put her on that bloody thing for?' blurts out Helena.

'You're not watching the funeral, are you?' you ask.

'What, Princess Diana's?' I ask incredulously. 'Course not.' Helena turns down the volume. I scan the video shelves. 'We're watching *Dumbo*. Helena always cries at the bit where they lock the mother up.' I can't possibly rally the thinly scattered arguments which explain our fascination with this woman's death. And anyway, we're Republicans, for God's sake, aren't we?

'How's it going?'

'Badly. We're way behind. We had to do about fifteen takes of the massacre scene.'

'You know why she died, don't you?' says Helena to the television, blowing her nose noisily. 'She died because she wouldn't keep quiet and let her husband get on with shagging who he wanted to shag. Her trouble was she was a modern woman trapped in a Victorian world where men still treat their family like a third-world colony.' I glance at Helena. She is very red and blotchy. I fear she is over-identifying with Princess Diana.

'Look,' you say, losing interest in this conversation which is more disjointed than usual, 'I think my plane gets in around ten on Thursday. Is that too late for you to meet me?' The camera pans the crowd of grief-stricken women throwing flowers at the passing carriage. It's a strange, eerie sound. Then the wailing begins again. 'Are you sure you're not watching the funeral?'

'You know why they're crying, don't you?' Helena asks the television. I hold my hand over the receiver, watching the screen intently. 'They're crying for the death of hope . . . hope for a bit of democracy between men and women.' Blimey. Helena seems to have had the reverse of a lobotomy since David shacked up with the twenty year old.

'OK we can be there. Ivan only goes to sleep in the car

anyway, if you remember. It'll make a nice change to go down the M4 rather than the A1.'

'Mummeeeeee!!!'

'I've got to go, Mark.'

'Come and wipe my bottom!'

'Good luck tomorrow.' I put the phone down hurriedly. 'Tell me what happens,' I say, looking longingly at the screen before running up the stairs two at a time.

When I get back down, Helena is untransfixed all of a sudden. I look at the screen. Celebrities are shuffling into Westminster Abbey. Helena has filled up her glass again.

'Genevieve. Is it my imagination or do boys get their mothers to wipe their bottoms more than girls do?' I hate it when Helena starts on at me about this. She hasn't got sons so she doesn't understand. 'I mean, surely there can be no physical reason why at the age of six he still has to have you wipe his bottom.' It's true. Molly wipes her own bottom. Helena doesn't do it for her and Molly is four. But boys get their mothers to do it for, well, I suppose I have no idea how long for. And it is true that I got the job of scrubbing the shit off the lavatory bowl for the whole family. And it's not a job I remember applying for.

'And then they get to rule the world.' Helena is shaking her head in disbelief. 'I think there must be some connection. And if there is, we should be told.' She swallows another mouthful of wine and turns up the volume again.

'Jesus, that's not the Queen Mother at the piano, is it?' I ask, peering at the television.

'No you moron, that's Elton John.'

Twenty-One

12th March 1998

FROM UP here on our roof terrace the whole of the Angel is spread out below. Beyond it, London trembles in its sulphurous shimmer. I'm sitting on the small mound of hardened cement that the builders have left in the hole where they ran out of tiles. David is here because he knows someone who might help finance your next film. He's brought the twenty year old with him. Boo is charming, beautiful and friendly. An early version of Helena. In one hand she holds a packet of Marlboro Lights and in the other hand a self-help book which ought to be called *How To Have It All Your Own Way All Of The Time And Not Look Like You're Snatching*. I'm a bit shocked that David's brought her actually and feel I should say something but of course I don't. I'm struggling to maintain what I hope is a frosty welcome. You and David behave completely normally. As if nothing has happened. Helena airbrushed out of his life.

I watch the three of you turning in a small circle, your feet leaving little prints in the cement dust as you point out the landmarks to them.

'St Paul's, the Post Office tower, Canary Wharf and that's the beginning of the Millennium Dome,' you shout above the roar of the City Road.

'When will it be finished?' squeaks Boo, lurching for a foothold in the boy zone of your conversation.

'By December thirty-first 1999 they hope,' you explain kindly.

'Unless they have your builders. In which case they're shafted.' David barks out one of his laughs. 'You're rather blighted by that Colditz edifice,' he bellows, pointing with his champagne glass towards the sixties tower block fifty yards away. 'Can't you have it demolished or something, Mark?' More barking.

'Yeah, but if you face *this* way, and once the plants have grown up the trellising,' you make expansive, upward gestures with your hands, 'it'll be really private in here.'

'You know what?' You both lean towards Boo, eager to catch the wisps of her words. 'The orange haze? Hanging over the centre there? Actually looks kind of beautiful? Sort of surreal?' David puts his arm round her. Thank God Sid isn't here. Boo would be sausage meat.

'Well, Mark,' yells David, 'it's a crazy project this roof terrace but I have to hand it to you, you certainly make things happen. I admire your determination and sheer lunatic vision.'

A police helicopter circles overhead drowning out the sound of the traffic. You all look up, laughter and voices snatched away by the acker-ack rhythm of rotor and blades. It's like a war zone up here.

'Mark, I'm going down,' I shout. 'I've got to fetch the boys.' You don't hear me. You're laughing enthusiastically at David. You're happy. You've made it. Finally, your last film was well received. And suddenly there's a lot of money sloshing around. Since *Icarus*, you are officially 'hot'. *Arena* said so. Or *The Face* or one of those and the other evening the phone rang and it was bloody Nicole Kidman, for God's sake.

I make my way carefully down the ladder to the landing, and on down several more flights to the basement. It's a long way. These houses were designed with servants in mind. A roof terrace was not part of the plan. In the kitchen I open the dishwasher and start to unload it. David is right. Not about Helena obviously, or Boo, but about you. That you see the way that things could be and you make them happen. Against all odds. Sid may sneer. It is, I sometimes think, her only expression. Other than the snarl. I gouge the gunge out from the thing at the bottom of the machine. I feel like I'm losing Sid. Or rather I feel like I ought to lose her. She's making me self-conscious. The other day she started doing the voice-over to an imaginary Sunday supplement profile of the 'Precociously Prolific Mark Morrison. Here's Mark and his lovely wife relaxing with friends and family round the pool in Tuscany . . . the premiere of Mark Morrison's latest film was held amid tight security due to death threats from Animal Rights activists . . . the couple's adorable children love to visit Daddy on set and here they are taking cover from enemy fire in Angola . . .'

'Sid, envy is not a good look,' I told her, laughing despite myself because she reminds me of a part of me that is possibly still packed up in one of those boxes we never opened when we moved to the Angel. 'It doesn't really go with your non-matching eyes and witchy hair,' I add.

But Sid's off. She knows I'm enjoying it. '"It was at about this time that imperceptibly things began to change for Mark and Genevieve." There will be a shot of Mark, eye clamped to his viewfinder, hanging from a harness in a speedboat, while an actress simulates sex with a dolphin. "Increasingly, Mark began to seek out the bizarre, the dangerous and the downright odd." There will be a shot of you seated in front of a catatonic Mabel followed by a close-up of the screen of your laptop as you type, *With a knick knack paddy whack give a dog a bone* . . . "Genevieve's groundbreaking research, titled *Why Was Mary So Contrary?* was getting nowhere."'

'So who's in your next film then, Mark?' I straighten up from the dishwasher to find you and David standing in the kitchen. 'According to the piece I read on Sunday, "the world is Mark Morrison's oyster." Apparently you can have anyone you want.' Cue another bark. 'I heard it might be that girl, you know, was in that film with, oh shit, what was it called? Blonde. Legs up to her neck . . . Oh Genevieve, there you are. Boo wanted to know what those plants are out in the back.'

Boo is standing alone in the yard, her face in the remains of a waxy red camellia bloom with brown edges.

'It's so strange?' she says as I go out to her. 'It's got no scent?'

'I know, they're weird flowers. What's your book?' I ask, smiling my Wicked Stepmother smile.

'Oh this? Just some junk I picked up at the airport? You know, I wanted to say how sorry I feel about the way things worked out with Helena? And, like, I know it's been a really difficult time for Molly . . . but I feel like I kind of connect with her? Thing is, I know you were Helena's friend and everything but I hope that . . .' Boo is blinking back tears. With a little shake of her shoulders she begins to cry, very quietly and only screwing up her face a little bit.

'Oh don't worry. It's fine. Really.' I put my arm round her and give her a hug. 'No honestly. You know. David is obviously really happy with you . . .'

How could I? Why did those words come out of my mouth? I wait for a sensation of guilt and betrayal to make itself known to me. Nothing happens. I leave go of Boo and wander over to a seat. She's telling me what a great couple me and you are. And how she wishes that . . . well, that she wants some of that too.

High overhead, a plane arcs its way silently across the sky, trailing a fine scar in the blue. Boo probably thinks our lives have always been cruising comfortably. Just like David's. I look at her and consider telling her that is not the case. But Boo is blinking thoughtfully and thinking up a question to ask her new friend and it's you I should be talking to, telling you that the captions are not enough. A Happy Family. A Lovely Couple. Two Beautiful Boys. It feels greedy. Like we're asking for it. We should be vigilant. Listen carefully for any clunks and knocks as unidentifiable things begin to loosen and drop from the undercarriage of the plane.

28th May 1998

No expense has been spared. As we climb out of the limo the air is heavy with jasmine. Bowers of white roses deck the walls and twine round the pillars of the entrance. The path is strewn with white petals and lit with glass lanterns. You hold my hand tight and kiss me. Your bow tie is charmingly skew-whiff and the hair on one side of your head still flattened from where you fell asleep on it. I press my face to your neck and inhale, feeling a rush of excitement for you; for all this.

'Mark, do I look OK? Are you sure I don't look like Marge Simpson?'

'Well, when I said try getting rid of the grey, I meant go back to black.'

'But it said Raven on the packet.'

'You look fine. Relax.'

'Not too blue then?'

'You don't look like Boo at all,' you laugh.

A sudden wind lifts the fairy lights from the top of the walls and the villa door is opened by invisible hands. Once inside, the exalted roar of success and good fortune fills the air. Our coats are taken. Someone calls your name and you are swallowed up in a feeding frenzy of wheelers, dealers and players.

I'm not sure where to put myself and feel even more like Marge Simpson than I did in the car. I curse my genes for making so much of me. Less is most definitely more round here if you happen to be female. Uniformed staff drift about with trays of shimmering champagne flutes and tiny, but perfectly formed things to eat. They seem to be under strict instructions to get us all as drunk as possible. I stand by a pillar and survey the crowd.

LaLa, the star of your film, is leaning over a table of canapés trying to light her cigarette from a guttering candle. To each side of her stands a man in a dinner jacket holding out a cigarette lighter. She says oh fucking shit a lot as the candle threatens to send her head up in flames. Seeing me, she switches on a headlight smile and comes tripping towards me, clasping her neck. I grin with gratitude and relief and attempt a hug with a glass in one hand and something cream-cheesy with antennae on it in the other.

'Hi!' It's a little like embracing a ghost and there's the pause for me to compliment her on her performance but I am very pleased to see her. I look over her shoulder at a giant photograph of her face, one of a series that line the walls. In the stills she does look extraordinarily beautiful. In real life there's the slight shock of ordinary flaws. That and the shortness. I bend down to her and shout in her ear.

'I thought you were great in the film by the way.'

'Really?'

'Yes. Really really great.'

'Oh thank you.'

'No really.' Well she was good actually. Especially the naked rock-climbing scene. 'Fantastic.'

'Did you really think so?'

'Yes. Amazing . . .' Er, that's it LaLa, your turn.

'I really loved doing it, you know?' she says earnestly. I've noticed that ordinary mortals tend to bluster and turn a deaf ear to compliments but actors absorb every word with childlike seriousness as if it's their life-blood. 'And how are the children?' she asks with a brief expression of concerned sympathy. 'And you? How are you? You look . . . amazing. Hey!' she lifts her chin and rolls her necklace between her thumb and finger. 'Do you like my diamonds? Like these are so sleazy? They come with the dress and, like, I have to wear them for the photos? They're worth twenty thousand quid!' She claps her hand over her mouth, wide eyed with mock horror. 'Fuck! Like, I'm not supposed to tell anyone that? Hey,' she beckons me closer and jabs her thumb over her shoulder towards a man staring at her, 'gorgeous, isn't he? That's François, my bodyguard? Gets to sit next to me and everything? In case I do a runner with the rocks?'

'LaLa!' says an American, doing an elaborate double take and coming forward to kiss her on both cheeks. 'You were just stunning . . . honestly . . . I was a blubbering wreck by the end . . . amazing . . .'

'Oh *thank you*. It was such an incredible part? Just totally blew me away?'

I wander off trying not to stand too near anyone with a designer frock or expensive sandals which means I have to stand on my own or next to a man. Each time a tray passes I knock back another glass of champagne and toss a canapé into my mouth. These events are a bit different to the annual hospital knees-up at the Pizza Express in Tooting Bec and they often make me a little reckless in terms of food and drink consumption. I can't quite believe it's all free. When I said this to Sid she scowled at me like I was an idiot and said, 'Course it's not free, Genevieve. You'll pay. Just wait and see,' which pissed me off a bit actually because I know what she was implying. I think she's just a little jealous. I mean Angus is still mainly making false legs and the Kunt Tulips, well, they have a small cult gay following and they were on *Later with Jools Holland* once but nothing major. I probably shouldn't have told her how much my dress cost. Although I realise I might as well not have bothered in fact because everyone here is wearing seriously expensive dresses. Several thousand pounds' worth of dress. But the actresses haven't had to pay for them. They've been lent them for the night. That doesn't make sense really given how much they get paid for the film.

'How is it that when the seriously rich get seriously rich

they suddenly get given everything free?' I ask someone I vaguely recognise who is looking at me trying to work out where he's seen me before and whether I'm a useful person to talk to.

'Fucking outrageous, isn't it?' he shouts, chucking a couple of quails' eggs into his mouth. His eyes return to scanning the room.

'Mmm! Oh my God! These are bloody fantastic!' I momentarily come into focus and he says, 'Oh! I know you! You're Mark Morrison's wife. I met you before, didn't I? What is it you do again?'

'I work in mental health,' I say, looking hopelessly round for an escape.

'Really?' He blinks rapidly then leans towards me conspiratorially. 'You do know you are married to a genius, don't you?'

'Am I?' I ask, genuinely interested to hear more. It's unnerving talking to someone whose gaze roams over my shoulder and up to the top of my hair but never meets my eyes.

'Not only is he a genius . . .' There's a pause while a whole baby squid is popped in followed by some whelks on a spoon of caviar. 'Oh my God. Delicious. Not only is he a genius . . .' He lurches suddenly to the right. 'What the fuck? Christ did you feel that? Earthquake or something! Hey. No, but Mark, I mean, he's so grounded, you know? He is a genuinely nice guy. A really nice guy. You can't say that about many people in this business. Myself included. Just ask my wife! Oh shit. That's probably her now. Excuse me.' He claps his hand over his crotch, fumbling at it madly. He pulls a bulky mobile phone from his pocket. 'Gus! Yeah! Good to hear you! I'm at Mark Morrison's pre-screening thing! You got invites to the Scorsese thing? You bet! Sure! See you there!'

I can see you out on the terrace, surrounded by lilac blooms, lined up for a photo opportunity. You have one arm round LaLa and one round the producer. The camera flashes and you all laugh and gulp your drinks. You look bedazzled and deliriously happy. There's a shout from one of the photographers and you all line up again. LaLa dips about grabbing herself and gasping quite a lot. She tosses her hair back out of her face like a naughty pony and does pastiche pouts for the camera. She speaks in funny accents and makes everyone laugh. She's very good.

'Mad as a snake,' mutters Jack, your assistant cameraman. He puts down his drink and envelops me in a giant embrace. 'And talking of mad,' he says, giving my hair a funny look, 'how's work?'

'Ooh they've let me out. I'm being cared for in the community – doing university research, paid for by the government's mental health strategy.' I beam up at him.

'What are you trying to find out?' LaLa is dragging her bodyguard in from the terrace and trying to do something with her breasts and the ice bucket.

'I'm not really sure yet. It may be nothing but I *think* I'm trying to find out why so many women have been locked up for going mad . . .' We watch as LaLa pulls the front of her dress forward so he can retrieve diamonds or ice from her bra. I can see him checking her out, struggling with a smile, wondering whether he's in with a chance or not.

'. . . and why some are paid a fortune,' says Jack.

Outside the villa there's a fleet of cars waiting. A police escort sweep us all down the hill towards La Croisette. You and I sit in the back giggling at the absurdity of it.

'Last time I was in a police escort was when we had to fetch Mabel. She was running naked round The Hollywood Bowl in Streatham.' Onlookers wave at us. 'Do you think they've mistaken you for some head of state, Mark?'

'I was just speaking to the guy from Universal.' Your eyes are shining with excitement and champagne. 'Looks like he's going to give us the money to do the remake of *Snow Queen*.'

'Really?' My insides lurch. 'When? Where?'

'The autumn. Lapland and New York.' You read my face. 'It'll pay a lot of money.'

'Is this the one where Kay is a Hollywood agent and the Snow Queen's a film star?'

'Yeah. And Dilly Nettles says she really wants to be in it.'

'That's great.' I stare out at the giant billboards of American blockbusters and crowds of people behind the crash barriers.

'She'll have to play the grandmother though. She's a bit past it for the Snow Queen now.'

'Past it? How old is she?'

'She must be nearly thirty by now, twenty-eight at least. She's had a kid. Looks a bit knackered.'

I squint down the front of my dress and wish I hadn't gobbled up all those little things with tails on.

'But it'll be good if we do it because it'll mean we can afford to buy a place in the country.' The car pulls up at the entrance to the Palais.

'Mark, there's a red carpet, for God's sake.' Photographers line the crash barriers. 'And is that a bit of lobster on your trousers?'

The car door is opened by yet another flunkey.

'Where do they get these people from? Don't they have proper jobs, for God's sake?'

We climb out of the car and you whisper in my ear, 'Hold my hand and don't let go.'

Club class is dotted with the odd celebrity slumped beneath a large coat. Occasionally a pale, trembling hand emerges to take a cup of coffee. You're reading *Frank Capra: the Catastrophe of Success* and I'm reading *Easy Riders, Raging Bulls*. The anxiety and sense of doom that it is filling me with is managing to utterly erase my fear of flying. We've taken off, plummeted a couple of thousand feet, buffeted our way through dense cloud and are now swaying wildly in some kind of French airspace vortex. But I hardly notice.

'Is that good?' you ask.

'It's horrific.'

'What do you mean?'

'Well according to this, being a great movie director involves taking lots of drugs, shagging teenagers and leaving your wife and children. Repeatedly. It's a tale of utter carnage.'

You giggle. 'Great! Sounds like fun.'

Twenty-Two

19th August 1998

'OH FOR God's sake—' says Sid, slapping her hand down on the paper and lighting up a Silk Cut. 'Omagh's been wiped off the front pages by President Clinton's blow job.' Sid is supposed to be reading the first draft of my thesis which is currently called *Voices from the Asylum* but she keeps reading the newspaper instead. I can't blame her. The news these days is kind of distracting. Sort of Shakespearean. So much more interesting than the television or the cinema. Not to mention real life. A close-up of Monica's face which can now only denote one thing, looks up at us. Clinton's grizzled, fifty-something 'What *Me*?' face sits alongside. Yesterday's horror is history.

Sid is momentarily lost for words while she devours the column inches. I take this opportunity to push my pile of papers towards her. I turn and fiddle with Sid's collection of china tulips and then examine one of Angus's wooden limbs. Somehow what I've managed to put together about the psychopathology of grief in mothers is not quite as interesting as the Hans Christian Andersen version. And also, my main characters, Octavia, Alice, Lily, Mabel . . . well they're just not that good at dialogue. Sid's going to be disappointed.

The room is silent apart from the prairie gallop of my heart.

Sid leafs through the papers and smokes. She really should think about stopping. We're not getting any younger. After a while she looks up at me and leans back in her chair.

'What does Mark think about it?'

'He hasn't read it.' She thinks it's crap.

'Why the bloody hell not?'

I don't have an answer for this.

'Oh hello, Angus,' I say registering how terrible he looks. Sid hands him my work.

'Look what Genevieve's done. It's not bad. Not finished mind, but not at all bad. And you said she'd never manage it.' Angus throws Sid a cold look, gives me a kiss and sits down at the table. He starts to read.

'My great fear is,' I begin, anxious to fill the uncomfortable pause, 'that after listening to their stories I may be left with the embarrassing conclusion that the reason so many more women are locked up in mental hospitals is because female insanity *is* linked to puberty, pregnancy, childbirth and the menopause.'

'In which case you're fucked,' says Sid, getting up to graze in the fridge. 'I mean think of the hoo-ha, Genevieve, if the world really knew how mad we go just before a period.' She stands behind Angus and mimes the *Psycho* shower moment.

'So it's all the fault of the menses after all,' says Angus, which is possibly the first time I have heard him make a joke. I laugh. Sid doesn't.

'It would probably be enough to have us all locked up on a monthly basis,' I say.

'No need for that now we've got Prozac,' says Sid, chucking Angus a fag and lighting another for herself. 'Do men go mad, Angus, or does a regular dose of footie and the occasional war keep the demons at bay?'

'I'm sure men do have similar crises in their lives,' says Angus, turning his back on Sid, 'perhaps similar reactions, but they are not locked up in mental hospitals as much and most don't find their way to the doctor's either. They commit suicide or do other things.'

'Like shelling Iraq, getting caught having blow jobs,' says Sid, 'or disappearing off the face of the earth like your dad.' I shoot Sid a look.

'Talking of shells,' says Angus, 'you know that the term "hysteria" fell out of favour during the first world war when soldiers started displaying exactly the same symptoms? They couldn't bring themselves to say that soldiers were hysterical so they called it "shell shock", despite the fact a lot of the soldiers had been nowhere near a shell. Much more manly.'

'If you for one moment try to suggest that childbirth is analogous to fighting in the trenches, Genevieve, you will render yourself completely unemployable for ever more,' says Sid.

Angus reads aloud from my work.

'*Margery Kempe's autobiography is an account of a medieval woman experiencing post-partum psychosis. She says she had a difficult pregnancy, a difficult birth, was convinced she was going to die and "went out of her mind"*. Are those the actual words she used? That's incredible.'

'I know. She writes about childbirth as a sort of death of self. As if post-natal depression or whatever it was she was going through is a kind of bereavement.' Sid rolls her eyes and hangs her tongue out of her mouth. 'Maybe the thing to do, is to draw no conclusions,' I say hopefully, turning my back on Sid. 'Let the analogies speak for themselves. What the experiences have in common for men and women are fear, proximity to death, loss of identity, violence, alienation and—'

'The impossibility of being understood,' says Angus, returning to my work again. I watch his hand turn a page.

I lift my coffee to my lips and it happens again. It keeps happening. His fingertip tracing a line downwards from my neck. Face burning, I look away.

'Your coffee, Gen,' he says, handing me a tissue. 'It's all down your front.'

30th September 1998

On the tube to the theatre I read in the newspaper about a theory that explains why it always rains at the weekend. The reason, apparently, is because of the volume of car exhaust produced by commuters in America during the week. The pollution warms the air which rises and spends the week blowing its way across the Atlantic in pollution particle clouds which arrive as rain about Friday teatime in the UK. So maybe the answer really is blowing in the wind.

I'm thinking of you as I wait in the hiss and swash of London traffic, longing to see you. Although leaving Karl is always fraught. For him it really seems as though this could be the last time he sees me and I wonder at my heartless capacity to walk away. But while my heart is torn by his voice beseeching me not to leave, it yearns for you too. I don't get enough of you. Perhaps the endless leavings and reunions are what hold you and me together.

You're late and I'm afraid you'll miss the beginning of the play. I find a phone box inside and dial your office. His plane's not landed yet, they tell me. There's a one-hour delay for all flights from New York. You're still up there then. Somewhere. I wait outside among the throng of meetings and greetings around me. Sparks of desire, eddies of uncertainty, the occasional snarl. I wait till the last minute because often, many times, you just make it just in time. At the sound of the final bell I enter the darkened auditorium, find my way to our seats and sit down next to your empty one.

To my relief this Shakespeare production has dispensed with period costume and complicated sets. I wish you were here to see it with me. There are things I want to tell you that I cannot find the words for. Can't find the quiet space to speak them in. Thoughts that are barely formed until they're spoken. The play begins with a shipwreck, the cries of the dying, the inky chaos of disaster and imminent death. I pray your plane stays safe in the sky. I suffer a kind of vertigo on your behalf in my attempt to imagine how high above the earth you are at this moment. Acted out before me is the story of lost twins. I keep checking the Emergency Exit sign with the green man running. You do not come. On stage, Viola tells Olivia how she would woo a woman. Not with actions but with words. 'I would call upon my soul within the house.' It's true that the phone doesn't quite get through to the soul. I'd like to disconnect it. It makes us lazy. 'Write loyal cantons of contemned love and sing them loud even in the dead of night.' I still keep the one letter you ever wrote to me. It's in my bag actually. I know it off by heart. It says, 'Car parked round corner Love M X.'

The man next to me begins to snore quietly. His wife stares straight ahead, glasses flashing. In the silent space that follows Viola's speech the faint wail of a London siren reaches the audience. For some reason my eyes are filled with tears. The man on my left is reaching the staccato piggy stage. His wife gives him a nudge and he returns to consciousness with a snort of surprise, staring in embarrassed bewilderment at the erotically charged scene between the two women on stage in front of him.

You miss the play but afterwards I see your boy's face in the doorway, wet from the rain, anxiously searching the crowd for me. Sometimes I think you must look like my brother. Sid says we all seek out partners who resemble our siblings – it's a gene thing. 'Do I stand there?' said Sebastian, when he saw his long lost twin. I'll never know but you feel like my other half and I cannot imagine you not being in my life. We reach each other through the crowd. You are flustered and apologetic as we kiss. You smell of aircraft cabin which I suppose is several hours of two hundred and twenty other people's exhalations. In your hand is a battered copy of *American Psycho*.

'How was the play?' you ask as we pound the pavement at high speed searching for a bar that isn't closing.

'It was really good . . .' I struggle with the words. As always. '. . . it was about . . .' How can I tell you? I look at the programme.

'I can't stand all that cross dressing—',

'No but it's about the accident of love, twins, madness and—' A taxi roars past soaking both of us. 'Rain—'

'And the box tree stuff. Sir Toby Belch. Just not funny.'

'Oh no. It's not. It's tragic. Unrequited love, the transience of youth—' You disappear inside a bar which is closing. I follow you. You turn round impatiently and walk out again.

'This bloody country. Come on, let's try round the corner—' I look at my watch and think we ought to get home. The babysitter will be wondering. Karl and Ivan might be waking. 'In New York you can get a drink and food any time of the day or night.'

I follow you. My feet hurt. It hasn't stopped raining for days.

10th October 1998

The hotel is vast and absurdly luxurious – like all the places we stay in these days. The view, we tell ourselves repeatedly, is fantastic. And the bathroom's incredible. And the bed's enormous. But the hotel is empty. We are a little at a loss. Each day we play cards with the children by the giant outdoor pool which is too cold to swim in. Or we take them for bike rides round the hotel's extensive grounds. Nobody else is here. Today I am going riding.

You all walk me down to the corral. I am nervous because although I used to be able to do this riding thing as a girl, even then it was a battle to overcome my fear of the physical danger the animal presented to me. Each Saturday, I would cycle, jeans tucked into wellington boots, legs turning on and on, stomach churning.

'There was this programme on telly called *White Horses*,' I tell the children. 'I used to sing the theme tune on my way to the riding stables when I was little. I'd have butterflies all the way there.' I sing what I can remember of the song.

'That's a nice song, Mummy.'

'Did you watch it, Mark? How does it go?'

'Karl, stay on this side of the road!' you shout.

'What's it about, Mummy?'

'Have you got butterflies now, Mummy?'

'Yes I have, strangely enough.'

'I can't see them.'

'Butterflies, Ivan, is what we call a figure of speech. Not real. A comparison,' you explain.

'It's funny really,' I say to you. 'But now I've got children—'

'Don't touch the dog. Don't touch him. Hold my hand, Karl. Genevieve, hold Ivan's hand. Just keep walking. That's it. Don't look at him. Genevieve, for God's sake, don't let Ivan touch him.'

'Everything I do is with the added fear of what will happen to my motherless children,' I continue as we circumnavigate a completely harmless-looking dog that has passed out in the heat. 'Plus, I think I have just become – afraid.'

'Mind the horse poo!' you shout at Karl who is trying to jump on flies.

'I can't work out what of, though. It's like a sort of vertigo. Like a fear of flying. Do you ever get that? It seems to be getting worse.'

'What's worse, Mummy?'

'Nothing, darling. I was talking to Daddy.'

'Oh please tell me.'

'Mummy doesn't like heights. Now remember, boys, *never* walk round the back of a horse.'

When we get to the stables, the powerful equine smell hits us like a wall in the afternoon heat. The corral looks deserted and the oak and olive forest on the mountain looks sort of wild and I'm not sure I either want to or can ride any more. Those horses look seriously prancy. White Spanish dancing horses. Their veins stand out round their eyes and on their necks. Their ears are back and they don't look pleased to see me. I can see their hearts beating. They stamp their feet and flick their tails in the cool dark of their stalls. Out in the trembling glare behind us, cicadas stutter their castanet chorus. I feel a bit sick. We walk into what looks like the office. A curtain across an inner door is pulled to one side and a tall man stands there. He smells of leather and tobacco. He ignores me and the children and looks at you questioningly. You talk to him in broken Spanish.

'Don't tell him I'm really good, Mark.' There's a framed photo of the man before us astride a rearing, ballet-dancing stallion. In the picture he's dressed as a matador or a general and now he looks at my feet and says something, pointing to a cabinet of gleaming leather riding boots. Then he slaps a pair of leather gloves on the table and a long whip.

'*Chapeau*?' I ask hopefully, patting my head. 'Mark, for God's sake, what's Spanish for hat?'

'Mummy needs a hat, Daddy,' says Karl firmly. You say the Spanish for hat. General Franco looks at you, purses his lips and shakes his head. Presumably the hat will spoil the effect although in the picture of him as rampant conquistador I notice he has what looks like a baking tin on his head.

I sit and struggle to get the boots on, the smell of horse sweat making me feel about eight years old.

'You look nice, Mummy,' says Karl squatting down and studying me.

'Nice, Mummy,' says Ivan, trying to climb onto my lap.

We all troop out of the dark office and follow the man to

one of the stalls. It is like being led to the guillotine. And in fact there is a large block by the rails of the yard. In the gloom of the stall stands a pale, quivering horse with a rolling sideways eye. Like a slap in the face, a waft of ammonia hits us as we hold the children up and lean over the half door.

'Earrr! What's that terrible smell?' squawks Karl.

'Pooohh! What's that smell, Mummy?' asks Ivan.

I follow Don Juan to the block. With a sickening feeling I notice the bridle is equipped with complex emergency braking systems of a kind I have no idea how to use. I climb onto the block and clamber into the saddle. As soon as I'm in the saddle the horse goes up one end and down the other and I feel a mouth of steel on the end of the reins.

'Mark!' I cry. But you are bending down instructing the children in Spanish vocabulary.

'What's the horse's name?' asks Karl. You ask the man. Funny how much better you are at speaking Spanish and French than at speaking English, I think unkindly. The reply to your question makes you fall about with laughter.

'What?'

'What, Daddy?'

'Why are you laughing, Daddy?'

'I think she's called Psycho.' You are spluttering with laughter. 'And he says keep to the path. It's signposted!' you shout after me as I disappear round the bend.

Psycho carries me off at a jangling zippy trot down a path towards the woods. I turn to take a last tearful look at my motherless children. They're waving at me while you wheel around, clapping one hand to the side of your head talking loudly to yourself. Your mobile means we need never be away from your work. It comes with us on holiday. I expect they'll start making them so small one day that you can have one round your neck like a crucifix. Or implanted into your thorax.

I give up trying to make the horse walk and concentrate on Enjoying Myself. This is all Very Beautiful, I tell myself.

Oak forest and olive trees stud the gently rising hillside. There's the occasional stone villa screened behind cypress and lemon and the heat of the sun is softened by the breeze. We follow a track that has a wooden post with a blue splodge pointing somewhere indefinite on it every now and then.

It's about an hour later that I imagine everyone will be missing me and anyway I've had enough of the sight of stunning scenery and sweaty horse neck. It's a while since I've seen one of those blue splodges on a post. That's because I have lost the path and the sun looks as though it will sink below those hills before too long. I seem to have found myself in some damn fairy tale. Wouldn't be surprised if I see a gingerbread house any minute now. Psycho is still champing at the bit and my legs are flecked with froth from her mouth. Dread begins to settle like lead in the pit of my stomach. Maybe if I follow the line of trees in the valley that'll lead me back to the hotel. I'm sure there's a river in the grounds somewhere. We descend the hillside and I try to steer her round the outcrops of rock that obscure what faint path there was. At the bottom we find ourselves in a dried riverbed and begin to pick our way along it. I let her go the way she wants. The cicadas have changed key which means it must be around six by now. I wish to God I had a sense of direction in wide open spaces. My inability to read the signs, interpret the map and go the right way is a cause of profound irritation for you. We had our first seriously nasty row a few months ago during a map-reading incident in the country. And I sense that Ivan's tendency to run the wrong way when called drives you crazy too. Must be the mutant gene he's got from me. I wonder what the reason is for it still surviving though. Maybe discovery of unknown places. I'm sure Columbus turned right instead of left when he set sail from Portugal thereby discovering America by mistake. Or was that Marco Polo?

Just then Psycho sits down, which is alarming. Horses don't sit. I snatch myself up out of my reverie to find that her back legs and tail are tangled in barbed wire. Jumping to the ground I lean down and discover the situation is serious. She cannot move and her legs are bleeding, for God's sake. Visions of leaving her to bleed to death in this gully pass through my mind. I have no idea at all how I will get out of this situation. There are a lot of flies.

Bells. I can hear bells. I stumble up out of the riverbed and stand looking around me. And then, over the brow of the hill comes a little sea of sheep, threading their way down towards us, emitting a melancholy bleating and donging, and behind them walks a shepherd. I don't quite believe the story I have got myself into, which seems both unlikely and sentimental but it appears to be happening. I start staggering up the hill towards him, waving my arms, wanting to shout 'Help!' but only managing 'Hola!' My voice sounds alien in this strange landscape. I wouldn't blame him for thinking I'm mad and herding his flock off in the opposite direction but when he sees me, he starts galumphing sideways down the hill and it crosses my mind that the story might end with us getting married.

I show him Psycho who I feel very sorry for and think now might actually be called Psyche. My shepherd is wiry with skin like leather and very little hair on his head. He looks like the mummy in the British Museum. When he sees what has happened he takes his knapsack off his shoulder and produces a penknife. He cuts away at Psycho's tail, releasing the barbed wire, and then hacks away at the wire encasing her legs. Suddenly she is up on all fours and we are free. I thank him profusely and ask the way to the hotel. He gives directions and a few points with his hand. I'm reluctant to leave him but Psycho and I set off, she with a limp and me with a resolve to go to church the very next day.

Don Juan has gone home when we finally reach the ranch. By now it is nearly dusk. I'd like to apologise to someone about her shortened tail and the tears on her legs but no one is about except for the flea-bitten old dog so I take off her gear and put her in an empty stable.

Back at the hotel, I wander into the courtyard, expecting to find my distraught family being comforted by the padrone but there they are, playing cards by the fountain. Ivan and Karl look up and bullet towards me gratifyingly crying out 'Mummy Mummy Mummy', threatening serious head injuries to all three of us. There is one last ray of evening sun which you are sitting in. You look golden. You glug on your beer bottle and smile at me.

'Hi. How was it?'

With a jabbering child attached to each leg I hobble towards you and collapse into a chair.

'I was lost—'

'Mummy, I swam without any wings.'

'Did you?'

'He did. He was very brave. And it was freezing. What was the temperature, Karl, do you remember?'

'It was cold.'

'I got completely lost—'

'It was in centigrade, wasn't it, and centigrade is what . . . ?'

'Mummy, I rode that bike.'

'Did you, Ivan? You clever thing. Yes, and I didn't think I'd get back at all—'

'He did. And at the end I let go so he was riding on his own. Centigrade, centimetre, centipede. It means what . . . ?'

'I fell over, Mummy, look.'

'And the horse had an accident.'

'You weren't riding on your own, Ivan, Daddy was holding on.'

'I was riding on my own!'

'I only held on for a little while and you did ride on your own in the end, didn't you?'

'But fortunately a shepherd rescued me.'

'Mummy, I just spat in your water.'

'Oh. Otherwise—'

Your phone bleats.

'. . . I might never have made it back before dark . . .'

18th November 1998

The evening is careering out of control. Angus is here, which is fine because he adores you and encourages you to talk endlessly about the film you have just made. Which stops you hiding in the kitchen like a shy wife and fills me with a warm kind of pride. It's taken several years but now at last you do speak at dinner parties. Sometimes, indeed, it's rather hard to get a word in edgeways. Like tonight. You thoughtfully gave Angus a job on the last film making a boat and a pair of giant wings out of wax and feathers. Right up his street. And he had a small part playing a ploughman. The film is in the can and tonight we're having a dinner party with them and Helena and David who are Trying To Make A Go Of It. Except Helena hasn't brought him because he's in New York, that great repository of husbands. Luckily we have invited someone called Todd. He works in television and being forty-nine and three-quarters is newly divorced for the second time in ten years.

Helena sloshes more wine into her glass, knocks it flying, and leaps up shouting, 'Oh no! Look at this!' She slaps her soaked breasts with her hands. Todd's eyes keep sliding over her way but mainly he is immersed in his monologue about his job. He tells us he has a rather *sexy* idea for a new version of *Blind Date* where the contestants actually are blind. Helena almost falls off her chair laughing at that one.

Meanwhile Sid has her sights fixed on the cosy techno talk between you and Angus which has slowed to a crawl because by now Angus is completely stoned. The words are coming out at approximately one per minute. Sid has obviously got it in for you. Maybe she's jealous. Maybe she's firing a warning shot across any film career ambitions Angus might have.

'Mark,' she says, exhaling up at the ceiling and balancing

her packet of Lucky Strikes on their end, 'the Line Producer's job. I mean, looking at the schedules on the *Icarus* shoot, I could not believe that it is just one person's job. Are you telling me the Line Producer has to make sure everyone is at the right place at the right time every single day for the entire shoot? Co-ordinate the cars and wardrobe and makeup and equipment and catering and Fire Brigade and everything? And then type it all up every day and make sure everyone gets a copy?'

'Er, not sure what you're getting at exactly but yes. Why?' You offer her an amazing-looking dish of marinated herrings and olives.

'But why would anyone want to do a job like that?' Sid stubs out her cigarette.

'Lots of people want to do it. It's experience. It can lead on to jobs in production.' You get up and pull a bottle of champagne from the fridge.

'Is it always done by women?'

'Not always no but quite often, yes, but . . .'

You try to get the cork out then hand it to me.

'Why's that then?'

'Just always been like that.'

'How often do Line Producers become Producers then?'

'Well not that often. But some do. I mean look at Sally.' Two red spots appear in your cheeks. You're getting rattled and I want to spring to your defence. But I can't help admiring Sid's chutzpah. Especially as your last film just helped pay her mortgage.

'Does it ever lead on to directing though?'

'No, not really.'

'Why aren't there many women directors then?' Sid leans back in her chair and absent-mindedly adjusts her bra, dusting down her enormous cleavage.

'What do you mean? There are some.' You name two.

'Yes, but is there some reason that generally speaking women *don't* get to be directors?'

'Sid, if you're trying to imply that in the film industry there is some kind of conspiracy to keep women out you're talking rubbish. And anyway, how many female Consultants do you know?'

Sid names four. 'All I'm saying is does it ever occur to you that you work in probably the most old-fashioned industry of all of us. It's as if the sexual revolution never happened. Actresses over the hill at thirty-four. I mean look at Sukey Sukovitch in *Sniper*. She was, what, twenty? And her screen lover was fifty-three, for God's sake. What's that all about? Whose reality is that? You should know better, Mark. It's bad for men and it's bad for women. You're perpetuating a poisonous myth. Think if you had daughters.'

'A very nice myth she was, too, as I remember,' snorts Todd, probably shoving his foot up Helena's crotch. 'Drop-dead gorgeous.'

What does Helena see in men who still say things like this?

There's a small pause as Sid turns towards Todd.

'Actually . . .' We look at Angus, praying he'll get a sentence out before Sid dismantles Todd. 'There is a theory . . .' We hold our breaths. Come on, Angus. You can do it. I hear Ivan beginning to cry on the baby monitor. '. . . that the reason . . .' Sid is staring at Angus holding an unlit cigarette to her mouth. '. . . younger women go for older men . . .'

'Apart from the success and money conveniently already established and the fact that they are always going to look better than him, however old they get,' says Sid, moving things along a little. The cries become louder.

'. . . is because they don't have to . . .' I get up slowly from the table, hoping not to distract Angus. '. . . do so much . . . fucking,' he concludes.

There's a pause while we join all the bits together and then Helena bursts out laughing which is mainly what she's been doing all evening.

'Well done, darling,' says Sid, lighting the cigarette. 'We weren't sure you were going to make it but I *think* it was worth the wait. Philanderers are just disguising a decreasing sex drive then. Where do you stand on that theory, Todd?'

But Todd and you are deep in audience ratings talk. Ivan's crying is now unignorable and so I climb the stairs for a welcome nap on his bed.

Twenty-Three

7th March 1999

SINCE WE moved to Six Mile Bottom it hasn't stopped raining and I have become dependent on email for my daily fix of human contact. I've become gene@bottom and I log on several times a day, like a patient eager for medication. Usually there's one from thekunt@tulips and for the few minutes it takes to read Sid's email, I feel sane again. She writes long diatribes about Angus, Monica Lewinsky and the trials and tribulations of being a Kunt Tulip and they make me laugh. You sometimes send very short ones addressed to all three of us and signed 'Daddy'. So life is measured out in the beep beep doy-oing shhhaaaaa of electronic connection, no doubt a completely artificial sound effect to dupe the population into thinking this wizardry by which so many of us now live has some similarity to the safe and familiar systems of days gone by. Like the dial tone. Yeah right, as Sid would say. It's lucky email was invented, in fact, because it came along just as there stopped being anything good on the telly.

Apart from the rain, absolutely nothing happens in Six Mile Bottom. Strangely, I quite miss the thundering traffic, the foul air, the filthy pavements and the heaving swell of suffering humanity. The other possible villages, apart from Six Mile Bottom, which had the requisite prettiness and gigantic properties for sale in which you could invest your suddenly excessive quantities of money, were called Little Snoring and Great Snoring. They're not that good on names in this part of the country. Not a lot to choose between them really, but by the time I'd finished stalling for time and forgetting to ring the estate agents and the bank, the snoring side of things was no longer an option. You'd spotted an absolute bargain. A rural idyll if ever there was one. My future was to be Six Mile Bottom.

When I told Sid she was predictably scathing, said I'd become nothing but a passenger and that no good would come of it. I tried to argue back, I'd even written down the points in favour of moving that you had used to persuade me. I had to write them down because for some reason I could not make them stick in my head. Sid told me to tell you I will die of loneliness in a village in the country where everyone votes Tory and owns a gun. And as she says, guns was one of the reasons you said we should move. Guns, drugs and dangerous dogs. But it's not much different here. Except the guns are twelve bore, the drugs are single malts and the dogs are Jack Russells. I told Sid that actually I held out for a long time against me and the children being evacuated. Which I did. But last summer there was a heat wave and the Angel became a fume-filled furnace. A hell, in fact. And I allowed myself to be persuaded that Karl and Ivan would be happier with a garden and fresh air. It's true that there are songbirds in the garden here instead of the magpies and squirrels which we had in the Angel. And traffic is not the problem it was. Well none at all goes past our house. In fact, we are the traffic now and what I hadn't fully understood about living in the country is quite how much time we would have to spend in a car. But here at the end of our lane, traffic is a rarity. On the odd occasions that a tractor with a trailer full of turnips does rattle past, it's so exciting that all three of us rush to the garden gate to have a look.

It's the rain apparently that is holding up the builders.

Arthur and Brian did come when they said they would and they performed a lot of enthusiastic demolition. Knocked down the end wall, erected scaffolding, removed the window frames, took off half the roof, disconnected the heating, delivered a whole beach of sand and wheeled their cement mixer into the hall. Then it started to pour.

'So, when do you think you'll be able to start again, Arthur?' I ask, handing them their cups of tea. ('Never give a builder a cup of tea, Gen,' said Sid. 'They won't respect you for it. It confuses them. You've got to treat a builder like you'd treat any man. Badly.') Arthur looks at the deluging rain and shakes his head from side to side, pursing his lips.

'You never can tell in these parts can you, Brian?'

'Well, they do say,' begins Brian sagely, '"If it rain the first day of March . . . then your crops you must watch." That's what they say, in't it?'

'That's true, that is,' agrees Arthur, nodding.

'So you'll be coming back, what, end of the week maybe?'

There's a pause and then Brian says, 'Well, it don't look too clever at the moment.'

Spoons are stirred in cups and tea is slurped wetly as we stare out at the small lake where the garden used to be.

Sitting here, miles from anywhere, listening to the rain, I look at your phone number and try to work out which country you're in and whether it's night time or day time where you are. The children are finally in bed, the house is still and my mind is too slewed by wine and exhaustion to do any work. I pick up the phone and hold it to my ear. At the sound of the dial tone I ring off. I can't quite face another hotel receptionist or voice mail. And I don't want to have to have another of those conversations where one of us has just been woken from a deep sleep. And also . . . Well, also, I'm not sure that we haven't exhausted the phone call side of our relationship. Maybe I'll write.

Funny really. Here I am living the rural idyll and here you aren't. Gone again. Being a hero somewhere. Boldly going.

And in order to do that you've annexed us, the boys and me. We've been partitioned. The phone rings.

I let it ring until it stops.

21st May 1999

The three of us snuggle together on the sofa, watch the blaze in the grate and listen to the typhoon raging outside. It's true, the real fire is lovely but we do spend nearly all our time in front of it. We're like cave dwellers. Arthur and Brian are back. They decided to start on the kitchen, given the permanently weeping sky, and so this room is our refuge from the cement dust, wet concrete and the unseasonably cold weather. Luckily Karl and Ivan like camping.

A small hand gently points my head down again towards the book on my lap. I look down at the page but I can't focus on the words. I want to go to sleep but should really do a few hours' work before bed. Angus, rather shockingly for him, said he's decided that women *are* mad and that there's a simple reason for this. They are all under the influence of a very powerful drug. Oestrogen. I can't completely disagree with him there. And it's probably not a good idea to medicate my oestrogen habit with Chardonnay but it's all Six Mile Bottom offers by way of drugs. Obviously I could go to the doctor and get something but I'm not that desperate yet. I read somewhere that Prozac is being prescribed for PMT now. Helena's on it. Not for PMT, just for general unhappiness. She says it's great. Just stops you caring about anything. Oh, libido completely disappears, apparently, but she says that the Prozac stops her worrying too much about that. Says she can't imagine not being on it now. Especially since she's going to move in with Todd. Maybe, if Helena took Todd's Viagra and Todd took her Prozac . . .

'Mummy.' Karl points at the page and I continue reading. '*That night Psyche's new husband came to her, but the palace was so completely dark that she could not see him.*' The phone rings.

It's my mum. We talk in hesitant circles. I try to keep my voice neutral but when she says, 'Are you all right darling?' it wobbles and I say something about builders and research deadlines and she says, 'You sound tired.' The call doesn't last long. Sid's last email implied that my mum and I should go to family therapy. That we've never confronted the grief around the death of my brother. And she said I'm psychologically blocked and addicted to the fantasy of a man who might one day return. So much so that I bloody well went and married one. I sent her one straight back saying that if she's an example of what happens to the psychologically unblocked then I think I know what I would rather be. Come to think of it, I haven't heard from her since then.

I carry on with *Myths and Legends*. '*Still, he was kind and gentle, and his words were loving and sweet.*' Karl's eyes follow the words, absorbing their shape and sound and God knows what else. Was there a day, an hour, a minute when all that sweet stuff between us stopped? '*She soon fell in love with him.*' There's a high-pitched squeal from the garden. Ivan looks up at me in alarm. Another squeal, this time abruptly curtailed. I have a feeling there's some sort of Ted Hughes type rabbit death going on out there. Strangely comforting to know that nature is tearing itself apart. '*He promised that he would give her anything she wanted, but warned her that she must never try to see his face.*' What's it called? A screech owl. Or would that be the noise the rabbit makes? '*She must not ask to know him.*' Is that all men then? I bet that's not Angus or Leon. But then would one really want to know Leon? Probably not. Just dance with him every now and then. '*If ever she should look upon his face, they would have to part, and she would then live in loneliness and misery.*' What exactly is the moral of this story? I'm beginning to lose my patience with this bloody Psyche woman. I can see exactly what's going to happen. And it won't be that she dumps Eros and finds someone who doesn't mind the light being on.

You ring.

'Hi.' Both boys look at me. Your voice is tired and distant. Out of reach.

'Where are you?' It's Daddy, I mouth at them. 'We're just reading our bedtime story.' Karl tenses up in pantomime excitement and stretches his hand out for the phone. He elbows Ivan in the eye who thumps him in the ribs and starts to wail with an intensity out of all proportion to his injury.

'Daddy!' shouts Karl, taking the phone from my hand and turning his back on the wrath of Ivan who has recruited his feet as well as his fists to avenge his hurt. 'Today, at school, we did about the Romans. We're doing everything Roman at the moment.' Ivan makes a grab for the phone. 'AND TOMORROW I'M DRESSING UP AS A CEMETERY!'

A piercing scream and floods of tears from Ivan drowns out the rest of this conversation. I leave Karl to it, get to my feet and haul Ivan off up to bed.

22nd July 1999

I press the bell, prompting a riot of yapping and deep-throated barking from inside the house. I know the Book Club is a mistake but I am Making An Effort. As you suggested. Getting Involved A Bit. The yapping and barking continue but other than that, nothing happens. I crunch my way round to the back of the house and squeeze between the van and the bushes showering myself in raindrops. At the back window two men and a boy stare blankly at me. I wave and point towards the front of the house. Making my way back towards the front door again I wait. For a long time. Taking my mobile from my pocket, I find the number and dial it.

'Hello?'

'Hello. Margaret? It's Genevieve O'Dowd. Is it the right night for the Book Club?'

'Yes. We're all here. Are you lost? Where are you?'

'Outside your front door.'

The door opens and a head and shoulders leans out into the damp air. She has a phone to her ear.

'Come in!'

We smile and wave phones at each other and I step into Margaret's hall.

'Nimrod! Sniffy! Stop that!' she growls, hauling at the collars of a black Labrador with a head like a bear and a Jack Russell that seems to be on springs. I try to keep their muzzles out of my crotch with one hand while undoing my coat with the other.

'Come through.' Margaret hurls the dogs into a room and slams the door. 'I'm so glad you could make it.'

Holding my copy of *Intimacy* like a Bible I follow her down the hall and into her front room. Inside is a thin scattering of women, some of whom I recognise from the school gates.

'Hello,' I say to everyone, exuding smiles and what I hope is a general air of apology for being late, for being new and for recommending a book I haven't read yet. I look around for somewhere to put myself. Up one end of the room a few people are putting slices of quiche and lettuce leaves onto a plate. I wander over. No one looks up.

'Hello,' I say to a woman wearing a mauve pashmina. 'You're Sam's mum, aren't you? I'm Gen, Karl's mum.'

'Oh, hello. Yes I've seen you at the school, haven't I? How's Kurt settling in?'

'Karl. Well, it's still a bit strange for him I think, but he's OK. Have you read the book, by the way?' I wave *Intimacy* at her.

Sam's mum puts a paper napkin to her mouth then holds out a glass to me.

'Cider?'

I nod gratefully thinking that the last time I drank cider was when I was fourteen and ended up being sick into the plate rack. 'We brew it ourselves.' She laughs nervously.

'Mmm. This takes me back! Actually I have a confession to make about the book—'

'Oh do excuse me a minute. I must just . . .' And she scurries off to speak to Margaret. I edge closer to the three women left up my end of the room who are all discussing secondary schools. My heart sinks. I know this conversation off by heart. It's the same as the one about mortgages, just different nouns. I wonder whether I can muster the enthusiasm to intone the responses required of the School Litany and decide that I definitely can't. I begin to plan my getaway, composing a fiction in my head concerning Ivan and an ear infection.

'Do you think we should make a start?' announces Margaret. The three women make an undignified dash for the sofa leaving the rest of us looking around for somewhere to sit. One of the men I spotted earlier throws what looks like a space hopper into the room followed by a beanbag.

'Here you are, ladies. You can sit on the poufs. Rather you than me!' He laughs uproariously, goes out and then wheels in a hostess trolley. I lower myself carefully onto the beanbag and recline in the only position it will allow with my feet up above the level of my head and arms akimbo. Margaret begins to pull the thick maroon curtains closed. A single bulb in a fabric shade lights the room. The man with the poufs, presumably her husband, is plugging and unplugging cables, bending down and peering into sockets, switching buttons on and off and generally displaying Technical Expertise.

'Lights, Margaret,' he commands. The light is switched off and an ominous hum accompanies a shaft of light directed at the wall.

A quiet voice is speaking. It is Sam's mother.

'When Margaret asked me to show the slides of our holiday in the Maldives,' she pauses, dips down, sips some cider and continues, 'I thought, Won't that be boring for everyone? But she was most insistent,' she beams at Margaret who beams back, 'and so, here goes. Are you ready, Don? Could we have the first slide please?'

'Oh, beautiful,' murmurs Margaret as the first slide appears upside down on the wall.

'Oops. Whatever's that, Don?'

'Angela, I did tell you to put these in with the black dot at the top.'

'Oh I'm hopeless with technical things, Don. You know me. Oh that's better.'

'Oh, gorgeous. Are those tulips, Angela, or something more exotic?'

'Well, we weren't sure what those were but according to the man in the hotel . . .'

I look round the room trying to spot copies of *Intimacy* in the semi darkness. Perhaps I've come to the Flower Arranging night by mistake. When Margaret urges Angela to take it slowly and fill us in on all the details of each slide I realise it's no good. Intimacy is obviously not going to occur. And anyway I can't stay here. I know I should and that these are good people with kind hearts and that unless I start mixing with the locals I will never feel I really belong but I feel like I'm in a foreign country and I very much want to go home.

I tiptoe over the legs in the gloom and bend down to whisper to Margaret on my way out.

'I'm really sorry . . . I've just had a text from the babysitter . . . Ivan's ear . . . I'm going to have to go . . . thanks ever so much . . .'

She nods me off in a no-nonsense cheerful kind of a way. The dogs are waiting for me in the hall.

'Nimrod! Sniffy! Get back in the pantry!'

Outside, the night is dank and starless. I trudge back home, fishing out ten quid for the babysitter. The house lights glow at the bend in the lane. I can hear the phone ringing as I reach the gate. That'll be you, Captain Scott, ringing base camp.

I'm beginning to think I'm in need of a serious adventure of my own.

11th August 1999

We stand in a row on the high bank of shingle looking out over the mercury sea. Me, my mum, Karl and Ivan. All four of us wear cardboard glasses with green lenses and stare up at the sky waiting for the moment we've all been promised. The sea swells and retreats at the stones beneath us and I grip the boys' hands hard. In the lull between the sea's roars I can hear the faint call of a bird high above us.

'Oh look at that.' My mum points upward as the moon slowly, slowly, discs the sun black. All four of us bend back our heads and stare at the sky.

At the moment of totality, when the sun is an end-of-the-world-ish black orb, colour drains from the day, the sea becomes still and the temperature drops. It is eerie, unearthly, lunar. The bird is silent.

As colour, warmth, movement, sound return, I take my mobile from my pocket and press Search. As I do so it rings. 'Mark calling' is illuminated on my screen.

'Did you see it?' I ask, labouring through the shifting pebbles away from the others.

'Did you see it?' My voice. The time lapse. I imagine the threads of our two voices circling the globe. I sit down on the stones. I turn to watch my mum crouching down, holding the boys' hands.

'I miss you.'

'Are you all right?'

'No.'

'Miss you too. Did you see it?'

'Yes. It makes you realise—'

'I can't hear you.'

'It just made me think—'

'Are you still there?'

'I want our old life back. I want to go back to the Angel.'

'We should talk—'

'Where are you now?'

'I can't hear you very well.'

'Can you hear me now?'

Your voice is torn and scattered in some wind tunnel. I wait, phone held tight against my ear.

'Mark—'

'Are you still there?'

'Mummy!'

'Hello?'

'Mummy! Mummy!'

'Mark?'

'Karl says he's gone blind, Mummy!'

'Can I talk to Daddy, Mummy?'

'It's all right.' My mum is laughing and lifting Karl's glasses, peering into his eyes. 'Open them now. Open your eyes, Karl. Karl. Don't be silly. There. Not blind after all.'

Twenty-Four

14th October 1999

YOU PUSH your chair back noisily to get another bottle of wine. Orchestral and choral swirlings drift in from the television room where the children are watching *Bambi* for the twenty-sixth time.

'Has the farmer got back to us about selling that field yet?' you shout from the kitchen, pouring copious quantities of Extra Virgin olive oil into a pan, and pausing to study the *River Cafe Cook Book* which is propped against the wall. ('Mummy, was Mary an *extra* Virgin?')

I don't answer you. I don't want to buy a field. I don't know the farmer's name. I'd hoped you'd forgotten about the field project. And I'm afraid of the farmer. I glimpsed him one dark morning thundering out of his yard, gravel spitting off the wheels of his Jaguar, he didn't smile and he reminded me a bit of Mr McGregor in *Peter Rabbit* or the scary gardener in *Bill and Ben.* I feel guilty enough about living in this village without colonising their potato field. Anyway, it doesn't look like he needs the money. Maybe he's growing opium.

'It'd be great to build a tennis court and a swimming pool in that field. There'd still be loads of space left for the children to roam about in. Don't you think it'd be good?' You're standing in the doorway, wine glass in hand.

What I think is that I don't want any more projects. I want us to catch our breath, be still for a bit. What I say is, 'Mmm. I suppose so,' in a feckless, spoilt brat of a wife kind of a way. As you walk past the back of my chair to reach the wine bottle, you pause. I look up and see you looking at me.

'I don't think you should wear that jumper,' you say, throwing a handful of nuts into your mouth and topping up our glasses. 'You need something with a higher neckline.'

'What do you mean? I love this jumper. I've had it for years. It's made of special sheep.'

'It's not flattering.' You move over to the CD player. I flinch as you walk past the back of my chair. Leonard Cohen starts up.

'What's wrong with this jumper?' I feel the current of alarm with which my brain instructs my stomach to prepare itself. Bloody Leonard Cohen. I used to quite like him when I was eighteen but now he gives me the creeps. Here he is at sixty still droning on about sleepy golden clouds and ways not to say goodbye. I can tell that you're dubbing the soundtrack to some disaster movie in your head.

You wander back over to me and lift my chin up with the tips of your fingers. It's a while since you touched my face like that.

'Your neck's going.'

A laugh rises up in me. With relief I understand that this is a fond bit of fun. I lift up your jumper to reveal your soft white flesh. You take your hand away from my face and take a step back, pulling your jumper down irritably. Your face is white and drawn. The room suddenly feels cold. But you're still studying me. Your next project. I think I preferred it when you didn't look at me at all than when you look at me like this.

'And your eyes.' You touch the soft skin above my cheekbones. 'Just . . . here.'

I push your hand away. 'Piss off, Mark.' I can hear a chute

opening at the base of my skull. 'I can't quite believe you just said that.'

'Maybe you should find out about, you know, getting something done. Everybody has it these days. All the actresses, once they get past thirty. It might make you feel better.' Your mobile trills from the kitchen.

'Like Helena you mean? You didn't see her the day she came back from the clinic. Her torso was bandaged like she'd been sawn in half and her face looked like it had just gone through a windscreen. She couldn't stop shaking.'

'She looks amazing now.' You return to the kitchen and begin sweeping oven gloves and children's drawings off the kitchen table in the rush to find your bleeping phone.

'Her breasts are completely numb, Mark, and she can't wink any longer!' You're already talking to someone else. 'And Todd's still screwing the au pair!' I shout, loud enough for whoever it is to hear.

I swallow some wine and look up at the dark, blank window opposite. My reflection stares back, a little confused and indistinct. Oh shit. It really has never occurred to me until now. And if it had, I'm not sure I would have thought of it as a problem. Isn't that how it's supposed to be? Us growing old together? But my eyes and my *neck*, for God's sake. I had no idea that I had to worry about them as well as grouting floor tiles, resuscitating my career and keeping the children alive.

After years of sailing through life not giving a toss and thinking that body fascism was for sad people addicted to the fear and envy sold in the pages of glossy magazines, am I to understand that they include me? I can hear you jabbering to some agent or actor or investor. I watch you pace the kitchen enthusiastically, warming to your own theme. I've gone off you a bit now actually. You've gone and ruined everything just like Scottie did in the playground all those years ago. He had Elastoplasted glasses and a permanent bubble of green snot plugging one nostril and one dark December playtime he charged towards me, stopped an inch from my face and shouted that Father Christmas didn't exist.

Suddenly it's not a marriage of true minds any more. I have inadvertently gone and got myself a love that alters when it alteration finds. Oh. My. God. As Sid would say.

I pull the neck of my jumper up to my nose and wonder whether they sell burqas in Six Mile Bottom. Karl's eyes appear over the top of my jumper. Looking through his elbow are Ivan's eyes.

'Mummy, we've paused the tape. Can you come now?'

'The deer mummy is going to get shot, Mummy.'

I'm not sure whether I can sit through the Bambi moment yet again but having instituted the no viewing the death of Bambi's mum without Mummy rule, I allow them to lead the way solemnly through to the television room where I take my appointed place between them, one head under each arm as if I am breast feeding a pair of giant twins. On screen, Bambi and his mum are frozen in the meadow eating the spring grass. Karl points the flicker. Bambi's mum lifts her head. The shots ring out.

'Bambi! Quick, the thicket!' cries Bambi's mum.

Rather typical that The Great Prince of the Forest appears to be out of shot at this moment, I think, scowling in the direction of the kitchen.

'Faster, faster, Bambi! Don't look back! Keep running!'

Choirs of angels sing, the orchestra plays, snowflakes fall sadly.

'Mother! Where are you?' calls Bambi.

'His dad's coming.'

'That's Bambi's dad.'

'Got 'normous antlers.'

'Where's he been?'

'Your mother can't be with you any more,' says Bambi's dad.

'Karl! Ivan!'

You are bellowing distantly to the sound of crashing pots

and pans. It must be lunchtime in LA because the daily cliff-hanger narrative of whether *Snow Queen* will or will not get made and which manifests itself in a stream of phone calls from America is beginning in the kitchen. 'Supper's ready! Wash your hands! Turn it off now!'

We can't actually. Now is a very inappropriate moment. We are in the recovery position and need a little time. I'm wallowing in a little unconditional love. They're being reassured that although terrible things may happen, I will always be there. As long as I'm not actually shot. Or something.

A steaming saucepan comes in the door, followed by a dripping wooden spoon, followed by your irritated face.

'Genevieve, it's getting cold. Come on, boys. Turn it off.'

'But, Daddy—'

'It's the Great Prince of the Forest—'

The boys start to wail. In an instant you put the pan on the floor, clamber clumsily onto the sofa and envelop them in hugs and desperate cries of 'What's the matter?' smearing all of us with sauce. On cue, the boys weep and wail copiously. This is obviously going to take some time so I get up to tackle the kitchen where some kind of atrocity seems to have occurred. Charred remains line two pans, something has exploded up the handmade Mexican tiles and the *River Cafe Cook Book* has taken a direct hit.

Twenty-Five

31st December 1999

IT'S FINALLY come then. The day we've all been waiting for. The Millennium is nigh. We've been whipped up into a complete and utter paroxysm of anticipation. And when the clock strikes twelve tonight, the entire population of the planet will experience some sort of . . . *thing* after which nothing will ever seem as monumental again. Furthermore, due to the much-feared K2 bug, we are warned that there may be apocalyptic events in the skies, imploding bank balances, and many pedestrian crossings stuck permanently on 'cross', causing total mayhem. Burglar alarms will go crazy, medical records will crash and mobile phones may spontaneously combust. In America, Christian Fundamentalists are eagerly preparing (again) for the long-awaited Rapture, during which they will ascend to heaven in a fiery Armageddon. Like the Millennium Dome in Greenwich, New Year's Eve promises an epiphany worthy of the cultural and spiritual climax of two thousand years of Western civilisation. And the boys and I are thirty-three thousand feet up in the air which is probably quite a good place to witness the cosmic realignment that will no doubt accompany the event.

The problem is that New Year's Eve has been so hyped that everyone has been even more equivocal than usual about what they're doing to celebrate. To be caught not having a good time on this New Year's Eve would obviously be a curse worthy of at least a thousand years' bad luck. Therefore no one has dared to make any firm arrangements for fear of missing out on one that might be more meaningful. We had an argument about a New Year's Eve party. I put my foot down about spending it with your mum and dad and suggested we have our own Millennium party. I knew that if we invited everyone we knew to Six Mile Bottom it would be a laugh. Kind of chaotic and mad. The Kunt Tulips could play and Angus could bring his kilt and his bagpipes and no doubt Winston could organise some outlandish dancing of a Jane Austenish nature.

'Oh go on, Mark. It'll be great,' I said. 'Well, I'd enjoy myself.'

'If we're going to do something like that it's got to be properly planned—'

'We are planning it—'

'We'd need a marquee and we'd need to book hotels so people could stay over—'

'We can sort something out – half of Six Mile Bottom is going to be away.'

'And I'd have to ask people like LaLa.'

'So?'

'You can't just *invite* famous people. There've got to be other famous people there who they can talk to. Just one famous person in a room is very stressful. For them and for everyone else.'

'Well you're famous.'

'No I'm not.'

'You are. I saw you on telly the other night.' At which point you ran your hand through your hair in exasperation at my sheer stupidity.

'What are you looking at?'

'Don't move.' I'm seeing them everywhere now. It's a

national epidemic. 'There.' I hold it up for inspection between my thumb and forefinger. 'You've got nits.'

In the end it turned out that you had to be in Lapland just before New Year for some last-minute recces for *Snow Queen* or *Snow* as it looks like being called and which keeps on being delayed and at one point was not going to happen at all because the three stars were wrangling about who will be paid the most and who is, in fact, the star of the movie. And the financiers were getting cold feet about the budget. And then someone had the bright idea that Kylie Minogue should be in it. And the financiers were suddenly OK again because they're sure she will guarantee a decent return at the box office. Some of the other stars, however, were not so pleased. Dilly Nettles feels it is compromising her professionalism and has insisted that her part be rewritten. And the actor playing Kay is being very difficult. He is The Next Big Thing apparently. Well according to his agent who is now insisting that unless his client is paid more than the others he will pull out of the film. Fortunately, Sugar Rush who is playing Snow (Queen) is incredibly nice. Just really really normal. But also really really mature given that she's only nineteen. And she's got a brother with Down's Syndrome whom she takes everywhere. He kind of keeps her grounded, you know?

So when the filming was brought forward to the first week of January you thought we might as well abandon Britain for the Millennium and take advantage of the Lapland connection, seeing as you've got to be there for something or other anyway. Besides it's somewhere snowy and different and Karl and Ivan will love it. And that is how the boys and I come to be on our way to meet you in Lapland after a three-hour delay in taking off due to severe weather conditions at the Lapland end. I don't like to think of the possibilities for disaster that landing in Lapland may incur. The boys, for whom the excitement of Christmas, the Millennium, Daddy *and* seeing Father Christmas at the North Pole, have proved too much, are prostrate, white-faced and unconscious on the empty rows either side of me.

I look at my watch, stare down through the night at the featureless planet beneath me and have a funny feeling that we're going to be spending the Millennium apart.

At half past eleven, Rovaniemi airport is deserted, apart from a large red-faced man with a beard, driving a vacuum machine in slow circles. I can't quite remember the plan for arrival. I stop to search in my bag while the boys lie slumped on top of the luggage trolley.

Suddenly there you are. Jogging towards us, thick coat flying, gloves stuffed in both pockets, face flushed and brimming with excitement. You are waving two gift-wrapped boxes at the children. The three of you fall to the floor in a confusion of heads, arms, mouths, cheeks, kisses and voices. You are yammering at them about the Arctic circle, the Northern Lights, dogsledding, reindeer rides and how everyone here speaks Lappish.

'And Santa. Mummy said Santa was here.'

'No, not now. Santa's been, hasn't he?' You look up at me with irritation. 'What did you tell them that for?'

'But Santa lives here, doesn't he, Daddy?'

'Santa's village is closed now because he's resting. He probably likes to go somewhere hot for New Year.'

'I don't believe in Santa, Daddy. It's sad but I don't.'

'Shuttup, Karl! Shuttup! Shuttup!' Ivan wails.

'Hey! Don't thump him, Ivan!'

'And don't thump him back, Karl.'

'I wanna open my present!'

'Let's open them in the car, shall we? Come on, we don't want to miss the New Year! And I tell you who you might meet in a few days' time. Not Santa, but someone much more famous . . . Kylie Minogue!' You scoop both children up in your arms and start running for the exit, tunelessly singing 'Locomotion'. Squeals of laughter trail behind you as all three heads bobble and jiggle through the empty building. I follow with the baggage trolley.

'We've got a special car that goes over mountains and snow. How was the flight?' You wheel round and wait for me to catch up so you can give me a kiss.

'Do you mean an ORV, Daddy?'

'Fine. Apart from the three-hour wait at Heathrow.'

'Do you know how to drive it, Daddy?'

'No, Jazz is driving us. He works on the film.'

'What's his job?'

'Driving mainly. You've met him before. Look, there he is!'

Jazz is young, good looking and eager, with perfect public school manners. He leads us out of the airport doors where the cold momentarily silences the boys before they are bundled into the leathery warmth of the jeep. You sit in the back between them. I sit in the front with Jam, I mean Jazz. As we accelerate silently into the night, I enthuse about the scenery. It looks as though it expects it.

'Wow. It's incredible.'

'Amazing, isn't it?'

'Really beautiful.' Please don't say 'awesome', Jazz.

'Awesome.'

We cruise along the snow-carpeted road with no sound but the slow beat of the wipers. The dashboard is lit up like a pilot's cockpit. As we round a bend, up ahead at the limit of the headlight beams, there's a flurry of snow from the dark forest margin.

'Look at that,' says Jazz, slowing down. 'Look. See?'

Ahead of us, in the deep drift by the side of the road, but clearly visible, lies an elk, blood darkening the snow around its rear legs. It has an enormous muzzle. Among the trees, I can just make out the shape of another elk, its massive, ungainly antlers hovering among the pine trunks.

'Oh God. Poor thing.'

'Must have been hit by a car. Happens quite a lot.'

'Can you see its mate there?'

I turn round. All three of you are sleeping. It's five minutes to midnight. I look at Jazz.

'So. Looks like we're going to miss the New Year then.'

'Can't be helped. We sort of did New Year last night. There's quite a few us out here already. Now that the shoot's been brought forward. Dilly Nettles came out a few days ago. Brought her son.'

'Her son?'

'And her nanny. And her mother. And her bodyguard. You know, because of the K2 thing.'

We continue our silent route through the snow, leaving the elks in the dark behind us.

'Met Kylie yet?'

'I met her in New York. She is such a laugh. Really really . . . normal.'

I sit back in the deep soft leather of the passenger seat. The jeep takes us on silently, effortlessly to the hotel. I wonder whose job it is to clear dead elk off the road.

Twenty-Six

19th February 2000

KARL AND Ivan have been asking what time Molly and Helena are arriving since seven o'clock this morning. What is it with children and time? We have several clocks in the house but they don't want to read the time for themselves, they want me to tell them.

'What time is it, Mummy?' asks Ivan as though this is a completely new question that has just popped into his head.

'I don't know, Ivan. I can't see the clock. Please eat this apple, Ivan.'

'But roughly, Mummy. What time is it roughly?' He shakes his head at the apple.

'About five minutes later than it was last time you asked, Ivan. Can you remember what time it was then?'

'No.'

'Well, a banana. Have a banana then.'

'Once upon a time,' says Karl. 'Why don't we say that any more?'

'Because that was in the olden days when they didn't have clocks, Stupid,' says Ivan.

'Karl, don't thump Ivan,' I say, holding out a pear to him. 'And Ivan, don't thump Karl. Karl, please eat this pear. It's lovely.'

'Don't like pears. They're disgusting.'

'Mummy, it's one hour twenty-five minutes until Molly gets here, isn't it?'

'Yes, Ivan, I expect it is. Look, just take a bite, Karl. It's lovely and juicy. Look.'

'One hour and twenty-five minutes?' wails Karl. 'I can't wait that long.'

'Did you know that time bends?' I tell them, eating the pear myself. At least I think it does. Or is that space?

'Does it?'

'Bends? How can it?' Ivan presses his face to the clock.

'Well, that's maybe why it goes at different speeds,' I say, relieved to have moved away from the literal. 'Why don't you run outside and play football?'

'Oh. You mean it stretches. Bends like something stretchy,' says Karl, sticking his fingers in the peanut butter jar.

'Molly doesn't play football.'

'Yes but she's not here yet. Don't do that, Karl. Actually I have a feeling that it's space that bends,' I confess.

'Space? Bends?'

'But that time is space,' I add putting the kettle on and wondering whether I should prepare some wholesome meal for lunch. But then, Helena doesn't eat.

'Yeah, that's right. Time is space,' says Ivan, sticking his fingers in the peanut butter jar.

'How do you know?' says Karl. 'Mummy, what's for lunch?'

'Ivan, don't do that.'

'Karl did it.'

'You're just saying space bends because Mummy said it did.'

'No. When I look down the road to see if Molly's coming round the bend yet it's just empty space. That's how I know it's not time yet.'

'Let's pretend time doesn't exist for a couple of hours, shall we?' I wonder whether I can get away with baked beans on toast again.

'Yeah! Let's pretend time hasn't been invented yet!'

'OK. But before we do,' says Ivan, 'how long is Daddy away for?'

'Daddy's back on Friday night.'

'Friday night! I can't wait!'

22nd February 2000

Helena's been here for three days now and I'm beginning to wonder whether she's ever going to leave. She spends a lot of time in bed, in the bath and on the mobile in the garden, huddled inside her cashmere duffle and elegant wellingtons. You would have thought elegant and wellingtons were a contradiction in terms but not where Helena shops.

Every now and then Helena gets off the phone or out of bed or out of the bath and drifts into the kitchen which is the only room in this giant house that anyone occupies. The door opens and in she comes.

'Ooh, that smells lovely,' she says, watching me pour water into the coffee pot. 'Oh. Your hair,' she adds.

'Who was that on the phone?' I ask, checking the top of my head. Helena's hands are long and slender. How does she get her nails like that? They're perfect. Where's the dirt?

'Well, it looks like Daddy's got him that job in the States.' She pulls her hair back from her forehead in a languorous gesture.

'Really? That's great.' I look at Helena's face. Her skin seems translucent, as if it's in soft focus.

'I know. It'll mean we'll all go and live there for a year. I'd love that. Course, we'd have to get married.' Jesus. Married to Todd. A living death. But in the Land of Helena, that is better than living alone.

'So this is the fly-on-the-wall documentary he's doing, is

it?' How did all these shrivelled bits of garlic get into the sugar bowl?

'Yes. The Americans are really keen apparently. Todd gets on so well with my dad. And Todd's boss can't believe his luck. I mean it's quite something to get access to the CIA.'

'But a fly-on-the-wall documentary about the CIA, Helena? Is that possible? Won't it just be a PR job?' I put the pot of coffee on the table.

'Is that decaff?' Helena peers at it suspiciously. For someone who's taken as many Class A drugs as Helena, she's oddly puritanical about coffee. Thinks it stops her sleeping. Ha!

'Oops. Sorry, forgot.' I get up to make another pot.

'Thanks, Gen.' She wraps herself up in her capacious, soft cardigan and gazes out of the window. Molly has been captured and imprisoned in the tree house. Ivan guards the entrance with a scaffolding pole. 'Ooh. It is lovely here. I could stay here for ever.' With a tumultuous crash, the coffee pot smashes on the stone floor. 'Oh no! Are you OK, Gen? Oh, what a shame, that was such a beautiful pot.'

'No, don't get up.' But she isn't. 'It's fine.' But it's not and my heart contracts in woe. We bought that in Greece, years ago. I pick up the pieces and lay them on the counter.

'It's so brilliant to see Molly enjoying herself here with the boys. She adores them. But how are *you*, Gen? I keep reading about Mark. I'm dying to see him again.'

'Well he's gone through hell with this bloody film. You know they had to abandon the shoot halfway through because one of the financiers pulled out. Mark only told me the other day that for a while he thought the company was going to sue him and we'd be ruined. But,' I bang on the window with the dustpan and brush in my hand and gesture at Ivan to put the scaffolding pole down, 'it looks like it's probably going to be all right.'

'Thank God for that.' She sniffs the hyacinths in their pots on the window sill. 'Mmm. You're so lucky you know, Genevieve.'

'I know.' I make a Do Not Use That Pole As A Sword sign through the window at Ivan. 'It's lovely here. But I do miss London. Time can pass rather slowly in Six Mile Bottom.' I swab up the coffee grounds from the floor and glance at the clock. It is still only quarter to eleven. The day yawns ahead of us. What the hell can we do today? Helena doesn't do mud.

'Oh, but it's beautiful here. You'd be mad to go back to London.'

'I know.'

'And it's so good to have so much time with the children.'

'Yes, it is.'

'And so much space too.'

Twenty-Seven

20th April 2000

THE MUSTY smell of old cloth and damp stone always reminds me of Christmas at Uncle Frank's. On the altar stands a tin vase of yellow chrysanthemums and fern leaves, the kind you can get in the garage. There are only three of us, apart from the vicar and the woman at the organ.

I've never known Sid cry before, but she stands now with her head up, tears streaming down her face, mouth stretched in pain, occasional gasps escaping from her. I look at Winston's sad profile, eyes lowered, hands clasped in front of him. He wipes away a tear.

The plain, veneer coffin looks huge and is supported by two trestles, its feet-end pointing towards the curtained entrance to the furnace.

The vicar looks down at his piece of paper and says that Mabel knew great suffering in her life yet found comfort towards the end of it and that now her soul was resting in everlasting peace in the care and love of Christ the Lord. He nods over at the organist and the incomprehensible wheezings and blowings of that infernal instrument begin. We look to the vicar for guidance as he sings out the first words of the hymn.

'He-e who would valiant beee, 'gainst all dis-aster.'

Winston joins in, then Sid, voice breaking and swerving,

and then me. In between verses, there's a noise at the back of the chapel and we all turn round. Octavia stands in the doorway, half turns, steps out again, turns back and with a dip of her head, totters haltingly up the aisle towards us. Halfway up she stops, adjusts her yellow hat and veil, looks down at the bunch of dandelions in her hand and says, 'Oh Mabel.' Winston steps out of the pew and goes towards her, holding out his hand. She takes it and shuffles into the pew next to him, holding tight on to the wooden rail in front of her, joining in the hymn with her oh dear oh dear oh dear oh dear oh dear.

And then I start to cry too. Terrible wrenching sobs that drag themselves out of me so that my throat, my skull, my stomach ache with the effort of it. Sid puts her arm through mine and squeezes it, but I can't stop. The second verse is a total shambles and when the hymn staggers to an end the vicar looks at his watch and presses a button under the table by his side. With a judder, Mabel's coffin moves forward and then stops. We watch. It moves forward again and passes slowly through the curtains. The vicar says thank you and the four of us wander out of the chapel, blinking into the sudden brightness and colour of the hospital cemetery. We stand, blowing our noses, unbuttoning our coats and pulling our gloves off in the unexpected heat of an Easter sun.

Much of the hospital is a building site now, the development of the Exclusive Luxury Living estate is well underway. Acute Admissions has gone, so has Geriatrics and Out Patients. In their place a spa and health centre is being constructed. Mabel and Octavia were among the last to leave and were waiting for their places in a Residential Therapeutic Community. We stand in the heavy London clay, watching the bulldozers climbing the slope where the patients used to walk. I try to think of something to say but nothing seems very appropriate apart from silence.

'You'd better hurry up and finish that damn thesis or

whatever it is, Gen,' says Winston. 'There's going to be nothing left of the place soon.'

'Yes,' says Sid, lighting up a cigarette. 'For God's sake, stop composting out in the sticks and get your arse into gear.'

Octavia puts her bunch of dandelions down on a grave.

'Let's go down the caff and have a fry up,' I suggest. 'Are you coming, Octavia, or do you have to hurry back?'

'I'd love a cup of tea,' she says.

Sid and Winston look at me in amazement. I beam at them, take Octavia's hand and lead the way.

5th July 2000

When I see you step off the train I can't help smiling at the sight of your face. You look tanned and happy after your trip to LA and you've brought presents for all of us.

'Did it all go OK then?' I ask on the drive back to the house, once Karl and Ivan have been plugged into their technology.

'Yep. It all looks like it's going to happen. The deal's been signed and we should start shooting again in, well, that's not fixed yet. But it's looking good anyway. We won't have to sell the Angel after all.' You put your hand on my thigh and look at me. 'You look well.'

'It's all the sun we've had,' I say, linking my fingers in yours. 'We've been in the garden a lot. And I think I've cracked the research thing.'

'How is the garden? Have we planted those shrubs yet?'

'The garden's lovely. Full of life and colour.'

'What time will Sid and Angus be here?'

'In two hours fifteen minutes. I can't wait.'

The smell of rosemary, garlic and olive oil drifts out onto the lawn and I feel full of happy expectation. I've nearly finished the research, we're not going to be sent to Debtors' Gaol, you're back for a whole week and soon Sid and Angus will be here. Karl helps me wrap Sid's present, a first edition of Hans Christian Andersen fairy tales with woodcut illustrations. Ivan is drawing forty tulips on a card he's made for her. At the sound of their car on the gravel I leap up and race the boys over to the drive.

'My God,' says Sid, lifting herself out of the passenger seat. 'There's nothing like a long drive to really get acquainted with someone.' I laugh and hug her hot, smoky body tight to mine.

'Happy Birthday, Sid, you old shrew. You have no idea how much I've missed you.'

'Sid,' says Angus, hands still on the wheel, staring ahead at the windscreen, 'You are poison incarnate. Don't speak to her, Gen. You have no idea . . .'

'Oh dear, did you get lost?'

'Did we get lost? Gen, Angus *is* lost. You of all people must know that by now.' Ivan hands Sid her card. 'Oh, hello, handsome boys. Now wait a minute, I've brought you a couple of teeny weeny presents.' She walks round to the back of the car, the boys jumping and scampering around her. Opening the boot she pulls out a pogo stick and a metal detector. 'There you are, my darlings. Now you can jump for joy all day long and find buried treasure in the woods.'

'Oh this is so cool,' says Karl, bouncing off onto the pathway. Ivan chases after him firing the metal detector at him like a ray gun. Angus gets out of the car and lifts a cardboard box of wine and food from the back seat.

'A few supplies, Gen.' He bends down to kiss me. 'You look gorgeous. What have you done to your hair?'

'Right, you two. When you've stopped snogging, someone could pour me a birthday drink.'

You come out of the back door wearing oven gloves and waving a spatula.

'Mark, you look younger every time I see you. You're not on some youth drug, are you, by any chance?'

‘It could be the aspirin my mum tells me to take when flying.’

‘I’m so glad to see success hasn’t changed you, Mark.’

‘Perhaps one day, Sid, success will change you,’ mutters Angus. ‘Hey, Morrison, don’t you bloody disappear. I need a job.’

‘Hey, Sid, we’ve got you a present,’ I call after her as she sweeps into the house in search of a bottle.

‘How lovely. Is it a new lover? I do hope so. I’ve completely grown out of my old one.’

Twenty-Eight

10th August 2000

IT IS a tiny distance to slip from my restless unconscious state to full consciousness and the transition is made with a cold stomach-rinse of fear. Tomorrow is the day of the local health authority conference: *Mental Health Strategy for Women – The Way Forward* and I am giving a talk on my research. I have promised to email my paper by eight o'clock this morning so that it can be approved and distributed in advance. Consequently I was up until one this morning finishing it. It is so easy to say yes to these things: the flattery, the small payment, the line in the CV, the excuse to buy some new clothes. But these things come nowhere near to compensating for the horror of the actual giving of the talk. And it's not just the giving of it. Like pregnancy and childbirth rolled into one – the preparation is colossal. For weeks I have slaved over my books, tapped the tips off my fingers writing and rewriting, handed the children over to be cared for by drug-addled teenagers and completely abandoned bedtime stories and de-nitting routines.

Half-heartedly, I bury my face against the cool skin of your back. Perhaps the best thing is to go back to sleep. I put an arm over the hard bones of your ribs but I can't tell whether you're asleep or not. You're turned away in what looks like a bit of an angry lump, if not an actual hump. We had an argument last night about the Folly being built in the garden. You want it to be made completely of glass but I know I'll be too paranoid to sit in it at night if it's see-through. I'll feel like I'm in a goldfish bowl, an aquarium, a bell jar. 'Don't put me in a bell jar, Mark,' I said to you in the bath last night. Your head was wedged between the taps while I soaped your feet. 'Remember what happened to Sylvia Plath.' You looked a bit like some Aztec sculpture, kind of compressed and tortured, face wet with steam, mouth open, eyes closed. After a bit I realised you were asleep. My feet and our conversation would have to wait.

My paper is called *Rising Hysteria – Women and Madness in the Twentieth Century*. As I stare at the filter of pale light showing through the gap between the curtains, I understand with the alarming clarity that only dawn brings, that my title is complete and utter bollocks, surpassed only by the sheer idiocy of the content. Corpse-like, I drag myself out of bed and feel my way downstairs. I open the laptop and press the On button, keeping my feet four inches above the very beautiful but very cold stone floor. The machine welcomes me with its portentous chime and wide-awake glow. It is 4.30 a.m. and I have three hours to salvage my career.

By the time I finish it, I am about six pounds lighter than I was when I woke up. The title of my paper has changed many times since my dawn awakening. It's been *Shut Up, Shut In and Shut Out – Five Women Speak about Madness*, *She Sells Sea Shells on the Sea Shore: Women Get Shell Shock Too* and *Silence and Lies – Gender and Mental Illness*. At this point in time I'm still not completely decided on the final title. Or even what it is I'm trying to say.

11th August 2000

My schedule for the day informs me that it all kicks off at 10.00. I have half an hour to kill and so I sit in the car in the carpark, check my bag and stare at the back end of the delegates' cars. All sensation is centred in my stomach. I don't know why it's called butterflies because that does not describe the sensation inside me. Butterflies is what it feels like when you first feel your baby kicking at twenty weeks. A gentle fluttering. What I'm feeling now is a dismantling, a liquefying of all my essential organs, including my brain. I sit in the car and look in the mirror. I look about a hundred and seventy-six. Your last words to me were, 'Don't worry, Gen. Just smile and it'll be fine.' I try a smile. That looks even worse. I try a bit of makeup and wish Sid were here to show me how to do it. The lipstick makes me look like a prostitute. It makes Sid look like a prostitute too but somehow it suits her. I rub it off and have another look. Now I look like a prostitute who has just performed an act of fellatio. I run my hand through my hair, pick a head louse off my lapel and climb out of the car.

The first shock I get as I enter the room where the conference is being held is that it has already started and the Director of Mental Health is giving his introduction with a PowerPoint presentation.

'. . . a whole raft of measures and a range of issues . . .' He glances at me as I come in. The first few rows of chairs are empty and the rows behind are thinly scattered. I sit down at the side and try to look composed, wondering how I could have got the start time wrong. A few delegates are trickling in, sipping coffee and taking up very temporary positions near the back and round the edges. The atmosphere in the room is of terminal exhaustion and resentment at yet another government initiative. The language of New Labour management-speak is floating across the wall in soothing pastels and cursive fonts. 'Challenge and Accountability.' I scan the audience. 'Planning and Partnership.' They look shattered and wary. 'Delivery and Access.' Thank God there's no one here I know. I look up and realise the Director is winding up his introduction and turning towards me.

'Before we get down to the main business of the day, Genevieve O'Dowd is going to talk to us about her research conducting interviews with long-stay patients in London. And I'm sure Ms O'Dowd will understand that in order to keep to our tight schedule we should break for coffee as arranged promptly at 10.30.' There's a spatter of applause and three people, bent double, make for the exit.

I walk to the front, wondering how to rearrange my talk so that it can be compressed into half an hour. I take a deep breath in but my lungs appear to be full already. I try a deep breath out and with shaking hands put the first transparency on the projector and switch on the light. Behind my head the word *Hysteria* is illuminated on the wall. I turn to look at it. The audience gazes passively. It's at a bit of a crazy angle and so I move it across the glass a bit. I look at the wall. Whoops. Now it's completely wonky.

'Whoops!' I say, twitching it the other way again. Hysteria judders to the left and then slides to the floor. I pick it up and stick it back on again. Looks OK on the projector. I check the wall. It's upside down and back to front. My head hums and I have the strange sensation of actually being somewhere else.

'Oh dear. Hang on a minute . . .' Whichever way I move it on the glass, it moves in the other bloody direction on the wall. I fiddle and fumble some more. 'There. Right . . . now that I'm completely hysterical . . .' I risk a laugh and sneak a look at the audience. A woman near the front beams encouragingly at me. Heads are bowed over clipboards and briefcases are rummaged in. I look down at the copy of my talk and freeze. I have no idea how to begin or how to actually deliver it.

'What do we think of when we see the word Hysteria?' Blank faces look back. As well they might. For God's sake. 'Right.' I say, fishing out another transparency. 'OK. Now, what do you think of when you see this?' I place it carefully in the middle of the glass, tossing the first one aside. Wearily, they raise their faces to look at the nineteenth-century lithograph of eight women in the grounds of La Salpêtrière Hospital, Paris. 'And no, it's not the checkout at Budgens.' I grin desperately. 'I don't know whether you can read the caption,' my voice is shaking like one shortly to be executed, 'but it says, "Eight women representing the conditions of dementia, megalomania, acute mania, melancholia, idiocy, hallucination, erotic mania and paralysis . . ."' There's a shifting of bottoms on seats and the slight stir of interest.

A man in the front row who arrived late raises his hand with an expression of urgent enquiry on his face. His eyes are fixed on me. I glance at him and feel a bit annoyed because I think I could continue now that they don't seem so bored and hostile. He takes my look as permission and into the hesitation inserts his question. I catch a whiff of something burning. The canteen must be preparing lunch already.

'I'm sorry,' he begins, pausing to look round until everyone is quiet, 'but could you just tell us what it is, exactly, that you were trying to find out in your research? I mean, what was your initial hypothesis? It isn't at all clear.' Blood rushes to my face and then rapidly retreats. I think I may have to sit down. I offer a sickly smile and search desperately for Page One of my talk.

'Well . . .' I begin. There is most definitely something burning somewhere. 'Studies in the general population show that men and women present differently in terms of mental illness.' Where are all those statistics I had this morning? 'Um, women are more likely to suffer depression, anxiety . . .' Don't tell me I left them in the bathroom. I did leave them in the bathroom. 'Er, eating disorders and of course,' I gesture vaguely up at the wall behind my head where the women are still falling about in various postures of lunacy, 'post-natal depression and post-partum psychosis.'

'Excuse me.' Another delegate has her hand in the air and is trying to interrupt. I ignore her and plough on.

'Whereas men present more often with—'

'Excuse me.'

For God's sake, do they want a talk or don't they? I flick my eyes away from her, determined to get the rest of this sentence out because it is one that I can remember. 'Whereas in *men* we see more substance abuse and anti-social personality disorders.'

'Sorry.' It's that man again. 'But we know all this, don't we? Are you going to tell us anything we don't know?' He uncrosses and recrosses his legs and looks round the room triumphantly.

'Well that is interesting actually . . .' I hope desperately that inspiration will visit before I reach the end of my sentence. My talk is in a hopeless muddle at my feet. 'Because you see I think that my research does reveal things we already know but may have chosen to forget.' His features harden as he considers the small grenade I've just lobbed into his lap. I wince. Now I'm for it. 'Given that madness is historically considered a particularly "female malady"—'

It's the woman again and she's standing up and pointing anxiously.

'I was interested in finding out whether—' I stop and look at her desperate hand waving.

'The projector. It's burning.'

I turn to my left and sure enough, a thin plume of smoke is rising from the eight women on the glass. The man from the front row leaps up and switches off the machine. The room erupts in laughter. I take a gulp of water and wave away the acrid smell of burnt acetate.

'Well. I'm sure that was a metaphor for something,' I say when the mirth has exhausted itself. A mobile phone sings its insolent tune. A woman makes her escape, bent double, hand held to her ear. A caretaker with a clattering trolley of teacups and urns enters as she exits. Slowly he makes his way the long way round the room. I look at the Director. He looks at the man with the trolley and then at his watch.

'In view of the situation with the technology,' he says, 'I think perhaps we might break early for tea . . .' Several people with 'I cannot believe it's started already' expressions on their faces are arriving through the doors looking harassed and holding letters and maps out in front of them. The room is filled with a buzz of chat and laughter. He thanks me for my thought-provoking contribution to the day and suggests that if I stay for the Plenary at four o'clock, delegates could ask further questions.

I have no intention of staying a moment longer and bend down to collect the scattered transcripts and transparencies of Lily, Octavia, Mabel, Alice and Mary. The years of my life I spent in that place were no different to the years of their lives that they spent there. They were just mad. End of story. Their little dramas – grief, betrayal, loss – were just that. Little. And here was I trying to turn Ophelias into Hamlets. Truly, I was a fool to think that any of their mumbling and stumbling could be made to mean anything. A woman is standing over me. She holds out a sheet of paper of mine that I've missed. She's saying something kind that I don't hear.

In the car I sit and wail. I dial your number on the mobile. You're probably halfway to London by now. I wait, sniffing and listening to the rain on the roof. I switch on the radio and switch it off again quick. Kylie is back. And she's still smiling.

'The Vodafone you are calling is switched off. Please try later.' I consider calling Sid but can't face the barbed wit and snipe of one of those conversations.

All at once I am consumed by a visceral need to be tangled on the sofa with Karl and Ivan, eating baked beans on toast and watching *E.T.* I can send the teenager home early. I start the engine and head back to Six Mile Bottom.

1st October 2000

The distant sound of the telephone eventually penetrates my subconscious. I struggle to disentangle myself from where I have dozed off mid-sentence in between Karl and Ivan.

'You fell asleep again, Mummy. Are you going to finish *Peter Pan*?'

'Oh. So I did. Sorry. Hang on. I'll just get the phone.' I clamber off the bed. 'It might be Daddy!' I shout back at them as I hurry to our bedroom, throwing myself across the bed just in time.

'Hi.'

'Mark?' It's a moment before I am sure it is your voice. 'Are you back?'

'I'm at the airport. I'll be there in a couple of hours.'

'Great. I'll cook something. Are you OK?'

'Fine. Are the boys awake?'

'Just about. Hang on.' I hold the phone out to Ivan who is bouncing up and down on the bed. Karl intercepts it and starts bouncing too.

'Karl! Don't snatch. Give the phone to Ivan.'

'I want to speak to Daddy!' wails Ivan.

'Karl!' I warn.

'What? I'm talking to Daddy. What?' His face is a vision of self-righteous indignation. Ivan is bouncing up trying to reach the phone and shouting, 'Daddy! Daddy!'

I leave them to it and get back into their bed. Their pillows smell of wood smoke and nit lotion. I pick up the book and look at the cover. You'll be cross I'm reading this to them again. According to your mum you had read all of Dickens by the time you were Karl's age. Karl is still struggling with *Harry Potter.* On tape. But they seem to like their bedtime stories and often ask for the old ones they already know. And anyway I'm reading the very end from the original *Peter Pan.* The bit they never include in the Disney video or the Christmas productions. The bit that reveals that, at its heart, *Peter Pan* is a horror story.

Ivan and Karl come back into the room still bouncing.

'Daddy's got us a present.'

'Come on. Into bed. I've got to go and clear up downstairs in a minute.'

'He's got us a present from Japan.'

I start to read.

'*And then one night came the tragedy. It was the spring of the year, and the story had been told for the night, and Jane was now asleep in her bed.*'

'Will I be awake when Daddy gets home?'

'No. You'll be asleep.'

'I wanna see Daddy before I go to sleep.'

'You'll see Daddy in the morning. Shall we finish the story? *Then the window blew open as of old, and Peter dropped in on the floor. He was exactly the same as ever, and Wendy saw at once that he still had all his first teeth. He was a little boy, and she was grown up. She huddled by the fire not daring to move, helpless and guilty, a big woman.*

' *"Hullo, Wendy," he said, not noticing any difference, for he was thinking chiefly of himself; and in the dim light her white dress might have been the nightgown in which he had seen her first.*

' *"Hullo, Peter," she replied faintly, squeezing herself as small as possible. Something inside her was crying, Woman, Woman, let go of me.*'

'Wendy's old now, isn't she, Mummy?'

'I don't want you to die, Mummy.'

'I'm not going to die, Ivan,' I tell him, sealing my lie with a kiss.

'I dreamt Daddy had died, Mummy.'

'Daddy's not going to die either. He just works a lot. Shall we get on with the story?'

'I dreamt you left me in a boat in the sea and you didn't hear me calling you. Why didn't you hear, Mummy?'

According to Freud, the clever parent understands that it's the questions children do not ask that are significant. Freud had obviously never met children like Karl or Ivan. I cannot think of a single question they haven't asked. Especially since moving to Six Mile Bottom. It's a bit like the way the police are trained to keep a dialogue going with the suicidal jumper or the hostage taker. I think that's what they're doing. Just keeping a dialogue going. What do they think is going to happen? I read on, the tears pricking my eyes.

'*Then she turned up the light, and Peter saw. He gave a cry of pain; and when the tall beautiful creature stooped to lift him in her arms he drew back sharply.*

' *"What is it?" he cried again.*

'*She had to tell him.*

' *"I am old, Peter. I am ever so much more than twenty. I grew up long ago."*'

'I've got a sore eye.' Ivan pulls his lower lid down horribly.

'Have you?' I give his lashes a lick.

'Peter wants her to go to the Neverland doesn't he, Mummy?'

'But she's forgotten how to fly.'

I sneak a look at my watch, wonder what I can make for supper and speed up the reading a bit. '*But he supposed she was; and he took a step towards the sleeping child with his dagger upraised. Of course he did not strike. He sat down on the floor instead and sobbed; and Wendy did not know how to comfort him, though she could have done it so easily once. She was only a woman now, and she ran out of the room to try to think.*'

Ivan is curled towards me, one hand inside my jumper, his eyes closed. Karl breathes heavily through his mouth, his eyes fighting sleep.

'*Of course in the end Wendy let them fly away together.*' Nearly at the end, I speed up, planning the supper and the resurrection of my career in my head. Scott Fitzgerald told Zelda that work is the only dignity or something and Sid told me to stop stagnating in Six Mile Bottom and damn well finish my thesis and then things will become – well, things will become clearer. I must email Helena. Things are obviously not working out with Todd and she sounded so down last time I spoke. Drunk or drugged or something. Perhaps she and Molly should come and stay for a few days. '*And thus it will go on, so long as children are gay and innocent and heartless.*'

Closing the book I listen to the silence. The boys have crashed into the abandon of sleep, heads thrown back into pillows, mouths open. I lie with them and contemplate the chaos and labour that awaits me downstairs. It's not just the Duplo, the Brillo, the Playmobil, felt tip pens and Star Wars weaponry. It's the bloody builders' dust that is impossible to defeat. Each day I swab the floors with a mop but I can never entirely get rid of it. It's sending me into a bit of a Rumpelstiltskin-like dementia. It leaves a chalky smear all over the floor. And each day, Brian and Arthur come and create more dust. And, on the days they don't come, there's the oak worktops to clean, seal and polish, curtains to hem, shutters to paint, wood doors to oil. Doing it is boring. Thinking about it is boring. Talking about it is boring. It is all very boring.

This must be what Laing meant by 'the hell of frenetic passivity'.

Twenty-Nine

1st February 2001

'IS EVERYTHING all right now between you and Angus then?'

Sid and I are standing before a cattle grid. I'm waiting while she photographs a sign that says, DANGER DEEP SLURRY PIT AHEAD. Sid finds this highly amusing. The giant expanse of air about our heads is filled with bovine groans, birdsong and the distant buzz and putter of a small plane. I wait rigidly for a reply, half expecting her to turn on me and tell me it's none of my damn business.

'Well it is now.' Sid swings her arms like you're supposed to in the country and stares up at the grey wash of sky looking for the plane.

'What do you mean?' Come on, Sid, talk to me. I haven't had a decent conversation for . . . well, it seems like a very long time. And I could do with the consolation of someone else's calamity right now.

'Since I took him to the dentist and the osteopath. Pre-emptive action you see. I couldn't help noticing that just before a midlife crisis, at the age of precisely thirty-nine and a quarter,' she turns to look at me, one eye green, the other blue, 'there's the Tooth Scenario, swiftly followed by the Back Emergency.'

'Funnily enough . . .'

'Both these intimations of mortality,' Sid continues, 'leave the man deeply traumatised and compel him to shag someone unsuitable in a frenzied attempt to negate the forces of death. Or if you're a woman, of course, there is the sudden need to conceive the third baby. Are you sure you don't want an E?'

'No thanks. Not at lunchtime. On a Tuesday.'

'Sorry but I've already had one. Now that I don't smoke.'

'Too many Es damage your serotonin production, you know.'

'Nah. I've got a specially adapted metabolism. Anyway, I only take them on special occasions. When an experience needs heightening. You know, if we have to go to Todd and Helena's for dinner.' Sid stops and produces a yawn of gigantic proportions.

'Or coming to see me.'

'Not you specifically. But a walk in the country. Yes definitely.'

'Thanks.'

'Oh. And there's these job adverts.' She pulls a crumpled copy of *Nursing Times* from her bag. 'You've probably seen them already. There's the Crisis Resolution one in Camden and there's a Senior Lecturer one in Camberwell.'

Over our heads, high in the sky, a tiny plane is performing loop the loops. We can hear the engine strain as the plane struggles vertically upwards.

'Now who would want to do a thing like that?' I ask, scanning the sky and filled with dread for the pilot.

'Well Todd the Tit for one. He's got a bloody Tiger Moth, for God's sake.'

'He hasn't, has he?' We are both standing with our heads bent backwards, eyes squinting, watching the plane's progress.

'Yup. All his teeth fell out just before the second divorce and so then he bought a Tiger Moth.'

As the plane reaches the top of its climb, it seems to pause and the noise of its engine ceases entirely.

'Oh my God.' I clutch Sid's arm.

'He's gone and done it now,' she laughs.

I hold my breath as the plane begins to dive towards the earth. It simply falls, straight down like a silent arrow. Just before it is too late, the engine sputters back into life and the plane draws gently out of its headlong plunge, banking lazily beyond the woods.

Sid is marching on ahead. 'Don't stare, Gen,' she shouts back. 'It just encourages them. So, the thing to do is get the job first and then tell Mark that you and the children are moving back to the Angel. How much notice do the tenants at the Angel need?'

'Does the E mean that you never shut up, Sid?'

'That is one of its benefits, yes.'

I hurry to catch up with her.

'So, back to Angus then. Has his crisis been averted completely or just postponed, do you think?'

'What the hell is that bloody banging?'

'I think they're culling the cows. Foot and Mouth.'

'This is the thing about the countryside. This is exactly the thing. It is so brutal. Give me the Elephant and Castle any day.'

At this point Sid's voice is swallowed by a sudden bellowing from the cowshed alongside the lane. What sounds like gunshots ring out. One, two, three . . . four. The mooing is deafening.

'Jesus, Genevieve. Glad you brought me the scenic route. How can you live in a place like this? Are they going to have a funeral pyre later? You know the emissions from those things are absolutely toxic, don't you? Anyway, how is the Boy Wonder? Don't tell me how you are. I can tell the country air isn't doing *you* any good.'

'Mark is fine. Away, but fine.'

'Fine? Ha! He probably wouldn't notice if you all move

back to the Angel anyway. In fact, you needn't even tell him. That'd be hilarious, wouldn't it? I keep looking out for *Snow* or *No* or *O* whatever it's called now. What exactly is the problem with that film, Gen? I mean it's been a year now. When's it going to be finished?'

Sid's voice rants on and on. I let the gap between us widen as she turns the corner in the lane. A spasm of missing you comes over me. Or is it just the idea of you that I miss now? At the thought of our house in the Angel I feel suddenly, leadenly sad. I look up at the sky again. There is no sign of the plane. I curl my fingers round the mobile phone in my pocket. It rings faintly. I turn it up in my palm and look down. Your name glows green from the semi-dark. I pop the Off button.

You've been gone too long.

27th February 2001

'It's beautiful here. Find out about flights and come now,' your email says. 'I'm counting the days. Love Daddy.'

I ring you. It takes a while for you to answer.

'Hello. It's me,' I say.

Your voice, when it comes, is heavy with sleep. Something falls in the dark.

'Hi. Sorry. Dropped the phone. You still there?'

'Did I wake you? Sorry. What time is it there?'

'Not sure. It's dark. It's nice to hear your voice.' You sound pleased. 'Did you find out about coming out here?' I breathe again. Girlishly pleased and relieved that between the email and the phone call you are still talking about us. I can't remember the last time you used my name. That's so strange.

'Where exactly? When?' And is this a Money Isn't An Issue Trip or a Go Through The Motions Of Trying To Find The Cheapest Flight Possible Because We Used To Be Poor Remember Trip?

'New York. It's snowy and amazing.'

'Like a Woody Allen film—'

'When could you get here? We finish on Thursday. Why don't you come for a long weekend?' Because: the dentist appointments, Ivan's rumbling ear infection, the interview in London, the plumber who has absolutely promised beyond all shadow of a doubt to come and fix the washing machine the day after tomorrow but whose visit necessitates a twelve-hour vigil by the front door and complicated arrangements for Karl to be collected by someone else which involved a lot of grovelling and many cups of tea in Six Mile Bottom because the washing-machine man can't say for definite whether it'll be an a.m. call or a p.m. call, it all depends and my mum is on the verge of coming to stay so that I can go to London and has for several weeks now had her bag packed, cab ordered and train fare paid in preparation for this complicated and rare event.

'All of us?' I say. No. Just you. Just the two of us. Sex, drugs, music, the occasional art gallery if we can really be arsed and then back for more of the above. You know. 'The Way We Were', 'I Just Want to be Adored'. Et cetera.

'Karl and Ivan'd love it,' you say. 'There's skating in the park, some amazing shows, a zoo . . .'

I'm not convinced that City Breaks are their thing but lately you've been trying to make Family Life our mission. I think you suddenly realised that your family is actually me and Karl and Ivan rather than you and your mum and Marion and that if you didn't watch out the children would grow up and leave home and think of you like the dad in that Cat Stevens song. Of course, Family Life in practical terms is a bit of a Mission Impossible, but I still love you for trying. Reluctantly, I let the fantasies of morning sex in the SoHo Grand dissipate. Bid a fond farewell to us walking arm in arm through the snow, gazing at the iconic skyline. It'll still be fun, wandering around Central Park with two jet-lagged children on the ends of my arms. Instead of Budgens bags on a buggy. I know that I am A Very Lucky Woman.

People you work with often tell me this. As if being an ordinary mortal I don't deserve the fidelity which obviously rather surprises them. And not many internationally acclaimed film directors would suggest the wife and kids coming out for a weekend to New York.

We say goodbye and I begin the frenzy of pointless activity that precedes trying to find a flight at short notice.

'Mummy. It hurts.' Ivan is standing tiny and tousled. His pyjama bottoms are sodden. I extend the arm that isn't holding the phone to my head and beckon him over to me miming Oh You Poor Thing and I Love You Sweetheart faces.

He is burning hot as he folds into me, staring blankly at the page of scribbled flight numbers, prices, arrival and departure times. Scrawls that began at the top of a clean sheet of paper with confident optimism and which have dwindled one hour later into a scatter of impossible connections and insulting prices. Ivan paddles my breast with one hand, sucking his thumb and stroking his nose with the other. I put the phone down, place my hand round his head and breathe him in. He smells of small boy, urine and Calpol. His eyelashes are unbelievably, exquisitely long. Each night I fall in love with this boy who reminds me so much of you.

Thirty

13th March 2001

'I'M SORRY. We cannot connect you at present. Please try later.' I replace Sid's phone quietly and climb back into Sid and Angus's spare bed, taking care not to disturb the boys.

I haven't been able to get through to you for three days. Unheard of. Time differences, weak signals, last-minute relocations or something. We're cut off and I don't really know where you are now. Sometimes it's the unobtainable voice and sometimes it's just the cold, outer-space monotone of disconnection. Still, we come, as arranged, the boys and I. I assume we'll meet up somehow, like we always do. And I hope you remember we got flights to Belize and not New York, Vietnam or Costa Rica.

Angus helps me tug them from their beds at dawn then drives me to the tube. Swaying half asleep on our way to Heathrow, our faces stare back at us from the window opposite. Motion, distance and sleeplessness have scrambled our features. We look like wet clay heads, which have been dropped, face downwards. With an arm round each of the boys, I look at us and think of you, connecting us all together. I am anxious, a little breathless, not sure whether I'll manage this journey or what the point of it is exactly. Except that after so long apart this time, I do see that coming home to Six Mile Bottom would be a bit of a let down.

At the airport we haul our bags and clutter, push our trolley here and there, lose Buzz Lightyear, find him in Sock Shop, queue for *pains au chocolat* and juice and tepid latte for which we are asked such an absurd amount of money that I almost laugh aloud and tell a joke of my own except that the face of the Kosovan serving me prohibits mirth. And I quite agree. None of this is funny. Occasional and completely incomprehensible announcements fill the air above our heads. Incomprehensible that is apart from the ones addressing the two passengers with no vowels in their names who have probably done a runner and escaped back to real life. It informs them that their flight to Wherethesunshinesbrightly has boarded and is awaiting departure and if they don't get their arses over there quick their bags will be tossed on the tarmac and run over by the aircraft. We chew and drink and swallow. Karl and Ivan tear up the sugar sachets and knock their drinks over and get crumbs down the fronts of their T-shirts. We stare up at muted screens Breakfast TV-ing us with shock revelations of some celebrity coke and blow job and general what a whacky world it is and over to you Johnnyness.

We trail round WHSmiths, Boots, Body Shop and Dixons which relieve us of shocking amounts of money in exchange for huge quantities of packaging. We lose Owl. We retrace our steps but in doing so become distracted trying on sunglasses in Duty Free and I'm just wondering whether ninety-eight quid is really so much to pay for a label that, if I stand this way, possibly transforms me into the not unattractive wife of a famous film director until Karl tells me they make me look like the lady who killed those children near Granma's house. And he is right.

We drift back the way we came and find Owl by the hand dryer in the ladies' toilets at which point we are seized with great excitement because a number that sounds a little like our flight might have just been announced although it is harder to hear than normal above the roar of dryers, toilet flushes and cubicled calls of 'Maureen? Is that you in there?' The excitement makes Karl want to pee again and I give in to irritation, tell him he can't, he's had an hour and a half to do a wee and our plane is leaving NOW because we've got to go and see Daddy. Wailing and tripping over their Virgins R Us knapsacks they follow me across the concourse where I start marching in urgent but aimless circles staring up into space looking for the gate number. As every mother knows, being horrible to small helpless creatures every now and again can be strangely invigorating and soon I'm nice again and returned to myself and carrying Ivan, Owl and Buzz, all three bits of hand luggage and the Boots bag, the Body Shop bag, the Dixons bag, the WHSmith bag and holding Karl's hand, giving secret squeeze messages as we take the acrylic and concrete trail to the gate, Karl stumbling with anticipation and excitement at what we will find when we get there.

I'm too occupied picking up crayons, juice and Owl to take any notice of take-off. Once we are cruising, the meals consumed and the films viewed, the boys fall asleep, their bodies jammed between armrests and I read up Belize and Guatemala, the Maya and the Spanish conquest with the guidebook balanced on top of one of their heads. Reflected in the blank TV screen in the seat back in front of me is my tired face watching me. I look exhausted. When did I start to look so damned tired all the time? I turn the screen on and select the flight path map. A creeping dotted line leads from the UK across the North Atlantic Ocean, Sargasso Sea and Caribbean. I fight off a rising horror at the thought of the space and uncharted depths beneath my feet.

Over Belize City, within the belly of the plane, two hundred and eighty of us sit packed, stupefied by nine hours of Hollywood, in-flight food and cabin-crew courtesy and prepare to be discharged onto the scrub, swamp and concrete of Belize's capital. We land and queue at Passport Control. The boys look in trepidation at the guns. At the empty and motionless baggage reclaim carousel we sit on a trolley and wait. I'm not sure what system of baggage reclaim is being employed out on the tarmac but it takes a long time whatever it is.

Outside the airport we look around for a taxi. The taxi drivers pick the passengers as far as I can tell. We wait for another long time, listening to the lilting Creole which though based on English is tantalisingly incomprehensible. Eventually one of them decides he might as well pick us. On hearing our destination the driver becomes blank faced and drives at ninety miles per hour past endless billboards exhorting us to visit lagoons, Mayan ruins, Cayes, Eco-Archaeological Parks and Baboon Sanctuaries. We thunder past mile upon mile of plastic bags and half-built breezeblock houses.

On arriving at our rendezvous ('Las Palapas – the romantic holiday hideaway, the perfect haven for seekers of rest and relaxation'), I know immediately that I have made an appalling mistake. You will be furious. Locations are everything, obviously, to you and this is not the setting you had in mind to enact our long-awaited reunion. Impossibly verdant, happy-houred and brochured – I seem to have booked us into a village of lost souls faking it. Alsatians patrol the high perimeter fence and signs on the beach warn us not to stray alone from the tourist village. The children scamper with glee in the sand while I look at the roiling sea in which no one is swimming. Here and there, elderly Germans lie on towels like dazed survivors of a shipwreck. They do not lie on their backs in the glorious abandon of the sun-starved in the Mediterranean. They lie on their sides and blink up at us with the stunned and desperate look of the holiday maker who has another ten days to come to terms with the terminal boredom that is the dreamy get-away-from-it-all beach-front idyll. There's no sun here. Just heat. And a hurricaney look to the horizon.

The children love it. They exclaim at the little thatched cottages, the tourist shops, scummy green swimming pool and the prospect of a self-service buffet three times a day. You're going to hate it. Never mind, tomorrow night you'll be with us and then we'll leave and maybe head west to Guatemala or at any rate discover the real Belize, whatever that is.

14th March 2001

The boys and I have been lying on the sand staring up at the night sky. I'm trying to read *A Brief History of Time* with Ivan's torch. We've done Black Holes and now we're doing White Dwarfs.

'A White Dwarf is a stable cold star, supported by the exclusion principle—'

'Daddy! Daddy! Daddy!' I roll over and feel the cold sand trickling from my hair down the back of my neck. Karl is tearing towards you, followed by Ivan who is stumbling behind, holding a tangle of seaweed up in the air and shouting, 'Look! Look! Look what I found, Daddy!'

I don't recognise you at first, standing with your bag in your hand in the semi darkness beneath the 40-watt bulb of our hut's porch light. You look lost, like you might have come to the wrong place.

Seeing the children, you call their names, drop your bag, squat down and stretch out your arms. I watch them hurl themselves against your body and wait for the hysteria to die down. You straighten up and look over at me as I walk towards you brushing sand from my dress.

'Hi.'

'Hi, I wasn't sure if . . .'

'How are you?'

'We missed you.'

'Missed you too.'

Within our embrace we feel shy. You have lost your familiar smell. Without kissing, we allow the boys' small hands to tug us apart.

Checking the boys' sleeping forms sketched behind mosquito nets, we finally close the door on them, turn to each other in the half light and look. You place one palm against the back of my head and the other against the small of my back and pull me down onto the bed with a kiss. At the feel and the smell and the taste of you I hear you say my name, 'Genevieve.' Closing our eyes we slip back into the warm salt water years of us. We can do this. It is much easier than words.

The shower drips on our soaked bodies and the faint stench of sewers rises from the drain. Through the tiny window a hard white moon stares low in the sky. You try to pull me back to you. You run your hand down my back and mutter something about loving me against my hair. I hold myself at arm's length and look at you.

'What are those?'

Wide-eyed and motionless, a gecko holds the ceiling, padded fingers splayed. I understand that in this small moment everything about us is being reconfigured.

There are marks on your neck. Small bruises. Like the first signs of decay. There are more on your chest and your arms. Time falters like the slow-motion seconds before impact and what I have long dreaded rushes at me in a stammer of blows. Marked on your body like a map, is a record of your frenzy together. Her mouth was here, and here, and here. All that is left to my imagination now is to conjure up the places where you put yours.

You look at me. I read terror in your shining eyes and I see your mouth wobble.

'I got a bit drunk,' you murmur, 'at the wrap party.' You breathe out, a small exhalation, half laugh, half sigh.

'Who was it?' I sound like someone else already.

You give me the name of some runner. We both know you're lying. You're ashamed to say it was an actress half your age. Ashamed to have written such a crap ending for us all.

'It was Sugar Rush, wasn't it?'

You hang your head. You sigh.

'Sorry,' you whisper, swallowing noisily.

Fury rushes in to fill the chasm left by love. Thumping you hard, I try to obliterate all traces of her on your lying body. I want to hurt you too. I want to mark you too. But my blows bounce off the strange, hard surface of your body. Bewilderment, shock, anger and then indignation pass across your boy's face. You grab my wrists with that steel strength. Whatever you expected, it wasn't this. Whatever I expected, this is the exit I will take.

'Don't bother lying!' High-octane rage consumes me.

'Genevieve, shh. You'll wake the children.'

But rage feels good. Better than fear. Better than pain. I take a deep gulp of contempt.

'You,' I hiss. 'You . . . and your look-at-me child-prodigy!'

Holding my wrists tight, you push me hard against the wet tiles. You are saying your stupid lines and noises are coming from your throat. Plastic shampoo bottles clatter round our feet. Outside the Mayan Musical evening is in full swing. Somewhere, down along the beach, the Alsatian barks into the night.

Later, we stand, leaning into each other, broken and wordless, afraid of the chaos and the long trek that awaits us.

'Genevieve, it didn't—'

'Don't. Do not. Do not tell me it meant nothing.'

You sigh and hold me tight. I concentrate on not saying that in her you thought you could buy a little time. Experiment and taste some manna. Before your shadow tapped you on the shoulder and said, 'Boo. I am Death.'

15th March 2001

The breakfast buffet laid out on palm fronds is stacked with sliced mangoes, pineapples, guava, eggs, rolls, bacon, cheese and sausages. Other guests meander about with their trays, balancing as much as they can in precarious piles onto the small plates. We sit at our table overlooking rampant bougainvillea and hibiscus. A shiny bird grips the rail and eyes our plates with sideways jerks of its head. From the giant magnolia tree something is whooping repeatedly. The coffee tastes of ash.

'What's the capital of France?' you ask eagerly. It always takes a moment for me to realise you are not talking to me.

'Poland?' suggests Karl.

I look at you. Her stupid love-bites look back. You seem compelled to display them like some badge of courage or club membership. I'm ashamed and embarrassed for you. It looks like you've been shagging a fourteen year old. And in the face of my contempt for you I know it will leave you no choice but to invest the scene where you shagged Sugar with a dignity and significance it doesn't deserve. Humiliation. Men just cannot stand it. Who said that? James Baldwin? Men cannot stand it and so women must instead. I cannot bear to look at you.

'What's three times three?' you say brightly.

'Nine,' I say, sullenly.

'Not you.' You laugh a nervous laugh. 'I was asking Ivan.'

All at once I am aware of a new emotion. No, not new, just never named. Not pain, not shock, not anger, not fear. They are still there. It's in addition to those. For a moment I can't work out what it is. It is leaden. Terminal.

'Ivan can't do tables yet, Dad,' says Karl.

'Pardon?' you say, looking taken aback. Ivan pushes an entire mini croissant into his mouth and looks at you. Then I realise what it is.

It's boredom.

All four of us are drawn and tear-stained as I drive the VW Beetle down the empty road. I drive fast, failing to see the metal speed bumps that smash the chassis at irregular intervals. I'm getting us as far away from Lost Paradox or Las Praecox or whatever it's called, as fast as I can.

Driving is good. The pitted tarmac leads us, takes us, absorbs the swerving, leaping flight of us. The noise of the engine and the wind through the windows renders talk impossible. The children are behind us, focused quietly inwards on small toy animals between them. The speed makes looking at you unwise. My mind hovers, watches the still, safe places we made of us. You rest your hand on the naked skin of my thigh and keep it there.

We drive through blizzards of blue butterflies, see buffalo, families on mopeds, mud huts with corrugated iron roofs, naked children staring from the mud and curled shapes lying listless in hammocks.

We flee south where we turn off the road and judder in first gear down a sandy potholed track, the turquoise sea like a wide brushstroke beside us. To our left are cabanas, thatched adobe huts. The further we go, the fewer there are. Where the track peters out into breath-taking beach, I swing off the road and stop the car. This place is the last one and the best.

Like sleepwalkers, we follow the woman through the soft sand path bordered by the spikes and colour screech of tropical plants. We pass sleepy, secluded huts painted pink, purple and lemon. She shows us ours. Painted magenta, surrounded by palms and banana trees, it overlooks a broad expanse of deserted beach, the sand like powdered zinc. Beyond stretches the sea, spread like sky, ending with a distant line of white where the reef meets the horizon. A family-sized hammock is slung above the veranda. Inside there is wood, muslin, sisal, tiles and coral. Two beds, one double and one god-sized, are suspended by ropes from the beams. Above them, cascades of mosquito netting caught up in a giant knot. The sudden, strange beauty is like a gift and it feels as if we've found paradise.

19th March 2001

The children play for hours in the shallow water. They seem happy. In the afternoons and at night and at dawn you pull me back to a place we once knew a long time ago. Our history holding on. Heat heavy, limbs wet, you sedate me with margaritas and sex and try to make me believe this might be the beginning, not the end.

But in the blank stillness of the nights sleep does not come. I try to catch the rhythm of the children's sleep. Karl's breathing is steady and slow, every now and then a limb flung at random. Ivan's breath is shallow, almost silent, broken sometimes by an abrupt fragment of speech, sent out into the pitch. Surprisingly, as soon as the sun sinks, a wind howls in from the sea. All around, things flap, rattle, creak and sing out.

I watch your sleeping face, barely there in the dark. You are worn out, oblivious, and snore quietly, beside me. You look content and I can feel my grip slipping. Can't hang on to the raft you have thrown. Waves of madness and grief engulf me and I feel myself sink again as I rewind and replay the scene between you and her. I think of the film, like an albatross round our necks, dragging us down through the months of editing and dubbing and premieres to come. I am haunted by you with her, by her face, her naughty revolutionary spirit, her bloody website.

I give in. There is a perverse relief in letting go. Of you. Of your impossible dreams. Of our hopeless, unspoken histories.

You have always been careless with your possessions. Lost more wallets, sunglasses and jackets than I can remember. An endearing lack of concern about material things. But now you seem to have mislaid us. Such bad timing.

Didn't you notice I was already losing it?

Thirty-One

30th May 2001

THE EARTH feels warm and full beneath my cheek. I can smell the soil and somewhere near, bees rattle and hum, drunk on early summer flowers. A ladybird makes its way up a stem of grass and waits upside down at the curling tip. The blackbird hurls his ribbon of song out into the space around the apple tree. That sound always used to make me glad, with its promise of long summer days, but now it jars and triggers a roller-coaster drop low down in my guts. I raise my hand above the bright green blades and watch it tremble. You'll be here soon. I must go and fetch the boys.

Outside the school, cars sit parked on the verge, each containing a mother sitting with a phone to her ear. Holding my own phone in my palm, I stand at the entrance, under the sycamore tree and scan the tide of heads moving towards the gates. Some charge headlong, butting obstacles out of their way, animate or otherwise. Some trudge, red-faced and sullen, eyes on the path. Others meander by in clumps, jostling for position with elbows, bags and shouts.

I like it at the gate. I feel solid at the gate; not made of air or liquid as I do at our house. I like the certainty of our children's faces; the uncomplicated, uninhibited, genuine connection when their eyes meet mine. Sometimes, if I'm very careful and don't say much, don't move too fast, I can make the moment last until we reach the car.

We drive home at speed, a convoy of mothers and children, the fields of pigs and cows, green shooting barley and spiking wheat streaking by our windows. The radio has something new to tell us each day. Fresh events squeezed out of the future, several of them every day.

My mobile rings.

'Where are you?'

'On our way back. Where are you?'

'Waiting at the house.'

'We're just coming up the hill.'

I slow down, not wanting to get there, dreading the dumbshow until bedtime. Sick at the thought of the slow fall of us through the 'we both just need some time' and the 'but I want to see her again' and the 'what about this house and the boys?' as we sit close and afraid with the blank night air at our backs until I choke on the bitter cud of us and of you and of her and our past and the suddenly disposable future and vomit up something vile that should have been left unsaid.

'There's Daddy's car!'

'Daddy's back!'

And there you are, coming out of the house, smiling, tanned, slim and beautiful and unable to disguise the helium hope in you that is her.

4th July 2001

In the scruffy little chapel of Monterchi, the *Madonna del Parto* is a shock when I see it. A series of revealings. Both boys hold your hands. You keep your distance, telling them how Piero della Francesca was a very famous painter who lived more than five hundred years ago and challenging them to do that sum, work out when he was born and I feel like dying.

The painting is smaller than I expected and held behind curtains in a dimly lit room at the back. All four of us stand in the gloom and it's a moment before I realise that we're looking at it. Within the painting, two angels stand on each side of the Madonna, drawing back curtains to display her. She is child-like and she is unlacing the lower half of her dress, parting the secret layered folds of it. She stares at the four of us. Her look is disdainful, erotic, proud.

We sit on a restaurant terrace in the village, an elaborate seafood dish before us, warm bread, velvet wine in our mouths and the scent of thyme and cypress in the air. The children do not stray far from our side. Our eyes skim each other's, restless, unsure. Occasionally we grope for words.

We've been here before in happier times with Sid and Angus but now we're here to see whether we can lay the ghost of Sugar Rush. I'm under strict instructions to Be Happy and Enjoy Myself. I'm on probation and I know I'm going to fail.

'It's beautiful here, isn't it?' you say.

'Mmm. It is.'

This is how it ends, I think. Not with the storm or the battle but with a tired surrender. A weary dismantling and packing away of the bricks and mortar of us.

'If you're happy and you know it clap your hands . . .'

You sing tunelessly on the drive back to the house. The children join in. Knowing that you don't do irony, I look at you and wonder if I ever really knew you. Perhaps you were just an idea I once had.

When we get back, seeing the pool and the neighbour's children in it, the boys hurry down the sharp, stony path to join them. The couple from next door wave us into the house. 'They'll be fine,' they shout. 'Go and have a nap.'

Once we are alone I am compelled to say the things that perhaps should be left unsaid. Words that have been filling up in me like gravel in a quarry. Out they crash. A torrent of questions, accusations, derision, pleas. Then there's the weeping. It all makes the most terrible noise and mess. You pat my shoulder and sigh. You really cannot stand the weeping. And I cannot stand your inability to comfort me. I'm supposed to have stopped the crying by now. According to Winston. I snatch up the packet and study the pills.

'I think I'd better up the dose.'

You look on sympathetically as I burst a capsule from its bubble.

'Or maybe I should be giving them to you, Mark. Perhaps it's you that's gone mad.' I offer the packet to you and have a go at laughing. But I can't for the life of me remember how to do it.

'Look, just try to be happy for this fortnight,' you say. 'Then, if we're getting on all right when we get back, I won't see her again . . .'

'I can't be what I don't feel, Mark. I'm not a fucking actress. Not that you need reminding of that, I'm sure.' There. I just did it again. Poisoned little darts of gall.

'If we can just enjoy the holiday then . . .'

But no, I'm crying again. All of me is leaking outwards through my skin.

'I'm sure it's going to be all right,' you say.

I lie shaking in the crook of your arm, not sure if I want to believe it. Bravely, we attempt kind lovemaking. This. This is the worst of it. How do we get back from here?

Chest aching from the weight of you asleep on top of me, I shift myself from beneath your inert body and listen to the distant shouts and cries from the garden. Through the window, the view is unchanged, its beauty, stolid and unmoved. Beyond the olive-studded hills, thunder threatens. Hanging by their necks from the closet door, our clothes watch me. We seem ghosted in them already. When the lightning comes like a synapse leap, screams and laughter rip from the pool. The lights go down and the wind begins. Raindrops like bullets fall.

'Shit!' You leap up, throwing the sheet in a tangle from you. I know you've remembered your mobile which lies outside somewhere, still warm from your texts goading each other towards the final act. You pull on shorts and race to its rescue. I hear you struggling through the doorway which is jammed with squirming, glistening children – all seeking shelter from the rain. Behind them hurries their mother, laughing and shepherding them indoors.

I go to the window and watch. You cradle the small heavy weight of it in your palm, checking its secrets with tiny twitches of your thumb.

Assassin.

20th July 2001

I wake and watch your back that is becoming a stranger to me. Foreign territory. I doubt we could even touch one another now. Already, our history seems a fifteen-year blink.

Supporting my head on two pillows I can see the garden framed by our bedroom window. The pearl sky is threaded with darting swifts and a plump pigeon waits on the wire for its mate. At the centre is the old apple tree which is contorted and nearly hollow from age. A few small apples hang in its leaves. We don't eat them. They are maggoty and sour. The tree's bark is pale with lichen and from its one strong branch hangs a rope and tyre. Both our children cling to the rope and to each other, their thin bare legs dangling from pyjama bottoms, laughing as they slip lower towards the damp, scuffed patch beneath. The sun breaks through and scatters trembling shapes and shadows over our ceiling. I shut my eyes and move my head out of its way. I shall miss the garden.

When I open them again, the swing is empty. Then the stocky stomping figure of Karl runs across the frame shouting

Ivan's name. And after a moment from the left comes Ivan doing his hesitant, loping run, holding up his pyjamas with one hand and clutching Owl with the other. He falls giggling and Karl topples on top of him, wrestling Owl back. Karl takes a running jump at the swing and swings in and out of my line of vision, leaning right back and looking up into the tree. Ivan stands watching, waiting for his turn.

Thirty-Two

2nd August 2001

YOUR FEET pound the chewing-gummed pavement of the Angel, bag bumping against your side, jacket collar turned under. Your battered trainers strike the ground hard, sending a judder through your body and up to your head, which bobs rhythmically as if being punished. You keep your eyes down, weaving a meandering path through other pedestrians. I can see you thinking, Christ, the ugliness of this place . . . this sodding litter . . . how is it we're living in the twenty-first century and the council employs a guy with a broom to deal with industrial quantities of rubbish? Yet you couldn't live the life you want to lead, your Sugared life, in Six Mile Bottom. You need the Angel, although you can't quite decide whether you can entirely do without Six Mile Bottom, by which I assume you mean me and so, here I am and we've arranged to meet to Talk About The Future.

You've got a whole new wardrobe, I notice. Stylish, but studiedly unflamboyant, your clothes have a crumpled, loose look to them. A careful casualness battles with the familiar air of chaos that threatens to overwhelm you. Clasped under the other arm is a newspaper. Occasionally, leaflets drop unnoticed from it onto the pavement. I mean what is this all about? Crisp packets, sweet wrappers, that's a half-eaten chicken, for God's sake. I'll see a human corpse in a minute.

Who drops this stuff? Why can't England be more like France or Italy or Spain? They know how to do it. A bit of beauty, a bit of tragedy, some food for the soul. *Stupenda e misera.* Could get a decent cup of coffee at nine in the morning in any of those places. Distracted momentarily from your favourite rant, you catch sight of your reflection in a shop window and flinch, pulling at fistfuls of hair on your scalp. The beginnings of a beard shadows your jowl. Your eyes are hidden behind sunglasses which give you a mean look at odds with your shambolic gait. As you walk, your mouth moves, rehearsing the conversation. You stand at the kerb opposite the café, taking care to cross only when the road is completely clear. Looking up, you lift your sunglasses onto the top of your head and open the door.

Sitting down at a window table, you rummage in your bag and bring out a copy of Shelley, letting the newspaper fall to the floor as you bend over the table to read, hands clenching into fists in an unconscious rhythm. You glance up and notice the face of a young woman two tables down. You study her briefly. Self-possessed and still, she stares out of the window. You admire her youth, her features. The mouth, especially. And heavy lidded eyes. You do not need her to remind you of Sugar. Sugar fills your head already.

Without your sunglasses, and despite the tan, your face looks worn and tired. It's finally beginning its descent towards middle age. The clatter of cups, hiss of the coffee machine and the chatter of mothers fill the air. Still you do not see me. A small girl sits down with her father at the table next to you. Father and child rest easily in their seats, staring neutrally around them. You indulge yourself in a little moment of guilt: Christ, but no one could say I'm not suffering too. And so's Sugar. It's not easy for her either you know. From the depths of your bag a mobile phone rings. You tear open Velcro flaps and zips. Hands fumble among the invisible clutter stuffed in the darkness. *Sugar.* You check the clock. Midnight her time. Where the fuck is my phone?

What is all this crap in my bag? The ringing continues, becomes louder, more urgent, insistent. One or two heads turn to look. You hold your phone in your hand.

'Hello? Hi.' You listen briefly. With one palm on your forehead you hunch yourself over the phone, speaking fast. A work call.

You finish the call and hold the phone. It rests comfortably in your hand. Smooth, curved, solid. Holding it feels reassuring, familiar, like the feel of your cock. You press the small button near its head. Search. The list of names and numbers blinks up at you, peeping conspiratorially. Your mobile is the one possession you are learning to look after. Faithfully, every night, you plug it into its charger. Without it, you know that you could not be . . . free. Cordless. Mobile. You look down as her name is illuminated in the liquid crystal of the tiny screen. Sans serif, cool, digital. Sugar. Call. Calling.

I try to imagine the mysterious connection taking place across three thousand miles of sea, snow and forest.

Winged messenger. A connection that would take you tedious hours, whole days of your lives to make flesh by plane. Unbelievable. Metaphysical. You look up and see me. The distance between us is unspeakable.

10th August 2001

'Why the hell didn't you say anything before?'

'Because once you say it, it becomes true.'

'But all that time, you just kept it to yourself?'

'We agreed. To give us a chance to sort it out.'

'To give him a chance, you mean.'

'Seems like that now, I suppose.'

'But you must have gone mad.'

Sid and I sit side by side in the garden at Six Mile Bottom. She flips the top of her cigarette packet open and shut, then pulls one out and offers it to me.

'No thanks.'

I watch her light her own, take a big lungful of smoke, hold it and exhale a white fan of Don't Say I Didn't Warn You. The act of smoking, when Sid does it, looks strangely like an affirmation of life. I take the packet from her and light one, wincing at the foul first taste. God, how did Bill do it all those years? Come to think of it, how does Sid? Nevertheless, I inhale the toxins deeply with a gratifying sense of physical damage being done.

'I thought you'd given up, Sid.'

'Well, I bloody well had.'

'Can you hear that funny chewing noise?' I think I can hear a snail eating a leaf although I'm not sure if such a noise is audible to the human ear. Sid looks sideways at me. 'You look a bit tired yourself, Sid,' I add, hoping to shift a little of the Wronged Woman persona I seem to have been landed with.

'I don't look as bad as you.'

'I know. I do look extraordinarily terrible.' I pull my waistband out. 'But film-star thin now. Look at that.'

'Mm. Very alluring, obviously. Actually, I haven't been sleeping either.'

I look at her. There's that crunching noise again. It occurs to me that if I could carry on sitting here, like this, with Sid, for a very long time, everything would be fine.

'I've been seeing someone else.'

I lift up my dark glasses and squint at her.

'Who?'

She puts three cigarettes in her mouth and lights them with the flame up high. I don't laugh.

'Charlene.'

Jesus. Everybody's doing it. There are snail trails and ants everywhere.

'Don't hurt Angus, Sid. I gave him to you for safe keeping, remember?'

'I have no intention of letting Angus go. Just performing a minor adjustment.'

'What the hell for? What if he finds out? Which he will. No one likes being the other woman, you know. She'll be accidentally leaving her knickers down the side of the sofa in no time.'

'Genevieve, if you'd had any sense, you would have had a fling with Leon when you had the chance. It's all about the balance of power.' Just by my foot, a snail slides out of the pot of basil.

'I think it's a little more complicated than that.' Don't make me say it's different if you've got children, Sid.

'Don't kid yourself. It's all horribly simple.'

1st September 2001

My immediate reaction to the moment of impact is surprise at how little it takes to render the car immobile. It hadn't felt like enough to make the wheel come off. But I knew it had even before I got out to look. The car had no more than clipped the parked van and then just sort of sat down like an animal. And it had made a strange noise, like a final exhalation as it came to rest. Oh, I think, well, that's that then. I've crashed. My next reaction is a feeling of relief. Relief that the wild night of rage and grief has finally been brought to a stop. It wasn't supposed to be a wild night of rage and grief. It was supposed to be one of those Let's Talk Things Through dinners for two.

Hauling myself with some difficulty out of the car, I look with shock at the skewed wheel, crushed metal and spreading stain on the tarmac. I sit on the kerb, feet in the spotless gutter of the pretty market town and wait, wondering how you got back to Six Mile Bottom after I slammed on the brakes and told you to get out. I regret it slightly now, but when you told me that Sugar really really wanted to meet the children I suddenly really really wanted to dump you in the dark. Preferably near to that dangerously deep slurry pit. As the flashing blue light of the police van silently fills the night air around me, it feels like the moment before going under anaesthesia. A child-like surrender to a group of strangers in uniform who know what to do. Thank God they've got a plan.

The two police officers and I go through the routine by the side of the road. Obediently I blow into the breathalyser. Not too hard. Just in case it makes a difference. One of the officers delivers the speech about not saying anything if you don't want to and I suddenly want to laugh. Just because it is such a cliché. As indeed my entire life appears to have become.

Much later in the interview room, my liveliness wanes. Exhaustion hits me. It is going to be a long night. On the wall is a poster of Kylie Minogue and a calendar. At the sight of the photograph on the calendar my stomach gives a lurch. It's the colours I recognise first. The same iridescent blues and greens as the ones in the holiday brochure I studied all those months ago. Enhanced, unreal, impossibly intense. It wasn't a picture of that unspeakable tourist village we'd gone to that I was looking at now, but of the ruined temple near by. Focusing with some difficulty, I can make out that the caption confirms it. *Ruins at Tikal, Guatemala.*

I look at the policeman in front of me, his head bent diligently over the paperwork. His badge says PC Wright. His hair is cut short on his square head. I notice the vulnerable places, just behind his ear, his neck – where the hair has been closely shorn. He is laboriously writing down my details, concentrating hard.

'And how much alcohol had you consumed before your arrest?' he asks, looking at me. I try unsuccessfully to hold his gaze for a moment. Automatically dividing the truth by about three, I give him an answer. There is a pause while he writes.

'And in the last twelve hours, have you taken any drugs?'

I shake my head. Just as his biro touches the paper I pipe up.

'Do anti-depressants and tranquillisers count?' He stops writing and I register the look he gives me. This is how the world will see me now. Hogarth prints of asylums and gin-soaked women leering as their babies drop unnoticed from their breasts pass through my mind. Well, too bad. It is a version of the truth.

'Look, I disapprove of drink driving. Obviously. I've got children. I'm horrified at what I could have done to someone. It's not something I make a habit of.' My voice is shaking. I hate the person I must appear to be. It occurs to me to tell him my story. I've kept silent about it for long enough. Out of shame mainly. And a belief that to put it into words, place it inside other people's heads, would make it real, the truth.

'Where were you driving when the accident occurred?'

'Back home. To Six Mile Bottom. I was upset. My husband and I argued . . . he got out of the car . . .' He waits, forearms resting on the paperwork. He avoids my eyes. I study the blue serge of his sleeve and continue.

'We're separating.' Sounds like I'm describing a surgical operation. Are we separating? I don't really know. I think you call it Having Some Space. You want everything to be conditional. Just in case, as your mum would say. 'The children are staying down near Bristol, with their grandparents,' I add, just in case he thinks I had abandoned them as well.

He doesn't say anything. Perhaps he is relieved to be spending the next hour in here with a melodrama rather than out on the streets with a corpse. I feel like I've done him a favour. I tell myself to shut up while he resumes the task of writing down my story. The strip lighting hums. It seems to be affecting my vision. I can feel myself detaching from the scene, as if I'm behind a gauze screen.

During the silence, I try to focus my eyes on the calendar

again. What a ridiculous aura of romance and history that photograph gives to those ruins. Like our marriage. It is not the truth. While you were away making *Snow* we were held together by increasingly fragmented emailed I-love-yous. Telephoned I-miss-yous, hesitantly, hopelessly uttered. I bet you send Sugar several Hotmails a day. What has our marriage been then? Surface gloss like that picture up there? Well it had looked incredible from a distance, rising out of the rainforest like an ancient skyscraper. But there was a lot at those ruins not visible in the photo. The rip-off guides, the litter, the look in the eyes of the traditional dancers and the slow, solid invasion of tourists like us desperately seeking authenticity. And the misery that had hovered over the children and us on the day of our visit there.

I rub my eye with the heel of my hand and wonder if I'm ever going to be allowed to sit down. PC Wright straightens up, picking up the paperwork as he does so.

'I'm going to need to fingerprint you and take a DNA sample.' He looks at me. 'Just wait here a moment.'

I nod, wondering which particular part of my anatomy is going to have to offer up my genetic code this time. He holds my hand in his. I let him press each fingertip in the inky pad and then onto the record sheet. Like potato printing at school.

'You been there then? Where is that? Greece?' he asks, nodding up at the calendar.

'Guatemala. A bit of a mess. First the Conquistadors, then Tourism.'

I open my mouth while he scrapes the inside of my cheek with a wooden spatula. Eyeing the broken stones and silly, fallen splendour, my heart starts thumping at the thought of Sugar, tramping like some sixteenth-century invader all over our marriage. Loaning some youth to you. Christ there should be a law against it.

'So what happens next?' My legs are lead.

'You'll receive a summons in the next couple of days. A

driving ban and a fine are automatic. A custodial sentence is up to the discretion of the magistrate. You can go now.'

Fear washes through my veins like hot ice. He gathers up his notes and my sheet of fingerprints, looking back at me as he leaves the room.

'There's a payphone in the waiting room. Cab company's number is up on the wall.'

A moment later the door opens again and he comes back in.

'Forgot your DNA,' he says, picking up the vial and giving it a little shake.

The clock says 3.15. I look at Kylie's irrepressible smile and arse and at the Mayan site in the calendar photograph. I think of Sugar and watching take after take of her in the snow on your rushes. And then I think, this is nothing to do with Sugar. She's not a conqueror, she's just a tourist. The ruins of our marriage lay undiscovered long before she came.

Thirty-Three

5th September 2001

THE DAY is slipping towards dusk and Angus and I are sitting on a bench overlooking the Thames, waiting for Sid. Down here, with the thick Bankside masonry at our backs, the torrent of traffic is silenced and the only sound is of the passing feet and voices of people on this hidden riverside walk. Opposite us squats the monolithic Tate Modern, joined to the north bank by the slender troubled spine of the Millennium Bridge. To our right the steel and stone buttresses of Blackfriars stand firm against the convoluted currents of the Thames. And beyond the bridge, dwarfed by office blocks but still distinctive against the darkening sky, rises the Oxo Tower.

'I read about me and Mark in the paper today,' I say, handing the piece to Angus. 'My five minutes of fame. At last.' I consider a sardonic laugh then think better of it. Angus lets the paper rest on his lap. He doesn't look at it. Faintly, the bells of St Paul's chime eight. The top of the Tate's chimney is a glowing slice of light sending a beam over the stricken bridge towards St Paul's. Angus's large body stays firm against my side. He doesn't move. He is looking upriver at that strange art deco Oxo Tower. I follow his gaze and as I do, the tower is flooded with uplights from its base. There's a pause, like the moment before Curtain Up, then a flickering pulse of red. After a moment the lights behind the wrought-iron windows glow red. Oxo.

'How lovely,' I say. And it is.

'I used to be so sure I knew what that meant,' Angus says. A splutter of a laugh escapes me followed by a noisy sniff. Angus hands me his hankie. 'I was so sure it could only mean something bad.'

'Oh, yes. What was it again, Angus? The CIA? A meat rendering conspiracy?'

A smile spreads over his large gentle face. It looks runnelled, like the timbered wharves, and I lean against him, tucking my arm through his. He squeezes it tight against him.

'Something like that. But also . . .' He looks at me, checking that I won't mock. I won't. 'Well, those two circles,' he traces their arc in the air, 'archetypal symbols. All cultures have them. They represent the soul.' He slides an uneasy look in my direction and feels in his pocket for a smoke before remembering he's given up. He breathes in deeply and I really hope he's not going to go all astrological on me. I stare at the iron work silhouetted against the red and all I can think of is the Conran restaurant and the night we celebrated one of our wedding anniversaries in there. 'And the cross stands for the body. Reality.'

I don't say anything. He lifts one huge foot and waggles it in embarrassment.

'But, Angus, the circles can just as easily symbolise nothingness, the void. And as for the cross. Well, don't tempt me. X-rated? No connection? Wrong?'

'Yes, well. It didn't look too good to me either that night when . . .'

'And you were a vegetarian then, Angus,' I say nudging him. 'No wonder it upset you.' He gives me a shove and I smile at the memory of that evening all those years ago, when Angus was mad with grief for Helena and thought OXO held the answer. He nudges me back and we settle into silence to watch the river. A gull, wings outspanned, suspends itself on invisible columns of air. London is becoming quite beautiful in the twenty-first century.

'I wonder where Sid has got to?'

'Being late is a matter of principle for Sid, as you know,' says Angus. He turns and looks at me. 'I'm so glad you'll be back in the Angel, Gen. And it's great about the job. It's what you're good at, after all.'

'What, madness?'

'Definitely. You do madness beautifully.'

'Well having no driving licence certainly makes Six Mile Bottom impossible. I would leap for joy at this point, Angus, but as you know, I can't stand on my own two feet yet.'

'I'm not sure what your plans are, but I should warn you that Sid has said we're coming to Six Mile Bottom on the eleventh to help you move back.'

'No, really, you don't need to do that.'

'Well, how are you and the boys going to get back to London? You can't drive, can you?'

'Oh. I hadn't thought of that.' I wonder if you'd thought of that? No, of course not. You'll be away by then. With the fairies.

'And, Sid says, could we look after your car?'

I grin at him. 'Please, Angus, be my guest,' and I take the keys off my keyring and hand them to him.

Towards us, like a barge in full sail forging a channel between the drift of theatre goers, comes Sid, smiling, shouting something inaudible, her arms outstretched. I get up and wave at her. She's wearing a T-shirt which says I CAN'T BELIEVE IT'S REALLY A TULIP. She strides through a gaggling school trip of FCUK'd Italian teenagers. They stare after her, first in irritation and then in amazement and horror at the back of her T-shirt.

I laugh out loud at the thought of what's on it.

11th September 2001

Tongue-tied, we avoid one another's eyes and busy ourselves with tasks that allow us to keep our backs turned. I tape up the last of the moving boxes and write on them. Kitchen. Bathroom. Bedroom.

I look out at the sky. A wide expanse of afternoon September blue. You turn the radio on to fill the silence. President Bush has snubbed Blair's request for peace talks on Palestine. A plane has flown into a building in New York.

I see Catullus go in your bag, watch the nape of your neck and wait for the oyster reflex of pain. It doesn't come.

I hate and I love.
  And if you ask me how,
I do not know:
  I only feel it, and I'm torn in two.

You feel your pockets. Ticket. Passport. Phone. I move my eyes to look at you. Your face is lowered. You check the time.

Your mobile rings. The landline rings. Your cab blows its horn outside.

Acknowledgements

Thanks to Alison Samuel at Chatto & Windus and Simon Trewin and Sarah Ballard at PFD for their enthusiasm, expertise and steadfast belief. To Lesley Moors, Ardashir Vakil and Nicola Green for their tact and friendship despite having to read the early draft. Also Wendy Brandmark, Judy Cook, Stephen Knight and others at Birkbeck for their inspiration and encouragement. To Susan Everett, Justin Fisher, Elizabeth Gee, Leisa Rae and Val Rutt for their advice on tulips, madness and biplanes. To the Wellcome Library for the History and Understanding of Medicine for being full of knowledge and free. Thanks too, to Ruthie and Anna for their patient guidance on child-rearing.

*

CREDITS

Page 2 & 8: extracts from 'What really happened on Flight 103?' by Cay Rademacher and Christoph Reuter, from the *Observer.*
Page 11, 199–201: thanks to Zvi Har'El for extracts from Hans Christian Andersen's *The Snow Queen* and *The Child In The Grave* (www.HCA.Gilead.org.il).
Page 38 & 287: extracts from *Wisdom, Madness and Folly* by R.D. Laing, permission of Macmillan, London, UK.
Page 39 & 323: extracts from Poem 85, *Poems of Catullus* translated by Peter Whigham (Penguin Classics, 1966) Copyright © Penguin Books Ltd, 1966.
Page 95: extract from *Freedom And Choice In Childbirth* with permission from Sheila Kitzinger.
Page 110, 115, 116: extracts from *Baby And Child* by Penelope Leach (Michael Joseph, 1977) Copyright © Penelope Leach, 1977.
Page 169: extract from 'This Be The Verse' by Philip Larkin, *Philip Larkin: Collected Poems*, Faber & Faber 2001, used with permission of Faber & Faber.
Page 231: extract from *The Book of Margery Kempe* translated by B.A. Windeatt (Penguin Classics, 1965) Copyright © B.A. Windeatt, 1965.
Page 282: reference to the title of *The Female Malady: Women, Madness And English Culture 1830–1890*, by Elaine Showalter, Virago Press, 1987.
Page 285–287: extracts from *Peter Pan* by J.M. Barrie, (Penguin, 1995) reproduced with kind permission from the Great Ormond Street Hospital Children's Charity.
Page 298: extract from *A Brief History Of Time* by Stephen Hawking published by Bantam Press. Used by permission of Transworld Publishers, a division of the Random House Group Limited.

Every effort has been made to trace copyright holders and we apologise in advance for any unintentional omission. We would be pleased to insert the appropriate acknowledgement in any subsequent edition.